The Impossible History of Trotsky's Sister

By Maree F. Roberts

Photograph of Olga Kameneva (left) with a comrade.

The Impossible History of Trotsky's Sister

Second edition

Published 2022 by RR Imprint

ISBN: 978-0-6541533-4-7

 A catalogue record for this book is available from the National Library of Australia

Cover design © Conor Roberts.

Find contact details and more about Maree Roberts and her work at: mareefroberts.com.au. The website has links to information about the characters and times remembered by Olga as well as short stories by the author you might also enjoy, and news about other projects.

You are pitiful isolated individuals; you are bankrupts; your role is played out. Go where you belong from now on — into the dustbin of history!

— Leon Trotsky addressing the Mensheviks at the 1917 Soviet Congress of Soviets. (Trotsky was a Menshevik from 1903 to 1904).

The only historian capable of fanning the spark of hope in the past is the one who is firmly convinced that even the dead will not be safe from the enemy if he is victorious.

— Walter Benjamin, On the Concept of History. (Soon after writing this work in 1940, Benjamin committed suicide rather than be captured by the Nazis).

This book is dedicated to:

— my extended family and my partner Robert Hodder.

two people taken too soon, who would have appreciated the spirit in which this book was written, and laughed at my pretensions:

— Colin Richard Hodder and Peter John Roberts.

Maree F. Roberts has been writing fiction for many years. With a long career in the public sector, she spends her time reading, writing, sewing and playing music and trying to fix the world. She writes about what makes her curious, following up loose threads from history and culture, to reveal the fabrics, textures, colours and shapes.

TABLE OF CONTENTS

BEFORE

Air. Sharp as hail hitting flesh. Biting like a wolf. Voiceless, and — it surprises her — odourless. The cold has obliterated even her sense of smell. The hot stink of animal warmth — a signal of life in the coldest of places — absent.

A line of silent people waiting in the open, Arctic air — soft snow falling like sugar on the ground, on their rough clothing — and she can smell nothing.

Robbed of external cues, she turns inwards, recalling a time crushing rock for the road. She had seen a calf in the lake. It bobbed in the water lapping at the muddy shoreline. The calf had fallen in and drowned and was thawing in the weak sun. The eyes had been torn out, and there was only half a face, but the body was intact, so when the overseer was not looking, three men took their knives and carved hunks of meat from its flanks and stuffed them in their coat pockets. The stink hung in the wide, cold air and now she remembered it, standing in this line. The last time she had seen the calf, three ravens had landed on it, cawing and pecking.

In this human line she cannot feel her fingers or toes either, but that is not unusual. People are standing close in unwashed clothing, mostly to keep in the orbit of each other's body warmth, but she cannot smell them, even as the freezing air enters her narrowed nostrils.

The food arrives, and it brings her sense of smell back swiftly and violently. The return is emphatic. A smack on naked skin. As the lids are removed from the dirty, blackened cauldrons, Olga begins to gag. She can barely control herself, but the thought of being torn from the queue and beaten brings back her senses.

And she remembers that the men had shared the calf meat, stinking and raw, huddling in silence. But the meat had been so cold, she'd barely tasted it.

In this new country memories come and go. They reach out their hands pleadingly, trying to draw her back.

This cauldron of sleep, of memory, of dreams, of life — prisoners who live in the same cell for so long they copy each other's speech and wear each other's clothes until finally, they are indistinguishable. In sleep, her dreams wear the clothes of memory, but she had learned not to trust them.

Why even the day before she had daydreamed about those very events. On a visit to the delicatessen to buy sausages and brown bread, she saw the half-eaten head of a calf in the display case instead of the neat rows of sausages, and when she looked up at the man serving her, she saw the face of a camp guard, his eyes gleaming, circled by darkness.

It was the snow she remembered most — its cold breath as it swirled around then settled on the hard ground. It seemed that her most vivid memories involved snow. Now, she had trouble remembering what it looked like — its infinite forms. But she remembered what it tasted like.

The snow had been her playground. The thrill, the freezing snowmelt catching the tops of their mouths as children dared each other to stuff it in. As it melted in her mouth, it was even colder. How could that be? She never asked. She just knew that it caused pain when she swallowed it. But that did not stop her.

She'd held the child carefully at the neck and under its rump, picking him up and fitting him to the curve of her shoulder and arm. She stroked the baby's shortish neck, at once strong and fragile. It was a Sunday afternoon, snow sleet at the windows, her body inert from the fire-heat as she sat on the floor between her mother's chair and the hearth; her mother's hand idly stroking the back of her neck — she felt her mother's fingers ripple through the fine hairs, as if she were the young child.

Olga was not long married to Lev, with an unknowable future and a tiny baby. Her mother's fingers said: I do not know what you do now, I am not part of your rushing-around, your dangers, your fears, but I still know the shape of your neck.

She never saw snow in this new country. If she ever had money or people who would take her, she would visit the snow on some low mountains she had heard about, quite a distance away.

HAPPY BIRTHDAY, OLGA

What a morning. She had performed an emergency tracheostomy on the train to help a fellow commuter whose throat had closed over with asthma. She had killed the greengrocer who looked at her sideways when she had politely asked if he had any kohl rabi. Then, when she had finally reached her own doorstep after the long train trip back, she had encountered the postman and after asking him in for a cup of tea, they had retreated to the bedroom where…well, enough of that. She really must learn to switch off her mind. It had been a problem since her earliest years and, as she had chided herself many times, it had even interfered with her work.

This heat! Mosquitoes! Sweat in ribbons like she'd never seen! It completely tired her. Exhausted, simply by a morning's trip to the shops. She who had done more than her fair share of work, some of it back-breaking, and still she had gone on. But now, the heat made it harder. Or perhaps that was her age? She did not like to think about that. Even today, which was her birthday.

Slowly, Olga unpacked the groceries she had brought home, lifting them from her plaid-patterned shopping trolley. She had bought nothing more than she'd had on her list:

Cheese.
Tea.
Pork sausages.
Eggs.
Onions.
Cabbage.

She, an Old Bolshevik who had once been in charge of relief activities in the Great Famine, who had seen whole families starve on nettle soup, now feasted on unimaginable plenty. Sausages and eggs for breakfast almost every day. And why not? As she tasted the first mouthful of the day, she would say to herself, "Here's one in the eye for you, Kremlin Highlander."

Today Olga Kameneva is turning seventy. She may be older. Officially she is dead, she knows, so what age does that make her?

Her friends have organised a little celebration for her. She told them she was turning seventy over a month ago. She knows it will involve the square, coconut-covered cakes the women call almingtons. Is that right? Today, she will confirm the name. If there is one thing she has been afraid of in this country, it is standing out, not getting things right.

Betty has organised what the women call 'a spread' — tea, more tea, and everyone will bring a plate except her because it is her birthday. And Betty will shout "Surprise! Happy Birthday!" when she opens the front door to find Olga standing there. She already knows which cake stand Betty will use, and the special red and gold-patterned teacups kept in a frosted glass cabinet will also be produced.

It is all so dull. Olga feels like crying. In the middle of it all, she will feel like shouting at them: do you not know my children are dead? That trust is just a lullaby for babies?

But she will get through it as she had done for each one of her birthdays and her children's. She will chew and swallow an almington, though she thinks they are a very dry kind of cake she needs to wash down with the muddy tea they will serve. The women will sing a song, *Happy Birthday to You.* 'To you-ou-ouoo', they will sing. She will smile and thank them. They will have 'chipped in' for a present for her. She will thank them, 'from the bottom of my heart.'

The thought of it touches her deeply. She calms herself. Sometimes, it is all just too much to bear. But today, she will make it bearable.

Olga walks to the end of the street to Betty's small, wrought iron gate, the fence barely of knee height. It would never keep out intruders! But then, she did not suppose that intruders — soldiers or the secret police — were in the habit of overrunning these suburban bungalows. She is still cautious; her small flat with a foyer and a door with a latch suits her just fine, and with a window overlooking the front path she can observe any visitors. And of course, there are boards she has nailed across the door in case anyone thinks of trying to kick it in.

Betty's house stands behind a patch of grass called a lawn. Olga thinks it is the oddest concept she has come across as a use for land. Do they not have parks for the people to promenade, covered with just such grass? Yes, they do, she knows that. So why do they use their own land in this way? Why not plant vegetables and fruit trees, so that you do not need to pay for your food? If she had land, that is what she would do. But she has none. She has never owned land in her life.

Betty wears an apron and greets her with the expected words. Betty, who is of middling height, looks down at Olga, then at her apron.

"Whoops!" she says and reaches behind to undo the knot and take off the offending item. Olga is the first to arrive. This is often the case. She was so used to getting to meetings on time. Why break the habits of a lifetime? It was her brother, he who called himself Leon, who was notoriously late. She could never bring herself to call him that. Or Trotsky — the underground name he retained even after the Revolution.

Olga looks around. She can see the flash of Betty's orange-red hair in the corner of her eye as she busied herself with her preparations. The table is being set for a ladies' afternoon tea. The husbands made themselves scarce on such occasions. Olga knows where they will be — at their clubs, or the hotels. Once, she went to a hotel with Betty, to the Ladies' Lounge. They had drunk something called a shandy. Olga thought it tasted like a drink for children. Where was the vodka?

The other women arrive: Iris, Helen and Clarissa. Beverly was visiting her married daughter on the other side of Melbourne. Beverly had two daughters, but only one, Olga noticed, was referred to as *my married daughter*. How is your *married daughter*? her friends would ask. That daughter was always very well, thank you, and the children, also, both of them growing big and strong.

Olga met Betty when she first moved to Box Hill. Betty's husband, Eric, was retired and Betty had time on her hands, she said. Betty had proudly told Olga that as a retired business owner, Eric had invested enough to make sure they did not have to rely on the pension. Odd to be proud of such a thing, Olga thought, but she kept her thoughts to herself on that occasion. These people had taken her in, they had even helped her collect a secondhand sofa from a shop in High Street. Eric brought a van he borrowed. Nothing was too much trouble.

Olga would be pleased that after a lifetime of work and sacrifice, she might receive a pension from a government. Olga had worked for four years after her arrival, two of them as a condition of her acceptance as a Displaced Person. Now she was too old to work, she had a small monthly allowance, which she viewed as a human right. She was a world citizen now. She had once told Helen, who was Betty's sister-in-law, that she did not believe in nationalism, that she was happy to take money from any government.

"Nationalism, dear?" Helen had asked.

Olga had explained the heart of the problem, that nationalism was the antithesis to the brotherhood of man (as she had heard it called by a Methodist minister once, and that seemed easier to explain than the international proletariat).

"I'm not sure what 'problem' you mean, Olga. I'm an Australian, dear. There's no changing that. I might wish I was a Fijian, but that would just be wishful thinking, wouldn't it?"

Olga's train of thought is interrupted by Betty offering her a plate of the dreaded cakes.

"Almington?" asks Olga.

"Lam-ing-tons," says Betty. "They're called lam-ing-tons, Olga dear."

Betty was so gentle with her rapprochements, Olga barely noticed that's what it was.

"L-amingtons," Olga repeats, rolling the 'l'. She knows she has been corrected before, but the correction never stuck in her mind.

Olga had made a hazelnut torte for the ladies once, soaked in brandy.

"Oh, my goodness!" Betty had exclaimed. "Very continental! So much alcohol! My Eric will wonder where I've been!"

Soon, they get down to the business of the day — polishing off the 'spread'. The lamingtons are indeed dry; the tea like bitter mud, only made drinkable with the addition of spoonfuls of honey. Olga loves honey. She makes a mental note to buy some for herself. She could not think why she had not done so before.

"Beverly left a card, Olga. Here it is."

Olga opens the scented envelope. The card is embossed with a sparkling, pastel bouquet of flowers and has bevelled, gilt edges. Her fingers tickle as she runs them over the card.

"Thank you, Betty. I will treasure it."

The women have gifted her some personal products called Yardley Lavender Soap and Yardley Hand Cream. They have an English smell, which Olga had decided meant not very sophisticated. She, who once chided Coco Chanel for presiding over a factory! At least the French knew how to blend real perfume. She thanks the ladies warmly for their gift.

"Olga, how do you sing Happy Birthday in Russian?" Iris asks.

Iris is British and 'quite proper', as Betty described her. She and her husband were referred to — when she was not around Olga noticed — as Ten Pound Poms. That meant that they had paid a token amount of money to travel on a ship for six weeks to get to Australia to make a new life. Olga thought this would mean she and Iris had something in common, but then, how can you compare six weeks on a boat with three years in displaced persons camps across Hungary and Italy and a year at Bonegilla? (Olga would always, in this country be referred to as a 'DP' and Iris as a Ten Pound Pom).

But that had been Olga's journey to Box Hill. Iris was always more inclined than Olga to comment on the things she missed and how the small things in life were different in Melbourne than 'back at home'. Iris's husband, Rex, had been a shipbuilder in their hometown of Newcastle Upon Tyne and was still employed at the naval dockyard in Williamstown. Olga thought this a good working-class job, even if Rex was a supervisor. Did he not have a workers' council to advise him? Olga asked. Iris, puzzled, had emphatically assured Olga that he did not.

Iris had remarked that Australian tea was not as good as English tea, that the sausages had more cereal in them and not nearly enough pork fat. But Olga, who had many things to miss about her former lives — her sons, her political positions, (her *outstanding contributions* to the Revolution, she wanted to say) — largely kept her opinions to herself. Except when she could not.

Olga breathes deeply a few times and starts to sing in a low voice, "*S dnem rozhdenya tebia...*"

When she finishes, the women clap.

"That was lovely, dear," Betty says.

That was the only time the women had asked her to speak Russian. She did not mind that they did not ask again. There were many Russian émigrés in Melbourne, hidden in the tide of refugees and DPs. Olga could have sought them out if she had wanted to hear the language. But Olga had very little to do with them. Occasionally she went to a little shop in St Kilda run by some White Russians. She did not make friends with the shopkeeper or with his haughty wife. She bought sauerkraut and passed the time with them warily. In truth a void separated them; one filled with war and betrayal, dead bodies and the groans of the wounded.

In this country, you had to act as if nothing whatsoever had happened in your life, even if you had lived through the greatest events of the twentieth century. Olga knew this better than most. She met a few other women in the shop, but she was evasive if anyone made enquiries. The questions were quite superficial anyway. People didn't talk too much about the past. As shopkeeper and customers, what would be the point? They were simply people exchanging in the marketplace. After the Revolution, everyone had an opinion on everything — a marketplace of ideas — and a lot of hot breath was expended in furious conversation by the shopkeepers and butchers and gardeners and soldiers as much as anyone else. If only it were like that now!

Olga Bronstein. Olga Davidovna Kameneva. Lev Kamenev. Yuri. Aleksander. Bronstein, Olga Bronstein. That was her, but these were not the answers she could give to the questions the authorities asked her. Your maiden name? Your husband's? And your children's? They did not ask who her brother was: Lev Bronstein. He who became Leon Trotsky.

The questions always led in one direction, as if her life had followed one path: young woman; a father's daughter; young wife, then mother. But her life had turned back on itself, as if an arrow had flipped in mid-air and flown back the way it came. But no one was interested in that.

Her answers were well rehearsed, as she took on the identity of another displaced person she had known in Italy, another Olga. The woman had died of an illness that swept through the camp's drinking water. Olga Chernenkova had been around the same age and had also lost her husband and children. Olga was the first one to find the few papers the dead Olga had on her, and she used them, as anyone else would: to survive.

Here, she is called Olga Chernenkova for official purposes. But she has never disguised her identity from her friends. To them, she is Olga Kameneva, though she and Lev had divorced when he left her for the painter. Mrs Kameneva, they call her. But why should she mind? Here, she would sometimes fantasise, her name is no longer a problem.

But who was she fooling? She might as well have her real name, or Come and Get Me, tattooed on her forehead.

The last time the women held a birthday celebration, Betty had offered them some cheap, sweet white wine. It tasted a little Germanic to Olga, but she could not be sure if it really was Moselle or an imitation. It had been too many years since she had drunk the real thing. She thought that the wine must have loosened Betty's lips, because Betty started asking about Olga's brother.

"Leon? Was that his name?"

"Yes. Or Lev. The name he was born with," Olga replied.

"He was in the army? The Red Army, Olga? My what a sight they must have been in their red uniforms!"

Olga did not say "My brother was the Commander in charge of the whole Red Army". She did not say "They were lucky to have a warm coat let alone proper uniforms". And to not understand the significance of the colour red: a colour she had given her life to defend? She did not say "No, they did not have red coats. Red was the colour of their politics!"

Instead, she answered Betty's last question, "No, not red uniform. Normal army colours. Brown. Grey. You know."

"Oh. Was he handsome, your brother?"

"Yes. Very handsome."

"He must have been a terror as a child!" said Betty, then, "I bet you miss him."

"Yes. He was a real terror, and I do miss him. He is dead of course."

Betty had put her hand on Olga's forearm and leaned across to her and said, "I'm sorry, dear."

Olga had held back her tears. No need for crying in front of kind people who knew nothing of what it was to be a target of political assassins, to have that target follow you, as it did her brother, wherever you fetched up in the world.

By the time the food is finished and third cups of tea offered, Olga wonders how long she should stay at her own birthday party, and as she stands near Betty's sitting room window, she spots a blue car parked across the street and a man sitting in the front seat reading a newspaper.

Finally, they have decided to notice her. When it suited, she had fooled herself that in this distant place she might be left alone, that she might live unnoticed by holding her tongue (for once in her life). Her friends, these kind women, had lulled her into a false sense of security, as had the visits to the shop in East St Kilda where she could rub shoulders with White Russians, Russian and other DPs and talk to them about the weather and go home afterwards at her leisure. What a laugh!

But here — in the form of a man with a newspaper, sitting in a shiny new blue Holden — here was the past and the future all rolled into the present.

Helen is standing beside her.

"That's a nice car."

Olga says nothing, sipping the tepid liquid.

"Fresh cup?"

"No. No thank you. I've had plenty."

Helen takes the cup and saucer from Olga. The man has folded his newspaper and is looking towards the house. Olga lodges behind the curtains knowing that he will not be able to see her. Hours of boredom await him in the service of his country, thought Olga. Possibly peppered by a few moments of drama, perhaps even of brutality.

Betty walks over to her.

"You seem a bit preoccupied, Olga. Don't worry, there is life after 70."

"Yes, I am fine. Thank you, Betty."

"I wonder who that is over there in that car. Do you see him, Olga?"

"Oh, I see him. He is here because of me, I think."

"Is he a friend of yours? You can invite him in if you like."

"No. He is not friend exactly. I think he works for your government."

"Whatever do you mean, Olga? Our public servants don't work on Saturdays, perhaps they do in your country, but…"

"No. He is special kind. He is…spy."

Betty's mouth opened in shock. "Oh, my goodness me! All because of your brother, I'll wager. I feel like giving him a piece of my mind…"

"No. It is really alright. He is doing job. Nothing more."

"Well, I don't want him to spook you, Olga. I'll walk home with you, if you like."

"No. I do not think he will trouble me. Spies in this country are really quite polite. At least here I don't think they kill you."

Betty looks even more shocked. Her brow furrows. "Well, before you go, why don't we have another lam-ing-ton?" she asks Olga.

OLGA AND THE WHITE RUSSIANS

Polish sausage was what they called it at the delicatessen, but it was so like the sausage from her childhood that she told her friends it was Ukrainian sausage. She fed it to the Box Hill ladies, sliced on thin brown bread garnished with pickles. She felt they ate it just to be polite, chewing the sour brown bread for a long time. Such stupid politeness, she thought. She felt like she would never understand these people. If there is too much garlic in the sausage or you want another type of bread, why you don't just say so?

Smell-memory lured her back to the delicatessen each time. The perfume of home, of her youth, and dinner with her family on the farm in Yanovka. The rare times as an adult she had been able to join her parents for Easter celebrations.

The scent was bread, sugar, cinnamon, part animal fat, sausages and pickles which were sold from large containers. Olga would take her time to fill her basket so she could breathe its alchemy. She fumbled the delicatessen's products in her fingers, examined them, put them back. Picked up something else. Read the description in Cyrillic letters, Polish or Hungarian on the back, replaced it where she had found it.

On this occasion, she was looking for a quality chamomile tea, some salami and a good dark bread. She waited at the counter for her turn. A woman stood next to her trying a slice of what they called Polish sausage, talking in a low voice to the shopkeeper behind the counter in Russian.

"Did you hear that Radomir died? If I was still living in the home country, I would spit on his casket."

"Yes. Good riddance. He was one of Stalin's men. We all felt his reach. It is a pity he was beyond ours: I hate to think what I would do to his body," the shopkeeper whispered over the counter.

"They even murdered their own. No loyalty. No shame. My cousin, Maria Spiridonova, she killed a landlord for the Revolution, and how did they reward her? By lining her up and shooting her in the forest…" said the woman, providing uncharacteristic detail.

Ah, thought Olga, it was not quite like that.

"Well, she was one of them, and you know what they say? You lie down with dogs…"

"Yes. But she was still my cousin," insisted the other woman.

Olga thought Maria would have soon died anyway had she not been shot, she was so ill. Should I tell this woman? No, the fact is she *was* shot but she did not die straight away. She lay groaning for quite some time. But she saved me, by being on top and shielding me from view. I who had been wounded, but not dying quite as quickly as she was.

And here was Maria again, in the portly shape of an elderly woman who still wore a headscarf when she went to the shop. Olga had looked sideways at her and thought she could see something of Maria in the woman's eyes and mouth.

The Maria that Olga knew was at the end of her life even before the soldiers got to her. She was gaunt before she joined Olga at the gulag. Of course, Olga had heard of her; the once-young, revolutionary assassin, the woman who had been beaten so badly by the Cossack guards that a wave of sympathy had freed her from prison.

The woman in the headscarf, Maria Spiridonova's cousin, ordered some of the Polish sausage. As it was being wrapped for her, she looked across at Olga and said, "*kolbasa ochen' khoroshaya zdes.*"

Olga nodded to her and smiled. Yes, at least the sausage is good.

Ah, Maria! Politically, Olga's enemy. But in the camp...in the camp! Olga had befriended her, Maria, a dark, hobbling old bird ready for the pot. She made sure Maria had broth when she could, or some extra gruel.

But Maria had not been long for this world. She'd had few teeth left and eyes that haunted you as a constant window into her pain. But there was something that had burned bright. An ember at the core of her being that Olga recognised.

Maria Spiridonova had reproached her, "In the end, you, Olga, were part of the problem that we, the Socialist Revolutionaries were trying to solve. Some of my SR comrades would have killed you if they had come across you in a dark alley."

Olga reminded Maria that the SR had tried to blow up her brother, Trotsky's train — twice.

Maria had replied, "Well, he was your brother, not mine. It is a struggle for life and death. That's what a revolution is."

"In the end, Maria, who knows when the end is? You think you were right because of what transpired, because of Stalin? Stalin bubbled to the surface of the Party like so much grease on the top of the soup, but I do not share your conviction that we are doomed just because of him. We had hopes of better life…that we all did. All of us had the glint of *idealism* — even you, Maria. People suffered under the Tsar. We thought we would put an end to the suffering, but here we are. Is it the end? We don't know when that is. Not even Koba knows that. If he did, he wouldn't be constantly looking over his shoulder."

Maria, Olga remembered, had become very angry.

"Nothing good. There is a right way, there was a right way, and you deviated from it, Olga Kameneva. You and your husband. And now we are all paying for it."

Maria was as unshakeable as the great pine tree that had stood in Olga's grandfather's front yard, immovable even when burdened with snow or whipped by the Arctic winds. That tree, so mighty! She could smell the pine even now. The tree could no longer be there; such things were cut down in the great famine or since, in times of shortage, to sell or given as fuel for local families to heat their meager portions of food.

But what use are these memories? She resolved (as she often did) not to think of them anymore.

Now it was her turn at the counter, and she put the tea and the bread and tinned fish in front of the shopkeeper. She heard the bell over the door trill as Maria Spiridonova's cousin exited the shop, and when Olga left just afterwards the cousin was nowhere to be seen. And what would Olga have done if the woman had still been there? Would she had told her tales of Maria in the camp?

Olga saw only the crooked trees marching in a line to the end of the street, nearing the end of losing their crisp, dead leaves.

OLGA AT HOME

In the privacy of her own home, Olga Kameneva did what she pleased. Up to a point.

She placed the lavender hand cream on the window ledge in the kitchen. The lavender soap, she slipped into her underwear drawer. She would keep it for a special occasion, and in the meantime, she could smell it on her undergarments and perhaps it would keep out the moths. Finding practical uses was what she had been doing her whole life.

Olga washed the dishes every second day, and afterwards she smoothed the lavender hand cream on her hands. She knew how to conserve water. Her neighbours let their hoses run on their gardens as if there were an endless supply. Betty's husband, Eric, washed his car in the driveway of their house every Sunday, and the water ran in rivulets through the street and gutters. The water was so sweet, she wished she could drink all of it instead of watching it rush away needlessly.

Olga wondered whether they were nihilists, her neighbours. There was a thoughtlessness in the way they went about things. They would be shocked to hear what she thought. They wasted food the same way they did water, throwing it out in the garbage bin instead of keeping it to dig into the soil to feed the worms. They washed their clothes each time they wore them, whether they were dirty or not.

There were things she could do in her flat but did not. She did not dance around the room when she heard music she liked on the radio. She did not like to stay up late at night nor get up late. Her work ethic was well-honed through her early years as a Party worker and looking after her family while her husband was frequently away, as well as through her work with the famine relief committee and the theatre and in the labour camp. There were many who did not survive the work of the camps. You needed to pace yourself, to take it slowly when the guards were gossiping. That wasn't all you needed — there was bribery, and luck as well. Fate, as the peasants would call it.

Maria never had much by the way of luck, but she would never shirk the work, though she was the frailest of all the women in the camp. She, of whom the peasants would perhaps have said, "see what happens when you try to escape your Fate? Something worse happens!"

It was the memory of Maria, and women like her, that kept Olga on a straight path now, that kept the piles of magazines and the ornaments and string and brown paper bags and other things she hoarded in some kind of order.

Maria: her tormentor and her saviour. And she, Olga, was still a prisoner of sorts. She would serve her own afternoon tea with a cheap samovar she had bought in St Kilda, and she would quickly suds the cup, saucer and plate and the bone-handled cutlery and set them aside for the next morning as if she were still sharing a communal kitchen. That was her fate- now written by a tea cup, not by tea leaves…

She had bought these little luxuries at a secondhand shop in Box Hill run by what she could only describe as a Christian sect (what else would you call a group that called themselves 'The Salvation Army?') Army! She should show them an army. She could flick a switch in her head and there they were, marching into Stalingrad, marching to stop the advance of the Nazi hordes. Once they were real with flesh, sound and smell. Now there was only the warm suds slipping through her bony old hands.

If only you had listened to your brother.

If only my Yuri had stayed in America and not returned to Russia.

If only I had never been born.

The buzzer to her flat rang. She wiped her hands on her apron. She stood before the door, without opening it.

Once, she had opened the door to the Okhrana.

Once, she had opened the door to the NKVD.

Once, her husband, Lev, had slammed it in her face. After that, he was her husband no more. Koba, (Stalin's benign nickname, which they all kept using — desperately hoping it would win them some favour), soon slammed the door in Lev's face, and her brother's. *I do not know you.*

Would that they had all been able to find a way past that man. But he was always there, the doorkeeper, our Koba. Many tried to get past, but usually tripped over his heavy foot. Lev and her brother, and all the others.

In Box Hill she should have nothing to be afraid of. She had no contact with Australian socialists. Commies, the newspapers called them. The Reds.

Olga opened her front door.

Iris thought that her friend looked a little ashen, but she did not inquire further. Perhaps Olga had been ill. That would account for it. She could revive her with tea and chat. It always worked. There were many, many times, when confronted with an ashen-faced woman, Iris had worked her magic. She had made the tea, counselled the woman to think of the children, of their welfare, to understand the pressures on her husband and why he might treat her the way he did.

Iris had a suspicion that Olga and her husband, the one called Lev, were parted long before he died. She suspected that Olga didn't talk about it because of the scandal.

Iris tried not to associate with divorcees. It was unfortunate, but such women provided the kind of temptation that other marriages could well do without. Iris saw a divorcee once at a distance. She had been a Mrs Potter, but had reverted to her maiden name. The woman was standing on the platform at Flinders Street Station waiting for a train, her eleven-year-old daughter in school uniform standing next to her. Iris was glad that the Potter woman, or whatever she called herself now, did not see her.

"Are you alright, Olga? You don't look well, dear."

Olga waved her hand and smiled. "No, no. All is very good. Thank you."

"Yes, the colour is coming back to your cheeks," said Iris as she walked into Olga's living area.

"Is there something you are worried about, dear? Anything we can help with?"

"No. I am a little nervous. Living on my own, you know."

"Oh, yes, I see. Well, perhaps you should join us at the Returned Services Club, Olga? Rex is a member, as is Eric. There are many retired veterans there who have lost their wives…glad of the company…"

"Lost?"

"Yes…you know, men whose wives have passed on…"

Olga looked perplexed.

"Their wives have died, dear."

"Oh. No thank you," said Olga. "All the same," she added — she had worked out people added that phrase for the sake of politeness.

"Tea, Iris?"

"Just a small one, thank you, Olga. I must get home to put Rex's tea on, dear."

By which Olga knew she meant his evening meal. Sometimes concentrating on what people really meant exhausted her. She had a vision of what Iris would experience had she been a foreigner in Russia. For a start, she would know nothing of the language and few people would know English. She would be offered strange food, and from street vendors. She would be awed by the Red Square and the candy-cane spires of St Basil's. And the cafés where the artists and activists gathered, with cheek-by-jowl fervour. That would test our Iris, Olga thought.

Iris had come to visit to ask Olga to a picnic that Beverly was hosting in her backyard.

"It's a…well a chop picnic," explained Iris. "That means we cook the meat outside."

"Outside? In the fresh air? That sounds wonderful," replied Olga.

As Iris left, Olga followed her out to wave goodbye. She noticed the blue Holden once again, pulled up across the road. Waving to Iris, she walked back inside and bolted her door.

OLGA AND THE CHOP PICNIC

Olga finished her preparations for her outing as she usually did: with the slap of cold water on her face as she stood in front of the bathroom mirror. She had become used to cold water in the gulags, and besides, hot water had been a rarity when she grew up, and even later, in Leningrad. There was one difference here: the water was pure as Ukrainian snow. In the gulag it had been dark with other people's muck besides your own. The DP camps in Europe had been little better. Bonegilla was bearable for an old woman — young men were goaded by the guards and young women harassed for sexual favours. But occasionally, there was hot water. Olga considered herself an expert on the water quality of camps.

She felt the sun warming her up as she strolled down the street towards the tram stop. She was on her way to Beverly's house. Beverly, with the two grown-up daughters and the jolly husband called Leslie. Others called them Les and Bev, but Olga did not. As a name, Bev was too close to Lev for her liking, and she preferred longer names that rolled more easily off the tongue.

Beverly's house was three tram stops away. In her younger days, Olga would have walked, but not now, not with the arthritis in her hips and knees, and the relentless puffing when she walked longer than half a mile or so. She was overweight, which she had not been for many years. Not since the early days of the Commissariat had she been overweight, when there had not only been enough to eat, but meat as well. And not only horse! And vegetables, even fruit — apples, and once, figs. She never found out where the figs came from, but she had often wondered.

The tram slid to a slow halt and she alighted. Beverly's house was bigger than those in Olga's street, with three solid brick rooms across the front, and a large entrance hall off the substantial porch.

Smoke wafted around the corner of the house. The smell of charred meat followed. Next, she could hear voices. There was a phonograph set up, some jolly music playing. Was it called music hall, that style? It made her heart skip.

Beverly greeted her at the front door. Olga was surprised to see the apron missing, and when she was taken through to the backyard, it was Leslie who was sweating over a 44-gallon drum. The men had gathered around him, beer glasses in hand. Most of the women were seated away from the wafting smoke. They sat at the kitchen table, which had been brought outside, piled with bread and empty beer bottles, glasses and plates all on a red and white chequered tablecloth.

Olga offered up the sweet biscuits, which she had bought for the occasion from the delicatessen, and she was warmly thanked.

"We call it a chop picnic," said Leslie. "A cove at work —Iti or something, New Australian, anyways — he started having them, invited me and I thought this is not such a bad idea. Man in charge of a fire — better than an Empire Day bonfire! Just a chop or sausage between two bits of bread and a bit a salad. But it tastes lovely, Olga. Specially after a few beers!"

And Olga did indeed think it tasted lovely when she finally bit into a chop. The caramel-charred outer layer of meat encased fleshy juiciness. The bread was normally tasteless, like uncooked, white dough, but today it soaked up the meat juices so was completely delightful. The meat was lamb from a sheep, of which she had heard say there were thousands for every person in Australia.

Olga could see blood-red juices trickling down Eric's chin and neck and she laughed as he attempted to clean himself up with his handkerchief. Then he pretended to swat her with it.

It was very pleasant and easy and reminded her of the times she and her family had cooked outside in the summer, especially venison, hot potatoes and apples toasted in the coals of the fire.

It was then that Olga noticed the women had been joined by someone whom she did not know, a young woman. Olga estimated she was in her early twenties. She wore a large blue coat, which Olga thought odd, given the warming weather. The young woman looked pale, as if she had never been exposed to the sun. Brown hair hung over her shoulders in wisps and she wore black-framed glasses atop a long thin nose separating her brown eyes. She reminded Olga of an owl, so much so that Olga startled a little when she looked at her, because of all the animals that seemed to be absent from this country, the owl was the one she most missed.

Beverly saw that Olga was looking at the girl intently.

"This is my daughter, Vera," she said.

"Vera, this is Olga. Olga is from Hungary. No, Ukrainia, Russia... Oh, which one is it?"

Vera looked through her thick glasses at Olga and held out her hand.

"Ukraine...Russia," she said with an extra roll on the 'R'.

"So pleased to meet you. *Privet*," Olga added.

Vera smiled. "*Privet*," she replied, and her eyes — yes, her eyes! They told Olga something. A look, almost conspiratorial. She knew conspiracy when she found it. To the right person, its cry was as loud as a newborn's.

Vera, the *other daughter*, refused anything her mother gave her to eat. Olga observed that she looked out of place amongst her robust, ruddy-faced elders. She looked fragile and breakable, even in her heavy coat.

"Vera's not staying. Just popped in to say hello," Beverly said.

"Actually, I didn't know there would be company," Vera replied, taking a seat next to her mother.

Olga ate until she was fit to burst, but she felt that her hosts would never notice how much she ate, there was so much food. She finished off on the chocolate cake that Betty had brought along.

Eric said, "here, have a shandy, Olga. You're one of us now!" Olga nodded and took the weak urine-coloured drink, drank and pretended to like it.

"Is good, eh? Olga?"

"Yes. Good, Eric."

Once the women had cleared the main table, the men started a card game, sitting around a small table with folding legs. Olga had seen something similar played amongst the English in Paris. They had called it 'Crib'. She herself had played cards as a girl and young woman. That was before she joined the Party. There was not much time for cards after that, except occasionally in exile before the Revolution. She liked card games. She liked to think they had given her a taste for politics, so that when it came along, she was ready with her knowledge of tactics and her poker-face, which had come in very handy — especially when she had to face her husband's accusers. Playing card games had introduced her to systems and signals, to know how to improve on a weak hand — which she had managed to do, more times than she could count.

Her brother, Lev, (he who called himself Leon) had never been interested in cards. It was he who introduced her to politics. But perhaps he had never needed a vector to it, as she did.

When she played cards now, she played as her own woman. She'd had several games with Betty, though for some reason the women preferred something they considered more of a women's game called Euchre. Confidence was as important in cards as in politics. But after all, these were only card games! Not life and death. Not like politics. But perhaps her childish pursuits had played their part in preparing her, both for defeat and for victory.

She watched the men play for a while and noticed Vera was leaving. As she made her way past, Vera said, "*Do svidaniya.*"

Olga replied the same way, and taking Vera's hand in hers, she looked at it as if she were about to read the palm.

"When you feel like it, you should come and visit me," Olga said, and whispered her address.

VERA'S VISITS

"You were a…how you say it? Muggins."

Olga had learnt that word at the chop picnic when the men were playing cards.

Vera had come to visit her twice now. The first time, they had talked about Russia. Vera told Olga that she was interested in languages and asked to visit again for the purpose of Russian conversation.

The second visit was made after dark, on Olga's insistence, and Olga let Vera in through the laundry at the back of the flats.

Olga knew better than to ask direct questions. She bided her time with Russian tea and small, sweet, sticky almond cakes bought from the delicatessen. Over the second cup, she said to Vera, "I buy these cakes from the White Russians. You know who they are?"

She saw that Vera knew — her eyes widened then narrowed in focus — and that fierceness told Olga, in a phrase coined by her own brother, that Vera was a 'fellow traveller'.

"Oh, you mean the cakes?" Vera said playfully and with a slight smile, then continued, "no… I mean, I have met…some of those. Kids at school who, you know, called themselves White Russians, protesting when other kids called them Communists."

There. The word had been spoken, and not by Olga.

Olga nodded as her eyes darted around the room. But there was no one else, no one listening.

"Oh? And you know about the Communists?" And in Russian, Olga followed with "*Kommunisty*?"

"Yes. Of course I do," Vera answered. "We had the war, and they were our allies. And the referendum against it? I was old enough to understand."

This was like a dance, or an inquisition.

Vera was chewing gum, like many teenagers who had adopted the habit from the American soldiers.

"I know about this referendum, to ban Communist Party. I read about it. What you think?"

Vera shifted her legs. She said, (carefully, Olga noticed) "I thought it was not democratic, I thought that people had a right to their views, and they had a good reason to…well, Hitler was a monster and…anyway, I went to a protest against it. In the city. My mother and father were furious when they found out."

"How old?"

"I was sixteen. I went with a friend from school. As a dare."

Olga thought of herself at sixteen. A dare! Ah, the middle classes, she thought. They get bored so easily, the dare is what they have…hunger is a better frisson, that gnawing and sick-making feeling so you think you can focus on nothing else but your stomach. But you can be distracted — even from that. She focussed again.

"You met people, there at the protest?"

"I did, yes, they gave me a card with an address on it. I had to pretend I had gone to bed with a headache, then got out through my bedroom window to attend their meeting."

"And?"

Vera knew she had to tell Olga everything. There was no one else now.

"And I joined up. But you knew that already, didn't you?"

Olga nodded. "More tea?"

"Yes. Thank you. I went to the classes. I told my parents I was studying with a friend they didn't know. I made up a name — Evelyn — at the State Library. Which I did do for half an hour before the classes, so it wasn't a total lie."

"Strictly speaking," said Olga.

"Strictly speaking," Vera repeated. "I learnt a lot. I really did. Except perhaps how to protect myself."

"You know, I was in the same situation myself. Oh yes. I met my husband-to-be, Lev, when I was eighteen. He was already an important figure in the Party. He turned my head. What can I say? Along came the baby."

"Oh, Olga, I knew you would understand! I just knew!"

Vera leaned over and threw her arms around Olga's shoulders. Olga leant into Vera. No one had touched her in such a way for many years.

"So, you were…right in the thick of it all? The Revolution?"

Olga nodded. "Not only that, but yes. My husband and I were…important people. But that is in the past. We have to talk of the future now."

Vera poured herself more tea but said no to the cakes. She ran her hand over her midriff, absent-mindedly.

"Yes. It's all happening too quickly… I'm not ready…"

"We were not ready for the Revolution either, Vera. And yet it came."

Vera briefly opened her mouth, Olga could not tell whether it was a shock response, but in any case, no words followed.

"How old are you now, Vera?"

"Nineteen."

"Same age as me with first child. You are old enough to make your own decisions in life." Olga stood up. "In Russia, you would have been married and already have your own brood by now."

"I'm not twenty-one, so here I still have to obey my parents."

"And yes," Vera added with resignation, "we aren't in Russia. And this is 1953, not 1917. At the other end of the Earth."

The young woman had the same mix of uncertainty and certainty as Olga at much the same age. What was the expression? With the world at your feet.

Olga could see that the young woman was on the verge of tears, her cheeks flushed.

"So. Old Russian expression — what is to be done, Miss Vera?"

"I don't know. I just know that whatever it is, I need to be quick about it."

"How far are you?"

"I would say more than three months."

"Yes. As you say. Your parents know?"

"No. They don't. I was hoping you would tell them."

"Me?" Olga was shocked. "Why me?"

Tears had welled in Vera's eyes. Her cheeks had gone red.

"I'm sorry to drag you into this, Olga. I don't have anyone to turn to. I can't do it myself. I just can't! My parents have paid for me to live on campus, they have made sacrifices…this is how I repay them? They will be devastated. My mother…she will feel I've humiliated her. I don't know what they will do, but you must help…"

Olga felt a little ill. She had held her tongue in her adopted homeland — Box Hill, Melbourne, Australia. The other end of the earth! She had not wanted to come to anyone's notice. After all, what threat could an old lady Bolshevik with bad legs possibly be? But she had already come to someone's notice, and she did not know why. And here, in front of her, was someone that needed her help. *Hilfe* — a good German word.

"Yes, yes, I will do so," Olga said reassuringly, though she had no idea what help she would be.

Vera sighed, then relaxed her breathing. She felt as if this were the first time in over a month that she had been able to breathe properly.

Vera got up to leave and Olga walked her to the back of the flats, carrying a small torch. Vera turned and kissed Olga on the cheek, contact so brief that Olga had time to only register it and the moment was gone.

"What happened to your baby, Olga?"

"Ah." Olga swallowed. She turned off the torch. The moon, she decided, was light enough. "My sons...I had two sons. Both executed."

Vera had a sharp intake of breath and she felt a stabbing pain in her stomach and reached beneath her coat.

"Oh, Olga! I shouldn't have asked... I have no right..."

Olga waved her hand in farewell. "It is old news," and as she said that she could feel the weight of five-year-old Yuri as she carried him to bed after he had fallen asleep in front of the fire. And she could still feel that beautiful weight against her stomach as she said goodbye to Vera and walked back to her flat, locking all the door locks behind her.

AT OLGA'S THRESHOLD

Vera had never seen anything quite like Olga's. First, there was the front door. It was made of wood, but Olga had hammered boards across the front in criss-cross. Vera assumed they were for reinforcing. Then once past the door, it was an obstacle course. Olga had accumulated a lifetime of possessions in a few years. On her third visit, Olga had remarked she was a frequent visitor to the second-hand shops around the suburbs and that the books were particularly cheap. And, she added that if the shop happened to be a religious one, she usually took what she wanted and left without paying.

"The priests have enough money already," she had said. "And no one here ever stops old ladies and asks to look in their bags."

Bric-a-brac was scattered in a semi-orderly fashion. Olga had clearly run out of space on the shelves. There were jars and vases and ornamental porcelain dogs and kookaburras and biscuit tins lined up next to the lounge and chairs and covering one end of the small dining table. The other end of the table was piled with magazines and some newspapers in varying shades of yellow and bone. In a corner, there was a pile of cardboard, neatly stacked, drawers were crammed full, so they were only partly shut. String hung from one of them.

Then there were the books. There were piles of them, even lining the small hallway. And there were chairs, more than Vera felt were needed for a single old lady, and some chairs also held piles of books.

The week after her second visit to Olga had been trance-like for Vera. After the first visit, during which she and Olga had not talked of Vera's condition, Vera had been determined to end the pregnancy and had even found someone to do it through the network of Communist women she knew. She had walked to the house, a shabby brick terrace in Collingwood. She had never been to Collingwood in her life, and just the walk along Johnston Street was enough to frighten her. Some men were drinking on the footpath and made as if to stop her from passing, whistling and leering. This is the working class! she had thought as she gingered past them. She had waited in the front room of the house, a threadbare carpet covering the floorboards and the smell of animal urine wafting from the chairs. There were cats everywhere. Vera had hoped the place would be cleaner, more sterile. She walked out, still not really knowing what she was doing.

On the third visit, Olga told Vera she had not seen Beverly and Leslie yet but was planning to drop in on them that very evening.

"I think that you think a baby would be a bad thing," Olga said.

"Well, I have my studies to think about." Then suddenly she was unsure of herself. "Don't I?" she added.

"Yes, you do. You must study no matter what. Someday, you will be considered the equal of men. But you will have worked twice as hard for same outcome. Believe me. One day it might not be so, but there will be…how you say? A reckoning."

Vera listened.

"I fought hard, you must see, for women to be mothers and workers, to have the joy of family and satisfaction of work…but I lost it all…my husband, my sons."

"Oh, Olga. I'm…so sorry. I didn't know you lost your husband, as well…"

Husband. Yes, he was I suppose, Olga thought to herself. Even after everything.

"Yuri and Alexei. If only my Alexei had stayed in America working for the Ford Company. But the lure of home was too strong…"

Tears had begun to flow down Olga's face and she brushed them aside.

"Let us not waste the joy of a new life. Sorrow is never far, but joy we take very, very seriously. In Russia, I learned how to do this. You have right to your own child. In the old days, if a girl fell pregnant out of marriage, and the father wanted nothing to do with her, or her family felt shame, the baby would be killed or neglected or farmed out for worse fate. I did not work to build the society…which kills the future…"

Vera was holding her visibly rounded midriff.

"I did not join the move-e-ment to see women carry on in misery. We made the new rights — childcare, children's programs, properly supervised. Help with the housework. Meals prepared in public kitchens. All these things. But perhaps the most important thing is for women to be able to bear children, freely and without stigma. Or shame."

Olga could feel a warmth from within, that she had not really felt since she had been in Australia. It was ironic in a way, that she had felt less able in this country than in Russia or in the camps, to express her true self, her deeply held views.

Vera was silent for a moment. "Mrs Cross, who gave us a talk on women in the Soviet Union, said that, well...doing away with the unborn child...is safe and legal."

"It was. Once."

Olga put the kettle on to make Russian tea. She usually did not serve it to her Australian visitors, but Vera liked it. Today, Olga made do with her Birko, she did not feel like using the cheap samovar. The Birko had been a gift from Beverly. Actually, Olga enjoyed using it perhaps more than the samovar. She loved to watch it boil, to watch the bubbles form and rise without the bother of a kerosene fire. Truly liberating!

Olga drank tea as many as ten times a day. It had been her staple, she told Vera; in the camps, a source of solace.

Olga told Vera that she had supported the ban on abortion in Russia. It was in 1936. She had continued to assert her views against those of many, including Kollontai.

"You have to know what we faced. It was not the chop picnic! We had lost many, many people in all of the wars and we had starvation and orphans and war-wounded and many other things to deal with while we forged new society. You could not imagine worse situation if you tried."

Vera arched her brow.

"You look at me like that, Vera. Women will always feel the sharpest edge until the dilemma of motherhood is resolved. This is what I tried to do. Women should be mothers if they want and get support they need. Full social and polit-ical participation. But there was official policy, then there was what really happened. Of course, women still had abortions. People will always find the way through.

"Nothing is straightforward. In Australia, too... Yes, Vera."

Vera sniffed a quick intake of air, as if someone had shocked her. "I told you...I went to someone to take the problem away...but it looked too...dangerous. But Olga, if I keep the baby...I won't be able to live at home. And no one will rent a flat to me. No one will employ me, except perhaps as a servant. Not much of a life for a child. Or for me."

Olga looked quizzical. "You mean, you might send the baby to an orphanage?"

Vera shook her head.

"First, we must tell your parents. Because whatever happens, the baby comes, and they will find out."

"Unless I go somewhere else…to the father, for instance. He's in Sydney. He was relocated, to work for the Party."

"Does he know?"

"No. No, he doesn't know. We parted before he was transferred."

"Is he in any position to help?"

Vera grimaced a half smile. "He has a girlfriend. She's a new comrade. Rising through the ranks. I don't know whether he would help. Or whether anyone in the Party would."

"We should ask. Surely there will be sympathetic women. No?"

Olga remembered Tatiana, for whom Lev had left her and with whom he had a baby. She, too, had been a rising star, a painter. But a baby had not stopped her painting. Why would it?

"So, you will not go away?"

"I don't think so. I love my parents. They do need to know."

Olga could hear it in Vera's voice, her belief that if only her parents knew, they would make everything alright.

"Promise me one thing, Vera. Do not lose hope. No matter what your parents say."

"Alright. If you say so, Olga."

Yes, thought Olga, I hope you know your own mother. She changed the subject.

"And at least now women can leave their husbands because of what we did," said Olga, thinking out loud, not especially of herself but of the peasant women who were able to leave, instead of dying at the hands of some half-starved, crazed, drunken wife-beater.

"I mean, in Soviet. We worked hard to end the so-called 'colourful ethnic practices' — the old ways like bride price and the marriage of nine-year-olds and honour crimes…"

"Well," Vera interrupted, "we are free to divorce here, too, it's just that it's not that easy." She surprised herself. She did not know why she was suddenly defending the Australian legal system.

Olga interrupted, "and as usual the woman is worse off…left with the children…same here, no?"

"My mother will probably tell me I need to marry the father. She will talk about making beds and lying in them…"

Olga already knew that Vera and the young man had had a political disagreement, but even if he did have someone new, Olga felt he had an obligation to Vera. She could see that Vera felt she, as an independent young woman, should bear this burden alone, but social arrangements had not caught up with this thinking. As usual, these lagged behind the human imagination, Olga well understood.

Olga realised she knew little of the laws of this country. She had fought for laws to protect mothers, the state to become the breadwinner when there was no one else. But she recalled, with the civil war the old ways had started to creep back in, like the errant drunk returning to his family, sneaking in through the back door.

The old ways. When exactly did they become the old ways? The sun is in its heaven and the Tsar is far away. She would do what she had promised.

BEVERLY

Beverly was at home when Olga arrived without an invitation.

"Olga! How nice to see you!" Beverly exclaimed.

"May I enter?" said Olga, trying to smile.

"Yes, of course. Come in!"

Beverly untied her apron as they walked down the hallway to the kitchen and folded it carefully and draped it on the back of a kitchen chair. Instantly, she sensed that this was not a social visit. There had been something in Olga's manner that told her there was something important to talk about.

As Olga's visit was unexpected, Beverly went to the living room to straighten the gold-coloured cushions on the sofa, (making sure they sat on their points, Olga observed).

It was a Saturday, and Les had gone to the hardware store to buy wood to repair the chicken shed. Beverly had been worried for weeks about stray dogs getting into her hens and had worried the life out of Les to get the problem fixed, she told Olga.

"Now, you could not have just been passing," Beverly remarked as she moved back to the kitchen to put the kettle on.

Olga detected a rise in her voice. "No. Not just passing."

Once they were settled with their hot drinks and a slice of tea cake, Olga divulged her reason for being there.

Beverly winced visibly. She told Olga that she had already suspected her daughter was pregnant.

"I didn't say anything to her. As long as neither of us said anything, I could live with it."

"That is so," said Olga, humouring her.

"Yes. But futile, I know."

"You would not be a human being if you did not have capacity to live in denial," said Olga.

She meant it kindly. Beverly would certainly not survive the camps, she thought, which brought a faint grimace to Olga's rounded face.

"Beverly, you have the chance to be a grandmother…"

"I'm already a grandmother, Olga."

"Yes, I know. But I mean to see another new life begin and grow before your eyes."

Beverly shook her head. "I know you are well-meaning, Olga. I'm still not sure why Vera has confided in you…"

"As you say, easier to live in denial, even if it is only until you get to a silly old woman's doorstep. You say to yourself, 'that didn't happen'. It allows you to keep going."

Olga was thinking of another time, another inquisition (what did she know and when?), of finally being allowed to leave the bare, windowless office to go back to her family, ignoring what she knew would follow for as long as she could. She brought her mind back to Vera.

Beverly spoke again.

"I know I should say thank you for trying to look after her. But she will have to face up to things sooner or later." Beverly's face had started to tighten.

"I don't really know what Vera wants to do…"

Beverly gulped her tea and clanked her bone china; rose-patterned, gold-edged cup on its saucer.

"It doesn't matter what she wants, Olga. It's about what's possible. And it isn't possible for her to come back here. Or to keep the baby. Or…" Beverly added with special emphasis, "for me to look after the baby while she works or studies."

"It sounds as if you have thought about it already."

Beverly smiled. "Even when you are living in denial, your mind is still working."

"Yes. I know it well."

Olga finished her tea and they sat opposite each other and did not talk for a few moments.

"I don't know what it is like back in your country," started Beverly. "But here, young girls in Vera's position are encouraged to give up their children to kind families who are not fortunate enough to have had their own children. That way, she can put the incident behind her and get on with her life."

Olga smiled faintly again. "In my country, as you call it, Beverly, there are so many orphans and children with no parents, there is no shortage of children. We do not need to encourage young girls to give up their children. They give them up when they are starving."

"Oh, I see. Well, it's different here. You must see my position, Olga. It would be very difficult for me to move in my circles if I had an unwed mother for a daughter. These girls are an affront to decent families — whether you like it or not — and we would be cast adrift. We have worked too hard for that. No, my mind is made up. I will find a place for Vera at a charitable home where she can wait out her...term. They will look after her. And then when the time comes, she will be able to return home — or even back to the University — as if nothing has happened. No, I know what to do. I will tell my friends she has gone to Sydney to finish her studies."

Beverly let out a strong sigh as if her airway had been suddenly unblocked.

"We have paid out a lot of money for Vera to live on campus and mix with the right people, and this is how we are repaid!"

She wiped a tear.

"It will be very sad for Vera, I think, Beverly."

"Well," said Beverly, pushing decisively against the table with her hands, "if you have come here to plead with me to keep her and the baby here, your pleas will fall on deaf ears, Olga."

Beverly stood, and Olga could see that even when she was in the safety of her own home, Beverly wore lipstick and rouge and her eyebrows were dramatically marked with dark brown pencil, lest she be caught out by her friends or a travelling vacuum cleaner salesman. Presentable, Olga had heard it called.

"We will be a family again, Olga. After this is all over. Thank you for your help, but we know how to take care of Vera, what is in her best interests," said Beverly as she showed Olga to the door.

Yes, Beverly, thought Olga, perhaps you would survive the camps, any way you could.

MR CHEKHOV MAKES HIS FIRST APPEARANCE

On Vera's last day before she went to the home for unwed mothers, she visited Olga again. Such a strange thing, Olga thought, Beverly sending her there instead of wanting to be close to Vera. Childbirth can be dangerous — you might never see your loved one again. Life and death are not the time for abstractions! Strange people, Olga mused.

Olga had offered for Vera to stay with her, but the confines of a one-bedroom flat with no prospect of anything to follow once the baby was born, was not a solution.

Vera had visited Olga for some Dutch courage. It would be her last alcoholic drink, and she had gained a taste for Olga's various types of vodka. They made her feel like an adult.

"You are quite the *connoisseur*," Olga said, handing a shot glass to Vera and using a word from the French language that she knew well.

Vera gulped a mouthful of the translucent, fiery liquid. "My stomach has butterflies in it."

"Not surprising."

They sat on the high-backed kitchen chairs and Vera finished her drink quite quickly.

"Another?" Olga asked.

Olga filled the shot glass again. She could feel the fear emanate from Vera like a wave, just as it had from the women in the gulag-bound train hurtling through the black night.

"I never ask about your study at the University, Vera."

"Oh, I'm an Arts student. Literature, history, languages — French, Italian. Taking International Literature, the French- Balzac, Flaubert. Americans. Tolstoi, Chekhov," she said.

"I met Rhys — the baby's father — in the International Literature class, and...well, you know the rest.

"But I'm afraid I found the Russians rather...I don't like to say it about such revered writers...but a little...melodramatic?"

Olga thought that Vera sounded as if she were parroting something she had heard. Perhaps from lecturers trying to discredit Russia and "the Reds", or from her Party ranks trying to throw out the old Tsarist authors. Everyone twisting the history to suit themselves — this she knew to her cost.

She sniffed, "I was present at the first production you know, of *The Three Sisters*. It was directed by Stanislavski. You have heard of him?"

"Oh, that is really something. But no, I haven't heard of him. Is he famous?"

"Well, he is dead, of course," Olga said. "But yes, Vera, he was a very famous man. He was my friend, Mr Meyerhold's *nastavnik*. You say mentor, I think. And rival, of course. That was in-evitable."

"And what of Mr Chekhov? Did you meet him, as well?"

"Oh, yes. I knew him. He was never a comrade. But he was, like many, not in favour of the old order. It angered him, very, very much."

"Oh, my goodness, Olga," Vera said putting her hand to her open mouth. "What an amazing thing to have met him!"

"He was doctor, you see. And he died of a disease he refused to have treated. He tried to ignore it, to pretend it was not as it was. It is very Russian, no?"

"Is it?" asked Vera.

"Our Chekhov thought of himself as a modern man, as so many of my fellow Russians did. So, he esch-ewed the old diseases. We are sometimes self-defeating, as if that bright future revealed to us can never be ours, and so we do our best to make it not so. Is it character? Or is it the snow?"

Snow? thought Vera, alarmed. She did not see what snow had to do with anything.

"I first saw *The Three Sisters* in Moscow. It was 1901 or perhaps two, directed by Stanislavski. I was around 18, and it was my first play. I must say it impressed me as much as the Communist Manifesto. Good writing can do that. Good theatre. In my opinion."

Vera appeared to Olga to be concentrating very hard on what she was saying to her. Or perhaps it was just heartburn.

"The sisters, their tiny world, the mess they make. The self-confining middle class! Never looking beyond their noses! I grew up next to them, I observed them, and I knew them like I knew my mother's own face. But when you see it on stage…up there, somehow you see it differently. It is as if you are seeing their world through a Gypsy's crystal ball, magnified. It very much affected me, and I resolved never to be like the sisters. Somehow, the outer world is there just beyond their reach, they both want and fear it at the same time."

"But Olga, so much has happened since then…so much more dramatic than those plays…the wars, Revolution — do you not think him a little pre-Revolutionary?"

Now she knew Vera was parroting someone. Olga dissented. "Don't you feel like we are all still living in one of his plays? I know I did when in Russia. The surface is nice, but underneath runs the sewer. Those humans. Their emotions. Their exp-res-sion happens, no matter what. But yes, there is nothing essentially thrilling about him. Perhaps you prefer the *sturm und drang* of a Mr Tolstoi?"

"Oh, perhaps. I love Anna. Her passion. But then she is a little dated, too, isn't she? I can't imagine having to make the choices she did…"

Olga could see Vera break off mid-sentence as her thoughts turned inward, to her own condition.

"Not in circumstances she chose," said Olga. "We make the best, though we fight for different ending. I have come to think that perhaps Mr Chekhov picked the *zeitgeist* — you know this German word? We are all concerned with the middle class these days. We all want to be middle class! So says our Mr Menzies! But Anton understood their real values, their deceit. They say they want the good world for all, but when it comes to giving up privilege…well, we know how that ends."

Vera downed the vodka shot.

"What was he like, Chekhov?"

Good, thought Olga. At least I've taken her mind off it.

Olga remembered Chekhov as contemplative, a praying mantis of a man, but occasionally a different man would emerge, though briefly.

"Well, *you* might say he could never have written 'The Cheery Orchard', but actually, he felt his plays were quite comic."

That brought a laugh from Vera as Olga hoped it would; a cheery cherry to her cheeks.

"Most people do not see it, but it is all in the production, you see? His characters, so infuriating! Some, so nasty," Olga continued, "but even the rogue deserves compassion, or some laughter at least. This is Chekhov."

The two women were quiet.

Vera smiled again. "Perhaps I should take him with me to the convent."

"You could do worse," Olga replied.

Vera declined another vodka.

"My mother told me they have a piano there and the nuns have agreed to let me play it. I don't know how often, though."

Olga responded, "I'm sure you will be able to cheer up the other girls with your playing."

"Not sure the nuns will like Jazz or Ragtime," Vera replied with a smile.

"Anyway, it might not be so bad. Mother thinks I can pick up my studies afterwards where I left off, and people will be none the wiser."

Olga walked Vera to the nearby tram stop.

"I don't want to be a marked woman, Olga. I know I should have courage, but I just don't!"

Vera started to cry, and they sat down on a seat part-way to the stop, and Vera wiped her tears, but they kept coming.

"I do want a chance of a normal life! I know I haven't exactly chosen the right way to get there, with the Party and everything, but that shouldn't stop me from having what others have?"

Olga swallowed hard. Mr Chekhov, please stop! Olga was thinking, laughing inwardly at the absurdity.

She admonished herself, on Vera's account. Olga knew that after having enthusiastically imbibed theories, that the maelstrom of practice, dreams and the dashing of them would suck Vera down. She would flounder for a while, just as Olga herself had done — when the attacks started on her brother and on Lev, when Lev was executed, when she finally heard of her sons' fates.

Olga was sorry and excited for Vera. Sorry for the ordeal, the humiliation that Vera faced, and excited to see how Vera would surface again after a near-drowning. Perhaps there will be the counterpunch! Olga had full belief in Vera.

Vera was talking again. "I remember going to a soiree last year," she was saying, "with my mother and father. We visited some of their friends in Kew. At a point, I became aware that the conversations had stopped. I was the last person to realise, but a woman they all knew had walked into the room and greeted the host. Mother told me later that the woman used to live nearby, and told them she was just passing and thought she would drop in.

"No one went up to greet her. She helped herself to a drink and stood awkwardly admiring some painting or other. One woman offered to re-fill her glass and after a while, she left. The conversations started again. I could tell they were all about this woman. I was expected to be looking after the children, but I overheard them talking. She had not only left her husband but taken up with another man and had a child with him. Then she divorced her husband. But she did not marry the second man.

"Later at home I heard my mother and father talking. My mother called her a schemer and said she wouldn't put it past the woman to have come to the party in search of another man to poach from his unsuspecting wife."

"Oh, the schemers are everywhere!" said Olga.

"I don't want to be cast out, Olga. Not like that."

At the corner of the street, a dog had stopped and began to bark in front of them, sitting on its hind quarters until its owner came past and coaxed it away, apologising to them for the interruption. Vera and Olga continued to the tram stop and sat in the shelter nearby.

"People are so polite here. It really is insufferable," Olga said suddenly.

"*Insufferable* is a bit harsh, Olga." Vera smiled at her.

Olga continued, "they try to cover up everything, like wallpaper over the crumbling walls. I think your mother's response is based on resentment. She resented the freedom this woman found, and now you. She is scared of the freedom. She still has the cage of expectations…what am I trying to say?"

Olga stopped her nervous prattling and turned towards Vera and held the young woman's hands in hers. "Pity your mother, as you pity that woman. Do you see?"

She placed Vera's hands back on her lap. "Try to do what you know you must. You will find the way.

"So, that is the end for now," said Olga in a tone that made Vera think she had just been told the story of Olga's whole life.

"Will you write to me, Olga?"

"Yes. I will write. In my poor English. I will write you."

Olga watched Vera leave, her eyes following that capacious, blue coat as she stepped onto the tram stop. The tram arrived, and she was gone.

Olga sat looking at her hands, her old gnarled hands that were once so young and strong, that had held her own children. For many years, Olga had wished that she had had a daughter but that had stopped when she knew her sons were dead. She imagined a beautiful, shining daughter, one who knew her own mind and faced no barriers to its expression. She would be so unlike the misshapen relics made by the alternating hammer blows of parents and priests and Tsars, as if from a dank feudal forge, those women Olga had worked to liberate, all her life. Vera was a woman so familiar, full of old ways and new thinking.

The women. It was always the women. Really, they had been Olga's only interest. As much as she had loved her sons, she knew that they would make their way on their own, but the young women filled her with so much fervency and hope, to see the light shining in their eyes, it was they who had powered Olga onwards, like so many tiny suns.

Yes, she had met many, many Veras. There were differences of course, but then not so many. Young women always, always became pregnant. But it was no longer acceptable for men to banish them to the dark corners. That is what had changed, that was what she, Olga, had changed. And she was proud of it. If she had the chance, she would shout it from the roof.

And yet, here, Vera was going away like a bad dog to do penance before returning to the campfire. And yet, that campfire will not be the same. It was something her brother had said to her: you never step into the same river twice.

PLAYING TO THE GALLERY

Olga peered at the painting closely, examining the folds of the land, the brushstroke-grass, the acrobatic shape of the trees. Landscapes! She had never been fond of them. She preferred the brief flowering, musically, artistically, of abstraction — her intellect had accepted that as if it had always been, just as it had the abstractions of Marx on surplus value and Stalin on historical materialism.

Olga was visiting Melbourne's main art gallery with Betty and the others. Beverly had pulled out, pleading an aching head at the last moment. They had caught the train, joining at their various stops, to Flinders Street and walked up over the bridge in the heat, and once inside, told each other how grateful they were for the cool, cavernous spaces of the gallery.

Olga loved art of any form (she, who had once overseen the theatre for all of Russia). She had seen so much — the radical movements like Constructivism, the shocking ballets, radical operas, modern orchestral works — and knew composers, painters, poets, playwrights, directors, costume designers, singers, songwriters. She made a mental note to see if Betty and the others wanted to attend an orchestral concert. Here in Melbourne it seemed that only the middle classes did so. But how she loved the orchestra above all! For Olga, it was the essence of collective vision and work punctuated by occasional individual brilliance like the glint of a diamond. That was how she liked her concerts. Symphonic, collective. She did not have any time for the Western model, where the orchestra provided the backdrop to the star. No, the ensemble was the thing.

Next to the landscapes was a painting by Degas, and the familiar world of the traditional ballet was set out before her in all its thrilling costume-y extravagance. Here was a man who liked to paint indoor life. The ballet, like an orchestrated war with the violence removed, but still the parry, the cut and thrust. Oh, how she longed to see it again!

"Monsieur Degas," she said to her friends as they admired the painting, "a good painter, you see? But terrible man to my people."

"Your people?" Clarissa asked.

"The Jewish people. He was very anti-Semitic man."

No one said anything for a few moments. Since the war, it was easier to be a Jew, but Olga knew better than to poke an ant nest. So, she didn't persist. But her principles had made her say just that one thing, and that was enough. Her recent experience with Vera and Beverly must have loosened her tongue, she thought. You will not get away with it forever, Monsieur Degas!

"Yes, but still, it's a lovely painting."

Olga agreed. "Yes. Yes, it is. It is very lovely."

Then she added, "I knew a factory worker in Petrograd who painted scenes from the ballet. He was able to attend for free because he offered to paint them. Then he gave his paintings away to the dancers and the set designers. They were so beautiful, even better than these."

"And he gave them away, you say? He could have been a rich man, Olga!"

"Yes, but he had a different view. Execution of your craft is an act of generosity, it should be freely given," Olga said, which drew smiles but no comments from the women. Olga had hoped for a discussion.

Even more landscapes followed. Each of Olga's companions had a word or phrase, she noticed, that they used to comment on the art works. For Betty, it was "oh my." Clarissa said, "how interesting." And for Iris, "now I really like that."

Each time she heard them, Olga had wanted to ask but what is it that interests you, or what is it specifically you like? She wanted discussion, debate. She wanted to forge a new opinion, to hear a new angle.

She asked her friends about one painting. The scene depicted the Australian bush, tall eucalypts in front of a clearing with a smouldering campfire, and Clarissa had said her phrase, so Olga asked, "but what is so interesting in this one?"

Clarissa looked at the painting again for a few moments.

"It takes me back, that's all. You know my people come from Bairnsdale? They were loggers. They cut down big trees like these — even bigger. I used to go visit my father in his camp. He would be away for weeks and my uncle used to take supplies to the camp in a horse and cart. It took most of the day there and back and sometimes I was allowed to go. We would watch the men with their crosscut saws. I remember their muscles glinting with sweat. My Dad would make us a cup of tea from the billy, and we'd eat the silverside and butter sandwiches Mum had packed, sitting around the fire on big logs. I can still smell those trees."

Olga could see that there were tears in Clarissa's eyes. See? She felt like saying, see? Clarissa's tears were very satisfactory to her.

They reached what the women considered more modern works, some of the latest acquisitions. The first painting they stopped to look at was by an American painter, Mary Cecil Allen, Olga peered closely at the title.

"What's it say, Olga?" Betty asked.

"Sea Studio. Winter," Olga replied.

A flat, triangular lamp hung amongst dull-coloured planes, windows at odd angles, a flat sea with waves of cursive brush strokes, like a child's first attempts at joined writing.

"Oh, yes, I see that now," Betty replied.

"Oh, it's positively frightful," said Iris. "It'd never hang in the Tate," she added.

Olga said, "the colours — too dull for me."

They all nodded and walked to the next painting. It was of deep, dull colours and intersecting planes — modernist, a scene from Italy.

"Well, I like the red. It's very ochre-y," said Betty, then she added, "What kinds of paintings do you like, Olga?"

Olga smiled. What could she say?

"I like the Russians, of course, but there are none here. Isn't it the case you always like what is most familiar? What reflects your own experience the most? How you say — you feel it more in your bones?"

The women smiled. More landscapes were to follow, and some large portraits of a few dead worthies dressed in colonial finery.

"Ah, the treachery of images," Olga said dismissively under her breath as they left the gallery.

Betty had already suggested they should go to the Hopetoun Tea Rooms in the Block Arcade as a special treat. They walked to the café, back across Princes Bridge and the muddy brown river called Yarra. They could have scones before they took the train home.

The sea breeze had started to move, and Olga walked with the women, talking little as they enjoyed the cityscape. It was all so different from the boulevards of Paris and the wide, open streets and squares of Moscow. Olga was glad to have left the gallery. She had been looking forward to it, but once she started to look at the paintings, it simply reminded her of what had been lost, and what had been extinguished bit by bit after the Revolution. She had heard that Hitler had burnt paintings. Stalin did not do that. His methods were more subtle. It was as if he hitched the hope of the Revolution to an old horse-drawn wagon and rang his bell as he stalked the towns, spreading fear and recrimination and shouting 'what makes you think your books and paintings are good enough for the Revolution, for the glorious Soviet people?'

Olga's mood brightened once they reached the tearoom. The patterned, dark green wallpaper, discreet lighting and solid, dark furniture, she felt could have been in Paris! If they had been, they would have lingered for hours, with so much to talk about, but the ladies did not intend to stay for longer than it took them to eat and drink. Olga enjoyed the scones and the fresh cream and the feeling of her full, distended belly. But she would have liked to stay longer.

Olga fell almost-asleep on the way home, the rattling train vibrating her body. Her head fell on Betty's shoulder and she woke up just as Betty was smoothing her hair and saying, "it's alright, Olga dear, we're nearly home."

Olga felt an anxiety well up in her. Where was she? Who were these people? She shook herself awake and looked out the window, quelling her fears with a view of her new world, the women chatting in the seats around her, and outside the window the black roads, the brick houses, the leafy green trees in rows and well-clipped gardens. It soothed her momentarily. Then she thought where are all the people? Here, the streets are empty, there is simply too much un-used, purposeless space and nowhere to come together in common purpose. Her anxiety rose and fell with each new thought and her internal response. Rise and fall, rise and fall.

As she exited the carriage and waved goodbye, she said something that surprised her. "*Mit chavershaft,*" she said, as the carriage door was closed behind the alighting passengers, and she surprised herself with an expression she had not thought about for years. *With friendship.* Vera had dislodged it from her brain. Perhaps that, the rattling train and Betty's soothing hand.

Olga finally fell asleep on her long sofa. The day had worn her out but had stimulated her mind, so she slept only in fits and starts. In her waking moments (minutes, perhaps hours), thoughts collided like atoms, creating new questions and codas. But nothing was ever settled. Not least, Olga.

She had not eaten, so when she woke at five am, she sawed a hunk of brown bread and slathered it with butter and red jam. She opened her curtains to see magpies hopping under the front trees and she felt the rising heat through the window.

She looked at the simple repast before her and thought of the still-life paintings that she had most liked. Cezanne, the pioneer, had been so much a nineteenth-century man by the time of the Knave of Diamonds exhibitions that she had queued to see in the snow. French painters, Russian, all together in a wild, free jumble.

The Picassos she had not much cared for (too strict, like a dancing school), but Matisse, here was a painter who could bring the still world to life with a few strokes and a flash of blue or yellow or dark pink.

She had been in awe. She remembered she had stood before one of the Russian paintings. It was of a flower vase so crooked and heartfelt — the flowers were so like the image of something fleeting stored in your mind, not solid, but an impression of colour and line — and she had cried.

Of course, Olga knew the flower vase's painter, Natalia Goncharova, and many of the others, and had followed the debates and machinations of the various competing aesthetics: the Blue Rose, the Knave of Diamonds, Donkey Tails and so on. She had even witnessed Goncharova topless on one of her promenades through Moscow, her chest painted with objects only she, Goncharova, knew the meaning of.

The Russians and the French painters — such an exchange of ideas, back and forth like a ball game where each time the ball was kicked, the goalposts moved. Figuratively speaking!

El Lissitsky, Rodchenko, even Malevich (the renegade). Such tumult, even fisticuffs — yes, she had seen it with her own eyes. What was the difference between his Black Square and the Red Wedge? Nothing to the eye. But behind the scenes, as they say, the people were not so silent. Could you not have both? El Lissitsky was the one who saw how to straddle the void, as Olga herself had attempted to do, but failed.

That moment had lasted only fleetingly. There had been debates about 'Art' — that it was a bourgeois invention and needed to be re-integrated with social life. But mostly they had wanted to just be painters and designers and left to express themselves, and not be martyrs! People do to human expression what they do with everything else: turn it into a competition — a war, but less people die. She wondered what would have happened if she and Meyerhold had held on. But that was now — what do you call it? A pipe dream. N'est pas un Pipe! The treachery of images indeed.

As she took a bite of the bread, she began to sob so violently that she had to spit it out. She collapsed back into the chair and cried as deeply as she had ever done.

The gallery, the company of the women. They were so nice to her. But she was desperate for the company of Goncharova and El Lissitsky and Meyerhold and the brilliant one, their dear Mayakovsky. It was not the fault of these women. They tried, in their own way, they tried.

Olga put down her bread. She walked to her front door and out to the trees where the magpies played. She breathed deeply and slowly to calm herself. The birds were carolling their early morning greetings as the sun peeped over the trees and houses. It took a moment for her to register that she was even part of this scene, this landscape, it was as if she floated alongside. Even the birds seemed strange, large, hopping, playful. They kept up their beautiful warble.

Olga sat on the brick wall and staunched her tears. Her Box Hill friends had reached out to her, but she had been unable to reach back across the space between them, as empty as the green lawns and as silent.

I have failed! I have failed Vera! she sobbed at the magpies who played, oblivious. *Mit chavershaft*, she thought. Solidarity. Camaraderie? The expression did not entirely translate.

And am I still even capable of it?

OLGA, ESTHER AND THE BUND

A letter arrived from Vera. It sat on the dining room table until Olga finally made up her mind that she would take it to the library and open it there.

Unless something prevented her, she visited the Box Hill Library every alternate Thursday. Today, a Russian-blue sky stalked her, rumbling louder as it closed in overhead. She shivered, although the day was muggy with the impending storm.

After queueing for her allowance at the charity office, Olga walked past the bakery where she would buy a meat pie on the way back home. These habits amused her; she seemed to be developing them all over the place. She, who had had few habits in the past because of her topsy-turvy life and the need to outwit her enemies.

Another habit involved reading the newspaper at the library. She sat in the window where the afternoon sun helped her see the words more clearly. The paper was so large you could almost hide behind it. Which was quite useful today, because she knew she was being followed.

She was sure the man was not MGB. He would not be any different to agents from the Okhrana, Cheka, GPU, OGPU or NKVD, she thought. But, she recalled, she had already decided he was an Australian spy. Still, she couldn't stop those old wolf packs from running through her mind.

He had been standing in a phone box across the street from the Post Office when she queued for her allowance. There were two men who followed her. They seemed to alternate. One was quite tall and very thin — even his suit coat could not hide the trousers bunched up around his waist, hanging from the belt buckled around his middle. They both wore hats, but the second man was always unshaven. *He* could be MGB. Such untidy, nasty characters.

She knew why the Australian government was spying on her. It had taken them some time but here they were. Today it was the turn of the tall man. She felt safe in the library — safer than at home because here there were people around her. She wondered if anyone would miss her if she disappeared in the dark of night? Only the Box Hill ladies, and then perhaps a week would pass before they did.

Olga had stood shy of the Russians in the diaspora. The only real diasporic friend she had made was a Holocaust survivor, Esther, now passed on.

Olga brought her focus back to the front page of *The Age,* which headlined with the Royal visit. The new Queen of the Commonwealth, an organisation that Olga had learned included Australia as a colonial outpost, was touring the country. At one of the ladies' gatherings, Iris's husband Rex, with obvious pride, had described the Commonwealth as Britain's children gathered around their mother. "The strength of the Empire is our solace," Eric had agreed. Olga would have had plenty to say about that but had held her tongue. Down with imperialism! Did they not know how many millions had been killed in its name, in India, Asia, Africa? South America?

Try as she might to read the paper, her thoughts wavered between the spy across the road, the letter in her bag and her memories of Esther.

She had been dead for over a year. Esther, who had been her only connection with the Jewish diaspora, and now that she was gone, Olga did not keep up with Esther's family or community, except if she saw them in the street.

What would Esther say about the Queen? Olga amused herself by thinking about it.

Her family were Nazi sympathisers, and we are supposed to love her now?

How would she like living on a bowl of greasy porridge and stale bread?

Why does she wave at everyone like that? Do we think so little of ourselves that one wave from her sends us into frenzy?

Esther was tough, almost as tough as Olga. Perhaps that's why Olga had warmed to her, even though their political views were quite far apart.

Ah, the Bund. Esther's family were members. The Bund and Olga had been on opposite sides in the Revolution. When Olga reflected, she admitted to herself she had never told Esther who she had been in Russia, nor that she was a Communist, though she suspected Esther had guessed as much. Once, their groups had been close collaborators, then mortal enemies as Lenin decried the need for ethnically-organised groups in the socialist movement. Here, the stakes were lower and the arguments were not about life or death, here they mostly ended in laughter or an irritable stand-off.

She missed Esther, and now that she did not see Esther's family or extended group of *Bundistn*, she realised she missed the warmth of their conversation and hospitality. Olga missed their *chavershaft*.

She turned to Vera's letter.

Miss Vera Watson
c/- St Agnes' Catholic Institution for Young Women
24 George Street
Fitzroy, Victoria

Dear Olga,
This is my second week at the convent. I have settled into my room, but it is very cold. I have asked for an extra blanket but have yet to receive it. I share the room with three other girls. They are all expecting of course. One is due very soon, and I think we all look at her with a little dread. She will go first, and while we are curious as to what it is like, to be further along, something also tells us that we don't want to know, and so she is the girl we least include in our conversations, which is probably quite unfair. We are from different backgrounds, but here ultimately for the same reason, and so I do feel a camaraderie with them. It's strange. It's a stronger feeling than I ever felt for others in my life…well, I don't need to tell you about that.

The other girls in my room are from the Western Suburbs: Footscray and Williamstown down near the naval shipyards. 'Mary' has worked at the Williamstown Naval Dockyard since she was 14. She fell in love with a cove there and now he's jumped ship and she doesn't know where he is.

I don't know the real names of the other girls and they don't know mine. We were told to choose a saint's name when we arrived and that is the name we use while we are here. Mine is Bernadette. I told the nun I didn't know any Catholic saints and she was very annoyed and suggested that name. It was strange, but as I didn't know them before, it's not difficult to get used to false names. 'Dymphna' is the youngest of us at 15, and she doesn't talk about who the father of her child is — I suspect it's someone who is close to her family.

I have seen the piano in the day room, but it's locked, and I've asked for a key, but so far one hasn't appeared. There is a library, of which I intend to make full use if I'm able. Up till now, I've been helping in the kitchen — preparing vegetables and the like — but tomorrow I'm going on laundry duty.

I hope you have seen my mother. It was all very difficult in the end, and she didn't really even say goodbye to me. Please pass on my best wishes. She didn't say she would visit me, but it's my fervent hope that she does.

Best wishes

Vera Watson

Olga folded Vera's letter and replaced it in her handbag. She picked up the newspaper and peered over the top. The spy had disappeared. It was safe for her to leave, and since the storm had cleared and the sun was high in the sky, she could buy her meat pie and walk back to her flat with the sun's warm kiss on her back.

CHAVERSHAFT

The contents of the letter weighed heavily. Olga placed it on her dining room table. She made herself an early dinner of hot sauerkraut, brown bread and sausages and sat down at the table with the newspaper she had stolen from the library spread in front of her. Well, she had reasoned, the newspaper would be out of date soon and she was not letting the spy get the better of her, unsettling her as he did. She would finish the newspaper as she had wanted.

Inside, there was a photo of the young Queen waving her white-gloved hand to the crowd from her car as it made its way through the city. The day before, Betty and the other women had made a special trip to wave their little flags at her. They had invited Olga, who politely declined. The photograph was underlined by a quote from the Prime Minister, Mr Menzies, about outpourings of affection for the young couple. There were more photographs of the onlookers, cheering, children smiling. "I'll remember it for the rest of my life!" said one.

This affection for the Empire perplexed Olga. That Australia would send so many of its young men to that War to die for a silly Queen and Empire when the country was not even threatened? Such a waste of young men. They had no choice, she and her comrades, but to fight the invaders coming from every country to help staunch the flow of Russian aristocratic blood and kill off the Revolution.

She scanned the Letters Page: usually it was full of complaints about workers shirking their duties and condemning the waterfront strikes. Alas, the Queen's supporters were everywhere! One letter made her laugh. The writer complained about the design of the Queen's bedroom curtains in the room where she stayed in Melbourne, which were graced with images of bicycles and steam cars. The writer thought the design would be more suitable if the Queen had brought her small son with her, which she had not. Oh, thought Olga, to only have the silly Queen's silly curtains to worry about, and not the man watching you at every turn!

A Bundist friend of Esther's had once remarked that there was no need for socialism when everyone had a little house in the suburbs with a garden that no one could take away from them. Olga could see the point...but too bad for you if your new country peers at you suspiciously, so you still have to look over your shoulder.

Olga put down her newspaper and finished her meal. She knew perfectly well, she admitted to herself, why the spies had finally descended on her.

For the first few years in her new country, Olga had kept her distance from almost everyone. She was lonely, she lived mostly on her memories, she grieved, she re-lived all the sad things in her life. She isolated herself, venturing out for work, errands, groceries and books. She had met Betty, and they'd had a tentative friendship. Then on the very anniversary of her move to her flat, she met Esther at the delicatessen, they chatted briefly about the quality of the bread, with mostly bad things to say about it. How Olga missed the smell of Ukrainian wheat, she told Esther. Olga saw her again near the Jewish cake shops in downtown St Kilda and they talked and finally sat their old bones down, weary from shopping, and took coffee and cake together.

Right away, Esther had said enough bold things to make Olga laugh. She was knowledgeable about the politics around them, more so than Olga. It was Esther who was responsible for encouraging Olga to take up the weekly habit of going to the library and reading the newspapers.

Esther was a tiny sparrow, even her voice was high, she had thin legs and a protruding belly, and walked quickly wherever she went.

"I keep five steps ahead of everyone," she said to Olga, and she meant this both physically and intellectually. Esther offered to share the books she ordered from the Left Book Club and the Australasian Book Society with Olga, who politely declined. She preferred Agatha Christie these days, she told Esther, though it was not entirely true. She had borrowed her beloved Russians from the library and found some in translation in secondhand shops, but they were a secret pleasure. Esther had laughed at the Agatha Christie reference as only someone who had been through what they had been through, could do. Murder, as they knew it, was not like in the books.

For over two years, they met regularly for coffee and cake, at the same appointed time each month, until Esther became ill. Then Olga started to visit the home of Esther's daughter when Esther moved there for care. That's when Olga became drawn into the world of the Melbourne Bund.

She had known from the start that Esther had Bundist connections. Through Esther, she came to know the family, and through the family, the Bundist community. Once Esther became ill, her daughter Judy, her earnest son-in-law, Pawel and their two children looked after Esther in an old house in Carlton, and Olga made the trek there once a fortnight until Esther died. Pawel had a job in a knitted garment factory in Brunswick. Most of the workers there were Bundists, and that was how Pawel secured his job.

Many of the Bund were Polish and none of them asked questions of Olga. Not even what her patronymic was. She was simply Esther's friend, Olga. If they had asked, it might have been a different story. Perhaps they would have rejected her as a despised Communist interloper. While Esther was alive, Olga didn't want to take a chance.

Olga found out quite quickly that the Bundists knew they were being followed by the Australian spies. It sent Olga into paroxysms of laughter (in private), because all she had ever heard the Bund talk about was whether or not they should join the Australian Labour Party, which did not seem much of a threat to public order.

Imagine that — in 1921 she, Olga, was fighting the Whites for the dear life of her countryfolk, taking increasingly desperate measures to save their fledgling revolution from being pushed from the nest too soon. And here, this so-called party of labour (whose politicians did not look to her as if they had done one day's real work in their lives), were busy proclaiming themselves 'democratic socialists'. Not even as worthy as the Mensheviks!

Not that this so-called party of labour had ever even attempted any such thing as democratic socialism. There was the shameful episode of failed nationalisation of the banks, which they botched. Olga had been very interested in this aspect and had discussed it with Pawel. He was disappointed, he said, that the courts had overturned the laws of the Parliament, made by good people with the best interests of the Australian people at heart. And did Olga not know that Mr Chifley had been an engine driver?

Olga simply nodded her head. This did not impress her at all. Chifley was a turncoat, against the working class he was supposed to represent, crushing their legitimate strike, using the army no less.

Olga had run her mind over the tactics of the failed bank nationalisation after she had heard the *Bundistn* discussing them. Why did Chifley not mobilise the people to support it? Where were the unions? Fancy relying on the courts, and the yellow press! And besides this, Pawel himself had told her that the sainted Chifley had set up the very spy agency, which now had the Jewish Bund in its sights.

Politics and religion made for strange bedfellows. Even the Kremlin Highlander made peace with the priests, for his own ends. Lev would not have predicted that, Olga thought. But her brother would have.

The conversation with Pawel had occurred about a year before Olga noticed her spies. Esther had been brought over from her daughter's house in a wheelchair for a gathering, a Bund function at their hall in Carlton. There was a small klezmer band, a few speeches about the need to combat local right-wing agitators and to write letters in support of Jewish immigration. The tables were laden with the food that they missed so desperately from their homeland and which was denied them in the camps. Now they were re-creating it in Australia, busy making this country look like the land of milk and honey. Poppyseed cake and challah and potato kugel and too many things to remember, all reminders to Olga of her childhood and her mother's cooking.

Pawel had approached her as she mused over which delicious morsels to put on her plate. She couldn't decide between the cholent and the brisket, hovering and thinking what kind people they were to her, to take her in. Pawel steered her by the elbow into a corner away from the noise.

"Olga, I don't know how discreet you can be," he started.

Olga felt her face colour and it was not from embarrassment but the opposite. She breathed slowly, as she had learned to do to quell her anger. What could she tell him? That she had been discreet when Lunacharsky overthrew her and Comrade Meyerhold, she had been discreet when Lev recanted (as he was wont to do), and oh, so discreet when her brother fled for his life?

Olga smiled and replied, "I believe I can be very discreet, Pawel."

"We think…we have been infiltrated," said Pawel, and he waved a fork at her, "no no no, not by the Communists, *Baruch HaShem*. But by the spies. The Australian kind."

"Oh," said Olga.

"Now that Menzies is in and he lost his referendum, he had turned his attention more widely, to those who have labour sympathies. Part of him consolidating his grip on power. And as you know, we have a few members who are wanting to be selected as Labor Party candidates…"

Olga nodded wisely.

"So, just be careful what you say to whom. I know that you and my mother-in-law talk often about politics."

Olga interrupted, "but not really about Australia. You know it is of little interest to me here," she said. "No, we reminisce about the old times," she added to reassure him.

When they first met, Esther had been effusive about her own background, how her husband had died in the thirties amongst a group of striking workers attacked by the right-wing thug government supporters, how she had spent years in DP camps with her two children and that Judith had rickets and her son stopped speaking and finally, they had boarded a ship to Australia and Esther had got down on her knees and thanked *HaShem* for their change of fortune, even though she was not religious. Then, she came to Melbourne and found the Bund and a whole community, and she thanked him again.

"You are Russian, of course. So, you know the Bund. If the Bund had been better recognised by the Communists, Jews would never have been persecuted the way we were. Stalin would never have been able to do what he did to us."

"I am Ukrainian," Olga had replied. "But we have the DP camps in common."

At the Bund's hall, Olga finished off her kugel and brisket and Russian salad (that, too!) and although her belly was as full as a boyar's wife's, she topped herself up with poppyseed cake.

Inwardly, she had been dismissive of the Bundist angst about the spies. The Bundist Mensheviks now hunted by the Australian Cheka! But she had quickly scoured the room, giving away nothing. Her eyes finally alighted on one man. He did not stand-out particularly. But when he thought no one was looking at him, Olga thought he looked as if he might be committing names and faces to memory.

Pawel need not have worried. Olga was not in the habit of gossiping with the Bundists or anyone else. She did enjoy the *Bundistn* hospitality and their music, and most of all Esther's company for as long as Esther could stay at the functions. Olga was sure that she was viewed as Esther's funny old Russian friend who didn't really understand what they do, and she just comes for the cakes, doesn't she?

Olga had told Esther in hushed tones what Pawel had said. He had said the same to Esther, but Esther wondered why he had bothered. What vital secrets could we have here? It's not as if it's life or death. They might be spies, Olga, but they are Australian spies. The women laughed, Esther through her tiredness, and shortly afterwards, her daughter wheeled her back home.

So, Olga concluded, she was probably being followed because she was thought of as a Bund fellow traveller, not because she was an ageing émigré who had never made any contact with Australian Communists, unionists or others Mr Menzies had identified as threats to the social order. But the Bundists? Their crime was to associate themselves with the Australian Labor Party, who were Menzies' enemy, rather than the country's. But Olga was familiar with politicians using state apparatus for their own ends. Why should the Australians be any different?

Olga picked up Vera's letter again and re-read it. It was already quite dark outside, but Olga had an impulse to walk in the night air. The flat felt small for some unaccountable reason, and Olga put on her coat, locked the door behind her and set out.

Olga had to admit that Esther's death had left her very lonely. Even though Olga had seen her infrequently, she felt an invisible thread connecting them across the suburbs, and would often think to herself, I wonder what Esther would think of that?

When she was with Esther, she did not have to be Olga Kameneva or even Olga Chernenkova. Hah! She could re-invent herself and feel the weight slip from her shoulders. She fantasised about a different life, one where she had followed the artists, perhaps producing theatre herself, perhaps marrying one of them and living in exile, like Goncharova. She had flirted with Goncharova's husband once, so it could have been possible.

With the Box Hill ladies, it was different. She did not want to offend them because they had been kind to her, but her mind was often in a foment when she was with them because she found their lives empty and wrong-headed. She felt so sad for Vera and sorry that they had met under such difficult circumstances. Once Esther had died, Olga had reconciled to never again having a true friend. She'd had so few of them. Meyerhold had been one. Her sons. Maria another — in spite of their opposing views.

Olga needed air. From her front door, she walked up the slight incline to a park at the end of her street from where, in the distance, she could see the lights of the city. The space around her was empty, and the only sounds she heard were the barking of dogs. The Nevsky Prospect had been busy with people day and night. In those days, she had felt no need for close friendships because she had been buoyed by the hustle and bustle of those around her, making a new society in the company of others, so she never felt lonely.

She realised now as the cooler night air filled her puffing lungs, that it was the most Jewish of things, *chavershaft*, that she missed — something she had held at arm's length. How ironic that the champions of *chavershaft*, the Bund, should have re-appeared in her life here, in this alien land. They had both been on a long detour to reach a similar, if not the same, place.

In this twinkling twilight of her life, her needs were different to those of the days of the Revolution. New situations, new tactics, new collaborators. By the time she had reached her front door again, her mind was made up. She took up the letter again and read it. She put it down. She went to bed.

THE MYSTERY OF THE PIANO KEYS BEGINS

In her second letter, Vera told Olga about her days and her work regime. Vera rose very early (she complained about this) and worked in the kitchen to help prepare breakfast, served the food to the nuns, washed dishes until her hands were sore and raw. But, as she also had to help other girls with laundry, it was hard to tell which was the worse contributor, the washing up water or the laundry. So far, she had been spared floor-washing duty. From what she could tell, the nuns took you off any heavy work in the last month or so of your pregnancy, she wrote. Thank God for small mercies, she added. She knew that would make Olga laugh.

She was young, Olga thought. But it was hard work like she has never known. She will survive — it is not the gulag, Vera.

My mother and father have not visited, she wrote. Perhaps I am expecting too much of them. And Barbara won't come to see me if they don't come. But you will come, won't you? she had written.

She also wrote that the piano, which she had been promised to be allowed to play, was still locked. One of the other girls had whispered to her that all of the black keys had been removed. I don't know why anyone would do that, wrote Vera.

Olga had a story about pianos, which she would tell Vera one day.

Beverly seemed to be pretending her daughter didn't exist. Olga wondered if any of Vera's friends knew, or what they had been told. It made her angry. She had opposed contraception because she was a fervent supporter of women, that women could be mothers and many other things besides. Why had she not been able to convince her women comrades? Women should not need to hide in the shadows, and here, especially, in the land of milk and honey!

Children should always be welcome, that was her firm belief. Had she not managed herself to bring up two boys almost alone and see them become fine young men? Her comrades had accused her of idealism, which was a crime almost as bad as murder. Had she been an idealist in her position on women? She admitted to being a dreamer. Idealism: it lurked in the background like a tiny sprite.

So, Olga rummaged in her over-stuffed wardrobe and pulled out her best coat, one she had been given by a Bund member to wear to Esther's funeral. She threaded the marcasite brooch that she had bought at a Bund charity stall onto the lapel. It was her only piece of jewellery. She would visit, and needed to look nice for the nuns, to convince them she was a respectable Box Hill lady. She would summon all the skills she developed in the DP camp, where she passed for someone else, the other Olga: a bourgeois country housewife on the run from the Soviets who had seized all her property. It had been, perhaps, her best acting, and now she sensed she would need to repeat it for Vera's sake.

Vera was worth the act of *chavershaft*, the creation of the bond of sacrifice. A selfless act. Lenin knew how many had been committed for the socialist dream! And this one, well, it was entirely borne of friendship.

Turn person against person as he might, cleave off their interests into separate atomised existences as he had done, Stalin had failed to eradicate solidarity. Like dust, it could be scattered but would always find its way back together and settle again. That's what I am, thought Olga. Human dust.

VERA FACES LIFE

Vera could feel the baby move. It was not the first time, but it was the first time she felt she was being kicked and punched from the inside out. After everything that had happened. She felt like punching back. She had already told the baby over and over it was not her fault (she was sure the baby was a girl), but sometimes emotion boiled over. She cried at night. The other girls did as well, as quietly as they could. None of them seemed capable of comforting each other, it was as if they had been designated a room in hell and locked inside it, alone.

When Vera was scrubbing the floors or stirring the porridge or hauling sheets out of the copper, she would tell herself that this hell was finite, more like that purgatory the Catholics would have her believe in.

Vera was an atheist, so it galled her to be cast amongst god-fearers and such specimens of submissive womanhood. Their position living on the coat-tails of the church was very distasteful to her. She tried hard to hide her contempt, because she had seen what had happened to other girls who seemed disobedient. She had heard from 'Agatha' that another girl put in solitude for her misdemeanours had miscarried late into her term and no one knew for two days because no one checked on her.

The only solace Vera had was the library. There she found Ruth Park's books, Judith Wright's poetry books, Henry Handel Richardson's novels. Some she had read before, but she gladly re-read them. Not that there was much time — all she had was the hour before evening meals when you were meant to be in your room, contemplating, and a brief period between breakfast and other duties.

Vera had a small drawer of clothes, mostly given to her by the nuns because she had outgrown her own clothes. The dresses were very ugly, shapeless and made of terrible, cheap cloth. For Olga's visit, she picked out one with a floral pattern that was slightly less ugly than the others.

Life in the convent had given Vera time to think. That was one thing they couldn't stop her doing. She thought about Olga, and her time with Stalin. Olga's husband had been an important man, Lev Kamenev, who had fallen foul of Stalin. Olga had worked out when to talk and when not to, but it was clear from their discussions that Olga never stopped thinking. Even Stalin hadn't worked out how to read people's thoughts.

But in truth, what did she know about anything of Olga or Russia, except the little that Olga shared, the partial accounts of people from the Party who had visited, the *Tribune* articles?

The physical tiredness did make thinking difficult, and Vera thought of Olga in the gulag and how difficult it must have been not knowing whether she would ever get out of there alive. At least, thought Vera for the nth time, *I will get out of here.*

Today was the day of Olga's first visit, and Vera realised how much she had been missing her company. They had fallen into such easy conversation, and what was it about Olga that had made Vera reach out to her? That she looked, and sounded like, the kind of person who could get things done. That she understood.

The visitors to the convent waited on a row of chairs lined up in the entrance hall. Vera saw Olga before Olga saw her. Vera's throat caught, and Olga looked up and smiled. Olga kissed her as if she were that Box Hill aunt.

Vera found a quiet corner of the garden where they might be able to talk. There was a stone seat under a glimmer of light slanting through the trees and together with the faint birdsong, Olga thought it might have been a scene straight from Chekhov or Pushkin.

Olga started, getting straight to the point. "How do they treat you, the religious women?"

Vera found herself holding back tears, she felt she had to for her own sake, not for Olga's.

"It's bearable, so far. The work is hard, but we are young women and I guess if we had families of our own already, it's not so different. I guess the nuns think it's good training for motherhood."

Except, Olga was thinking, you won't be mothers because your babies will be surrendered or taken from you, more than likely.

"Have you seen my mother?" Vera asked.

"Yes, she seems well," Olga lied. "She hasn't told her friends of course. She said you are in Sydney where you are continuing your studies."

"Oh, well, that's plausible."

"Do you have enough to eat? I have brought you some lemon cakes," Olga said, suddenly remembering, and she fumbled for them in her big, black bag.

"Oh, thank you, yes I have enough," said Vera. "I will share them with the others."

Olga knew that Vera was not telling the truth about the food. She had seen that hollow look so many times, many thousands of times. Women putting on a brave face. What had she herself done when Lev was executed? She went on with her own business, though her drive came from the sheer terror of not knowing what would happen next.

Vera did not have a look of terror, but of resignation. This, Olga did not like and profoundly distrusted. It could lead to bad decisions. Olga looked around her and saw a few other girls walking the gardens with their relatives, who had probably arrived straight from Sunday church where they had prayed over their fallen souls. He won't stop their bellies from swelling, your God, thought Olga.

"You should not be sorry for yourself, Vera. You will be able to finish your university. There are not that many young women who can say they do that! You are better off than probably the other young women here. What has your politics taught you, if not that? There will be a way through, if you are persistent and bold."

Vera bit her lip. She had never thought of herself as bold. Olga put her arm around Vera's shoulders momentarily.

"Olga, there is something I have learned," Vera said haltingly and quietly. "The girls are allowed to, well, have to, look after their babies for a month after they are born. We...have to feed them ourselves. And...do everything. Before you give them up...I don't think I can do it."

Vera looked into Olga's eyes, her own eyes darting and blinking.

Olga was silent for a few moments, then spoke.

"Vera, Vera. You are not dealing with the kind people! Do you understand they mean to punish you? It is part of the punishment for your condition, you must bond with the child then have it taken from you..."

Vera started to sob. "The way they speak to us...you would think we had committed a crime..."

"Which you have...in a way. You are an abomination, no?" Olga tried to make a small joke.

"Oh Olga, can I survive this?"

"You will. What of the other girls? Do they not go through the same thing? What makes you so special?"

Olga spoke this way to snap Vera out of it. Vera needed to get angry; otherwise, she would not act to save herself.

"I thought my mother and father would help me. Instead, they've left me to rot!"

Ah yes, Olga thought. Her brother was scathing of the middle classes and their pretenders — the fomenters of fascism, the handmaidens of despots, slaves of warmongers and, worst of all, a race of greedy shopkeepers. Such a declaimer! And, in Russia, he would berate that the middle class had been especially weak, not even up to the role of bringing about the shopkeepers' parliament like in England or France. Fighting them held us back! he would say, as they took advantage of every corruption. They were the continuity with the Tsarist structures. Only the workers were the point of difference! She could hear him now. Anyway, continuity won. Perhaps, Olga mused, the middle classes were the cockroaches of humanity, destined to outlive everyone else.

She wanted desperately to explain it all to Vera, who had one foot in either class. The Bolsheviks had parried with them, the professional classes who did not want to give up their privileges. Could you share your apartment so that others might not be homeless and die in a Moscow winter? Share your food — you have plenty! Stand in a queue with everyone else who needs bread? Ah well, the Revolution brought them all down a peg. She pictured Beverly in a bread queue, bristling at contact with the hoi polloi.

"I will think more. You cannot rely on your family. I will work this out," Olga said. "Do not worry. I will come back to you, here."

"Olga, I can't thank you enough for coming. I was so happy to hear from you. I thought I had been, well...abandoned..."

They walked back to the thick wooden door of the stone building that would be Vera's home for the next few months and Olga left her friend on its steps, standing on the brink.

OLGA'S BIG IDEAS

Olga had visited Vera by taking a tram and a train, and on her way back home Olga realised she had run out of train tickets. Eric usually bought her a bunch of tickets when he was going about his errands. So kind!

Olga approached the ticket box with caution. Since she left Bonegilla, she had avoided interaction with authority except for the welfare people. She could not avoid that, and possibly the workers there resented the money they doled out to her, but she took it all the same. She was an Internationalist, she reasoned, entitled to support wherever she washed up.

She rummaged in her bag for her identity papers and pushed them under the grille towards the man behind it.

"No, love, you don't need them here," he said and peeled off the tickets she had requested without any bother. Olga was relieved.

On the train, her thoughts turned back to Vera. Her idea — that Vera keep her baby and resume her studies — seemed far from being realisable. The idea had originated on that long night walk through the empty Box Hill streets. If Olga could not help a young woman such as Vera to overcome her circumstances, then the Revolution had been for nothing.

Why should Vera and her baby be ostracised? After the Revolution, even when they had so little, her comrades had still set up day care and communal kitchens to help women of any age, so-called 'married' or not, to take up their place alongside the men, at schools, universities or factories. And of course, what helped women helped men and children, too, *and* the Revolution, let's not forget that! Olga was proud of what she had done, in spite of Kollontai and Inessa Armand disagreeing with her on abortion. She, Olga, was the far-thinking one, though. Women would only have real choice when their reality was accommodated by the social order, when their children were welcomed with open arms. She had said as much to Kollontai, but she had been sidelined for her efforts.

But what did she know about the women here? Vera went to University and was of the middling, if not middle, class. But women of all classes needed liberating! But they do not always know how to make common cause — Olga was thinking of Beverly again.

Earlier, as she had passed through Flinders Street Station, Olga had bought a copy of the Communist newspaper on the steps of the station on a few occasions. She, Olga Kameneva, had handed over her pennies without a word about who she was. It amused her in a way. And it made her sad. She would not talk to them. What would she say? They were still followers of the Kremlin Highlander she knew, and one Old Bolshevik lady wasn't about to change their minds. A few trips to Russia, a little support for their conferences from the Kremlin. She liked the name of the paper: *The Tribune*, taking its name from those Roman brothers who sacrificed their lives for the people. Tribunes of the People, they were called. Olga approved very much.

Vera had told Olga she had written an article for *The Tribune* using a pseudonym, Sylvia Bresnehan. The article had been a review of an Australian woman writer's book about the goldfields in the west of Australia. Vera still needed to use a pseudonym even here, Olga noticed.

Olga had been dismayed that there had been very little about women in *The Tribune*. There was one article that made her bristle, about the necessity for women to support peace, because women were mothers and wanted to protect their children from harm. All people want to protect children from harm, Olga reasoned, not only women. It annoyed her that motherhood was used and abused in every way, to support any position anyone wanted to advance or argue against. It should not be so, and she had fought against it.

Until she saw the bunting in the streets, Olga had not realised that the next day, Monday, was to be Empire Day; British and Australian flags were raised high above, with others she did not recognise. As far as she could tell, it was an excuse for a holiday. Not even her Box Hill ladies seemed to mark it in any way except to bake a celebration cake or package-up sausages and bread for children to take to the local bonfire. As her tram passed through the suburbs, Olga could see the bonfires being built by men and boys in the small neighbourhood parks. A cracker had been lit in her letter box once. If anyone sang "God Save the Queen", it had been out of Olga's earshot, otherwise she would have told them a thing or two.

The Australians did not really know in their stomachs what Empire meant, Olga thought; slavery, the bloodshed that stains those flags, the conflagrations in countries far, far away — places still suffering from the fallout of the glorious 'Empire' on their own soil. Tragedy followed by farce — the horrors of Empire reduced to a bonfire and a few sausages.

Olga made tea when she reached her flat. The trip had tired her, she who could once walk twenty miles in a day. She had to admit she was getting older and the arthritis in her hands that had started in the camps, had started to 'play up', as Betty called it.

How she loved that expression! To 'play up.' It made her imagine a tiny figure on her hands hitting her knuckles and fingers as if they were xylophone keys. Ooch, ouch! Imagining that made the pain go away, so she had started to do this each time she had an attack. She imagined the figure tapping out old songs she knew, like *Kalinka*, or *Dubinushka*. She hummed along and soon forgot the pain.

She hummed, she made tea.

After the birth, Vera could come here, Olga mused, as she worked her way exhaustively through the options. Beverly would soon find out about it, and perhaps she, Olga, would lose the only friends she had. Well, she thought, so be it. I go with my principles, in solidarity! Vera would return to University, and perhaps her family would 'come good', as her friends would call it, in time.

She put down her tea cup. She started to hum loudly. Why, I can do what I like in my own flat! (She sometimes felt guilty that she had it all to herself and wasn't sharing her good fortune with anyone else). She sang:

Kalinka, Kalinka, Kalinka maya.

f sadu yagoda malinka, malinka maya...

Hmmmm...she realised then that she had not asked Vera what she wanted to do once the baby was born. Does Vera even want to keep her baby? Olga was sure of one thing: if Vera had to look after the baby for a month then she would want to keep it. Olga could not participate in the cruelty of removing Vera from the convent without her child.

She would liberate them both: what an idea! She, Olga Kameneva, would become the underground operative again. The thought made her feel twenty, not seventy. How would she do it? She could hardly waltz in and demand Vera and the child be released to her care. She realised she had to have collaborators, but that was where her big idea stalled. Who would that be?

She put the problem away and started on her housework, which she had delayed because of the visit to Vera. Sunday was the day for housework, partly as a poke in the eye of the priests on God's so-called rest day.

While she worked, she turned on the radio. The broadcast was of a piece she knew well, she had heard it performed in Paris. That time, before Alexander was born, was perhaps her happiest with Lev. They had attended the Palais Garnier twice. Perhaps they were given tickets? She could not remember, but since they had no money, that was most likely. And she had heard this very piece there, Ravel's *Rapsodie Espagnole*. She could still remember the swell of the violins and the rapturous reception it received. She regretted leaving Paris, if only because she missed out on seeing Diaghilev and the Ballet Russe and the Stravinsky works. Her heart would have swelled with pride to see them on the world stage. But political duty had called her on, to Switzerland.

The radio was Olga's constant companion. Usually, she listened to classical music, but she had also developed a fondness for radio serials. She liked their depiction of everyday life. Chekhov was the superior writer, but Olga thought the radio serial themes similar, the middle classes struggling as everything changed around them, their values unable to keep up, the overtaking of their lives by changed fortunes, often (but not always) unwelcome.

The serial she liked most was called "Portia Faces Life," but there was another she listened to occasionally called "Blue Hills." Of that one, she was more skeptical. The farmers in that serial were not like any peasants she ever knew. And country life? It was depicted as idyllic. She preferred Marx's view that rural life was mostly just idiotic — people weighed down by agricultural work and the sway of the priests, not able to interact, develop and exchange ideas. The cities were the place for that. She had confirmed it in her own life.

According to "Blue Hills", the Australian peasants wallowed in a sea of trivial concerns. 'How soon will lunch be?' asked the grandmother. 'Why don't you buy that dress, Rose?' The Russian peasants were kept uneducated by their overlords as it made them easier to manage, perhaps it was the same here? In Russia, they made sure the peasants focussed on the afterlife and not on the inequality they were yoked to, which was as stark as a raven in the snow.

Olga had tried to listen to "When a Girl Marries", but such in-depth questions as how to arrange the flowers, and the agony caused by the late arrival of the piano tuner led her to not repeat the experience. She did not need to hear such propaganda. She knew that there were people who have hard lives in Australia, many women besides, and she had no time for whitewashing.

But Olga found Portia a little different. If she were at home, she listened to it each morning and sometimes even arranged her routine around it. Portia was an oddity — a woman who has gone to university and become a lawyer, eschewing marriage with someone she is attracted to, but whose actions she disagrees with. Principled, independent. A glimpse of the bright, post-war future.

For her own amusement, Olga found herself wondering what a radio serial set in Moscow would sound like. There would be no shortage of characters in a block of flats built to house perhaps twenty families but housing one hundred. There would be talk of the queues, the search for fresh produce and privacy. There would be laughter, some raised voices. There would be political disagreements, and before it had become dogma, perhaps debates on the relative merits of Stalin's views on historical materialism; of the various artistic movements: the Futurists, the Serapions, the Smithy, the role of Prolekult, the so-called proletarian writers' association. Perhaps Olga would set her serial in some of the aristocrats' apartments the artists had taken over in the Revolution: seven rooms, seven families (instead of one couple and their arrogant, entitled children occupying all that space).

Recalling such communal life, Olga admitted to herself they had done little to prepare people for its close confines, for sharing what little was available. She had jumped right in. There was always someone to look after Alexei when she needed to go to meetings. Such a small space so almost no housework! And you did not need to cook, because there were plenty of cheap food places (the food was basic, but Olga was always in a hurry); however, she admitted that most people seemed to prefer their own cooking. The kitchens could sometimes be dangerous places. Watch out for the knives! But then, so could the private home for women and children with no one to hear their screams.

She amused herself with some dialogue: what's cooking, Olga? You, if you don't let me use the kitchen in peace! Don't be like that Olga. Just make me some extra kacha and I'll be on my way. I have an important meeting with Molotov, and he doesn't like to be kept waiting...

Her mind returned to the underground. Of course, if Vera and the baby were to be liberated, they would need to go into hiding for a time at least. Olga had no idea where that might be. First, she needed to find out more about whether the authorities would come after Vera, and whether there was any crime associated with the act of removing her from the convent. She must get busy and start the dance.

OLGA KAMENEVA IN CHURCH

Olga had not set foot inside a church since she was a young woman and had never set foot inside a Catholic one. As she looked around, it looked similar to the Orthodox ones. That helped relax her nerves.

She sat in the back pew of St Patrick's Cathedral for the last part of the mass. The place was full, and she had squeezed onto the end of the pew, a young man in a suit pushing his fellow churchgoers along so she could sit down.

The main purpose of her visit was to observe the rituals. 'You shall know them by their acts': she watched the priest in his robes bless the crowd, she stood up when they stood up, kneeled when they kneeled. She observed how they made the sign of the cross in response to the priest and the exchange of words; monotone Latin phrases: *Dominus vobiscum. Et cum spiritu tuo.* Vera, of course, would receive no peace at all if she were forced to give up her child, as the priests demanded.

Olga left as the last hymn was sung. On her way to see Vera for the second time, the cathedral had been only a short detour but a necessary one. Outside the cathedral, she caught a tram, alighted in Smith Street and made her way to the convent. She sat waiting for Vera in the foyer, next to a woman nursing a large straw handbag.

"Did you come from church?" Olga asked the woman.

The woman smiled. "Yes. And you?"

"Yes," Olga replied. "I come from the cathedral. We must still pray for the souls of our fallen girls."

The woman nodded in agreement. "Oh yes, I don't get there much these days. But isn't it so…majestic? You feel yourself in His presence."

The woman made the Sign of the Cross and Olga smiled. This time, Vera took longer than last time to arrive, and while she was waiting, Olga spotted a man in police uniform standing in the doorway of one of the offices. He was talking quietly to someone. Olga could not hear them well from where she sat. She moved to the row of seats on the opposite side of the reception area, just outside the office and heard him say "…take care of it… I told you I would, Father… Did you get the parents to shut up about it?"

Vera arrived finally, and Olga thought her face looked even more drawn than the last time. She could see that Vera's ankles were very swollen.

They walked to the stone seat in the garden. Olga pulled out some poppyseed cake and offered some to Vera who took it and ate it readily.

"You look tired, Vera. Are you getting enough rest?' Olga asked.

Vera grimaced. "No rest for the wicked." She shrugged her shoulders. "Anyone would think I was in here for murder."

"Vera, I have question for you," Olga started. She was normally good with words, but she had trouble with these. "If the world was perfect — nice place, nice people, support for you — would you want to keep the baby?"

"Oh, Olga," Vera replied as the tears welled in her eyes, "How can you ask me that? It's like torture! Aren't I being tortured enough?"

Olga took Vera's hand in hers and massaged the back of it with her strong, bony fingers.

"I not mean upset. I mean to know exactly the feelings. We will work out."

"Oh, I would keep the baby. After everything I've been through, and will go through, I feel like I have only one course now. But there's no chance of that, Olga. I saw a social worker yesterday and she asked me how I was and what I planned to do once I had 'rejoined society'. That's what she said. I told her I was going back to university, and she told me that was a good plan. Then she said, 'and you will be able to rest easy now as we have matched you to your wonderful couple, the O'Connells.' She said, 'just tell yourself you are having this baby for the O'Connells, and that will make this all the easier.'"

By now Vera was sobbing, her head between her hands, though before she did that, she had looked around to see that she wasn't being observed.

"*Your* wonderful couple," she repeated, whispering.

Olga rubbed the young woman's back. She pulled a glass jar from her large bag and put it in front of Vera.

"This is for you. To drink. Very good. I make. It's kvass."

"It's very dark." Vera looked sceptical.

"It is good for you. And baby. It is like the dark sky. But with the stars. You are in turmoil, Vera. This is natural. You do not know what is happening around you. You must think. Read if you can. You say there is library? Read, feed your mind. Use your time wisely. This is what we did in exile, and this is not very different, no?

"I will tell you a little something from my brother. He wrote a lot; you may not know that. He wrote about his life, a life I shared with him for a time. There is something you might like that he wrote, about politics, and reading politics. It is my favourite part of his memoir. I have it written out. I keep it with me. In that way, he is always here, in my bag," Olga said, patting the worn black leather.

"I will read," Olga said and rifled in the bag for a piece of paper. She read:

"One might perhaps liken my reading experiences during that period to a night drive on the steppes: squeaking wheels and voices crossing one another, bonfires along the road flaring up in the darkness; everything seems familiar, and yet one does not quite grasp its meaning. What is happening? Who is driving past and carrying what? Even oneself — where is one going, forward or backward? Nothing is clear, and there is nobody like Uncle Gregory to explain: 'These are drivers carrying wheat.'"

Vera nodded and smiled, but she wondered about Olga. So much she did not know about her, and how was this of comfort? Something about reading, when she was in such a bad situation? Still, Vera took it in the spirit in which it was meant. Besides, it sounded like something Chekhov might have written, not a soldier in the Red Army.

"Thank you, Olga. It is very moving."

"I go now. I will return next week. Nuns no suspect?"

Vera looked up. "No, I told them you are my aunt as we agreed, married to my father's brother. That accounts for the accent."

Olga stood up, suddenly overjoyed. She kissed Vera on the forehead.

"Vera, the signs are good. At last I see the revolutionary! You...the subversive..."

Vera looked shocked.

"Make sure you do not make the lives of the nuns so easy. But don't let them suspect anything," Olga added, tapping her nose.

"Next week," said Olga and she left quickly to catch the next tram. There was no time to waste.

OLGA'S HOMEWORK

Olga had a spring in her step when she boarded the St Kilda tram. She wished she could share her big ideas with her fellow passengers, most of whom were her age or older; émigrés or DPs like her, women sitting with their round wicker baskets and trolleys and bags that would not look out of place in the old countries. When she felt like putting her old country around her like a worn, loved blanket, she took the tram to St Kilda.

It was not only the Jewish community that drew her there, but many fellow émigrés — Russians, Ukrainians, Armenians, who frequented the cafés and shops, as well. It felt like home for the time she was there. And it was there she'd had coffee and cake with Esther.

This time, Olga was not here for gossip or camaraderie, her purpose was more serious. She had come to find Pawel's friend, Boruch, whom she knew was a waiter in a café in Acland Street. As luck would have it, when she bustled in with her shopping from the delicatessen, Boruch was working and Olga spotted his large frame, greying, coarse, wiry hair and black waiter's waistcoat as he walked towards her.

"Ah, Olga. Esther's friend? *Borekh-Habo.* Welcome."

"Thank you, Boruch. Can I please have a black coffee and some of your delicious chocolate cake, the one with the rum cream filling?"

Boruch smiled and walked away to place the order. Olga knew that he was a leading member of the Bund, a great organiser according to Esther. He would know who Olga would need to talk to about Vera's situation.

Sinking back into the leather banquette, Olga looked around her and listened and watched. So, this is what Jews have here, she thought. Good food, political talk, people who understand your past, your troubles, your loss of family and homeland, your present. Not bad, but it could be better, Olga mumbled under her breath. Don't limit your ambition, she thought, and willed those thoughts into the smoke-filled air around her.

Boruch returned with the coffee and cake. "Here you go, Olga. I do not see you in here for a long while?"

"No, Boruch. When you have time, I need to talk with you."

Boruch nodded and ten minutes later he sat down opposite Olga.

"I am on my break now," he said. "Go ahead."

Olga began to outline the situation with Vera, and Boruch interrupted her.

"It is a pity she is not Jewish, Olga. We look after our own."

Olga nodded and thought to herself that while that was true, the Rabbis still held ultimate sway and it would be up to them to accept or not. And that depended on the family, and the power relationships and…

"I wonder if you know lawyer I can talk to about it. The girl wants to keep her baby but is not sure of the legal situation."

Boruch raised his eyebrows. "Well," he hesitated. "Perhaps there is someone. Efraim Ford. He has a practice in Elsternwick. I can write his address for you."

Olga felt relieved as she sat on the tram going home. Her first recourse would not be to the law, but she had to know what she was fighting. First rule of the Revolution!

In the letterbox, there was a letter from Vera. It read:

Dear Olga,

I know you are planning to visit on Sunday, but I think you should wait another week. I was asked more questions about you — the name of your husband, where you live. The other thing that has started happening is that twice, an hour before I was due to finish in the laundry one of the nuns, Sister Mary Joseph, came to fetch me and took me to one of the offices. She sat next to me and stroked my hand and told me what a wonderful future awaited my baby with the O'Connell family. Mrs O'Connell once thought she had a vocation, she told me. Then, how she was still as devoted to the Lord as ever and went to church every day and twice on Sundays. She is apparently an excellent seamstress and has been given the sacred task of darning the bishop's socks and undergarments. She is a homemaker and is just waiting with excitement for the birth of my baby, so she can take him home and complete her family and her devotion to God.

My mother apparently told them she was very happy for the child to be baptised a Catholic! I found that hard to believe since she hates Catholics. But then I thought some more. I suppose she thought that if she put me here, there was less chance her Protestant friends would find out. So, I guess if the baby goes to a Catholic family, it's even further removed from her circle. And irretrievable. I cried in my room when I realised that. Even when I leave here, even if it was without the baby, my mother probably won't want me back. I feel so let down. I feel sick when I think about it.

After the nun told me all of that, adding more detail about the sainted Mrs O'Connell the second time, she handed me the adoption forms to sign. I had already thought about what I would say. I told her I wanted to make sure the baby was healthy before I signed the papers. I hope that hasn't raised their suspicions any further. The nun had told me that if the baby was born with any kind of problem it would be sent to a Catholic orphanage and well cared for. I thanked her and told her my plan stood for now.

I could tell she was agitated, and she stroked my hand ever harder. She told me God would reward me if I renounced my wickedness by giving up its fruit. And I've been given 'extra duties.' I now have to strip the nuns' beds each week and cart the linen to the laundry.

There was one strange thing. While I was sitting in the nun's office and she was talking and praying over me with her eyes shut, I spotted a hessian bag in the corner of the room and I could see that it was stuffed full of wooden battens, I could see that they were black on the front and I realised they were the black keys from the piano. I think it is so strange that someone would remove them and stuff them in a corner, things that have so much potential, just relegated to the dark spaces.

The fruit of my wickedness is keeping me awake at night, and I think I can feel an arm and leg. I will write again before your next visit.

Vera

Olga beamed with pride. Vera was fighting with the only things she had: her wits, her spirit. So far, Vera had held out. But who knew what further pressures would be exerted on her? Vera had several months to go until the baby was born, and for the last month, Vera had already told Olga she would be forbidden to have any visitors from the outside. Olga needed a solid plan. She walked to the telephone box and rang the office of the Bundist lawyer.

OLGA IMMERSED

It is strange, thought Olga, as she hurried back from the offices of Mr Efraim Ford, how the past tries to catch up with you, like the old tale of the tortoise and the hare. You can't outrun your life — that was some old saying. Hah! She had done just that, once or twice.

Mr Ford was a short, stout man who had sat behind a very large desk on a raised chair. He had a kindly face, thought Olga — twinkly eyes. He had charged her little for his services, no doubt judging her to be an old Jewish grandmother trying to save her grandchild from the clutches of the authorities, just as grandmothers had done thousands of times. She did not correct his assumptions. She just asked her questions.

Is it illegal for an unmarried woman to keep her baby? No, not at all.

Can she change her mind if she signs adoption papers? Yes, she has thirty days to do this.

What happens to the child for the thirty days? In some cases, the mothers look after the baby, but mostly that is considered cruel. I have heard that some places do that. Most of the time, the child goes to the orphanage until the legal period has expired, then the child is handed over to adoptive parents.

"What if the mother changes her mind? That can be difficult, and possibly expensive if she needs a lawyer to help her," Mr Ford had said.

Olga had finished her questions, but Mr Ford hadn't finished his answers.

"If she is in a convent, as you say, then your friend will need all her wits about her. They will not necessarily follow the rule of law, those priests."

As she left, Olga realised she needed to find a weak spot that she could exploit. After all, it was what the churches had done for millennia, so she was ready to give them some of their own medicine.

Her plan unfolded in her brain like a long piece of tapestry, except that she did not know the colours of all the threads yet. She regretted not paying more attention to the politics of this country. Churches, of course, were powerful. Even the Kremlin Highlander had started to dance with the priests again; though it had been a dance with very complicated steps. Beverly, Betty and the others called themselves Anglicans. They seemed to go to church on Sundays, though Olga recalled that they often recited excuses for not going. I had a sore throat; Eric/Les/Rex wasn't well; we had an unexpected visit from my aunt.

There were a few things Olga needed to find out. Who exactly was her enemy? Who were their apparatchiks, their henchmen? And her enemies' enemy? It was time to invite the Box Hill ladies for a visit to find out about Catholics and what her friends thought of them. She wondered whether Beverly would come but thought there was only a small chance. Olga was anxious — Beverly might suspect that she was up to something if she asked too many questions about the Catholics. But then, Olga reasoned, Beverly couldn't confide in her friends. It was a cage of her own making.

Olga prepared afternoon tea — lemon tea in ornate glasses that she bought at the opportunity shop, cheese blintzes and plum torte.

Betty arrived first. Olga took the opportunity to find out what Betty knew.

"Has Beverly heard from Vera?"

"Oh, I don't believe so, Olga. You liked her, didn't you? I'm sure she will find her way through…whatever it is she's gone to find out about."

"Oh, I'm sure she will do well with her life. She is such an intelligent girl."

Betty sat down on the couch with the lace doilies draped end to end at the top. Olga had cleared away the books and the newspapers and put away all her clothes, piling them on her bed, stuffing them in drawers and in already over-stuffed closets. It had been months since she had seen the top of her dining table. Her final cleaning act had been to make it shine with olive oil and vinegar.

"Yes, I suppose looks aren't everything. Now Barbara *is* a beautiful girl, such an accomplished housewife, too. She has those children dressed so beautifully, she makes all of their clothes, and keeps that house spic and span. Vera could take a leaf from her book."

"Oh, yes," said Olga, "that young woman certainly has some things to be proud of. Lemon tea, Betty?"

"Oh, yes. I do like it, since you introduced us to it. With a cube of sugar, please."

Helen, Betty's sister-in-law, arrived next and told Olga and Betty that her Ronald had suspected a flat tyre, so they literally crawled all the way from Bentleigh.

"Now he's going to a garage to get it checked," she added.

Helen had worn a matching hat and coat made of deep turquoise wool, which she took off and handed to Olga.

Olga served some tiny almond sugar biscuits with the tea, which the ladies loved.

"You know how to comfort my sweet tooth," said Betty.

Clarissa soon arrived in her husband's car. Olga wondered why it was always called Peter's car when Clarissa — often accompanied by Beverly — seemed to have a monopoly on its use, for shopping trips and visits to their married daughters. Clarissa used it to drive Peter to the train station each morning and to pick him up after work. Perhaps that was why it was deemed his car. Clarissa apologised for Beverly, who had been detained by the arrival of an unexpected guest. Olga was relieved to hear it.

Iris arrived quickly afterwards, sorry for being late, but the tram had been running behind, and she had even been thinking of hailing a taxi, but thankfully it finally turned up.

This was the first time that these women had all been together with Olga since Vera left. Olga overheard their conversation while she busied herself in the kitchen finishing the cake with a dusting of icing sugar, frying the blintzes and making more tea. She had created a real spread.

Olga had placed a copy of the *Catholic Weekly*, which she had picked up at the church, on the coffee table, and she heard Betty exclaim as she picked it up.

"Oooh, Olga. Where did you get this?"

Olga replied as she carried out the tea-tray laden with the food and teapot, "someone dropped it into my letterbox. I didn't read. Should I bother?"

Betty put it back on the table. Iris had an allergic look on her face, and said, "well, we are all Protestants, Olga," she said looking around at the other women. "We don't really socialise with Catholics. We have our own church."

She stopped short, and Betty added, "of course, we would socialise if we knew any. Just like with you, Olga, we don't really know any other Jewish people, but it wouldn't matter, would it, girls?"

The ladies nodded.

"My Eric worked with a Catholic," said Betty.

"Oh, I don't think there are any at Rex's work," Iris said. "His part of the firm don't employ Catholics. Generally, Olga, they stick with their own. Then there's the Irish question and the doings of their Cardinal, Mannix. He tried to stop the boys going to war to defend the Empire. No, they are generally considered to be against King and Country. They owe their allegiance to a foreigner. An Iti, as my hubby calls him."

"What about the Queen?" Olga asked quickly. "Isn't she foreign?"

Olga saw Clarissa and Iris bristle.

Betty interjected, "Olga dear, the Queen is our Queen. She is no more foreign to us than…well…we are part of the Commonwealth, you see."

"Iris added, "about the only thing we would agree with them about is their vehemence against Communism, very active opposing them in the unions. No offence, Olga — we know you had to be one, back in Russia…"

"Oh. Thank you for explaining," Olga said.

"And you, Olga? Do you practice a faith?" Betty asked.

Olga shook her head. "I do not bother the God with my small needs. You had Catholic Prime Minister, too, yes?" Olga asked.

"We did," said Helen. "For a short time. Labor Party man. That's who they vote for, you know."

Then she added, "they have their own organisations, too, to protect their employment. You know, girls, The Knights of the Southern Cross. It is quite a secretive organisation."

"Oh. They employ only their own? The police do this? As an example?"

"Olga, you are a curious one," Betty replied. "What would you say, girls? There are certainly some parts of the police where the Catholics dominate. I've experienced their biased behaviour myself," she said, and the other women nodded as if they knew what she was talking about. But Olga had what she needed and did not press the point further.

Olga had read the edition of the *Catholic Weekly*. It was full of anti-Communist propaganda (presumably because Communism wants to make belief in an imaginary being unnecessary, thought Olga) and something called the Rural Catholic Movement, (which read like a retreat to rural idiocy again, so the priests could control what you read and who you talked to). Iris had confirmed this was one of their primary political causes in Australia.

"That reminds me," said Helen. "I've brought you the old copies of the *Women's Weekly* you wanted."

"Thank you," said Olga, "that is very kind of you. Do you all read it?" Olga asked.

Clarissa interrupted. "Olga, these blintzes are magical! That cheese. I've never tasted sweet cheese before!"

"Yes, thank you, Olga, we must get the recipe. Well, I think we all read it? There are always copies to be swapped. And Iris gets the English *Women's Weekly* delivered, I think?"

"Oh, yes, I couldn't do without it. It's such a comfort to know I still have a link with London. I was born there, you know, Olga? My father was a cabbie. A London cabbie. He drove Mr Stanley Baldwin in his cab once, when he was Prime Minister."

"I love the knitting patterns," said Betty, as if the thought had just occurred to her.

"And I love everything British!" added Clarissa. "So much more sophisticated. And you, Olga, you must have travelled in Europe?"

"Yes. I lived in Paris. Zurich. Moscow, of course…"

"Oh, how lovely," Clarissa interrupted. "I've always wanted to see Paris."

At this point, Olga could not help herself.

"I remember my brother and the others recounting the stories of the Paris Commune that they had been told as young men just beginning in politics. Do you know that ordinary people took over those lovely places you see in the postcards — Montmartre, the wide *boulevardes* — they were places of struggle and death and execution, but now you only see the flower sellers and the cafés."

The clinking of cups. The knitting of brows.

Though she tried, Olga could not remain silent.

"They forgave the poor the rent owed and abolished child labour and gave workers the right to take over factories abandoned by their employers. And they let the churches stay open," Olga said.

Clarissa said, "there would be a reckoning if they'd closed them."

Olga added quickly, "but only if they opened up for public political meetings during the evenings."

The ladies took their leave soon after.

Olga smiled as she waved them off. Then she took the *Catholic Weekly* out to the incinerator in the backyard and placed it on top of the other rubbish. She lit the papers and watched as the singed pages of the magazine ascended skywards.

WHAT IS YOUR STRATEGY? AND YOUR TACTICS?

"Lev? Is that you?"

It was as cold as a Moscow day and the magpies outside her window were scratching at the dead grass and hard earth. And the black crows had also come calling.

"Yes, it's me, Olga Kameneva. Your brother, your Lev. But everyone calls me Leon."

She could barely make him out. He seemed to be hiding in the folds of her curtains, like the heavy brocade curtains that adorn any Moscow apartment.

She retreated to the warmth of her tiny kitchen and poured the hot tea from the steaming Birko gifted to her by Beverly. She took the hot cup back into the living room.

"You never visit me."

Leon laughed, deep, throaty and with a hint of sadness. "That would be a little difficult. Given your husband and his anointing as Stalin's henchman, and his role in my downfall."

"My husband is dead, Leon. Executed for his adherence to what we all believed in. My sons, executed for being the children of their father and their mother, our sister as well. Dostoyevsky couldn't have written a sadder trajectory for our family, or our comrades."

"Dead you say?"

There was silence between them, with only the cawing of the crows to break it.

"You were at the Congress, Olga. I was hounded. Mercilessly! Yet you said nothing."

Olga gulped.

"You had already lost, Leon. You lost in '23, not in '24. Your self-belief deceived you, blinded you to the manoeuvrings of others. Especially the Kremlin Highlander."

Leon laughed again. "Hah! That is what won the war against the Whites, Olga! My decisions, my confidence! Have you forgotten that? Besides, I realised his poison long before you did. You thought you could control him. I knew differently, Olga."

"My children are dead. Comrades Meyerhold and Mayakovsky. All our comrades. All the Old Bolsheviks, Leon! One by one. The Kremlin

Highlander separated us from each other, undermined our solidarity like a slow drip of a tap wears away the stone beneath. We will never recover what we made together."

She heard him sigh. "Kremlin Highlander! I like that!"

"What do I do now, brother? I have taken on this new task. I have taken on Vera, and I have promised her. Perhaps I will not be able to deliver."

"You are not correct, Olga, in your pessimism. You never aimed high enough, never!"

"And you...you were just another Icarus..."

"The time for argument is over, Olga. We can come together again in common cause. What is your strategy? What are your tactics?"

This is the time. Vera would never know what weight her thin shoulders held up, Olga thought, the hopes of an Old Bolshevik, and those of her brother cheering from the wings.

Olga's head was filled with the tasks she had to do and the plans she had to make before she visited Vera again. She busied herself flipping through the *Women's Weekly* copies left by Helen (her brother laughing over her shoulder, shouting and clapping his hands, "see, the hypocrisy! The hypocrisy!").

She sat down with a large jug of tea and a few of the sweet almond biscuits, reading late into the evening. It transported her, this experience of pouring over newspapers and magazines, back to Paris or Zurich to find the latest news from Russia. When they were together, she and her husband, Lev, would gather as many papers as they could, and they and their comrades would read late into the night, debating, drinking tea, sometimes wine. At one point they might be all for a rush back to Petersburg; at another, all for negotiating with the Duma. Tactics, always talking tactics. The strategy was clear, to work politically to build opposition to the Tsar. But how to do it? When to make the decisive moves to destabilise the old order? How to mobilise the youth, the soldiers, the unions of the working people? What should the tactics be?

But how different this material was — *no illumination of actual human conditions*, her brother was saying — just a steady flow of hypocritical stories for women: but contradictions and hypocrisies exposed the potential for undermining the old order. Her brother was clapping slowly.

The sources of hypocrisy were obvious to Olga; the war had shaken Australian morals at the same time as it had fought to preserve it. Wars open the box and let loose all manner of things: women who had taken on the men's jobs and then, according to the *Women's Weekly*, contentedly retreated to their homes at the end of the war. They reminded her of the upheavals of the Revolution; women finally given real work instead of slave labour in the fields or as servants, cooking — always cooking, as if for an imagined army. The potential for independence glimpsed on a production line — the camaraderie, the inkling of a sphere beyond the remit of their husbands and fathers. Then Stalin tried to exalt them as mothers and wives once again, just like these magazines. But not everything can be stuffed back into the box.

There were the 'homemaker' stories: their biggest problem seemed to be the price controls on bread, leading to bakers baking cheap, poorer quality bread. They should revolt, thought Olga. Many a revolution has started over bread (including her own).

One article compared different versions of the Bible. Olga did not finish it. She read the story of an Australian girl's life as a governess in Britain's stately homes (and now she is coming home after her big adventure to marry her sweetheart). There was a short story about a scandal at a private school involving a divorced woman, (if I were running a school, I'd only hire married women, it warned).

Advice-seeking letters: should girls dress to their own taste or with an eye to male appreciation? If a girl has no brains, at least she should try to look as pretty as possible, was the answer. Poor Vera! thought Olga.

A new recipe for Hawaiian grill: six chump chops covered with canned, crushed pineapple.

Pineapple in a can, Olga thought. I must try it. ("Pineapple! Pineapple!" Leon shouted behind her).

The Japanese wives and the children of ex-servicemen were profiled, still living in Japan and struggling to come to Australia in the face of enormous prejudice. A storm of letters about Blue Hills: outrage about a storyline of a young man who can't marry his next door neighbour, but it's not clear why. When finally, it was revealed that he was Aboriginal, the letters were filled with life's important question: "how dark will the baby be?"

Then, a cautionary tale of a married woman who befriended a young, unwed mother, but found that she was being used as a babysitter so the young woman could go out with her friends. The baby would be better off with a real family, the article concluded.

Olga put the magazines in the bin, ready for the incinerator. She knew all she needed to know. She called out for her brother, but he had gone.

Olga woke early the next morning with a swirl of tactics in her head. She had been a sleepwalker in this country. Now she was awake, and she recalled signals she had not registered previously.

At the chop picnic, Leslie had told Beverly to get him another beer, Olga recalled now, and Beverly had said "get it yourself," and Leslie had replied, "you'll keep," and Beverly had quickly risen and gone to the ice box. Olga recalled now the hint of menace in Leslie's voice. Vera's story about the shunned divorcee. So much to do to liberate the women!

Olga made her childhood drink, steeped in sugar, and kacha boiled in milk to which she added even more sugar. Maria had come to her in the night, waving her finger as usual. If Olga had been religious, she would have believed Maria was an actual spirit. Maria was so vivid, a product of her own mind sent to rouse her, as she had in life in the camp. Come on, Olga! Get up! No time for sleeping!

In the camp, all the women would eat together huddled up for warmth, but Maria's eyes never looked warm — when Olga would catch Maria looking at her, she could almost see the words forming behind her frown as it flickered then set, rigid. *See, Olga Davidovna Kameneva, they did it to you, too, in the end. If only you had listened to your real comrades in the SR! You and your haughty brother!*

They had argued, Olga and Maria, as if in the camps the old arguments still mattered. They would argue about the peasants and land redistribution and collectivisation, as if they both still had some influence.

The visitations of her brother and Maria had the effect of stirring Olga, and now she realised that in addition to helping Vera, this project would help her do something else — it would help make amends with them — her ghosts. By the time Olga boarded the train for the city to visit Vera, she had tactics lined up in her mind, like her brother's childhood metal soldiers. Her tactics were speculative, but who then doesn't cling to a bit of hope?

At the convent, Olga and Vera walked to the stone seat again. The seat seemed colder than the last time, resistant to any heat from the day, and as they sat Vera could feel the cold stone through her skirt and stockings.

"Why do you choose to sit here, Olga, when these seats are so cold?"

Olga lowered her speaking voice. "Because here it is more difficult for spies to hear what we are saying, Vera."

"Oh. I don't think there would be any here, but as you like. I'm uncomfortable. Perhaps we could walk a little? It sometimes helps the baby settle into the right spot."

They took a few turns around the garden while they talked. Olga had her wits about her when it came to the spies. She was all too aware she might be followed but had not spotted the men following her on her Sunday visits.

"Thank you for your letters. I know what to do now," said Olga, smiling.

"By the way, how do you get your letters out without being read by the nuns? You have not signed anything?"

Vera shook her head. "No. And I can drop the letters in the letterbox on the way to church without the nuns seeing if I fall to the back of the group."

"That is good. You must resist. With all your…how you say…wiles? Make them pity you."

Vera nodded. She was too frightened, too anxious, to ask what Olga planned to do. As long as she did not know the details, she could bask in a false dawn and believe that something good would happen to fix it all, like her parents simply arriving one day to whisk her back to Box Hill.

"They do not have much pity here, I fear. Even for their own, Olga," Vera replied, and then started to tell Olga about a young nun she had found crying.

"I asked her if she was alright. She couldn't stop crying. I put my arms around her shoulders, and she sobbed and sobbed. At least you'll get to have your baby, I've been told I have to get rid of mine, she said. I was so shocked. I didn't think the church would let her do that."

"Hmmph, the hypocrisy," said Olga. "Did she say who the father was?"

"No."

"Then," Olga said, "the reason they tell her that is because father is one of their own. A priest, perhaps. Scandal is worse if priest fathers a child. Better you get rid of the evidence."

"She told me she had prayed very hard and if it's God's will that she must do it, she will pray for the soul of her unborn child. I asked, haven't you thought of leaving and she shook her head and said no, this is my home, and my family would be humiliated if I did. They are so proud to have a nun in the family."

"So, you see what you are up against, Vera. Gross hypocrisy. This is good. Very easy to exploit. I will get you out. A few more weeks, and it will fall into place."

"I can't even think about it," said Vera, then asked, "did you bring me a copy of *Tribune*?"

Olga passed over the newspaper, which she had placed inside a cardigan she had bought for Vera at a charity shop. She had read it herself, and this time there had been an article about Soviet women and their advances in the professions that brought up such emotion for Olga. Even Koba had not been able to destroy everything.

Olga looked around slowly, glancing at a tree, and back and forth, to make sure they were not being watched. She shivered. It felt strange, as if the Tsarists were watching her again. She shook off the feeling as if she were a bird after the rain, shaking its wings in preparation for flight.

BEVERLY

Olga woke in the middle of the night. It was Wednesday, and the night terrors had returned. She had dreamed people were knocking at her door shouting 'your game is up', 'we know what you are trying to do, and we've come to stop you'. Who was it? This time, the priests.

The terrors often surfaced when she was restless, and she realised she was restless because she didn't have a plan. She had an objective but no solid plan, no real tactics at all. In her heart, and with her critical inner voice, she knew that so much was unpredictable, and she had to plan for events she didn't yet know about. Terror focusses the mind like nothing else.

This was just like politics, she thought to herself — you think you have a plan, some collaborators, then the ground shifts, other forces or events happen that you could never foresee. It all seems to be continuous, the way events unfold, but it isn't any such thing. There is simply a mess of events, accidents, coincidences and facts, some related to each other but many, not. Many converging then diverging paths and metaphorical streams and bridges were built then destroyed then built again in a different way. Perhaps it was the snow, perhaps it was the apparatus they inherited from the Tsar, centuries of torture and deprivation and resentment that twisted the people like corpses on a gibbet, swinging. Perhaps the war! Or the counter-Revolution! Of one thing she was sure: it had not been what they wanted when they created the topsy-turvy world, when they freed women, workers, artists. How long had it lasted? A mere ten minutes, it seemed to her.

You should know your history, Olga would tell anyone, if anyone would listen to her. Yes, we lived it. But how to tell the story? Olga had decided that was impossible. Stories are lies; so much is left out.

Her mind flowed back to Vera, whom Olga had convinced of a detailed plan. There was no sense in sharing her uncertainty with the girl, who had enough to fear already. That was politics — put on your most confident face, just like her brother. More poking around was needed — if you are afraid of wolves, don't go into the woods.

Olga rose to make tea. She turned on the radio in the living room and soon drifted back to sleep, listening to the low static of a symphony orchestra.

The next morning, her mind had calmed. She decided she had not given up on Beverly. She would give her one last chance. She sent her a letter asking if she could come to visit. Beverly replied the next day, and Olga knocked on Beverly's door at the invited time: two o'clock the day after that.

Beverly had not been able to decide what to wear to receive Olga. She knew quite well what Olga wanted. Should she wear the twinset? Her green tea-dress? Her pearls? She didn't want to appear flippant. Dark colours might be best. After all, she knew that Olga would be wanting to talk about Vera, and that was a solemn subject.

She swept up her grey-flecked hair and fastened it with a comb at the back, thinking it looked suitably serious.

When she answered the door, Beverly said quickly, "Welcome it's very nice to see you, Olga. Would you like tea? I've made a Victoria sponge with passionfruit icing from the last of my fruit, I hope you like it. I hope the tram ride wasn't too arduous? Not too busy out there, is it?"

"No. it is not too busy."

After they had been sitting for a few moments, Olga started the negotiation.

"I have visited with Vera."

Beverly sat back in her chair and drummed her fingers. "I thought you might have." She paused, then realising she had to say more, added, "I hope she is well."

"She is. That is the reason for my visit."

"I thought as much."

"She misses her family, of course. I am poor substitute."

"Oh, yes. We miss her, of course. And thank you for visiting. But I'm sure she understands. We couldn't be seen visiting a Catholic convent. It would rouse suspicion."

"But you not write? I can take a letter to her."

Olga wondered whether she was pushing too far, but as was her nature, she leapt into the breech and said, "I could take one with me now."

Beverly wrinkled her nose involuntarily. Olga had never minded making people uncomfortable. After all, how does anything ever move forward?

"Well, I suppose I could send a brief one."

Beverly rose and went into the bedroom for a few minutes. She emerged with a pale pink envelope.

"There." She sat down. "I feel like a secret agent. Passing messages."

Olga smiled and felt the envelope. There was one sheet of paper inside. "Do not worry on my account," she said. "This is not the first time I have by-passed the postal service."

While she wrote the note in her bedroom, Beverly had thought about the question she had been wanting to ask the whole time. She was pleased that Olga had come, though she didn't reveal it. She wanted to know what Vera's intentions were, after the baby episode was over and done, and this was her chance to find out. And yet, something had stopped her. She knew that she was frightened of the answer, that if Olga told her Vera intended to come home, she would not be able to bear it. To have Vera constantly in her orbit, like a question mark always in sight, challenging everything just by her presence. That was how she saw it. She did not want anything to change. She wanted it to be seen that Vera has simply moved on to other things, as was natural for a young woman, and especially one as intellectual as Vera. It was more natural for Vera to return to her own accommodation, though she knew Vera liked the comfort of home more than Barbara who had married at an early age, eager to set up her own domestic arrangements. Vera had left her old room much the same as it had been when she was a child — still the same wallpaper and fusty old, knitted toys on a shelf. Barbara had told her mother to turn her own room into a sewing den, which Beverly had done.

Why had God given her such a child? Many times, in church, she had tried to pray for Vera, but her prayers felt like empty vessels and no amount of faith could fill them up. Vera would not change. She had been willful as a child, Beverly remembered. She would not wear the clothes bought for her, she would tear them off and parade around in a pair of shorts day after day, an embarrassment to her and to Les. And to Barbara, who became more lady-like the older she got. She's just a tomboy, she'll grow out of it, Beverly's mother-in-law had said of Vera. But Beverly waited, and it didn't happen. Vera just graduated from one quiet form of disobedience to another.

Beverly blamed the times. There had been that girl next door during the war, who had gone off to factory work, wearing trousers. You would see gaggles of them at lunchtime down at the shops, all together, a swarm of them taking over the street with their laughing and shouting. In their *drill* trousers! The rector had even addressed it in one of his sermons and said mothers needed to be extra vigilant about loiterers who sought to exploit such vulnerable, unchaperoned girls.

Beverly had not always been a churchgoer. But she met Les at a church dance. It had been by accident — one of her friends knew about the regular dances and suggested they go. Les's parents helped organise them and his father, Warwick, had been on hand to serve the sparkling punch. Les's friend Brian had spotted the new girls and offered them a drink and introduced them to his friends. Les had hesitated to ask Beverly to dance, he told her later, because of the watchful eye of his parents. But once they had left, he made a bee-line for her.

When it came to their engagement, Beverly lied about the whereabouts of her own parents. Her widowed mother couldn't attend, she had said at first, because she had moved to Lismore in New South Wales to be near Beverly's aunt. Beverly had contemplated telling Les that her mother was dead, but she did love her mother and thought that would be a bad omen. She had lain awake wondering about the wedding, and whether to invite her. She decided bribery was the best option and had given her mother twenty pounds and bought her a new dress for the wedding. Beverly's heart had been in her mouth through the whole wedding, but her mother had revealed nothing of their former status. What did your husband do when he was alive? Beverly and her mother had agreed to say he had been a boilermaker.

After the wedding, she told her mother to write to her every so often, which she did. Beverly would meet her a few times a year until she died, and she never told Les. They would meet in a tea room in Seaford — not more than twenty-five miles away, where her mother lived in an old people's unit. Her mother understood. To get anywhere in life, you had to be just like everyone else, not stand out. They had invented a father for Beverly, when in fact he had disappeared before her mother even knew she was pregnant.

It was not something she could share with anyone — not with her husband, her daughter and certainly not with Olga. Olga was like a judging black crow, and Beverly wondered whether she might be the one who would be able to see through to the truth of the matter.

"More tea, Olga?" Beverly asked after she handed over the note for Vera.

"No, thank you," Olga said, her pupils widened as if her eyes needed maximum aperture.

Beverly caught her breath.

"The truth is, Olga, I don't want Vera and her…progeny…to suffer. You don't know what people are like here. Being an unwed mother is perhaps the worst fate to…befall a young woman. She would lose her circle of friends and her prospects. The…progeny…would be shunned by other children. Tormented. Lonely. It would be a terrible life. No, this is the right decision."

Olga nodded. There was a tinge of fear in Beverly's voice, and who could not but sympathise with the woman, stuck in a prison which she had helped to construct?

But Olga wanted to be able to say to Vera that she had done the best job she could, to push past Beverly's fear of loss. It was just as she had always done, even when she stood up for Maria in the camp and received a punch to the stomach for her trouble. Even after the punch, the guard had the good sense to retreat (after all, there were inmates all around him), and they had been able to resume feeding Maria, whom the guards had hoped would simply wither away.

Olga kept going.

"Alas, mothers alone with their…pro-geny — this is normal in Soviet. So many men killed, leaving behind the mothers to do all the work. Young women promised a home and family by young men killed at the front, these we needed to look after. And many women divorced when they were allowed to, to leave the abusive men. But I see is not the same here…Vera will most of all want to know if she can come home if the child…" Olga's voice trailed off.

Beverly's face seemed to twitch to life in a way to which it was not accustomed, and Beverly stood straight up and said, "I don't think so, Olga. Thank you for your visit. You have the letter. Now you must go. And tell Vera: chin up."

Olga pulled herself up slowly from the sofa. It felt as if she were hauling a dead body from a river.

At home, her brother was waiting. "A letter! That's the best you could do?"

Olga shrugged her shoulders. She knew it was inadequate. But her plan was crumbling like old paper and she had no idea of how to carry off the liberation of a young woman and her child from the clutches of the priests, in this city, amongst these people. For actions are always specific, Olga knew. They must be matched to people, time, place.

"This is such a small task, Olga," her brother chided from behind the curtains. "You of all people know what is to be done. You, who visited a lawyer. A lawyer, I ask you! What use are they when the law is made by rich people as a hammer for the poor!"

"This is not Russia," Olga whispered through gritted teeth. "And this is not the Revolution."

WHAT IS TO BE DONE?

Vera had not received a letter from Olga and did not know when she would visit next. She was finding it harder and harder to keep up her spirits. Olga had said she had a plan, but Vera did not know what it could possibly be.

She began to wonder why she was putting her trust in Olga.

Olga had shared just a few details with Vera about her life. She knew that Olga knew Stalin himself and many other of the original Bolsheviks, and she knew her family had been killed off by him. Olga had hinted at her importance in the Soviet Union: something to do with the theatre? Olga had been in exile, she knew, had been imprisoned by the Tsar and later by Stalin. Olga had told her that her brother was high up in the Red Army, and that had impressed Vera, though she had struggled to work out the backflip the Party had made from non-aggression to war footing when Hitler invaded Russia and they all fell in behind Stalin. She knew how hard people had fought not to be returned to Tsarist rule, not to have the Whites and Hitler exact revenge. But the cost — she had heard more than twenty million Russians had died. She knew that for a time, the Party had gone from being banned to being feted, once Churchill had shaken Stalin's hand. And then of course, post-war, it had all turned again. But where Olga was in all of that?

Vera had realised quite quickly that she had few friends in her current state. She had tried to confide in Ursula, another young Party enthusiast from Melbourne Uni who had joined at the same time. Ursula had shrugged and asked Vera if she needed to find someone to get rid of it. So much for asking Vera what she wanted, and after much wrestling with her own brain, and time having elapsed, she couldn't go through with an abortion. At the beginning, she had hoped the father would come back and help her, but she had hesitated to contact him for too long. The baby was already stirring in her, and it was too late to do anything but continue.

Her parents' reaction had truly shocked her, and when her mother told her about the Catholic convent, she felt as if her whole being had been dragged across a line, even though she wasn't religious. It was one thing to hear about shifting alliances; it was another to live them.

Beverly had chosen to give her up to a foreign church like a kind of human sacrifice, so that her own life would continue as normal. In the convent, she was meant to be reflecting on her sins, so the nuns and the priests had told her, and just to make sure, they made her spend hours kneeling on the wooden pews in the chapel. Vera would hum *"The Internationale"* in her head with eyes closed and hands cupped in the prayer position.

She knew that the nuns did not know what to make of her. She was compliant and always pleasant to them, even bowing her head when she entered the chapel. She had found they were easy to fool. Because of her compliance, they were nonplussed when it came to her refusal to sign the documents.

She had worked out her own strategy. She was leading them, like the proverbial lambs, and they were following. They believed that she would sign the papers because she told them she would. It was a source of great anxiety that they would see through her, but so far, they had not.

They believed the story of the pious aunt from the Eastern Bloc who had escaped the Communists so she could practice her Catholic faith, and who visited to make sure Vera prayed for forgiveness.

The worst part of it for Vera was having to keep up the fiction with the other girls. At the start of her internment, she had talked to the other girls in her room about how they could organise to withdraw from the punishing work they were being given and assert their rights. The girls, particularly "Mary" and "Theresa", were worried that they would be given limited rations if they stopped working. The most they could agree on was a go-slow. They communicated it to the girls in the other dorms. It didn't work. The girls complained that it just made the work longer and more torturous, and with the extra harassment from the nuns, it was abandoned within a few days.

Most of the girls seemed resigned to giving up their babies. "Well, it's probably better for the kid not to be brought up by a young girl with no support. I mean, I couldn't get a job with a kid, there's no care for them except with people you wouldn't leave your kids with, so it's for the best."

But there should be support for us, Vera had protested. They had looked at her as if she was from another planet. There was one girl, "Joan", who told the others straight out that she intended to keep her child and she'd go 'on the game' if she had to, to support herself and the child. She was so petite and slight, she looked to Vera as if she could be no older than twelve, but she must have been, Vera reasoned. She wondered if she should confide in 'Joan', but for the time being, Vera kept her own counsel.

Olga arrived home after her meeting with Beverly and slumped into her chair. Vera's own mother had given her final refusal of help. If Olga was honest with herself, she had thought it unlikely that Beverly would change her mind, but she had to try. There was a principle at stake.

She sat for a few minutes before rising to turn on the radio. As she did that, a wave of memory swept over her, of the old days when she was still in the flat with Lev and the boys. After particularly gruelling meetings — with Kollontai or Lunacharsky or the Committee for International Cultural Relations (of which she had been the chair) or the Famine Relief Committee (of which Lev had been the chair, but was really just a figurehead) — she would retreat behind loud music so that she did not have to think anymore or, even worse, have to recap all the ins and outs of the meetings, since Lev always wanted to know the latest.

The radio played Tchaikovsky, a piece she knew so well that she could anticipate the bars well in advance. Sometimes she wished she were more forgetful. At other times, her memories were her comfort. How she wished some of her women comrades were with her now! They would know precisely how to approach the problem of Vera — as a social problem, as a cruel oppression of the rights of a woman to have food and shelter and work so that she might bring up her own child. If this new country cannot do that, what use is it?

Her mind turned now to the Australian section of the worldwide Communist movement. She had been thinking about them more and more. Surely, they could be relied upon to help Vera in her hour of need, and perhaps even to help the other young women? Perhaps a campaign to get support? The conditions are not right, she chided herself: but when are they ever right?

She recalled how her own cadre had been called on many times to assist each other, especially in exile. Politics was important, but the personal was never far away. They shared their food, such as it was, and their rooms in their houses if needed.

She did not need her brother's presence to know what he would think of these Australian *Kommunisty*. He would be horrified at their fawning over Koba, at their flip-flopping behind the coat-tails of Stalin as he tried to out-manoeuvre Hitler and the imperialists. Her brother, Leon (as he insisted on being called), was capable of manoeuvre — he who started as a Menshevik and became a Bolshevik. He suited his tactics to the mission at hand.

She remembered the times he had returned to the family home with stories of his activism in the world outside, much to the anger of their father who considered himself a self-made man and deeply suspicious of anyone who wanted to change the established order. It seemed to Olga that her brother must surely have been to an alien world.

"It's very simple," Leon said once, devising a kind of game for his younger sister.

"Imagine I put a bean on the table. This is the Tsar. Around it, I place more beans. These are ministers, bishops and generals, and over there the gentry and merchants. And in this other heap, the plain people. Now, I ask, where is the Tsar?"

Olga had pointed to the centre.

"Where are his ministers?"

Olga had pointed to the other imaginary beans.

"Now, wait," her brother had said, closing his eyes. "I scramble all the beans together," he went on, moving his fingers and hands over the table. "Now tell me where is the Tsar? The ministers?"

"Well, you can't spot them now..."

"Just what I say. You can't spot them now." And then he said, "all beans should be scrambled."

All beans should be scrambled — hah! She had agreed with her brother on that. And here, she thought, I am about to scramble the beans again, to scatter the priests!

The music became more insistent, more urgent, like an advancing cavalry. How she loved Tchaikovsky.

Leon! Her brother, the staunchest defender of the Revolution — did she really abandon him? Or did he abandon her? Alliances shifted, and families found themselves on opposite sides. This had been common — children disagreeing with their parents. Sometimes betraying them. And they, Olga and Leon, found themselves on the opposite side of Stalin, until Stalin turned on Kamenev. And Koba had never forgotten that while she might be Kamenev's wife, she was also Trotsky's sister.

Both of them became exiles, a practice they thought had been ended when the Tsar toppled, only to see it resurrected. Olga never stopped thinking about rehabilitation and being brought back to make her contribution once more. She had seen it happen for others, so why not her? People came back from the dead all the time. She had heard that even Molotov's wife had been allowed back from the camps.

This time, Olga would take her cue from her brother. She would be resolute and self-confident when it came to Vera. It was a way back.

Every time Olga thought of Vera's child, she held her own belly, her mind full of the images of her swollen, pregnant body and the joy of her sons as little children. Other images followed just as quickly, of children who died in the camps, who silently passed with no surviving family to mourn them. No one, she thought, should be deprived of their own child, nor child denied the care of its parent.

If we cannot deliver that, we can deliver nothing! That is what she had said to Kollontai, and the other women who supported abortion. And she was worried, that it was working class women who would abort or use contraception, and then where would the future of the Revolution be then? Olga's beliefs were sorely tested during the Civil War, with the thousands of orphans roaming the streets, with Communism in place with its food rations and almost feudal labour assignments. But you cannot build a new society by dragging the worst practices of the past along with you — Olga had argued as much with regard to abortion. She was labelled an idealist, and the word still hissed in her mind like an unexploded bomb.

And as the old Bolshevik saying went: sometimes the tide is going out and coming in at the same time. Well, at least this was the saying of one Old Bolshevik.

So, perhaps Vera would be the incoming tide and Beverly the outgoing one. There were already signs. Beverly herself had remarked on how the Second World War had disrupted things. It was time to push it further.

The Party — it was time to see what they could do for Vera.

She travelled to the city the next day. She knew Thursday was the day that the *Tribune* sellers sold the new edition in front of the railway stations. Olga had noticed how forlorn they sometimes looked, with no eager mobs of buyers to trouble them as there had been back home. What a foment there had been when the fresh copies of *Isvestia* were fought over, so you wouldn't be the last person to find out what great leap the Party was making on behalf of the working classes and the peasants, (or whose name the Central Committee had disappeared from public comment).

The man selling the paper today at Spencer Street Station was a tall, gaunt man in an open-necked shirt with short black hair and thick glasses. Olga smiled as he gave her the paper and said to him, "I am from Russia, you know. I was Communist, back there."

He looked at her benignly and said, "that's nice."

Olga could see that he had already summed her up; she in her thick wool coat and mohair hat and faux pearl earrings — some old dear from the suburbs determined to chew his ear about the old days, and he was having none of that.

"Look here," she said in a loud voice. And he did.

"I need to talk to cadre. You know what that is? Someone who give their life for their Party? I am cadre. I need to speak."

The paper seller tried ignoring Olga, but that just made her voice louder, and as no buyers were coming near him, he finally shoved his papers in his leather satchel and said, "come with me."

She followed his quick pace until they reached a short, shabby, industrial street next to a grimy printshop whose large open windows exposed workers and acrid chemicals to the outside air. They ascended a flight of stairs and knocked on a heavy door.

The young man who answered the door regarded his comrade and the old lady he had in tow.

"Ehh?" he mumbled as the paper seller pushed past and Olga quickly followed.

The paper seller led her to a small back office and said, "this is Ron, our organiser. Ron, this lady is a cadre, she says. From Russia."

There was an almost contemptuous lilt in the young man's voice.

"Hello," said Ron. "What is it you'll be wanting with us?"

Uninvited, Olga sat down and placed her large red handbag on her lap. The paper seller left the room.

"Comrade—" she started. She paused. That word! It felt odd to say it here, and so many years between saying it. "Ron. I am CPSU member. In exile. I need help with private matter. But, not only is it private matter, it is of immense importance. Social issue which shows the terrible discrim-ination in your country for the unmarried women."

Ron had sat back in his chair, and at least seemed to be listening.

"I have evidence, young women forced to give up their babies. Church is involved. Perhaps even police. I have evidence."

"What can I call you?" Ron asked.

"Olga. My name is Olga Chernenkova."

"Well, Mrs Chernenkova. We have a well-established Women's Committee, and we support equal pay for equal work and additional rest periods for women workers. Support for working families. Our women are very devoted to the cause of peace, you understand. Perhaps you'd like to speak to the head of our committee?"

"No. This is human issue. Young women, enslaved for duration of pregnancy then forced to give up children. This is…you should not stand by while they suffer. We should — how you say — picket. We protest. Outside the convent. Mass protest. Embarrass the Government, force them to accede to our demands. You will see."

Ron leaned forward in his chair. The phone rang and he answered it.

Olga sat while she waited for Ron to finish the call. She knew that her plan might not be welcomed by the Party. The wrath of the State might rain down upon them, she knew. Her mind filled with images of the police and their batons, the horses trampling the starving, rioting peasants. Many died that day. She knew what a baton to the head felt like, and she was ready for it. But she also realised that here, state terror would not be risked. To embarrass a Government only? This is your best work, Olga? She could hear her brother whispering.

"Now, Mrs C. You are, I think, new to this country. Compared to women in your homeland, well, things are a bit different here. I know you fought for equal pay — I am well-read, you see — and child care, rights for working mothers and our comrades know it was hard." He paused.

"But it's not the time for that here. We've placed our women comrades strategically, where they are most needed, at the forefront of the fight against another war: a nuclear disaster this time. More imperialist wars. They understand and can speak to the impact of war on families. Boys ripped away to fight a war for the Capitalists and many never returning. You, I think, of all people know how devastating war is to a country, to its youth…"

"Comrade Ron, you do not need to lecture me on peace and war. I who was in Civil War in charge of famine relief for the whole of Russia!"

"Oh, is that so?"

"The most basic right of a woman is what we discuss. Inalienable rights. You must support this. I read in your paper, Women and children first. This is your slogan…"

"And support them we do. Through our policies. Our political campaigns…"

"No. You must actually fight for them. I am here to fight."

Ron sighed and nodded. He looked pained, frustrated.

"Comrade Chernenkova, is it? Frankly, we have our own battles: the unions, the waterfront. That's where the workers are under attack. I'm sorry, but it's a sad fact that we would alienate so many of the housewives and other women we seek to influence in the cause of peace. You, coming from the Soviet, will know how these things work. We have our priorities. Maybe we can talk more sometime? About the Party. Did you know Stalin?"

Olga pulled out her last card. "The young woman I am concerned about. She is locked up behind iron gate. She is one of you. She is cadre."

"Oh?"

"She joined at the university. She could be star recruit if you get her back. If you will not save all the women, perhaps there is a way to save your own."

Ron drained his tea cup. "What do you have in mind?"

Olga lowered her voice. "Well, if you will not protest, we must make a rescue mission. Comrade — your comrade — is in Catholic convent. She will be looking after her baby for a month once born, and that is the time we strike. What they do is illegal; I have research-ed this."

"That's never stopped any State…"

Olga raised her voice (as she did so, her lungs puffed up quite suddenly, they seemed larger, and she spoke forcefully). "Do not lecture me about State! I felt full force of Tsar's police and illegal detainment! I ran State! Communist State! My point, if only you listen…" Olga breathed deeply to calm herself, then continued, "my point is if we succeed, they will not make any fuss because fear of bad publicity. If they want to keep doing illegal things, publicity will not suit their cause. We must blackmail the church. And the police if necessary.

"This is the opposite of mass protest, I understand this," Olga continued. "But it can be equally useful to exploit the hypocrisy."

Olga thought that Ron looked a little scared of her, of what she was saying. He said a few vague things about consulting with others, and escorted Olga down the stairs. When she saw him get up from his chair to do that, she had said to him, "no need."

He replied, "good Communists don't forget our manners."

So, Olga fumed all the way down the stairs, trailing behind Ron. She could feel the hair on her neck bristle and wondered if she shouldn't poke Ron with her umbrella. These silly manners — all we need to do is get on with things! Did he think she was too old, so might trip down the stairs? Or that a feeble woman always needed an escort? This fake politeness irked Olga even more when shown to her by a fellow comrade.

At the bottom of the stairs, she shook his hand vigorously. He looked shocked. Perhaps she had broken some unwritten code between Australian men and women. Hooray for me! she thought.

Ron walked back up the stairs, his head filled with the business at hand, which was writing another pamphlet to support the waterfront workers. That Mrs Chernenkova — or Chernenkovich? She had been a real distraction, and he would not be derailed by a crazy old lady who had delusions of being a Soviet power broker.

Olga turned the corner of the street away from the headquarters and walked through the grubby streets in the direction of Spencer Street Station. It seemed from the surroundings that the comrades could only afford to rent in the poorest part of the city. This was no surprise, and Olga did not mind since it reminded her of home. In Australia, she had thought, people swept all of their dirt behind closed doors. Here it is out in the open, like in Moscow or Leningrad. She walked past garbage and rotting vegetables and trickling greasy water and could smell the sweat of working people as she walked past workshops open to the street — men fixing cars, printing works, cheap and dusty cafés.

She missed most of all the children playing in the streets; some of them war orphans, some with homes but no space to play, and they would all play together with whatever they could get their hands on — a piece of wood for a bat or a doll, trussed cloth for a ball, banging tin lids to make music.

She felt she would give anything to be back amongst it. Then she remembered how she had felt when she raised her voice to Comrade

Ron. She had prided herself on her rationality, even in the midst of turbulence, fear even; but this was something different, and she stopped and slapped herself on the forehead.

Leon — you were the air in my lungs just now! This is how we do it, you and I. How we respond to fear and uncertain times. We plot. We understand our enemy. We make many different plans, we adapt. Yes, you are alive again, Leon! (Yes, and you, too, Maria. I do not forget you). Her body did not feel like her own, it felt so light and young.

She had been walking the whole time, and as she rounded another street corner, she knew she had perhaps taken the wrong turn in her light, daydreaming state. She was in the patch of the streetwalkers, the women 'on the game' as they called it. There were brothels, too, she noticed, judging by the men she saw following women into dark doorways and up the stairs.

She tried to look her most confident as she made her way down the street. She had been late leaving the Party headquarters, and it was already gloomy, so it was easy for her to pick her way past the doors in the shadows and not be noticed. As she made her way, her gaze was drawn momentarily by a door squeak on the other side of the street. She looked across and saw a face illuminated by the dim light of the stairwell behind the door. She caught a glimpse of the face, a face she knew, but she could not immediately place it. The man wore a hat and dark coat pulled up around his neck, but his silhouette was so familiar.

Olga pulled herself into the shadow of a doorway, more from instinct than anything else. She waited for the man to walk the length of the street before she continued on her way.

HUNTER IN THE MORNING, CRITIC AT NIGHT

Alighting from the tram nearest to the convent, Olga felt renewed. She had taken her seat in the pale sunlight with the Sunday crowds — the churchgoers, the picnickers and the families who headed to the beach just for the ride there and back. She had a new purpose (she was three people! not just one!) and through the visit to the Party, she had advanced her plan to involve them in her efforts on behalf of Vera. This kind of activity, it never made her tired. It freed her, even if it did keep her awake — her mind abuzz with her vision of liberation.

Once, in an effort to relax, Olga had tried gardening, earnestly, but she had become bored. The flowers were lovely, but the flowers were the same each year, and what was the point once the garden was established? To sit back and enjoy? That she could never do. Political strategy and tactics — to her, it was like breathing out and breathing in.

Comrade Ron had been set back on his legs when she, Olga, followed up her visit with a call where she told him that he was betraying the most fundamental Marxist principles of dialectical materialism and failing to advance the position of women through specific actions to liberate Vera. That had really showed him who she was and that she would not skulk away. He made a phone call to see what could be done. He had called her not long afterwards and offered to set up a meeting with one of their comrades. Olga sent him a letter outlining the time and place. She set the terms.

Olga had a book in her capacious handbag, which she planned to give to Vera. In the middle of the book, she had placed blank pages for Vera, so she could draw a map for Olga and the rescuers   where she was in the convent, the entry and exit points.

Rescue seemed to be the only hope. Olga had failed to mobilise the comrades for a campaign (marching in the streets, placards, perhaps Molotov cocktails), though she thought again that perhaps she should have taken up Ron's offer to meet the women's committee. But time was running out for Vera (babies do not wait!), and given comrade Ron's reluctance, she reasoned that it might take her quite some time to persuade the women's committee to act.

When she was first sent to the institution, Vera told Olga that Sunday was the day for visitors, because both the girls and their visitors would have gone to early mass, confessed their sins and asked for forgiveness, and therefore met in a state of grace, as the nuns called it. Vera told Olga she quite liked singing hymns, which she hadn't done since she was younger when she stopped going to church with her mother and father.

"Why you stop?" Olga had asked.

"Because I listened to the minister droning on one day with his message for all of the young girls in the congregation, and he told us that we should look to our mothers as our role models. That they were the paragons of holy virtue because they had dedicated their lives to bringing up their children to love God and support their husbands in their work. I stood up and left and walked home by myself. I was twelve. I knew I didn't want that. And I knew right then and there I didn't believe in God, either."

Ah, thought Olga, the realisation of Godlessness often comes as an epiphany.

There was an advantage to the Sunday visits for Olga. So far, the Australian spies did not seem to follow her on weekends and seemed irregular on weekdays. Olga felt she must be a low-risk target in the eyes of the government, not worth the overtime, or of little value. This all worked in her favour.

Today, Vera's belly was very prominent, and her features looked drawn.

"So, we think only weeks now?"

"Yes. That sounds right, if you trace it all back."

"We have no time to waste," said Olga.

She handed over the book to Vera.

"Oh. *My Travels in the Emerald Isle*. Thanks, Olga."

Olga smiled. "Book is to fool the nuns. I stole from Catholic bookshop," she said, and she explained about the blank pages and the need for the map.

Vera looked alarmed. "That's your plan? To rescue me? Us?"

Olga took her hand and held it tightly.

"Who is helping you?"

"Your own comrades! Yes!"

"Oh," said Vera. "Really?"

"Well, why not?"

"Because they offered to help me, and I told them I didn't want their help."

Olga looked shocked. "What you say?"

Any colour Vera had drained from her face. "I…told them I would sort it out myself. They offered to help me…get rid of it. They even told me that if I decided not to do that, they would find somewhere for me to live, people to live with. But I said no."

"I still not understand…"

"I felt humiliated, Olga."

Olga did not say, you and your *bourgeois* individualism, but she felt like it.

"You decided to do it all by yourself?"

"To be honest, Olga I did think my mother would react better. I'm her daughter! No, once I'd refused their help, it would humiliate me even more to ask for it again. I needed to find my own way.

"I had my pride. I couldn't concede my mistake. Rhys, the father, had gone to Sydney by then. I felt alone, and I thought I could solve the problem. I haven't told you any of this, Olga. But I went to the social services and asked if they would give me some money to help me when I had my baby, and they told me I didn't qualify for anything because I wouldn't be able to look for work with a small baby, so I couldn't get any unemployment benefits, and I wasn't a widow or a deserted wife, so again, nothing. I went to the local Minister — yes! That same one who looks after my mother's parish. I asked if there was anyone in the church who might help me set myself up with my baby, and he told me that he could send me to a home for unmarried mothers run by the Anglicans and could find a good home and family for my baby. When I went back to my mother and told her all of this, she told me she had found somewhere herself, and it was with the Catholics and I had no choice."

Olga was silent. She knew she had only a few moments to reflect before she would need to respond to Vera. Olga felt the young woman had not learned the most basic of lessons about the long game. She was not as prepared for the world in the way Olga had been at her age.

No time now to reflect. Now is the time to act.

Vera had a frightened look on her face. A look that asked Olga not to judge her by her actions, but to understand her circumstances.

Olga had seen it before, of course. Lev and his recanting. (Sorry Comrade Stalin, it won't happen again). Then he would come home to Olga, and he would have that same look. His white, stretched knuckles. Pride goes before a fall, said Lev. He got that right.

Olga took both of Vera's hands. "None of that matters now. Perhaps you can go back to your comrades one day with your head high. What matters is our plan."

Of course, Olga had lied to Vera about her comrades actually agreeing to help, which had not yet happened. But it was a kind lie.

By mid-afternoon, Olga had made her way back to St Patrick's Cathedral. In her letter to Comrade Ron, she had stipulated that her contact should meet her in the Catholic cathedral she now knew and which was on the tram route. What better place? She relished the confusion that would go through the mind of her spy if he were tracking her today.

That part of Olga's plan was nothing if not exquisite. That was something she had seen the Kremlin Highlander perfect. Not just to plot, but to enjoy the reprisal.

She entered the church, which was between Sunday services. She did what she had seen others do last time: dip their fingers in a crevice in the wall and wave their hands up and down in front of their face in a particular manner. The comrade she was meeting would be carrying a burgundy-coloured scarf.

At this time, there were only a few of the devoted followers of the Virgin Mary in the pews. Some kneeling with heads bowed, others sitting quietly. A man holding a scarf sat at the end of one of the pews, far away from the aisle.

Olga hobbled around the pews and put her hand on his shoulder. "Hello?" she asked.

The man stood up and said quietly, "pleased to meet you. Mrs Chernenkova is it?"

He was very tall. Very noticeable. He wore horn-rimmed glasses, and his hair was slicked with hair oil, which Olga could smell as he leaned towards her. To her surprise, he was wearing a black clerical shirt with a white priest's collar and black trousers.

"The confessional is clear," he said. "No one seems to be using it."

He followed Olga towards the pulpit where she waited. He made the sign of the cross and moved to go into the confessional when a young man carrying a feather duster walked towards him.

"Can I help you with anything?" the young man asked.

The comrade replied in a heavy American accent. "Well, hi. I'm a visiting priest from New York. I am ministering to a small number of people out here and this little lady wants me to hear her confession. You don't mind, do you? *Pax vobiscum*," he said.

The young man made the Sign of the Cross and continued dusting.

Olga stepped up into the other side of the confessional, pulling the small door shut behind her. The comrade pulled the curtain open so that they could see each other through the grille.

"You are Mr Krachstein?"

"Gregor. Call me Greg."

"You are Jewish?"

"Yes. But my family are atheists."

"Of course. You know what I need?"

"Yes, I do. And as…our friend promised you, I have asked around and tried to find someone to help you."

"Thank you, Gregor. I will call you Gregor. Greg does not roll off the tongue easily."

Greg continued. "Do you like my garb?

"Well," Olga replied. "I am very amused."

Gregor stifled a laugh. "I got it from the New Theatre. It's a prop."

"Ah," said Olga. "The theatre! You are actor."

"Mostly I help with production."

Olga was immensely impressed. This man had embraced the absurdity of the situation like a real Soviet avant-gardist.

"I knew them all, you know, back in Russia. Meyerhold. Malevich. Mayakovsky. Lunacharsky."

"Ah. Impressive. And I gather you were part of the Soviet administration?"

He had ignored Olga's attempt to find common ground in the avant-garde, and she felt a chill waft across her neck.

"You are wanting my real confession, eh? Well, I tell you. My name is Davidovna, Also Bronstein before I was married. You know that name? Perhaps you know my married name. Kameneva? Wife of Lev Kamenev, executed by Stalin. Faithful servant of the Revolution, forced to recant his 'crimes' to save his children, then murdered as a traitor. Does that cause me a problem? Here? Am I exiled for all of this here, as well?"

Olga held back the fear from her voice.

"Wait…I…oh, Jesus Christ…"

Greg heard Olga stifle a laugh.

"I…well, it doesn't bother me, Olga. May I call you Olga?"

"Da."

"Let's say the Party and I, well we've had our moments. I was expelled once."

"Me, too!" replied Olga.

"You are helping one of our comrades?"

Olga told him Vera's name, but he said he did not know her. "I don't know many in the student branch. I stick to the unions, and theatre for the workers. That's my main interest."

"And mine is to help the young women who have been abandoned by their families and it seems by her comrades…"

"Hold your horses Mrs C… or K," said Greg. "I'm not sure anyone knew anything. Don't go making accusations…"

"No. I am not accusing. I'm stating fact. Some of you knew. Not least, the father."

Greg was silent. Olga continued.

"Vera must be rescued. And her baby, as well. On this I insist. You will know how to do this. You have been illegal organisation before — you will know how to do the clan-destine work which she needs…"

Greg interrupted softly.

"Yeah, I've thought about it. I've made enquiries. There are a few problems. For a start, we would have to find someone who isn't followed by the spooks."

"Spooks?" asked Olga.

Greg whispered even more softly. "Spies. Like Cheka."

Olga nodded. "Yes. I know them. But they not like Cheka."

"Hard to find anyone in the Party these days who isn't tailed. Except perhaps for some of the students, but they won't be of any help. I've made some enquiries already. There are a couple of young unionists I'm testing out. The spooks haven't cottoned on to them yet."

"I myself am followed."

Olga heard a sharp intake of breath.

"Thank you, Father Gregor. I will tell Vera we are on our way," Olga added, hoping to will him into action.

As she watched Gregor Krachstein make his way out of the church, she noticed some old ladies nod their heads at him. She stifled a smile. She hoped Vera would see some humour in it all. She would tell her after this was all over. Gallows humour was what it is called here. And she knew that people were still hanged in this country (the land of milk and honey!); she had read about it in the newspaper.

So, off to the gallows we go!

Olga was late getting to the convent on the next Sunday, but she smiled nicely at the nun and offered her some of the biscuits she had brought for Vera. After a long delay, Vera was informed she had a visitor and the two women retreated to the garden.

Vera did not want to talk about Olga's plan. She was distraught, but Olga could see she held back, telling her only a few snippets. Her dark eyes told Olga well enough. Vera told her that the baby was kicking her to death. She was able to eat a little but it made her feel uncomfortable. She had been put on reduced duties. They continued to pressure her to sign the adoption papers. Vera suspected that it didn't really matter if she signed or not, the baby would be taken anyway.

Olga sat next to her, holding her hand.

At night when she could not sleep, Vera had developed the habit of practicing relinquishing the baby after it was born, getting her mind used to it. In these hours, she had begun to view Olga's visits as a nuisance. Perhaps she should tell Olga she had changed her mind? It would make everything easier. Her mother would welcome her back. She could continue with her study and Party work.

Today's events had made it more difficult, but she did not want to share her turmoil with Olga, who, after all, was trying her best to help. Though what an old lady with few connections might be able to accomplish, Vera didn't have any idea. She sounded confident, but Vera wondered whether there was really anything behind it. Hence, she was practicing resignation.

Earlier, 'Teresa,' had said to her "my mother told me it's for the best." Vera had blurted out, "but best for who, Teresa?" and she realised she was speaking about herself. She had to admit that the Bolshevik in her wanted to keep the baby, perhaps exactly because everyone seemed so determined to take it from her. She was not just being oppositionist. Her mother had always said she was quietly defiant (agreeing up front but then doing what she wanted anyway), but Vera realised as she got older, it was a convenient tag that could be attached to anyone who wants to disturb the current order or point out what is wrong. And what about men able to shirk their obligations to children purely because women give birth? Any society worth its salt would correct that.

"I've been reading some interesting books," Vera said. "You'd be surprised to find what they allow in the library here. I don't think they really know what they have, or maybe the Librarian nun is compassionate. She seems kind when we go in there."

"Tell me about your books, then," said Olga.

"I read one called *Communism and the Family*. I think it must have been put there by someone who didn't read it! They must have looked at the title and assumed it was critical of Communism. Did you know the author? Alexandra Kollontai?"

Olga grimaced. "Yes, of course I knew her. Quite well. But how did this book come to be here? In Melbourne?"

"Our comrades translated it. We had a reading circle to discuss it, but I couldn't go because of an exam. I can't think how the nuns got their hands on it! Maybe someone put it in the library secretly? Have you read it?"

"No. But I know her arguments quite well."

"Is it true? What she wrote? Her critique of what was happening?"

Olga's shoulders slumped. She was feeling the weight of Vera's expectations upon her.

"It was true, and it wasn't true. We had such dreams, but society only half formed, like baby in womb. Baby forms from existing…matter, so when fully formed, it is not only new, but old…" Olga was gesticulating, and Vera could hardly keep up with her hands.

"Alexandra knew, as we all did, that the old morality is *bourgeois* invention, to keep working class in line. She did not obey rules and I admired her. She took lovers, a few husbands. She was fighter, though she and I did not agree on everything. Abortion, for example. She was pragmatic, and gave it support. So many war orphans, no one could look after them all. We were forced to divert the money to fighting, away from the social needs. Without war, we would have had so much! Me — perhaps I was idealistic, but I argued against legalising the abortions. We needed the children of workers to help the Revolution grow! But Kollontai looked at the hungry mouths and said enough. It was same with prostitution; she condemned it but knew the women had no money to feed themselves and their children. We tried to give better life to women so that the prostitution was not necessary.

"I wonder if she survived? I did not hear. Probably she did. She withdrew from the politics. Perhaps she saw future. She imagined one: the old peasant values gone. No more working from dawn to night and taking it out on the women. The divorce law was good. But it left so many women without means of support, as well. Solve one problem, create another."

Olga had risen and walked around during this speech, and now she sat back down on the stone seat.

"What about you, Olga? You never tell me much about you."

"Well, my story is not so interesting as Kollontai's. I lived in her shadow — Krupskaya's — Lenin's wife's, also. My husband died in the executions, I told you that. But we were not together then. The divorce law worked for him, as well. He left me and had another child with a painter. I met him once at the railway station where he had arrived with one of his lovers, and I kissed her warmly. We were still married then. But we were not hypocrites. Not *litsemer*."

"You mean, like we are?"

Vera was annoyed with the turn of the conversation. Hadn't she herself wished Rhys well with his new life and his new lover? Wasn't she also liberated?

"Why don't you ask me what I thought about the book?"

"Alright. Yes. Please."

"I was impressed. But I don't think she really knew how hard it is to be on the other side, like I am."

Olga replied, "perhaps you are right," but inwardly, she was horrified because Vera knew nothing of Kollontai's struggles or the dangers she had faced.

But Vera continued her train of thought (and Olga admired her for that).

"Everything that happened during our war, it hasn't really changed anything. We were full of hope for the future. But it was all just ribbons and bows! Now it's magazine articles about mothers and chubby babies and how wonderful. And here I am, about to have one of my own, but no one is celebrating. What's wrong with my baby?"

"Nothing at all," Olga replied, "I will get you and the baby out. You must trust me."

If Olga had her way, they would have continued this conversation for many hours and they would have argued and contradicted each other and shared new information and they would have changed each other's minds, even just a little. But there was no time left.

Vera sniffed back tears then nodded her head as if the very act would make her believe. And if she did get out? She would take Kollontai with her. The nuns didn't realise what they had.

OLGA'S SPY

Although it took some time, Olga's memory finally snapped into place: she had indeed seen the man before. He had sat in the car across the road from her flat, in the coffee shop opposite the library and once she had (intentionally) brushed into him on a tram to see what he would do. He ignored her.

This was the spy with the crooked mouth that seemed to droop to one side; a rangy figure with a prominent tapering nose and thinning hair that Olga could observe was combed over the top of his head when he removed his hat. My own spy.

Olga recalled that her first spy had started to follow her when she was just twenty years old, before she had been sent to the Tsar's prison the first time. He had been an old man with a limp. Clearly, they had not seen Olga as much of a threat. Not as much as her husband or brother, to whom the Tsar's police had assigned young, active, more vigorous spies. And she, as a much younger woman, had outpaced hers and given him the slip more times than not.

But here was her Australian spy again, and Olga realised as soon as she saw him that he was not just her spy, but he was the man she had seen in the doorway of the brothel near Spencer Street Station.

So, that's where the dog is buried!

Olga was sitting in the library. She was looking across at the café when she saw the spy remove his hat. The profile of his nose was unmistakable, as was his tall, hunched frame as he had made his way down the street that night.

Her mind was racing. She had found her collaborator — or perhaps her mark? Could this work? And the consequences if it did or didn't? The thoughts were coming too quickly now for one so old. One at a time, please! She breathed deeply to calm herself. "Tactics, Olga!" she felt her brother say again. She could hear him now as he instructed her, just like in their youth — if you find an obstacle, side-step it; even in the most hopeless of situations you will find there is a way through the labyrinth...

Leon: it was he that she was pulled towards, not Lev, the father of her children. The brother who had helped with her very first schemes. Helping her to play tricks on their siblings and cousins, on their parents, aunts and uncles — even cruel ones, like giving their father a written note, even though she knew he could not read. Their battles in the playroom, through the hallways of their house and later, watching Leon out-manoeuvre as he swapped Menshevism for independence and then for Bolshevism and all but neutralised the Kremlin Highlander. But not quite.

And when she joined him in the Party, she had already developed the habits that would later let her down. Her brother may have been guilty of poor tactics at the crucial time, but she, Olga, had submitted to more impositions than she had agreed with, an accretion like the layers of an oyster shell, just one more regulation forbidding something, one more committee convened to paw over someone's life and pronounce it good or evil. In the matter of Vera, she would not be compliant.

Ha! A compliant revolutionary! She could hear her brother snigger. But that's what we became, Leon.

She had not heard back from Gregor. When she thought back on the conversations with Gregor and Ron, she felt the Party was not really committed to rescuing Vera and her baby. What was it Ron had said? We are not a welfare organisation, we are a political party. She had no time to waste, and her calls to the Party office had rung out several times. When it was answered, she had left a message. But no call had come.

Olga slapped her own forehead: the dog is buried even deeper. Why had she been trying to use force, when blackmail might accomplish the same end? You could be mistaken for thinking it was force all the same, just dressed differently. A gentler form of blackmail — Koba had been the master.

First, she needed a camera. One with a light flash. She had days in which to organise herself, and hope this, her second (or was it third?) plan, paid off. If it didn't, she would fall back on the comrades, but they were not her best shot now. The spy was. She knew him now, and what he was. She knew!

It had dawned on her as she sat in the library looking at the spy's silhouette. Now she had her tactics! Olga wrote a hasty note to Betty to put in her letter box on the way home. She announced that she would call on Betty and Eric that night and see if she could borrow Eric's camera, which Olga has seen him using at the chop picnic.

Olga made up a hasty cabbage soup with some leftover pork stock that she had preserved in a jar. Then she went to see her neighbours.

"It's just a box brownie, Olga, but it's the latest model," Eric said as he showed Olga how to use it. "It's the Hawkeye Flash, the latest thing," he said proudly. "Here, I'll show you."

Olga took a picture of Betty and Eric. I want to take photos of my new country, to send to my friends back in the old country, Olga told them, even though there were none.

"There are spare flash bulbs in the pocket of the camera bag," Eric said, as he handed Olga the heavy canvas rucksack.

She was running a terrible risk, she knew that, (Leon and Maria, they were clapping. At last! At last! they shouted), and the weight of it all gradually dawned on her as she stood opposite the brothel once again.

She stood in the dark doorway, and she thought she was well hidden. But what would happen when the flash went off? Surely, he would rush her. Or she would be attacked by the pimps. And even if she got away, would they not come after her to retrieve the film? And if she was exposed as a blackmailer, might she not be deported? All of this is possible, Olga thought to herself as she stood in the cold with her warm coat pulled tight. She had taken worse risks, even with her own life.

On the first night at the brothel, Olga's stakeout drew a blank. The spy did not visit. And of course, there was no guarantee he would be back. Olga reasoned that her best chance was Friday night after the six o'clock close of the hotels. That would be the same day and time she had seen him the week before, and spies were nothing if not creatures of habit. But if he did not come to the brothel, Olga would come every night until he did. She was prepared. Lenin, how she was prepared!

Olga had gambled on seeing the spy on Friday, but that did not mean she didn't spend Thursday evening in the same cold place. Her brother had once called her a tamed cur, so determined had she been to follow the Party line. The cold was numbing, and she could keep going (as she always had), but her brain was tired, and she was trying to keep focussed on her one tiny chance.

In that dark place, intently watching each time the door opened, Olga felt as if every part of her life had prepared her for this. She would not be able to do this thing now unless she had out-manoeuvred the Tsar's men, the guards in the camp and then, as a displaced person, managed to get the authorities to accept her as a refugee. Poor Mrs Chernenkova, she would hear them say. And never let it be said that she had not striven or shirked her duty. She never missed a meeting of the theatre committees that she chaired, the women's committee nor the famine relief committee, and even stood in there for Lev when needed.

Olga was more than ready. She had slept well each night, dog-tired from hours of standing. As she had watched the women walking the street on Wednesday and Thursday night, bringing their clients back to the brothel, then seeing them out to the door, she realised the full extent of the problem she was trying to solve, whereas before, she had only focused on one part of it.

It is so unlike you, Olga! She admonished herself. Here I am, old lady who thinks she can take photo of the spy and get away? I cannot even run!

On Thursday, she had realised she needed to be better prepared. She had glanced around. What were her resources? Where were her weapons? She looked down at the heavy camera she was holding. She could batter him with it. But he would spring at her across the road. She could hit him in the face. It would have to be a well-timed shot and unless she disabled him, he would come after her.

Olga, Olga, Olga. How could you be so stupid? She had stepped out of the shadow of the doorway for a moment. She had seen smoke from a cigarette curling into the air at the end of the street. She walked towards it, and found it curling from a cigarette perched between the ruby red lips of a muscular woman with long dark hair.

Olga introduced herself. "Hello, I am Olga."

"Hello Olga. You want to do the business? Or are you on the game yourself?" asked the woman between puffs.

"No. Thank you, but no to both those things. I need help. Tomorrow night. I pay you. No sex allowed."

"Oh, it's always allowed. What are you paying for then? Are you a plant?"

Olga looked confused.

"A cop. Do you work for them?" The woman's voice raised a few notches.

"No. I not cop. I'm Olga. DP. From Russia."

"DP, eh? We've got a lot of DPs amongst our girls here. Some of 'em don't speak a word of…anyway. What do you want?"

"There is man. Bad man. He wears hat, like this. Tall, very thin. Stooped. Hair…" and she waved her hand over her head to indicate how he combed it across his crown.

"Bad man. Yeah. We know him alright. He's a cop of some kind. We have to keep him happy. But he's a wrong'un."

"What you mean, wrong. Un?" asked Olga.

The woman mashed her cigarette into the footpath and leaned closer to Olga.

"I mean he beats up women, you know? Uses his fists."

Olga nodded. If she had a shilling for every time she had seen a woman beaten or threatened by a man she would be a very, very rich woman.

"He may be here, tomorrow night? I take photo of him when he comes out. I stand there," and Olga gestured to the doorway opposite the brothel entrance.

"He will get angry, perhaps try to chase me…"

"And you want someone to help you get away? Stop him?"

"Yes. I pay. Here." Olga had handed over five pounds. It was all the money she had. She'd sold some furniture and added the proceeds to a few pounds she kept under her mattress.

The woman took the money and popped it down her tight-fitting dress front. "I'm Tessie. I'll be here at six." Up close, Olga could see that Tessie had a missing tooth and was perhaps older than Olga had first thought. Tessie said nothing more and walked to the next corner.

Olga found it hard to sleep that night. It could all go very wrong on Friday, she knew. It took her back, this escapade, to the days of important (life or death!) meetings and discussions and decisions, as if her whole life had been argument and counter argument and plan and counter plan. So many plans! Too many. But then, planning was something exciting, to think about a future, something new. How she loved to plan!

But this plan was better than Olga had imagined: the streetwalkers could be amongst the best fighters. She had worked with them before, she and Meyerhold had once cast the whole of *The Three Sisters* from amongst Moscow's prostitutes, even the male parts, as part of a rehabilitation program. Kollontai had approved of the plan. The women thought it was hilarious and laughed their way through the lines. They were particularly unhappy about the treatment of the old servant who was made to stand in Natasha's presence, so they took that part out. That was very acceptable! Even the prostitutes wanted to make the world into a just place.

The point of that exercise had been to build consciousness, not just in the audience but in the women themselves about their circumstances and what stopped them from having a better life. Not that Olga was able to find them other jobs — she was not influential where it counted. A few went to the factories, but she had wondered whether they lasted.

On Friday morning, she woke once again and saw that it was not yet light. She reflected that this exercise with Vera was more practical, more concrete. This is what seemed to her to flavour this new country; you can have any colour you like as long as it is practical. There seemed to be little time for poetry, no cafés crammed with enthusiasts for the latest Mayakovsky or Serapion poem.

She must throw herself into it, she reasoned. Her soul yearned for 'Art', for a time when everyone had the time to create. And yet, they — the dreamers, the poets, the intellectuals — had made something most practical: a revolution, a new order.

She rose as late as she permitted herself, which was close to nine o'clock. She had shopping to do, and she checked to see if the spy was anywhere in sight. Not today. That, she had often thought, was the strange thing about spies. You know you are being followed; it is an open secret. And even the spies know that this is the worst part: for you to know and not be able to do anything about it.

Olga went to the charity shop. It was high time she bought some baby clothes. She found some knitted jackets and little cotton dresses and a bonnet. She went to a local department store and bought six baby napkins. At home she put them into a small bag, for Vera when the time required it. She took some more practice photographs with the camera, including in the darkened communal laundry where she used a flash. She ate a hearty meal of chicken soup and stale bread and tried to have a short nap.

In the late afternoon, she took up the camera bag and pulled on her hat and coat and set out for the city. Her first stop was the comrades' office. She made her way there through those now familiar back streets of garbage and dirty water and little factories. Some thin men waved to her from the open windows, naked to the waist, sweating over presses and filthy machines. She wished she could talk to them, but she had no time. She knocked at the door of the office and asked for Comrade Ron. Someone fetched him and he led Olga back up to his office.

"I made sure I was not being followed," Olga said.

"That's alright Mrs...I believe it's Kameneva? Well, we won't worry about that just now. We do worry about the industrial comrades, so we are diligent on their part. We know we have spies in our midst. They're the more insidious ones. The ones you don't know about."

Ron lit up a cigarette. "Smoke, Mrs K?"

"No thank you," Olga replied. "I hear nothing back from you or from Gregor, so I go on with my own plan."

Ron looked embarrassed and started to apologise, but Olga cut him off.

"I have spy following me. He is tall man, hunch a little, long nose, thin hair like this...you know him?"

Olga simulated the combed-over hair.

"Ah," said Ron. "Nimbleby."

Olga was not familiar with such a name. It sounded like Nickleby, from Mr Dickens.

"Nickleby?"

"No. Nimbleby. That's our nickname for him. His name's Fred Quick. Nimbleby Quick. It's a joke. Like he is himself. So, he's your man, eh? I'm not being disrespectful Olga, but he isn't what you would call one of the best spies they have."

Olga smiled. "I am grateful for that."

Ron puffed on his cigarette, then stubbed it in a crowded ashtray as Olga looked on.

"Trying to give up. I wouldn't worry too much about it, Olga. The spy agency has something big going on with the government and the Soviets. Maybe you don't read the papers. It doesn't involve us. Not yet, anyway. Why did you want to know who he is?"

"I cannot tell you," Olga replied.

Ron raised his eyebrows. "Mrs Kameneva. Please don't get yourself into any trouble. We have enough to deal with, what with the attacks on the unions by the Catholics and the Royal Commission and the attacks on our writers...and this latest thing in Canberra, we're not sure where that's going either."

"Do not go on. I may need you again. But tell your Mr Krachstein it will be alright on the night. And I will need his help again. Do not worry, I will not endanger you..."

Ron looked shocked. "Don't put yourself in harm's way, Mrs K..."

Olga drew herself up and got out of her chair. "Comrade, I survive Tsar, Stalin, DP camp. You think I let a shame-fool spy stop me?"

Ron had more questions for Olga, but he could see she was in no mood for them.

"Alright, Mrs K. Sorry. And look after yourself."

Olga twisted and turned her way through the streets, periodically looking behind her, until she reached the greasy, dusty café at the train station where she planned to wait until dark. She ordered a pot of tea, the bitter black kind. They did not serve her light lemon tea here. The English, she thought to herself as she poured the bitter, muddy liquid, what do they know? She bought herself an evening paper. She had not read one for several days, not even at the library, because of the anxiety she felt about Vera.

Mother Russia, her glorious homeland, was occupying Page One. The stirring story of Russian spies and their heart-stopping defections. Mr and Mrs Petrov. They probably thought they would be killed if they returned to Russia. They may even have been supporters of Beria, who knows? Lenin help them if they were, now that Beria was supposed to be dead. And if they stay in Australia, Olga knew, their families could be killed or sent to the camps as hers were.

These are the strange choices we face, Olga thought. She chuckled out loud when she read what the Russian official who flew with Mrs Petrov had said. He had asked if armed guards surrounding an unarmed woman in an airport and ringed by a mob, could be considered freedom? He knew, perhaps as much as Olga, that freedom is sometimes found at the end of a gun or in the momentum of the mob, when you have nothing. Stalin still talked of freedom when his guns were pointed at everyone's heads. But, Olga was thinking as she read, this is not new, and not exclusive to the Russians! But there was no talk of the crimes of imperialism in the yellow press.

She realised once she read about the Petrovs, that it was even more important to strike the blow today — or in fact, she may have left it too late — as spies like Nimbleby would be re-assigned to more important work in Canberra, the capital city: finding Russian spies in their midst. The spies would be celebrating and thinking of who to target next. Diplomats, other embassies perhaps? They would want to widen their circle, in which case, minor fish like Olga might be let off the hook altogether.

The darkness thickened and Olga emerged from the café. She trudged back up to the streets where the women waited for customers. She acknowledged Tessie, stationed on the corner of the street then enfolded herself into the dark recess of the doorway opposite the brothel. She focused on breathing slowly, calmly. It was something she had learned in the trucks that took her to the gulags, and in the trains that ferried her from one DP camp to the next, always on the move and never knowing if this would be the last time.

She watched a few men knock on the door, wait, and each time a burly man would come to the door and let them in. There were only a handful, but it was still early evening. Olga took the camera from the bag and looped it around her neck, even though she knew its weight would make her tired. But she was always ready. Visits from the secret police, last minute ambushes hidden in the agendas of meetings, speeches where people changed sides, friends slighting you when Stalin pursed his lips: these had all taught her to be ready.

Mr Quick came along not long after. Tessie had lit up a cigarette, and Olga saw the smoke as if it were a signal of acknowledgement.

It was an hour before Mr Quick reappeared at the bottom of the stairs, and each time the door opened, Olga raised the camera. This time, she saw that it was him and she flashed the camera. Tessie came running and stood beside her, as Quick stumbled then tumbled across the street and lunged at Olga. Tessie stuck out her black-stockinged leg and tripped him and he fell in front of them.

"Not so fast." Tessie laughed, as if she had been waiting to say that her whole life. The pimp came across the street and Tessie told him to get back inside. "This is women's business, Ted," she snapped.

Olga saw that several other women had come running, she could hear the clack of their heels as they ran towards her. Quick was soon surrounded.

Tessie had her shoe on Quick's chest, pressing into its square heal with her whole body. One of the women pulled back her leg and sunk her shoe into Quick's side.

"Owww!"

Another of the women took her cigarette and stubbed it into Quick's forehead. He groaned.

"Off you go," Tessie said to Olga. "And Ted, he's not coming back here. got it?"

"This is for him," Olga said as she handed Tessie a note. Tessie shoved it in Quick's top pocket. Olga touched Tessie's fingers as she ran to the end of the street, caught her breath and then took herself away as quickly as her tired legs would go.

Olga took a tram back to Flinders Street so she didn't have to weave her way through the back streets and risk Quick catching up with her. But he knew where she lived. When she finally reached her own door, she took the film from the camera as Eric had shown her, she dragged some blankets and a pillow into the outside laundry and made a bed under the concrete washing troughs. She went back to her flat and locked the door and returned to the bed in the laundry. She had taken all precautions. She had isolated the spy; she knew that he would not be able to mobilise his fellow spies because of the threat of shame. Let him dwell on what it was like to be an outsider, a social pariah!

NICE OLD LADY, KIND TO ANIMALS AND SPIES

Olga woke early. She entered her flat quietly, dragging her gathered-up old bones and the blankets and pillows. No one had seen her in the laundry. That was a relief. She didn't want her neighbours to become suspicious. Better that they simply thought of her as the nice old lady in Flat Number Five. She saw that no one had tried to enter her flat, either. Her hammered-in boards were still on the door, nothing was out of place.

She brushed her mussed-up hair, and looking in the mirror, she realised she had become her own mother. The facial lines and gullies lay in the same places. The same pattern of grey flecked her hair. She looked and was, old; older than she had ever seen her mother become.

The prostitutes Olga had just encountered proved to her once again that the women had been up to the task. They were equally as magnificent as the ones who drove the trucks and became scientists and painters and who defied religious and family conventions, taking men and women as lovers and laboring alongside the men.

Olga poured warm water into a bowl and washed herself, daydreaming about the luxury of warm water and soap and lather and somewhere to tip it once she was finished, instead of on frosty, muddy ground or out of a window. She could see how this life could be seductive, of course she could. She was not made of spruce! But the younger Olga would never, ever leave her. No matter how tired she became, young Olga always had something to say to her: get up Olga! This is no time for daydreaming! Shatter those illusions! Go on!

Those who do not defy expectations are doomed to repeat them, Olga thought — and what a dull world that made for! In this country, everything *seemed* possible, but hopes seemed narrow. Perhaps that's why people here were content — content that they could change things *if they wanted to*. But what was there to change? they asked. This lack of consciousness of their *actual situation* seemed a poor state of affairs to Olga. Here she was, old Olga and Olga of old, making her way with sword in hand to smite a lethal blow for freedom. Joan of Arc without the priests and kings, but with the prostitutes as her chorus.

Even though she had spent the night on the cold, concrete floor of an outdoor laundry, she felt invigorated. Not even her sore bones could prevent this rendezvous. Olga had made sure that Quick knew that he had a date today. The note Tessie had passed over to him gave instructions to meet Olga at Berger's deli in Acland Street. She would make him stand beside her and receive his punishment, following her around as she did her weekly shopping in a public place so he could not put his hands on her.

She emerged from her flat, pouring milk into a saucer she kept for the stray cats and placing it carefully on her front step. As she looked up, she saw Beverly walking towards her gate. Strange, Olga thought, she has come without her hat. And her mouth was set oddly.

Olga met her at the front gate. Beverly spoke first.

"Vera has given birth," she said.

Olga clapped her hand to her mouth. "*O bozhe!*"

"Yes, well. It is a little early, they think. The baby is small and a little sickly, but the doctor said it does not need to stay in hospital."

"What kind of baby?" Olga asked.

"I don't know. It was a short conversation. As you know, Vera will look after the child for a month to make sure it gets mother's milk and a good start in life. After that, she will find a flat somewhere near the university no doubt and she will start her studies again."

"That will be inhuman, Beverly," said Olga. This time, she could not stop herself.

"Be that as it may, Olga, Vera will be thankful for what we've done for her. She doesn't understand it yet. One day she will."

Olga kept up her pretence. "Well. I go to visit."

"They won't let you see the baby," said Beverly.

Olga nodded and went on her way. She looked back at Beverly as she stood at the gate. Something about her told Olga that there was nothing simple about these matters; Beverly's slump and her face had told her that her emotions were not so silent, that perhaps a torrent flowed that could be barely contained. But there was nothing Olga could do about that now.

At least for Olga, the baby coming was good news. At least now, she could tell Quick a timeframe for the rescue. All of her puzzle pieces fitting together.

It was still early, and Berger's was not so busy. This delicatessen was large enough to have a quiet conversation but not so big that you would remain unnoticed. That was why Olga chose it. She found jars of herring and placed them in her basket and waited. Each time the bell rang above the door, she peered around the shelves. Clang! No Quick, not yet.

A woman wandered down the aisle browsing the shelves. A young mother, she was holding the hand of a small boy dressed in shorts and a shirt with a small bow tie. He wore eyeglasses and they talked incessantly together in Yiddish. Such a sing-songy sound! Olga was proud that the Soviets had established chairs in Yiddish and fostered Jewish culture, though of course, she had read that the Kremlin Highlander had crushed them since. A little flower, short-lived, but it is still a flower, she was thinking, and the bell rang again. She looked up to see the spy walking towards her.

"So, you come, Mr Quick," said Olga.

He dipped his head briefly.

"How did you know my name?" he asked, and his face was red with rage.

"You are not only one with spies," Olga said. She added, "you have something you must do before I give you photo."

"I thought that might be the case," Quick said through clenched teeth.

"I have friend you need to liberate. She is *comrade*."

Quick laughed softly and shook his head.

"Commos? We liberated you from Hitler. Not enough for you, eh?"

He was trying to bait her, but Olga continued. "My friend is in the St Agnes convent. She has baby and is alone. She wants to bring baby home. They hold her captive. You must rescue her. It will be quite easy, if you follow my plan."

Olga moved along the aisle, which obliged the spy to follow her. She could feel his annoyance grow again, and it pleased her very much. She asked him to remove his hat, in deference to the Jewish people who had been murdered in the war.

He took it off and held it in front of him like a schoolboy about to be punished.

"Mr Freed-erich Quick. My plan. My friend is called Vera Watson. She has a new baby which she is looking after for one month. So, you have not very much time. It must be done this week."

Quick stuttered. "I can't just take time off from my job for this. I..."

"I will mail the photograph to your agency, Mr Quick. I can do this."

"Well...when do I get it back?"

"After. I have one motive only. To get her out. You are what we call in Russia *litsemer*. Hypocrite. You have wife and government job, but you exploit young women. And you hit them, too. And you pretend to be upright, outstanding member of society."

"Steady on, Mrs…" mumbled the spy as he looked around and realised he could not move against her in public.

"Vera is Communist, yes. You must tell the nuns at the convent that she is suspected of being a spy, and that you have to remove her and her baby for the sake of the country. I hear the Catholics are not so fond of the 'Reds'?"

"Blimey… but steady on, I'll be risking my job if I do something like that for some stupid bint…"

Olga pulled two tins of sardines from the shelf and shoved them into her basket. "Well, it is your choice. Either you do it, or lose perhaps your job, but also your family. There is no problem with me sending the photo to your wife, as well."

Olga watched Mr Quick intently as he took a step towards her and without taking her eyes from his, Olga lifted her foot (which she had encased in a strong boot should the occasion need it) and slammed it down onto his.

She watched Quick wince. "You understand?"

Olga heard a begrudging 'yes' and raised her foot.

"Which day you go?"

"Next Thursday. In the evening."

"I meet you with Vera and the baby at Flinders Street Station. I wait until eight o'clock."

"And you will have the film? I don't just want the photo."

Olga replied coolly, "I will see you then."

She walked towards the front counter and waited her turn. Quick headed for the door, and she watched him walk towards the tram, then run, so that he could board one already at the stop and make his escape.

Did it occur to her then, that she might one day hear another stout knock at the door and realise they had come to deport her? It did. She knew that above all, Quick would hold a grudge and could manoeuvre to make her life as difficult as possible. Perhaps they would take away her allowance? Her flat? No matter. She had faced worse. She would make an extra photograph, as a little insurance.

Olga hastened back to her flat, her overladen basket full of food from her homelands and other local items she had grown a fondness for, such as the yellow butter and clarified dripping.

A man stood up for her on the tram and she did not refuse as she usually did. It seemed an arrogance to her that a man would give up their seat to a woman when they wouldn't do it for an old man who might need it. Just because she was a woman! She, Olga, was not frail! In giving up his seat to a woman, a man showed deference, not to her power, but to her lack of it. This infuriated her. Like the priests who wash the feet of the beggars once a year. The beggars have to sit there, Olga thought. Just make nice, that is all. Act as if you enjoy it! When you want to cut their heads off!

As soon as she had everything packed away, Olga hurried back to the tram, then to the train and into the city. She made her now familiar trek up to the Communist Party headquarters. By the time she got there, the camera bag felt very heavy, and as she approached, she saw Gregor coming towards her.

"Let me help you with that, comrade," he said.

She loved being called comrade! She blushed and handed over the bag. There was no such problem with this gesture from a true comrade, so the act of offering to take the bag from her was practical help, not fake deference.

Olga explained what she needed as they ascended the stairs. She had no time to waste. Greg was stunned by Olga's brief explanation of what she had been doing.

"You did what?"

"It is very simple. It is called blackmail."

Greg rested his wiry frame on the end of a wooden desk. There was no one else in the office.

"Are you sure you weren't followed here?"

"I am certain. Mr Quick will have found a reason to make sure I was not followed. He is only stupid when it comes to his...you know...down there. He feels entitled to have woman and that is a weakness. It will unravel him. You'll see."

Greg laughed. "You've got some nerve. But I guess you've bested better people than Quick. I'm sorry we weren't able to help, what with the trouble in Canberra with the Petrovs...well, the time just wasn't right for your...our comrade."

Olga nodded solemnly.

Greg stood up. "There is a darkroom here, as I'm sure you guessed. You would know better than anyone that we only trust ourselves with the photographs for our newspaper. Well, all our personal photos too, so that the spooks don't get hold of them. Follow me," he said, "this won't take long."

They walked to the back of the building. "Are you happy to come in with me?" he asked. "Only, there is no one else here, and it would be remiss of me to leave a non-member alone in the office, and I'd be balled out by an executive member if anyone else arrives."

Olga smiled thinly. "Yes. I have been executive member. I understand. And your secrets are safe with me, Comrade Krachstein."

They stepped into the narrow room, and Greg turned on a red glowing light as the door closed.

A chair was positioned near a long wooden counter, and Olga sat down. She really was quite exhausted now. She hoped that Gregor would not ask too many questions, but as soon as he processed the film, pouring the chemicals into the tray, taking the film from the camera, he started talking.

"I'm sorry we have not been very welcoming of you, Comrade Kameneva," he started. "We can't be too careful, what with the Royal Commission and the referendum and...well, the death of Stalin. To be honest with you, and I wouldn't say this to other comrades, but I don't think even Khrushchev will be able to change things."

Stalin, dead? Yes, of course she had known that, but now it seemed like news to Olga. She felt a wave of sleepiness as she sat in the red gloom.

Gregor continued, "everyone feels betrayed. It's not just the attacks here, but everything that's being said about Stalin now. It makes us look like fools. I had my own reservations, and to my cost, I voiced them. But we have no backing now, the West will exploit Stalin's death as much as anything. And we don't know what Khrushchev will do."

"You are not fools. You were fuel. Koba sucked on hope like a tick. But he didn't destroy the body. What did Shakespeare say? 'A peasant stands up thus,'" Olga said definitively.

She continued, "this was a most unusual act in Mr Shakespeare's plays — I have read them — because it is most unusual in the world. People able to stand up. But we will see more of it. Perhaps not me —

I am old. But the world will. The dead implore the living to act for them, that does not stop."

Greg was silent as he continued processing the photograph. He was listening but was not really sure what Olga was trying to say. Perhaps she was tired, rambling.

He placed the photograph in the second tray and came over to where Olga sat and leaned against the end of the counter.

"Some of us are still suspicious of Khrushchev. It's not that we don't trust the Russian people, but how can you undo what's been done?"

Olga was fully awake now. She replied, sounding irritated. "*You* cannot. How can *you* know what it is to be like Russian? I cannot really know what it is to be Australian. I am surprised many times, all the time, by what I do not know about you. That you have a native race amongst your people who you pretend invisible? That if you are a woman and you marry, you must give up job? That you lock up young women simply because pregnant? That your spies do not track the Nazis, but those who opposed them?"

Greg didn't say anything. He rinsed the photo and moved it to the last tray.

Now, she could not stop herself.

"I have seen many people who call themselves socialist, Comrade Gregor. Even Hitler, who took the name of socialism for his own shame-fool, nationalistic purposes! That most heinous man who shot Lev with his own hand, Blokhin, called himself that. With his own hands, he killed thousands. I suspected he came over from the Tsar's Okhrana to work for Cheka, but I never got evidence. There were many depraved individuals who did. We Russians, we dragged all the old ways behind us like the baggage carts in war: the Tsar's men, the peasant-slave thinking, all the stupidity that came along with it. Religion, those stupid aristocrats…and their wives who drove the serfs mad with petty concerns and cruelty…"

"Don't punish yourself, Olga. George Orwell wrote *Animal Farm* to save socialism. Now look what's become of it."

Then Greg asked Olga a surprising question. "Why did you not simply go mad? In the camps?"

Olga was crying, tears of exhaustion she thought. She paused for quite a while. If she'd had a pipe, she would have taken three or four puffs. Now, she moved to staunch her tears.

"People spoke up, for me, for others. In spite of the consequence! Is that not madness!? It was not straightforward. The camps were often badly run, some guards could be bribed. Sometimes you could get visitors. Not me, but others. Sometimes there would be a strike, the leaders would be rounded up. But authorities would get the message, hold off on the starvation rations, maybe. The promise of the Revolution lasted a long time. Even after my Lev was killed and 'the terror' started, people would write to the Central Committee protesting their lot and the bad local officials. Those sad, handwritten petitions, they came in their hundreds. The people continued to insist in spite of the consequences! They are like that! And you couldn't shoot everyone..."

Greg could see that there was no stopping Olga, it was as if a cork had been removed from a bottle.

"What did they want? They were not foolish enough to wish for happiness, only for long-promised justice and recognition — *priznaniye* — for their suffering. You will not recognise happiness even if it comes towards you in bright sun and presents you with a bouquet of flowers. It will last probably only as long. I have to tell you we did not waste joy! Even our songs, when they are joyful, sound...how you say, *seryeznyy*? In English: serious? Sad?"

Greg pegged the photo to an overhead string, turned off the red light and the white one on, a slow grin taking over his thin, taut face. Olga wondered how he could be so thin, here in this Land of Plenty. She had seen fatter people die of malnutrition!

"This is it. Good photo."

Olga relaxed, the heavy burden she carried had lifted from her shoulders, if briefly.

"You should eat more, Gregor. It is your duty to eat, to honour the many who died for the lack of it."

Greg took the photos down and opened the door, waiting for Olga to pass through in front of him. Olga accepted it as a true mark of respect and nodded her head to acknowledge it as she passed.

"To each according to his needs," he said, and he saw Olga's shoulders rock with a quick laugh.

In the office, Greg placed the photos in a brown paper bag and handed it to Olga.

"What will you do after all this, Olga?"

Olga shrugged. "I'm sure to find something to do." She added, "and thank you for asking," with uncharacteristic politeness. Perhaps she was learning new things after all.

"I must get Vera settled. And the baby."

Greg stroked his chin. "We are not a welfare organisation, we leave that to the unions, but if you want help, I'm sure I could get our women's committee to…"

Olga drew herself up.

"Women's committee should be engaged in propaganda against the shackles which capitalism attaches to them. Next, you will tell me they do your catering, too!"

Greg was embarrassed and Olga could tell by his silence that they did.

Olga sighed. "I have a plan for Vera. No need to trouble yourself."

SOMETHING IN HER POCKET

The next Thursday at 5.30 pm, Olga set off from her flat to journey to the place of assignation. She planned to observe the comings and goings at Flinders Street from the comfort of the seating in the train station's open entrance. Under the clocks, she had heard people say.

Olga knew she would not be followed, but she did wonder if Quick might have recruited one of his fellow spies to help defend himself against the old lady. She knew how to handle herself, even if it was only to put off the moment of reckoning. From the vantage point of one step ahead, sometimes you can see other possibilities. The future, Olga felt, remains a mystery until it arrives, saying "Well? What now?"

The rattling train made Olga sleepy, though it had been only a few hours since she had risen from an afternoon nap. It had been difficult to get out of bed, and she had risen once to make tea and kacha. She had returned to her bed and dozed eventually. The flat was cold, and she had grown used to comforts such as her warm blankets (though she still missed the goose-down quilt of her childhood).

Her bones had ached more than usual, and her ankle bone was red-swollen and throbbed as she pulled on her stocking. Then there was her tooth, which had ached once before, but the pain had come back with a vengeance like a jilted lover. She had chewed cloves before she left, and the pain had eased a little. She focused on the faint throb now to give herself the illusion of time.

The week had been busy with one action after another. She had even visited the Bundists again for final preparations for Vera, though she had not told Comrade Krachstein because of his anticipated reaction of horror. Now, all of the elements were in place. Hah! Olga had woken from her doze, startled. It felt as if the future had slapped her right in the face. The human mechanisms had been set in motion, and there was nothing she could do now. She had prepared — how she had prepared!

She pulled her body up and out of the train seat at Flinders Street Station and walked to the main thoroughfare. It was rush hour and the end of the six o'clock closing — or the 'swill' as her Australian friends would say. They had told her that women wanted this type of prohibition, because it helped to keep the men in check, on a 'moral' path. There is a first for everything, thought Olga. Finally, women get what they want!

This is what they *would say* — the politicians — hiding behind the dresses of women, when the employers benefitted, Olga was sure of that. How could you not see through this? Olga felt like shouting at her Box Hill friends when they voiced their Protestant approval of 'The Swill'. But of course, their own husbands would never be part of it anyway, it was just other women's husbands they were concerned about — the working-class ones. And what of those drunken men who did return home to their wives, having drunk a night's worth of liquor in an hour? It seemed to Olga that mostly people, including the police, turned a blind eye to the plight of these women.

As Olga walked towards the entrance, a man in a hat and suit bumped into her, shouting, "why don't you watch where you are goin'?" She could smell the beer as he jostled past. The close quarters of the front entrance were crowded with men leaving the hotel. The station stank of them.

Olga sat on a bench at the side of the entrance so that she could observe the traffic intersection in front as the jostling reached a crescendo. She looked at the ruddy faces of the men as they passed; some with their heads down, others with their arms around each other. A scattering of businessmen in suits tried to weave their way through.

A man stopped near the bench and emptied his stomach onto the tiles. People stepped around him as he bent over, then he slumped to the ground, sitting in his own vomit. He was young, perhaps just twenty-one, the legal age to drink. Olga could smell the sourness, so she moved closer to the entrance. She would have sat down on the steps, like a *babuschka* with her wares in old Moscow, but she thought the police would move her on. They were a presence, she noticed, though they did nothing to intervene in the fight that broke out just as Olga walked towards the steps. She looked up at the clocks, and saw that the time was 6.45 pm, and the crowd had started to wane. Someone was cleaning up the vomit. The air had begun to turn cold.

Olga paced to make sure her back did not start to ache as well as her tooth. She had become nervous since the crowd started to thin and decided to stand against one of the walls, out of sight. She was worried that Quick would double-cross her. She was prepared for it, mentally. She had done everything she could. In this instance she was not powerless; not like she had been when they came for Lev and then for her. She had tried with all her wiles to bring about her plan for Vera and knew she could do nothing more.

Suddenly, she saw them — Quick in his hat and a long coat, holding a suitcase and Vera right behind him, carrying a small white bundle, high up against her shoulder. She, too, was wearing a hat. One that her mother might have worn: a velvet cloche pulled down, shading her face. They had to stop at the lights just outside the hotel from where the drunks had streamed less than an hour before.

Olga had not seen Vera for weeks, and it was not the same person she saw coming towards her when the lights changed. Vera looked pale and bloated, like a body pulled from the water. She had a determined look on her face, as if her muscles had set in one expression. She walked straight up to Olga and kissed her cursorily.

Quick spoke first.

"Here she is, your little bint. Now where is my film?"

Vera held the baby tight, and Olga could not see its face.

"Well, Mr Quick. It is not your film. It is my film. I paid for it and I processed the photograph."

"Don't you cross me, Mrs. You and your streetwalkers, I will…"

"Here is your photograph. And *my* film. You must make sure I am not followed. Or Vera. I will not cross you unless you cross me. I have principles."

"You've crossed me…" Quick started to move towards her.

Olga shouted as loudly as she could, "Do you want me to call police?"

Several commuters looked at them, but hurried past.

Quick took the brown paper bag, looked inside, turned sharply without another word and left.

"Olga, I…I can't speak. I just need to go somewhere safe."

Olga took the young woman by the arm and guided her through the crowd towards a train platform. Vera stepped cautiously down the stairs, holding the small bundle tightly. Olga carried the suitcase.

Vera stood on the platform waiting for the train. She was wearing her own clothes, Olga recognised, though they hung off her now. The small bundle stirred, and Olga could make out an arm squiggling beneath the blanket and a bonneted head pushed through the folds like a new plant from soil. Olga held back her tears.

"Is baby boy? Or girl?"

Vera turned her attention from the train track for a moment. "Girl."

Olga was silent. She had so hoped it would be a girl. She could see the train careening through the tunnel, and Vera looked up at the platform signs and back at Olga and said "this is not our line…"

Olga interrupted. "It is not safe to go to my flat. I do not trust that man. I have somewhere for you."

She tried to guide Vera by the elbow, and Vera pulled away.

"Are you going to make me disappear? Are you doing my mother's bidding? Is this all for her?" Her voice was starting to wobble.

Olga picked up the suitcase. "I have somewhere safe for you, with Jewish people. Otherwise, I can pay for you to stay in hotel. But only few nights. I do not have much money."

Olga adopted a practical tone, but inwardly she felt something melting, as she had when she had been told about Lev, and then later about her sons. It was as if her resistance to life's deviations had turned into a puddle of water at her feet, and she looked down at it helplessly.

As she cast her eyes downwards, the train had pulled up before them and Vera said, "I have nowhere else to go."

Vera stepped across the gap and into the train carriage, and Olga followed.

Mr Chekhov would be pleased, Olga was thinking: move the walls! Move the scenery! Give her some room!

CONVENT RESISTANCE

The birth of the baby girl, who was not yet named, occurred in a Catholic hospital where Vera had been taken in a car once her labour pains had reached a certain point. The young nun who had been monitoring her and another inmate, was not allowed to go with them to the hospital. Vera felt as if every support was being stripped from her at every step, like Christ on the way to Calvary.

A week before the pains started, Vera had been moved from her shared room away from her roommates. She was placed in a single room at the other end of the convent and removed from all her daily duties, which meant she saw very few people during the day other than the nuns and domestic staff who rarely spoke to her. Luckily, she had a few books which she had secreted away in her suitcase, stolen from the convent library. She closed her door and sat on her bed reading them, shoving them under the blankets if she heard anyone walking along the corridor. Turgenev was her favourite, and there were other Russians, too — and why on Earth did the church buy Kylie Tennant's *The Battlers*? Written by a known Communist! Well, Vera had relieved them of the horror of discovering it.

Her food was served in the room by a nun who remained silent, and Vera had spent the days largely in silence. This was new. She had never experienced long, quiet days. Her sister, Barbara, had been the talkative one at home, and Vera had sat in her shadow, content with her 'quiet defiance'. Barbara had always sung, belting out a rendition of *"We'll Meet Again"* at any opportunity, then taking the lead role in many school plays, starting with Mary in the Nativity, and adding later roles such as Gwendoline in *The Importance of Being Earnest*. She had given it all up when she met Harry, and Vera had been horrified, deeply shocked that Barbara would abandon her talent. She had assumed her older, vibrant sister would go on to act in plays or study drama. But then it changed. Vera remembered Barbara in her late teens, sitting on her bed doing chest exercises, repeating to herself, "I must, I must increase my bust..." Vera thought it very strange.

When she left school, Barbara was already engaged, and the wedding followed twelve months later, just as soon as Harry had the deposit for a house. The children followed quickly, much to the delight of the grandparents. By the time Barbara was barely twenty-one, she was a housewife with two small children, a house to run and a husband to cook for. That's how she described it to Vera, anyway.

There was an exchange between the two of them, the only time they had ever raised their voices with each other. Vera had been sitting on her bed in their old room. Barbara had come in to see her. It was just after Sunday roast, and Barbara had told her she was pregnant again.

"Oh, Bub!" Vera had said, in a regretful tone.

Barbara had sniffed, "you can't congratulate me?"

Vera had tried to recover, but her voice escalated as she blurted out, "but I thought you had decided to join the local repertory…"

"Well, nature got in the way. Can't you at least be happy for me?"

"No," Vera had said. "I'm disappointed for you. Your dreams are in ruins…"

"What dreams? What *ruins*? It was just an interest till I started married life. Which I knew I would."

Vera later regretted her tone with Barbara, though she never said.

At the wedding, where Barbara shrank into the arm of her new husband after having been 'given away' to him by their father, Vera had watched Barbara spoon-feed her gawky, young man a slice of wedding cake. Vera vowed she would not follow her sister's example. It was a vague aim. She started to borrow books from the library. The first book she borrowed was called *The Man Who Loved Children*, and the main character, Sam Pollitt's daughter Louie, became her hero. She would never be Evie, the girl who stayed behind.

And now, at almost the same age as Barbara that day in their room, she had her own baby and her own ruined dream. And she'd had plenty of help from the nuns to reflect on it.

Vera could only describe the birth as brutal. She wasn't sure whether she could have been given an easier time. After a day in agony on a gurney, Vera had been told she was not yet dilated and that she should hurry up before something bad happened to the baby. She asked for a glass of water and after a few hours, a grimy glass appeared, half-filled with water.

She examined the water before she drank it to make sure it didn't contain any urine or spit, even though she was in agony. She tried to distract herself from the pain, remembering that in the convent, urine and spit were part of unspoken rituals. The laundry girls didn't only wash the nun's clothes and their bed sheets and tablecloths, they also took a consignment once a week from the archbishop's residence.

Whoever was rostered that day knew it was their solemn duty to foul up the laundered clothes. In the final rinse before pegging out the archbishop's singlets and underpants, a good dose of urine was added. Sometimes, if there was enough, it was added to the final rinse of the nun's washing, as well.

Then each afternoon, it was the responsibility of one girl to clean the chapel prior to early evening prayers. This involved sweeping between the pews and dusting, as well as replacing the holy water in the font. The holy water needed to be poured from a special bottle and the girls had their own small bottle, which they kept filled with urine and dropped in the font, with the holy water poured on top. There had been so much to learn about ritual and forbearance from the church.

The spit part was easier because you didn't need to carry a bottle.

Olga had laughed when Vera had confided in her about the spit and the urine. "People do same things to meals for Politburo!" she had said. And she added, also in rural towns, to the food of important visitors from Moscow — Koba must have swallowed a lot of it over the years.

Urine and spit! Urine and spit! Vera screamed as the baby pushed again. The nuns probably thought she had gone mad. When she finally reached the final stages of her labour, Vera was wheeled on the gurney to a bare room and left alone. She was screaming, and still no one came. She could feel the baby's head as it bore down on her and waves of pain like a hammer on an anvil again and again, and finally, a man in a white coat came in and ripped the baby from between her legs and cut the cord. He handed the baby to a nun and she left the room. Vera lay in the blood and faeces for a long time before the nun returned and said your baby was distressed and not breathing properly, so we took it to the incubator. The nun threw some towels at Vera and left again.

She had wondered why she was so despised, and nothing Olga had said resonated with her until that moment. It had all been theory until then. Wasn't she a shining example of the new woman? Educated, ready for the better life the war was fought for? It was all a fiction. And even Olga could not fix that.

What had gone on at the convent was an undeclared civil war between vastly unequal forces, and Vera had done her best to help the fight. She talked to as many girls as she could about whether they could think of anyone on the outside who might be able to help them get out, help them keep their babies. Some girls did think of friends, outside of the families who had put them there. Two of them managed to get themselves removed before their babies were born.

Of those left at the convent, Vera liked to think at least they hadn't gone down without a fight. Sabotage became commonplace. If ever experience was to teach her about the shell-thin values of her class, then this was it! She became as adept at sabotage as any — dirty oil smeared on wool tunics ("Just spurted out of the machine, Sister. Nothing I could do about it"), tears in clothing caused by the new washing machines or a well-aimed vomit during morning sickness. Once late at night, Vera sneaked into the kitchen with a hammer she had found in the laundry, and firmly pounded three stacks of plates that the nuns reserved for themselves. Then when it came time to serve dinner the next day, the plates were all found, one on top of the other, with neat cracks right through the middle. She was pleased with her handiwork, having never wielded a hammer before. That act had sent a wave of admiration through the inmates.

The aftermath of the birth revealed to Vera how alone she was. First, she wasn't allowed to see the baby and was told to express milk for her and hand over a jug of it three times a day. This went on for two days, and Vera didn't mind because she felt she needed to recover. On the third day she arose from her bed, put on a flimsy gown hanging from the back of the door and went in search of her child. She found a nursery at the end of a corridor off the main one and went inside. There was only one baby in the nursery, and when Vera moved closer, she could see that the tag on the crib read Baby O'Connell. They had already given her baby away! And she hadn't signed the papers. She hadn't signed anything. It amounted to kidnapping. Just as she leaned over the crib, the baby started to squirm, so Vera picked her up and swaddled her in her little blanket. She realised the baby was very cold. The blanket was thin, and all she had on was a singlet and napkin. There were a few baby clothes back in her room, so Vera rushed back, holding the baby. As she did, a nun came towards her and shouted, "where do you think you are going with that?" and chased after her. Vera held the baby tight as the nun burst through the door behind her.

"She needs to be properly clothed," said Vera, puffing a little. "And I didn't sign anything yet, so she is still my baby."

The nun came towards her. "Enough of that nonsense," and went to snatch the baby as Vera lashed out with an elbow and hit her squarely on the nose as she bent towards her.

"Sister! Sister!" screeched the injured woman.

Two nuns came running through the door, and by now, Vera was standing on top of the bed holding the baby above her head. The women stood back.

"Now calm, everybody be calm. Vera, this baby is promised to a good family. We don't want to see anyone hurt, do we?"

Vera screeched just as loudly as the nun had done. "I will keep my end of the bargain. But this baby is not signed over. I will go back to the convent and care for it. Then I will hand it over."

One nun stepped forward. "Alright, alright. Get down, and we will talk about this calmly."

Vera eased herself down the wall at the back of the bed and stood as upright as she could. "This baby is freezing and has no warm clothing. Hand me my bag."

The nun did as she was asked.

"The baby stays with me. I can feed her, the same as the other mothers. You have nothing to worry about. I will give her a good start. You'll see."

The nuns left Vera alone for the rest of the day. She lay on the bed with the baby in her arms and tried to attach her to the breast for the first time. The baby seemed to prefer the bottle, but Vera persisted, and finally felt the small lips engage and start to suck.

She looked down at the tiny figure, at her little, purple-veined eyelids and fine blond hair. After the feed, both Vera and the baby went to sleep. Vera was woken by a nun bringing her dinner.

Vera and the baby both slept well that night, and the next morning, Vera was told she was to be moved back to the convent. Her back ached as she picked up her one suitcase, and with the baby held up with her other arm, she walked to the waiting car, holding her body as straight as she could.

Vera was placed in a different wing of the convent. Two other girls were lodged there who were nursing babies about a week old. They sat together and told their birthing stories in muffled tones. Both girls seemed quite detached from their babies, which Vera thought a fair response, because they had both signed the relinquishment papers.

Vera's baby, who did not yet have a name, was the quietest of the three, which Vera put down to her being the smallest. The baby moved very little, and Vera found herself raising her daughter's tiny arms and turning her head, just to see her move.

The next day, Vera was summoned to the office next to the chapel. She knew what was coming, that she would be asked again to sign the papers. She had another story ready about why she wouldn't sign. She felt like Scheherazade — she knew she had to put it off as long as possible to give Olga a chance to come for her.

She was surprised to find a priest in the office where the nun known as Sister Gabriel normally sat. He was one of the priests who rotated through chapel services on Sundays and then stayed to dinner with the nuns. Vera remembered him. His red hair was parted to one side and cut short at the front, with the fringe plastered on his forehead like finely pointed teeth. Unable to sleep late one night, Vera had been looking out the window of the dorm when she saw him in the glow of the streetlight, having just left the convent at two o'clock in the morning. He'd had one too many and fumbled to find his keys and open his car door, then drove off erratically.

Today he reeked of sweat, and Vera noticed yellow stains under his armpits as he leaned forward with his forearms resting on the desk. He was solidly built, and his muscled arms stretched his too-tight short sleeves.

"Please sit down."

Vera sat down, the baby in a bassinette beside her. Such a light little thing, Vera thought.

"I understand that you haven't signed the papers for the adoption yet."

"That's right. I wanted to make sure the baby was healthy. I don't want her to end up in an orphanage if she's not, well…acceptable."

"That's very noble of you, I'm sure. But now is the time."

"I don't agree," Vera said. "I need more time. She is still so sickly."

The priest stood up from the desk and leaned towards her.

"Now look, you and your kind don't get more time. The child has to go to its home, a good God-fearing couple who you aren't fit to shine the shoes of…you little vixen…" and uttering those words he stepped out from behind the desk and pushed Vera back in her chair and ran his fingers up her thighs, then onto her breasts. She could feel her nipple burst a leak as she tried to push him away. He was just too heavy. Her mind blanked momentarily, then she saw the bag with the black piano keys in the corner and lunged for it. The priest, still clinging on, moved with her as she grabbed the bag and hit him on the back of the head.

He swore, sprang back up and put his hand to his head. Vera saw blood on his hand and his shirt wet with her milk.

"Why you…"

"If you try that again, I'll scream so loud your girlfriends will come running."

Vera threw the bag of keys at his head, picked up the bassinette and left the room backwards in case he attacked her again.

She said loudly as she did so, "patience is a virtue we all must learn, Father."

Back in her room, Vera realised how vulnerable she had made herself. She received only a small meal that night, deposited outside her door with a knock and a rustling of garments as the nun hurried away.

She woke to feed her baby at around midnight, and once fed, she nestled her back into her bassinette. The baby fell asleep before she could be tucked in. Vera marvelled at how contented she could look amongst all this misery. Babies know nothing, and how Vera wished she were able to go back to the time when her parents gave her certainty and protection, just like she was trying to do now. And why had they removed that from her when she most needed it?

After dark, Vera walked carefully to the door of her room, turned the handle carefully and silently padded downstairs to the kitchen where helped herself to leftovers. The roast chicken from the nuns' meals was particularly good. She was careful not to eat too much so as not to throw suspicion on any others, but as she savoured the chicken, she suddenly thought of herself as homeless. It had not occurred to her before. She had seen the de-mobbed soldiers in uniform begging for coins around the city train stations, but it never occurred that she had common cause with them. But she was worse off, because she had a baby.

This is not the life I was born to live, she thought. I have a brain. Why will no one help me to use it?

Olga had helped her — she still didn't really understand why. Olga had ideals in spite of her relentless practicality. Vera had been an idealist herself — the future that socialism promised was just around the corner. Why not? Surely people would wake up soon and see the postwar paradise they were promised was only for a privileged few?

Through her experience, Vera had come to see that the way ahead was not so straightforward. She had been so in love with Rhys, and she had fantasied about a life where she had told him she was pregnant and he would offer to marry her, and they would work hard together for socialism. She knew he saw other women and it had bothered her at first, then she came to see, after long discussions, that they were forging a new world where romantic allegiances could shift without recrimination. And guess what? His did.

Hope is hard to extinguish in the heart, whether it involves love or politics, but it can lead us down the rabbit hole if we let it, she thought. Hope requires eternal vigilance. Vera went back to her room and wrote that down. It seemed apt to her situation.

The next day, the priest who had assaulted her said morning mass at the chapel, and when she saw it was him, Vera sat right in the front row. She had begun the fight, and this act of defiance felt different for her. When Rhys said he was moving to Sydney with Gwyneth, Vera had shrugged and wished him well. She had been all 'New World' when the values she found herself actually subject to were ancient. She understood that now, and that she had to play a game. Her subterfuge of playing along with the nuns and the priests had worked so far. Dust off those old-world values, oh do! It became a show tune in her head, and she was smiling as the same priest blustered over some biblical passage, and no one could see her face except him. Her smile — a troublemaker's grin if ever there was one. She was learning to enjoy the game.

Late that afternoon, a nun arrived at her dorm and told her to pack her things and the baby, as well. "Leave the bassinette. It doesn't belong to you," the nun ordered.

Vera stood in the foyer cradling her squirming infant, who was now overdue for a feed. There was a knock at the thick, wooden front door of the convent, and as the nun opened the door, Vera saw a tall, thin man in a beige dustcoat and hat. He stepped inside and seemed to avoid looking at her as he followed the nun into Sister Gabriel's office.

Vera's heart was thudding as she moved to the other side of the entrance hall and put the baby onto her breast. She was seated just outside the office. Vera could barely hear what was being said, but she heard the word *Communist*, and Sister Gabriel raised her voice and Vera heard her say, *with one of our good Catholic families? I'll say not*, and she realised that Olga may be behind the man's visit.

The exchange of words became heated, and shortly after, Sister Gabriel appeared, followed by the tall man, her arms crossed, her hands hidden in her habit's sleeves. Vera hastily rearranged her clothing and re-bundled the baby.

"You've packed your things. Now go. This man will take you."

"Where?" Vera asked. She tried to keep the alarm from her voice and succeeded.

The man pushed the rim of his hat back and peered down at her. "To your own kind."

Sister Gabriel moved towards her and took her hand from her sleeve and poked a finger at Vera. "Whore of Stalin! A spy in our midst! Imagine us placing a Communist baby with one of our best families. You are not even worth our prayers and you will not be receiving them, though God loves a sinner. You have placed yourself beyond our compassion."

Vera couldn't help herself. She said, "Amen to that!" and she picked up her bag and turned towards the door. The man hurried to the door to open it for her, and Vera smiled her best smile and walked through. While she had been waiting in the foyer for them to stop talking, she had helped herself to a rather nice velvet cloche she found on the foyer coat stand. After she settled the baby next to her in the taxi, she pulled it onto her head.

HIDING WITH THE JEWS

"What do you think I should call the baby?" Vera had asked Olga once they were settled in the train carriage.

Olga relaxed. Perhaps Vera now understood that she would be safe.

"Do you want Russian name? That is all I can offer. But might not be good idea."

"No," said Vera. "It will have to be something that doesn't attract attention."

"Good for you," said Olga and she patted Vera's leg. "You are learning. What names are you thinking about?"

"My mother's mother was called Beryl, though I never met her. My father's mother was called Elizabeth, though we called her Granny Lizzy. But that's the Queen's name. So, if I call her that, people will assume I'm patriotic. So that would be good, wouldn't it? But I don't like the name."

"Beryl. It is precious stone. Found in Russia. So maybe?"

"Beryl it is," Vera replied emphatically. "I think my mother would like it too. So, where are we going? It's not to your flat, and not to my parents. I suppose my mother isn't interested in seeing me? Or the baby?"

Olga shook her head. "No. Not yet. But I am taking you to my friends. I cannot call them comrades, but they are very good people. They understand you have suffered. They have room for you and the baby. Then you can decide what you want to do."

Vera was silent for the rest of the trip. They alighted from the train at Balaclava and walked up Inkerman Road. Olga was tired but kept walking with determination. She had noticed that Vera fell behind a few times, and Olga knew that it was up to her to set the pace. How many miles had she walked in her lifetime? Even when she dreaded the destination, such as a new gulag, she would walk with determination to keep up the spirits of the other women. She knew only one way to put one foot in front of the other, and that was with a straight spine.

The family that Olga had found through the lawyer, Mr Ford, were Polish. They were the Slodkowicz family from Krakow: a mother; father; and one of their children who still lived at home, a young man called Joseph.

The family had prepared a meal for their new arrivals. After the introductions, Olga excused herself to catch public transport back to her flat. It had gone against all her instincts to place Vera with the Bundists, but Olga knew better than to hide something in an obvious place, like under a mattress or underneath the floorboards. Better in a pot buried deep in the dark earth.

Vera stopped. She could see Joseph Slodkowicz pushing his wheelchair down the opposite side of the street, navigating the curbs and having to use car exits in the footpaths to find a spot where he could cross the road. She hesitated, then turned the pram around, pushed it quickly to the end of the street and crossed the road.

"Joseph," she shouted. "Where are you going?"

Vera was returning from her visit to the child health nurse where Beryl had been vaccinated. Beryl had wailed all the way down Byron Street but settled as they turned into Hotham Street, to Vera's relief. And as they rounded the corner, Vera had spotted Joseph on the opposite side.

Joseph waved when he saw her pushing the pram towards him. "Just off to another meeting. Never bloody stops."

Vera smiled. "Will you be home for dinner? I'm cooking tonight. Just so you know," she said.

"Well, it'll make a change from the cabbage rolls," he said, waving, as he started pushing his wheels and headed in the opposite direction.

Vera had offered to cook only once before, but Mrs Slodkowicz had told her "no, you are guest." Then after two months Mrs Slodkowicz asked, "do you still want to cook for us?"

Vera had kept largely to herself during those months. Olga had visited but only twice, and Vera had not made the trip to Box Hill, lest she see her mother or any of her friends.

Joseph was an enigma to Vera, as she realised, she probably was to him. She judged him to be around thirty. There was an older sister, Sarah, who was married with children and it was Sarah's former room that Vera occupied. Sarah often came to the house for Shabbat dinners with her husband and two children, Moises and Yael.

Sarah's husband was a Bundist, quite influential and seeking preselection for the Labor Party. They had met at SKIF, the Bund's youth wing. He was setting up a new council to help Jewish people get into Parliament. At least that's how he explained it to Vera.

She felt that he thought he needed to explain it in very simple terms, as if she were uneducated. She found fairly quickly that the Slodkowicz family had not been told that she was a Communist. She had not asked Olga, because she had assumed that with a left-leaning family it would not be a problem, that they would be able to debate politics long into the night. But from that first conversation with Sarah's husband, Aaron, Vera knew she needed to be cautious as there was a lot of criticism of Communists, so she held her tongue at least until she understood more.

She'd had a lot of practice. She had never told her parents or her sister or the schoolfriends she was still in contact with, that she had joined the Communist Party.

Once, she almost told Julie, her best friend from high school. She met her in the city one day after work. Julie worked as a junior secretary in a law practice. Julie had thought about going on to university but didn't qualify for a scholarship, which was the only way she could have attended. She worked hard at school and used to come to Vera's place to practice piano before her school music lessons, and they had talked about the latest books they were reading, especially *A Town Like Alice*, which had been set for their exams.

When Julie left school, she gave up piano, because her parents couldn't afford private lessons. She went to Secretarial School for three months over the summer break while Vera had idled away her time at home, and when she finished, Julie bought some twinsets, wool skirts, court shoes and a new wool coat to wear on the tram, having secured a job at the law practice. Julie had been so excited when she'd shown Vera her new clothes and accessories. But the opportunity to tell Julie about her political leanings hadn't presented itself, because as soon as Julie sat down in Myer's cafeteria, she held out her hand so that Vera could admire her engagement ring, and the direction of the conversation was set. And of course, Vera could never tell her parents. Bev and Les were lifelong United Australia Party or Liberal voters, and her father had a deep antipathy for Ben Chifley. "A train driver!" he would say. "The man might be able to drive a train, but he can't drive the country."

What would there be to say? What to gain? She had never felt particularly close to them, until she had needed them the most (and then they had not been there for her). Her mother's fussing about her own appearance and that of her daughters had always chafed. Vera knew it was partly her own fault — she tended to find fault easily. When she visited home in the holidays from university, she felt like the haughty relative who became embarrassed by her mother dusting the house in her apron. She felt like shouting at her.

As for Barbara, they had quite grown apart, and Vera wasn't ever asked to babysit as sisters would usually do. They only saw each other if they happened to be visiting their parents at the same time. Yet, once they had been very close. She felt that Barbara had become suspicious of her when she expressed interest in going to university, as if that meant she were no longer to be trusted.

Vera wanted to know the Slodkowicz's daughter, Sarah, better, but she hesitated. Would she be able to talk politics, given Sarah's husband's Labor Party connections? Children would be a safe topic, now that she had Beryl. Books? It seemed to Vera that her old self had been shattered through her experiences of the past few years, and she was grappling with the way to put it together again, like shards of a mirror: once put back together, never the same and with joins everywhere, visible scars. And then it occurred to her that if ever anyone had ever had to do this, Olga must have been that person.

She wondered about Olga's despair once her children were killed. She must have known she would be next in the relentless pursuit of the families of outcasts. In some ways, Vera had dismissed Olga in much the same way she had dismissed her mother. Vera felt as intimidated by Olga's worldliness as she had her mother's certainties. That had spurred Vera on to find knowledge — more knowledge through the books she had been reading, as if the more she knew, the more she could control her own world and not let others take charge of it. She had felt that from such an early age. If only she could know!

Now she had Beryl, she felt she understood Olga; their paths were not the same, but Vera could feel the optimism radiate from Olga when she talked about what she had achieved, and Vera become infected with the same optimism for her baby daughter. But Vera could not imagine what it must have been like to lose a child, and she did not think she could survive that, as Olga did. But she hadn't believed she could survive the convent.

The Slodkowicz's have been so kind and helped so much, but it was company close to her own age she craved. She admired Sarah, her confidence with her children and with others. And Sarah had friends, real friends who looked out for her.

Olga arrived at the house, puffing from the walk from the train. "Sarah. Hmmm. You might talk about politics, in general. Perhaps not specific, as you know, her husband is Labor man. He is so-called reformer, not revolutionary. He is businessman, not worker."

"We can't all be perfect," Vera chided testily. "I won't frighten her off with revolutionary zeal. I really have so few choices for friends."

"Will you go back to the Party? They will have no problem with you. You know that. They reprinted Kollontai. They grapple with the 'woman question'."

Vera looked thoughtful. "Well, they understand the theory. But I don't know how to go back. I've thought about it. I'm neither fish nor fowl. I'm not a carefree student who can take on Party tasks, I'm not a worker who can help with union work and I'm not a married woman with a husband in the Party who can talk to housewives about the things socialism might change for women. So, I'm not sure what use I would be.

"And I'm not sure I would be welcomed? They do tend to be a bit moralistic…"

"Ah, yes," said Olga. "Much has changed since the twenties. Such stupid morality, coming in like the black clouds of the past! Ushered in by you know who."

"Besides, I don't think I have the courage to subvert my feelings to a cause. Not anymore. I don't think I'm cut out for … ideological work."

Olga sniffed and folded her arms.

"You listen to too much *bourgeois criticism*. What ideology? We made it all up! On the run, yes! In exile! Hiding from the police in stinky rooms! Many, many discussions and arguments. Such misunderstandings of how it all was! All incorrect! Perhaps I should write about it for *The Tribune*…"

"Perhaps. I'm not sure it would be welcome. We're still working Stalin out. To move from our previous position, well, it's painful. How do we say we got it wrong? We have to work out how to do it. People don't like admitting they got it wrong."

Olga noticed Vera said *we*. "You can't add it all together in a neat bundle like kindling! That's what the newspapers do. That is propaganda. What comrades need to do is to talk together and to truly understand together. That is the only way. *Chavershaft*. That's what the Jews call it. The Jews! I know. I'm Jewish!

"Vera, you have good people here, chosen by me because I knew they would help you. *Hilfe*. Help. You have here what I wanted in Soviet Union, support for women to raise the family, to participate. They are solid people, the *Bundistn*. Even though they not Communist and support A-L-P, they have extended hand of friendship. But life is strange."

"I think I knew you were Jewish…of course, and the *Bundistn* don't know I'm a Communist..." Vera said vaguely.

Olga shrugged her shoulders. "Jewish, schmewish. I don't really mind. I am, I am not. Who are they? Are they us? Are they you, Vera? You are honorary Jew. Welcome. And you don't need to tell them everything."

Olga's eyes twinkled and she took a deep bow and added, "collaboration is deep, but you never give up all of yourself. That is impossible. You are still young. You need friends. Solidarity. With Sarah. And others."

"Don't you need friends when you are old?" Vera dug just a little.

"Yes. But they are all in your head."

Vera felt she may have brought up painful memories for Olga. They were sitting in the Slodkowicz's sitting room in the sun, and it occurred to Vera that Olga had earned her rest now and that she had been badgering her instead. But then it seemed Olga liked nothing better.

"I was propositioned by one of the priests. You know what I mean?"

Olga arched her eyebrows.

"Well, not so much propositioned, as attacked. But I got my own back, Olga. It was in the office where he'd asked me to meet him, and when he attacked me, I saw the bag of the black piano keys in the corner, and I managed to grab it and swing it at his head."

Olga's eyes lit up. "Good for you Vera. So, experience has taught you much. How to fight like a peasant."

LET US PLAY!

Olga had returned from a visit to the doctor and had just sat down with a lemon tea when her doorbell rang. It took her several moments to get up from her couch and walk to her hallway. She was annoyed by this arthritis, because it seemed to take her longer to do anything now. "I feel like old lady when my legs don't work," she had told Vera.

And when I have nothing to do, she might have added.

It was a telegram, asking her to call Greg Krachstein. She made the short journey to the telephone box.

He had decided that it was time to call the old lady Bolshevik in from the suburbs. "The coming season of the New Theatre was being planned," he told Olga.

They were putting on a new Australian play, which would open the season. "It's a realist play," he explained, "very good, set in a newspaper office. The main character is a woman," he felt he needed to reassure her. The committee, of which he was a member, wanted to follow it up with something completely different, something experimental.

Olga agreed to come to the Party office to talk.

It was Friday afternoon before Greg could see Olga, right after he finished selling *The Tribune*. Olga was waiting for him when he arrived, and he was eating a pie as he came through the office door, with his *Tribune* bag slung across his torso.

"See. I took notice. Eating," he mumbled through the pastry in his mouth.

Greg made tea and they talked about how paper sales were going and about an upcoming public meeting on the Petrov scandal.

"We have a comrade just returned from Russia with some slides of what life is now like under Khrushchev."

"Hmmph," Olga responded.

"Anyway, you said you had something to do with the Soviet Theatre? With the 'thaw' in the Soviet Union, we thought we would try a performance that might attract some more artists to our cause. Create some collaborations that might play well in the arts community."

Olga smiled. "That is good. Good tac-tics. Show that you move *ahead* of the times."

"So, you produced experimental material? Back in the old country?"

What could Olga say? "Yes. Many times. I have the knowledge. And the practice."

"Good. Then you'll help?"

"No, Comrade Krachstein. I will not help. I will *lead.*"

Confusion, anxiety and foreboding all crossed Greg's face at once.

Olga added, "don't worry, Gregor. You will not regret your decision to appoint me as the head of your dramatic division." Olga stopped. "No, perhaps it is too soon for that. No. I will accept title of Honorary Meyerhold Playwright. For now."

"Ahhh, well, perhaps we could do that. It would have to go to the New Theatre Committee."

"That will be very satisfactory. I will submit myself to the wisdom of our comrades. I will work hard. You will see."

Greg suddenly thought to himself, you are strictly an amateur. You have no idea what you've just done.

He gave Olga the details of the next meeting of the committee and told her he would introduce her. The committee knew Greg had approached her, but it would be up to Olga to convince them she had what they needed.

"Hmmph. It is possible I will be the only person in the room who saw actual Russian theatre, who knew Meyerhold and Mayakovsky and Stanislavski. And Chekhov? And his wife, Olga Knipper? Perhaps I will be only one?"

Greg smiled. He thought of the characters who would be around the table when Olga appeared. He could hardly wait.

Olga woke the Thursday of the meeting with a new vigour. That she would, at least once more, be part of THE THEATRE!

It was Olga's first love, and nothing had come along in her long life to match it. When she and Meyerhold had been deposed by Lunacharsky, Olga had fallen into a deep crevice, as if all the promises of the Revolution were felled in one blow, which of course they were not. But Lunacharsky had been a harbinger. It's all downhill after him!

Olga had realised that now that Vera was safe, she had too much time on her hands to ponder. If she weighed up the thinking time and the action of her earlier years against what she was doing now, her current efforts would rival that lazybones, Oblomov, for indolence. No, perhaps that was too harsh.

Here she was, with new energy, crawling out of Stalin's dustbin. TA-DA!

It wasn't power she missed from the old days. Being a part of something truly new, forging on without really knowing where you were going, following some kind of light in your head — that was heady, more than Paris perfume.

Just look at what we did! In those productions, the images were mined from pure imagination (who wants reality, really — it's overrated — I should know, thought Olga); costumes from the cosmos; words smashed together in sequences never seen before; edifices of words built up or torn down as you needed. Nothing was sacred. Nothing! The ire of the priests and the lawmakers and the moralisers and eventually Koba himself — they seemed to take delight in inventing new ways to exile true expression from the human experience.

And now, she had been summoned to tell what she knew about all of it. This seemed fateful, to a woman who did not believe in fate. Or perhaps they would not have chosen a daring approach if Greg had not known of her background and promoted her? He seemed to appreciate her, and Olga was grateful for that, granting her a finale, a curtain call.

This assignment (for, in Olga's lexicon, there really was no other word for it), could be the full expression of everything left that she had to give, born of grief, disruption, anger, love, jealousy, resentment and humiliation, idealism and practicality, consciousness and the unconscious. Perhaps, at last, someone would listen to what she had to say, to the sum of her experience.

The situation with Vera and the other young women had struck Olga as such an injustice. Perhaps it could form the basis of this work for the New Theatre? And yet she was not sure about Vera. Perhaps the experience, instead of hardening her political instincts, had softened them, especially as she had not experienced the worst that could have happened through losing her child. Perhaps that meant she would still have *illusions*. But then again, Vera had displayed some remarkable traits, uncharacteristic of her class.

There were other possibilities, too. The committee meeting was not until the next evening, which gave Olga time to think about the focus, the locus, the hocus pocus! She set to work.

THE DAY ARRIVED!

Luckily, the theatre was not far from the train station, and Olga reached the hall at 6.00pm, punctual as she always had been.

Greg was already there. The venue was off a main street; a moderate-sized hall with a stage at the front, and two small windowless rooms on the side. It was sparse, not like the theatres she had frequented in Moscow, which were elaborately decorated with murals and posters — and colourful graffiti after Mayakovsky was through with them.

She stood looking around and asked, "Gregor, why you not decorate? Some colorful murals perhaps. Workers' stories."

"Well, Olga," he replied, "we don't know how long we'll be here; we could be shut down, we don't own the building…"

Oh, thought Olga, that never stopped us. We were always ready with our suitcases and hiding places and paintbrushes. These pessimists! Olga thought that a very British trait.

Greg and Olga waited for the rest of the committee to arrive, which they did one by one. There was a total of six, including Greg.

While they waited, Greg asked Olga if she really had known Chekhov well? And Stanislavski? Meyerhold? Lunacharsky?

She told him how she worked alongside them as a true comrade, being a particular friend of Meyerhold and of Chekhov's wife, Olga Knipper, who liked the comedic approach to drama, and as such was well suited to her husband's plays. Olga had seen the first staging of *The Three Sisters*, with the character of Masha based on Olga Knipper.

"He is being so praised now, Mr Chekhov," Olga remarked. "And Olga Knipper — so sophisticated, but able to make you believe she was anyone on the stage. Even a prostitute. She fought her family's expectations, as many women did, to break from traditional values." Some thought her too fierce, but Olga only admired her more for that.

"Yes. They were wonderful. Towering over the theatre. Wonderful, all of them. Except for that renegade Lunacharsky."

Greg blanched at what Olga must mean, a whole chasm of implication opening between them.

Olga filled him in as quickly as she could on her thoughts about the play, introducing him to her friends Comrade Meyerhold and Mr Chekhov.

Greg smiled. "Actually, that's exactly what I had hoped," he said.

A few people arrived and moved into the side room.

"Alright. Let's go in."

The office was sparsely furnished except for a mottled, brown pottery vase filled with large, dusty, dried flowers, that were a faded red and brown. The committee sat down around the table on hard wooden chairs, and the president, who introduced himself to Olga as Bob, asked the secretary of the committee to note attendance, confirm the minutes of the last meeting and introduce the agenda.

Olga immediately felt at home, from the hard chairs to the order of business. She felt invigorated to be back in the swing, as her Box Hill friends would say. This was the real Olga, she said to herself. Being appointed the head of theatre for all of Russia was the highpoint; it let her forgive herself all her political disappointments, such as missing out on a more important position in the women's section. And perhaps she had done well to avoid that, as the women's section had run its course in ten years, as the Party vacillated — the debate on the 'special needs' of women had flip flopped constantly — at one time special needs were in, at another they were out. Marx had known that the position of women was the mark of progress. It was one of the first things Olga had learned when she encountered politics, and it had stayed with her as a guiding light...

But the theatre! The theatre endured in spite of those who quashed its full expression and critical stances. Mayakovsky had as many people at his funeral as Lenin, such was the adoration of his work. The people's poet could not be de-throned.

Her thoughts ran on, but Olga heard her name being called.

She was being introduced to the committee as an invited guest. The first agenda item was the coming season. They had agreed previously that the opening play would be *The Torrents* by one of their own members, Oriel Gray. That was in the minutes, which had been read methodically and in their entirety. Olga did not mind the wait. She was nothing if not patient.

Greg gave the report on the plan for the second play in the season. It is time to be bold, he said. We need to show the people that Communism is not simply bread queues and military parades. We need to show the spark, the creative impulse that will become unleashed, like in the twenties in the Soviet Union. *Iskra!*

"And so," he continued, "I propose that we put on a more experimental work. There are many candidates, the plays of Mayakovsky, for example. Or even Meyerhold's *Cuckoo*."

Bob interrupted. "Meyerhold was discredited, wasn't he? By Comrade Lunacharsky? Mayakovsky on the other hand, remained popular. And we are very familiar with the work of Stanislavski. His methods were introduced to us by Dr Hilda Bull, one of our best directors."

Greg was conscious of a wave of heat emanating from Olga sitting beside him. "Well, we can talk about the play selection later. What I need now is your endorsement of the idea."

A woman spoke. To look at, she reminded Olga of Beverly. Well dressed, she wore a squarish, straw hat and gloves and took them off as she sat down. She was younger than Olga and wore a diamante brooch on her overcoat. Her overcoat, Olga noticed, was of good quality tweed.

"I feel it is in the spirit of the times. Let us show the Australian public that we are the progressive ones. We shoot for the stars!"

She was dramatic, and it left Olga wondering if she had been an actress, or perhaps still was. She would certainly make a good orator.

Another woman spoke from the other end of the table. Olga noted her German accent as she emphasised certain words. "I am concerned. After everything you — we — have been through. The bans, the refur-rennn-dum, Royal Commission. Maybe not the time to take risks. We are not in good position to win supporters. Mr Menzies still in power. Mr Evatt, discredited."

The woman with the hat and gloves interrupted. "That's precisely why we should go on the offensive, culturally. The Labor Party is divided...we have a chance with their young people."

"Through the chairman," said the other woman with deliberation. "I finish what I have to say. Gwen, you very optimistic. We should stick to basics. We did so well with our production of *Reedy River*. Why not do it again?"

"Yes, through the chairman, that is true," Gwen replied, then added, "but we have always courted controversy, culturally speaking. Lilia — Mrs Monk — was not here when we staged the Odets play. Our fighting spirit won in the end. We staged it, in spite of the wallopers and the spies. And the people loved us for it. And it's important we fight for artistic freedom, because Menzies has launched an assault on artists and when that happens it's a symbol, a ploughshare beaten into a sword to smite us. They fall back on outdated laws, sedition and libel, and the middle classes go along with it. They love laws that protect their property, others they don't care a fig about because the police turn a blind eye. It's our job to expose their hypocrisy."

Olga was very impressed with Gwen. Why was she not a Party leader?

Bob spoke next. "Well, if there are no other speakers, I will put it to the vote."

There was a show of hands: four in favour, two against.

"And now that's agreed, Comrade Krachstein is going to properly introduce us to our guest."

Olga sat upright in her chair and smiled as graciously as she could.

"Thanks, Comrade Chairman. Yes, as you see we have a very special guest today. Mrs Olga Kameneva was the...let me get this right...Director of the Theatrical Division of the People's Commissariat for Education in The Soviet Union. She worked hand in hand with Comrade Meyerhold to introduce new theatrical ideas. It is true, as Bob said, Meyerhold was later executed. And indeed, as Mrs Kameneva will acknowledge, as was her husband and she herself was sent to the labour camps under Stalin. But Stalin is gone now. And we are not sitting in judgement of Meyerhold and Olga — Mrs Kameneva. We know mistakes were made. We've made enough ourselves."

Greg had prepared his words carefully.

"My proposal is that we put Mrs Kameneva in charge of selecting and directing the play. As I said, there are a few candidates for the play. Mrs Kameneva knew them all, intimately..."

"And Lunacharsky?" Bob interrupted.

Olga spoke quickly. "Anatoly was a very successful man. But he did not like chaos. Theatre is chaos, creative chaos. He was uncomfortable. He couldn't control us. After so many years of Tsar's censorship...we wanted to be free to express..."

Bob interrupted again, "Thank you Mrs Kameneva, I've heard all I need. Order in the Soviet Union has been a positive boon. Five Year Plans. Wish we had some here! But we have agreed to an 'experimental' play. I propose that Mrs Kameneva be appointed as director, but that we do so under the supervision of someone else suitable to assist. We should have someone who knows the Australian stage, as well, as producer at least."

The lady with the gloves and the hat put up her hand.

"Yes, thank you, Comrade Shoebridge. I think we can put that to the vote. You are our most experienced producer, after all."

The rest of the meeting was conducted without Olga present, and she waited for Greg in the main hall. Around half an hour later, the committee emerged.

The first person to emerge was Mrs Monk. Olga smiled at her and she stopped.

"Don't worry, Comrade Lil-ya," Olga said. "I know you worried, and I understand," she said. "I understand."

Olga could see a tear begin in Lilia's eye. Lilia nodded and left. Olga knew that she should reach out to her, but it would need to wait, she thought.

Greg emerged next.

"Gregor, all is in order?" Olga asked.

"Yes, Olga. Most definitely. We needed to also vote on a budget," Greg said. "That's always the hard part."

Olga nodded. "The artists always want more."

She tapped Greg on the arm. "And I will be no different."

Olga had waited for Greg to take her home after the meeting, but instead, Gwen Shoebridge offered to do it. Gwen lived in Camberwell, so it wasn't as far as it was for Greg, who lived in the inner city.

Gwen had talked for the duration, and for once, Olga had been quiet. She realised, as Gwen talked away, that she could learn a lot from her. The library, her neighbours, the newspapers — you could only tell so much from those. You needed as many people as possible, their experience, contradictory as it may be, in order to make your own sense. Gwen could prove to be a real informant about the things Olga was really interested in — who holds the real power here? Who are the people behind the scenes? How are the comrades changing the world? Are they advancing humanity?

Gwen was voluble on the matter of women in the Party, and Olga was all ears. It was as she suspected, the same old story: the Party could not decide whether to give women 'special treatment' because of their role as mothers or release them from that burden. It amused Olga greatly, to be re-living this through Gwen.

"Well, Olga, there are many things we need to change in the Party and the first one, in my humble opinion, is to organise free child care for women who want to attend meetings and functions out of hours. We could have a roster. I proposed one, that we put the men on the roster, Olga. And it didn't matter what office they held or how inexperienced they said they were with children. Why, I even had one man, a senior official, tell me that he'd never had anything to do with children, because he was a bachelor. I know for a fact he had a liaison with a single mother in Bentleigh! Don't lie to me, just don't lie. I made Jimmy — that's my husband, James — put his name to the motion, though he was reluctant at first since he was afraid of a backlash from the other men. I told him, be more afraid of my backlash!"

"Do you have children, Gwen?" Olga asked.

"No, Olga. I was never what the Catholics call 'blessed'. You?"

"Yes. I had children," Olga replied. "Your husband, Gwen. He is employed? You?"

"Oh, yes. I'm a nurse. I work for a doctor in Hawthorn. Taking calls, organising appointments, lending a sympathetic ear, chasing their paperwork. Jimmy, my husband — well, we're not really married. We had a 'Red Wedding'. That's what we call it. The Party Secretary 'presided', as they say, and we had a great shindig. Thirty years ago, now. I go by his name, easier that way. With the neighbours. Well, Jimmy works as an accountant — his chosen profession — for a local meat-packing business. Been there twenty years. ASIO of course have rung Mr Flatman so many times to get him to sack Jimmy. They never give up. Flatman — well, I think he was German originally — changed his name. Oscar is a fellow traveller, as they say."

"Ah, *poputchik*! We all had the other names. Lenin. Stalin. My brother, Leon, as you will know. For a time, I was known as Ludmilla. Then another name."

Olga looked out the window, at her thoughts reflected back in the glass, and Leon was there, staring back at her. He was the one who first said that it was acceptable to have fellow travellers, she remembered, and many of the artists with vague notions of politics did just that: travelled with them. Those fellow travellers died, were killed, killed themselves, exiled themselves or were exiled...

Olga heard her brother cackle: "ahh, but how much fun they had been! Mayakovsky, and the others. Malevich — well, when he was in a good mood."

Gwen was still talking. "Anyway, I'm glad you're on board. The Party needs people like you, Olga."

"Oh. I cannot be member. Here, I am fellow traveller only. Stalin killed me off, and I am still an exile. Even here."

"Oh, Olga. I know. We cried when he died. Just think! I thought my heart was broken. Then more stories started to trickle out, more than just the rumours we'd heard before. But now…the famine…you knew about it I suppose?"

"Well, that depends which one you mean. I was in charge of famine relief during the civil war…"

"Ah, no, Olga. I meant the one Stalin created. The forced collectives…"

"Yes. Of course, I knew. My own relatives died! Stalin finished what the lack of rain started. And then there was that fool, Lysenko. Making the peasants plant their crops too close together. Because he proposed that biology was a mirror of human society, where we could all live together, not competing! He had Stalin's ear…"

Olga slowed her breathing.

"Of course, you may think Stalin decreed things and his wishes were carried out, as if people had no independent thought or ability to resist! That is what the West wants you to think. But there was so much resistance: underground, and o-vert, as well. Sabotage. Many people… used any methods possible to subvert. Humour even! The millions of tiny ways people struggled is hidden, but the West ignores it — it does not suit their purposes."

Gwen slowed the car as she coasted towards a set of traffic lights. "Yes, of course. And our hearts break all over again."

"Da," Olga said, and nothing more.

A period of silence ensued. But by the time they reached Olga's flat, they had started talking about the play and the various things that needed to be organised — auditions for the actors, leaflets to hand out at meetings and on the street to attract an audience, sets to paint and construct. But first, of course, the play needed to be selected.

"Leave that to me," Olga said finally.

"Yes, of course. We can rely on you, Olga. There is someone I want to introduce you to, as well. She's an émigré artist. I think you will get on well with her, and she is full of ideas for the sets. She has painted for us before. Such colours, such swirls!"

Olga had been unable to sleep when she got home after the meeting. And why should she? She sat up listening to opera on late night radio, dreaming of Chekhov and Meyerhold and the Moscow Theatre.

PLAY MYSTERY FOR ME

Olga's memory did not rely on the written form. She had never kept a diary. Diaries were dangerous things. Perhaps her words might be preserved somewhere in the great archives of the Soviet. She had written so much in her political life — speeches, minutes of meetings and letters to various departments and divisions from the women's section or the Ministry — but she had not been able to preserve letters from her parents, from Lev, or from her sons. All of that had been lost.

Life under the Tsar had taught her secrecy and not to commit her thoughts to paper. When she first arrived in Melbourne and isolated herself (she deliberately found work in after-hours cleaning jobs so she had little contact with people), Olga had started a memoir of sorts. But it was like inflicting a wound on herself every time she took up her pen. She burnt most of the pages.

Her memories of the avant-garde were sharp, and these were the pages she kept away from the fire. She had tried to list all of the plays she remembered seeing, where and when, and all of the writers, poets and painters she had met, where and why.

The day after the meeting with the New Theatre group, Olga set to work pulling out those notes. She would need to select a suitable play — a vehicle to tell her Australian comrades what it had really been like, the avant-garde. So much to choose from!

She had been lucky in her friendship with Esther, she now realised. Esther had managed to bring literature with her from Europe. Books in Polish, Yiddish and some Russian books. After Esther's death, Pawel had gifted the Russian books to Olga. There was Tolstoi, of course, and Dostoyevski, but Olga had never cared for him. He was no revolutionary, though he had something in common with her — that most Russian of experiences: arrest due to their political beliefs and exile to the camps.

Chekhov's stories and plays were among Esther's books, and this is where she turned most often. To have them with her, not simply borrowed from the library, and in Russian. That was a true miracle; a happy accident. She had seen all of the plays, but she had not read the stories. Reading them over and over, she never tired of the characters and their enigmatic responses, their lives shaped by dogged belief and capricious fortune and...

She didn't much like Tolstoi but had a small place in her heart for the chapters in *Anna Karenina* about Levin, the countryside, the work of the peasants and the Russian voting system. She cared not one jot for the love story — the dilemmas of middle-class Anna.

Chekhov was an odd one to Olga. When she started to read his stories, she found them dull. What's all the fuss? Those same middle classes, their silly dilemmas and misunderstandings. Where was the real world? The politics? She thought the stories were not as funny or absurd as his plays where the actors had Chekhov's own directions to follow (well, they were not always followed!). The stories were similar, but very flat, unless, Olga decided, you adopted the same perspective Anton had taken to his plays. Olga found that behind the dilemmas and the silliness there was something that spoke — Chekhov whispering again in her ear, "don't be fooled, Olga Kameneva. It is not what they say that counts, but what they do. They find themselves in circumstances they don't control, so watch the sparks! Don't listen to them!" Anton said. "Pay attention with your eyes!"

His patterns, his cosmology, were revealed to her. She stopped focussing on what was said between the characters. She paid attention to who was saying it, who it was being said to, what action had occurred and who had participated and who had not. There was politics, after all! And the focus on action — so like her beloved Meyerhold.

When Olga came to approach this project, a production for the New Theatre, she had Chekhov on her shoulder. She imagined what he would have made of the Revolution, since he did not live to see it. He would have observed the chatter and the action, who knew what about whom, whether they used or did not use the information they had to further their own ends; he would see how each person fulfilled their own character, how the conditions were still not right for transcendence. Even after all the upheaval, even as those on the bottom became those on the top.

And what would Anton make of the Russian avant-garde?

Olga could hear him clapping, slowly. Then coughing that wretched cough that would be the end of him. Now, reading him again — especially *The Three Sisters* — she felt she knew the terrain that the New Theatre play must traverse: the whole Revolution in an hour. Could the play be remade in just that way?

An adaptation. That was her idea. Olga turned her mind to *The Three Sisters*. She envisaged updating his play to a setting in Russia in the twenties with the sisters as Bolshevik fellow travellers whose husbands/brother/lovers don't want them to change, or to become political or to go to Moscow… but she could then alter the ending, so that the sisters really did leave.

This seemed like the right choice. The best of Chekhov's plays to showcase her themes of women and political liberation, although she knew it would be difficult, and perhaps even a betrayal of the writer, since his themes were more humanist than political. But then Olga told herself, that humanism, in its time, had itself been a political statement in the face of tyranny.

Could it be made experimental? Revolutionary? That was the question. She would need to get to work. There was nothing Olga liked better.

Olga had rehearsed her reasons for choosing the play and went over them in her head as she made her way to the theatre venue to tell her comrade, Gregor, and the others and to talk to them about what needed to be organised. *Sisters* was perhaps seen as a traditional choice, but Olga would stage it as if the avant-garde had written it. That was her plan. With a little over three months to opening night, which Olga thought quite short, pressure would be needed on the set designers and the carpenters and the rest, and it was likely they would be shocked by some of her choices and put under pressure to deliver them. But, if your labour has a point, who does not like to work hard?

Olga had even talked to Vera about becoming involved in the play.

"You spend too long here at home. With the baby. Come, you can help me with the production. You can design the sets. You can draw."

You always need to find a way back from exile, Olga was thinking as she devised this plan for Vera. It was a way to bring her back to the campfire, from the cold edges of the forest.

Olga was walking down Flinders Street towards the theatre when she saw a woman walking towards it from the other direction. The woman had flowing grey hair and wore a red woollen scarf trimmed with brown fox tails. Her black hat obscured her face. She turned on her heels and waltzed into the doorway.

Olga followed and saw that the woman was kissing her comrade, Gregor, on both cheeks. Gwen was there. "Welcome, Comrade Kameneva," she said.

The woman kissing Greg turned around and gazed at Olga with her big grey eyes.

"And I am Valentia. Valentia Vassilenko. I am pleased to meet you Comrade Kameneva."

Valentia moved towards Olga, and the two women shook hands, though as Greg looked on, he thought it perfunctory. They all walked into the theatre.

Everyone had arranged themselves around the committee table. Greg asked Olga if she had come to a conclusion about the play.

Olga explained that she had and went on to talk about the revolutionary potential of Chekhov and how they could show the sterility of the position of women through a modern setting — an adaptation set in a living room in Box Hill, which would be surrounded by a Russian garden decorated by Soviet artwork — the Futurists, Constructivists, and so on. She had just the right roles for the sisters: one would be a housewife, one a postal worker who has to leave work because of the marriage bar and one who has escaped the bourgeois net to challenge the authority of her father and make her own way in life.

Gwen spoke first. "That doesn't sound like much fun, Olga, if you don't mind me saying…"

Olga replied quickly, "we will have revolutionary songs and circus acts, people throwing each other into the air. The point will be in the *activity*. You will see. Besides, Chekhov is always the joker, but the joke is on us, so you should find much to amuse."

Lilia said, "the circus? What has that to do with it?"

Olga explained, "these were ideas developed through the Revolution, my dear Mrs Monk. Action is thought brought to the outside where everyone can see it, that is the point of modern theatre."

Greg asked, "other thoughts? Or do we go with Olga's idea: *The Three Sisters of the Suburbs*?"

Valentia spoke. "That title reminds me of Shostakovich. His *Lady Macbeth of Mtsensk*. Did you see it before it was banned?"

Olga replied quickly. "Of course, I saw. Yes, same themes: women who want to escape bourgeois morality. The women struggle and fall into the icy river and drown…"

Gwen shifted in her seat. "Well, perhaps we should just stick to *The Three Sisters*…"

"Yes," Valentia seemed to agree. "Perhaps."

Greg chimed in, "so that's settled then. Olga will re-work the script to add all the additional elements. We will need it in approximately four weeks from today. Then we will need to work with the set designers to, you know, make the vision a reality. That's where Valentia — Comrade Vassilenko — will come in."

Olga said nothing. She had wanted Vera to design the sets. Olga knew she would need to work closely with the set designer, and she was worried that she knew nothing about this woman, Valentia.

The conversation moved on to the budget. There were still profits at their disposal from Dick Diamond's *Reedy River*, the theatre's most successful production, but they did not want to squander those all at once. So, a small allocation was proposed, and an estimate made for box office sales and set design.

Olga steamed in her seat. Were her services worth nothing? She had assumed she might be offered a small amount in recognition of the work she must do. But to be offered nothing? It was an insult. Yes, it would be an adaptation, but artists' work is still work and should be recognised. Had she not fought for that? She imagined herself continuing to sit there without saying another word. That made her even more angry.

"Excuse me, Comrade Krachstein. Perhaps you have forgotten something?"

"Ahh, perhaps you could remind me…"

"Well, you have assumed the work of the artist comes free. It is work, is it not?"

"Ahh…yes. Well, what did you have in mind?"

"I would like some ack-now-ledge-ment that the writer should be recognised as worker. We, too, toil, not only the carpenters!"

"Well, Olga, the carpenters are volunteers. Apart from the head fellow. We have to pay him, don't we Gwen?"

Gwen nodded.

"My request is simply a small sum to recognise my contribution. And I be given a title. Honorary Meyerhold Playwright to the New Theatre. That will suffice."

Greg had forgotten to put this on the agenda. "Ahhh…I suggest we vote on the amended budget, and we probably don't have time to discuss titles or other recompense now? We could note it in the minutes."

Olga bristled a little, but not so that anyone else would notice.

"Titles are important," Olga continued calmly. "For linking past and present — *hu-man end-eavour* — to honour the memory of those great, *formid-able* people who came before you. Real people, title should not be province of silly aristocratic imbeciles!"

The business of the committee was hastily concluded. Gregor, Olga noticed, looked suitably shame-faced by his error. The committee members took their leave of each other outside the theatre. Olga saw Valentia swing her head briefly towards her as she walked away. Olga felt a quick movement behind her back. Perhaps it was Leon, come to warn her.

At home, Olga hesitated. It was not time for dinner, so she busied herself. She had energy, and she re-stacked some of the book piles that had subsided in the hallway. She even decided to take some books back to the secondhand shops. They would give her a little money for them. Now, she had decided to focus exclusively on the Russians and perhaps some Australian novels. She wanted a clean-out.

Olga was putting off what was inevitable: thinking about Valentia Vassilenko. Her first name was not strictly a diminutive. Olga was sure her name would once have been Valentina, daughter of Valentin. But who was she? Olga was worried that she should have known more about her before Gregor committed them to work together. Valentia, if that was her name, was a surprise entry in this particular scene; the unexpected visitor from Moscow.

Olga began to review Anton's play as she ate her carrots, potatoes and green sauce. She could not always afford meat, and neither did she always want it either. She was proud of how she stretched her small funds, the envy of any Soviet citizen!

She scratched out her own version of the play. She had moved away from the Box Hill setting and thought of locating it in the Australian countryside. She sketched her ideas until late into the evening before she abandoned that as well. She did not know enough, in spite of her attentive listening to 'Blue Hills'. She risked embarrassment, for writing about what she did not know. It would be like an Australian trying to capture the see-saws of Olga's own life or the twists and turns of the Revolution itself. Impossible!

SHAKING THE TREE TO SEE WHAT TUMBLES OUT

Olga was watching the magpies again. She had set herself up on the dining table so she could see them through the window. She was a lady writer. She could be Kollontai, writing *Red Love*. Everyone read that novel when it came out. Could Olga repeat the feats of Kollontai?

Olga sat there for two days and nights. She slept, and she prepared food, but otherwise she perched in front of a growing pile of sheets of paper and crumpled paper balls. She had nothing to show for all her efforts. She had tried many scenarios, even trying to model the sisters on well-known Australian politicians, who could be easily pilloried. She admitted to herself that the reason she had burned her own memoirs was because they were largely unreadable, a slow-paced litany of facts. And then, and then…

The morning after these writing sessions, Olga had retreated to the company of the magpies. Black and white, clearly defined. Olga longed for some certainty, like the starkly-delineated magpies, like Uncle Gregory's phrase in her brother's book, "they are drivers carrying wheat."

The magpies scratched in the dust beneath the tree. This tree, so different from those back home: the white trunk, the sombre, drooping leaves. A tree that did not shed in winter. Something enduring, which is what she wished for her play.

Vera had been summoned by Olga. She knocked on the door, noticing that there was an extra plank of wood now nailed across it.

When Olga answered her knock, Vera could see that she peered through the curtains first, then she ushered Vera quickly inside.

"Ah!" said Olga. "No Beryl?"

"Sorry, Olga, she stayed over with Sarah and her kiddies."

"So, you good friends?"

"Yes, we are. She is generous with me and with Beryl. And Beryl really loves Joseph. There is such a warmth between them."

Olga made the tea Vera liked, and they sat on the sofas opposite each other. They always did this. Olga had said, this is the way to have a real dialogue, to sit so that you see the full person and to participate in the debate that follows.

"Is there always a debate?" Vera had asked, a little wearily.

"Of course! We are human beings, aren't we?"

Today, Olga looked dishevelled; not her usual self at all. Her manner of speech was quite halting. Her hair had not been combed since she woke up, with a small bird's nest starting at the side of her head. Her face looked a little bloated and her wide brown eyes dimmed.

"Vera, you must help me now."

Vera was alarmed by the plea. "Of course, Olga. Yes, of course." She tried to sound reassuring.

"I cannot do this task alone, the writing of the play. I try. I fail. I asked you to help with the set design..."

"I said I would think about it..." Vera said, interrupted by a look from Olga. A strange, anxious look.

"The play... I am not writer. Not natural. There is no...poetry. I cannot rhyme to save my own soul! You must help me."

"Olga, I can't. I have too much to do now. The sets...I can design those at home. But to work on the script with you, I would have to come here every day."

Olga looked downcast. "*Hilfe*. That's all I ask."

A lump had formed in Vera's throat.

"Is there no one else? No one? I don't know the first thing about writing a play..."

"We just follow the master. We follow Anton and we up-date."

"But you told me on the phone they want something experimental."

"Yes. Da. I agreed, enthusiastically."

"What about the committee? Could you go back to them and ask for help?"

Olga shook her head. In her mind, she imagined Valentia on the other side of the table, smirking at her misfortune. That was something she could not countenance.

"Gwen? You like her. She sounds sensible. Surely, she would find someone?"

"Vera, I have so little time."

"All the more reason to go back to the committee."

Olga shook her head again. Vera got up from the sofa and walked over the Olga. She began to rub Olga's back. Olga started to cry and put her hand on Vera's.

"Olga, I know," Vera started, "that this is just your latest obstacle."

She sat down next to Olga and took her hand, rubbing the spiny, arthritic fingers.

"I know that what I've been through is very little compared to others. All I had was a bit of certainty taken from me. A particular family — a mother, father, sister, my niece and nephew. But I've lost my friends as well, my political organisation, my studies. In my loss, I have become a microcosm of you, Olga!

"I needed help, and it came from the most unexpected quarter. And if I could help, I would," Vera hesitated. "But I can't help with a task I'm completely unsuited for, Olga. We have to have another plan."

OLGA AND VALENTIA

The two women sat in a crowded cafeteria on Lygon Street owned by Sal, an Italian migrant known to Valentia Vassilenko. They chatted in Italian and he seated the two women at a table under the window.

Olga had asked Gwen to organise the meeting with Valentia Vassilenko, after resisting such a meeting with her very being (egged on by Maria), but it had been her brother who had finally convinced her, late at night, as she floated between sleep and waking.

"This is big project, Olga, even I recognise that. And you say it is beyond you. So, you give up? Or you find another way? You say Vera is not up to the task, you were clutching at straw. You need to find someone else to help. The Party could send another playwright, but not someone who knows the Russian avant-garde! Find out who she is, this Valentia. Is she White Russian? Is she spy? Is she old Menshevik? Apparatchik…"

Olga stirred.

"Dissident!" Olga felt Leon hiss in her ear, and she had woken with a start.

Here in the restaurant, Olga felt intimidated as Valentia talked with ease to the owner and his staff. And Italian was a language Olga had never mastered, so she sat there like a big lump of salo, waiting.

"So, should I call you Olga?" said Valentia as she lit a cigarette.

"Da. Olga. It is my name."

"Oh, I wondered, because of your high offices, whether you would prefer Comrade Kameneva."

Olga's thighs tightened. "No. I am just old lady."

Olga had no idea whether they were comrades or not. She jumped straight in with her questions. Her life-long hesitancies, the weighing up of alternatives, seemed to have left her.

"And you, Valentia? Were you comrade?"

"Ah. I knew you would ask. I was painter. I am…painter. I was minor figure in painting and involved in set design work. I took over from Chagall for some months when he left the Vitebsk Art School. I knew him and he asked me. I was a friend of his wife. Bella."

Olga nodded. "So, you knew Malevich and El Lissitsky? They were there, too, yes?"

"Oh, yes. But to answer the question, Olga, which I am sure you are wanting to ask, I had many friends who were comrades. I did join the Party, briefly. I moved cities soon after, and my records were lost. And it didn't suit me to rejoin."

Olga's mouth made an involuntary movement as if she had tasted something bitter. "So, you want to do the set design? You have done this for them before?"

"Oh, yes. They know me here. I designed the set, and I painted it for the last show. It was realist set, however…"

"Olga, I know your history. Greg told me. I know that from your point of view, I am not the ideal collaborator. But I had to walk a fine line in Soviet, just the same as you. I tried to stay true to my own ideals, which did not always bring me into favour. And I gave up on some. As we all did."

"Your family, Valentia?"

Valentia put her coffee cup back on the table and looked squarely at Olga.

"I knew you would ask that, too! And you, a Bolshevik! This is what still shocks me. We were all — me, you, all com-rades — supposed to be abolishing *class*…"

Valentia was vehement. "We could never escape our origins. Unless you were pure peasant! And no one was! And those with wealthy families who hid their origins to get ahead. You tolerated hypocrisy…"

Valentia stopped for a moment.

"My family were university professors — my uncle and my father — and there was land somewhere, as well. And yes, some aristocratic ancestry. But not White Russian, I can assure you of that. I should have been allowed to transcend my class. I was willing. But the comrades were not.

"You are silent, Olga Kameneva."

"You know about my sons?"

Valentia nodded. "I know the whole story. You survived, and so did I."

Valentia and Olga ate the small Italian biscuits served with the coffee.

"You know, we could be in a café in Vienna, Olga. Did you go there?"

"Yes, I did. I knew many artists, of course. In my time in the theatre and before."

"Oh, yes, I'm sure we knew many of the same people."

"But we never met, I think?" Olga's memories of her childhood and the first two decades of the century were sharp. It was the later decades she had trouble with, so she felt she would remember Valentia. But she did not.

"Did you know Alga? And Vladimir Kossich from the People's Art School?"

"Yes. Alga I saw in London once I moved there. I saw her in a department store! But Vladimir, he was executed. Not long after Kancharov disappeared."

"I know about Vladimir. You moved to London? From Soviet? What year?" Olga stopped herself. She was anxious to know, but she had begun to sound like an interrogator.

"Well, let me see. Was it 1940? Or '41? I had enough by '38 or '39, I know. I remember your husband's trial and the others. Many of us started to think about emigration or escape. I had finished with — what would you call them? Dalliances. Ah! Vassily — he broke my heart. But he was married and would never leave his wife. Willy came to Moscow from London on a cultural visit from one of the English museums. I was swept away. I did not think it would happen. As well, he was quite an old man. Almost sixty-five! Wilfred, he was called. So cultured, so…well, I don't mind saying…well mannered. Bourgeois, yes? But I suppose you can't escape all of your upbringing.

"And you, Olga. You stayed in the Party, after what happened to Lev and your brother?"

"I did. Leaving would have made no difference, except maybe I would have been hounded sooner than I was. And leaving would vindicate Stalin, and that I would not allow. We still thought the Revolution would defeat him. I *should* have died. They certainly tried to kill me. Heaven knows I wanted to be free of this world, after my sons were murdered. But I suppose some people had to survive so that Stalin would have mockers as well as mourners when he died."

"As you know, Olga, there were many who rubbed their hands at Lev's fate. Those who had lost so much because of Stalin, the families of the exiles, the émigrés I knew in London."

Olga was silent. She was prepared for recriminations, as if she hadn't also given everything, throwing her whole existence — her whole family — into the vortex. We tried to change the world, not only to make paintings…

Olga sighed loudly and wiped her mouth with a serviette. "We are all critics who are not actually writing the plays, Valentia."

Valentia smiled nicely. "And by the way, I would be happy to help with the script as well as set design, Olga."

Valentia could see that Olga's mouth was now set in a straight line as Olga moved to change the subject.

"And how did you yourself get to leave? How did you get the permission?"

"Well, I didn't. It was clandestine, you know. Willy and I fell in love. He went back to England and when the war broke out, he came back for me. We made the trip to Helsinki, bribing people along the way and finally some border guards. Money is good for some things! We went to London from there. I might as well tell you: he was an aristocrat. A baronet, they are called, and I, a Lady. The English are silly. They still have not abolished these hereditary titles! I tried to get Willy to surrender his, but his son would not agree, and so Willy would not do it."

Silly Willy, Olga thought, but she said, "we do what we can." She could feel her brother digging at her ribs. ("Very good, Olga. No need to make an enemy if you don't need to.")

You can talk! Olga pulled her mind away from admonishing her brother and re-focussed on Valentia who had continued her chatter.

"He had an eye for art. He left me some money and good paintings, which I sold. There was enough for me to get away — far away — to move here and to buy a house."

Olga asked Valentia, "tell me which plays did you see?"

Valentia sat back in her chair.

"Sooo many. Just before the February Revolution, the Arts Theatre to see *The Government Inspector*. What a laugh that one was! We Russians have a long tradition of bureaucratic idiocy to draw on! That opening night…it really was something…"

"Me: second night," Olga replied firmly.

"Oh, it seems odd that we didn't run into each other somewhere," said Valentia.

"Perhaps we did," Olga replied. "Go on."

"*Victory Over the Sun*? Who could forget? Of course, I had to attend, with Malevich having designed the sets. I am very influenced by him in my own design, of course. That language they used…"

"The *zaum* — made up language. Why not, eh? But so many disagreements, I recall…"

"And did you know Mayakovsky? And you knew Meyerhold…"

Olga nodded.

Valentia continued excitedly, as if she were just remembering events she had not recalled for many years.

"I remember a night at the Stray Dog, Mayakovsky was there. I didn't know him myself, but such an aura! Oh, you must tell me more about him. When was that? 1915? I got up on the bar and sang in my petticoat before someone dragged me off. I'd drunk a lot of vodka that night. But you, Olga, you must have seen so many of the plays. It was your job after all."

"Yes, I saw perhaps all of the most important of Soviet theatre. Until I was removed from office. Then not as many."

"But I do remember that it was a *heady* time. The biomechanics. I'm sure you would have overseen *Mystery Bouffe*?"

Olga raised her eyebrows. "Oh, yes. So incredible. Perhaps our greatest success — though you would never think so at the time. Some things need time to find their level."

Valentia leaned forward. "Olga, do we find our level? Is it possible?"

Olga did not answer the question directly. She still had her points to make. "When we were younger, both at the start of something, Valentia, we had imagined lives. Me, the head of the theatre and you, the head of a painting school. We perhaps seemed destined to change the world of art at the very least! But here we find ourselves."

Then she added, "perhaps not yet level. Perhaps still a little uneven."

Olga gestured to her surroundings. She was quiet again. She looked into her cup to see if there was any coffee left. Then she continued, still with points to make, "we thought we were breaking up the old machines and building new ones from all the parts. But the machines re-assembled themselves and came after us."

"I can see you are a serious thinker, Olga. But with this play, you and I, we just poke a hole in the canvas of history and draw a moustache on it," said Valentia, laughing.

Olga was not ready to respond to that but asked, "and what of Natalia Kroporondova? She was so promising! Those sets of hers…"

"Oh, don't flatter. She was adequate, I would say. She managed to get away. She took up with a man twenty years younger. Like Kollontai did. She flaunted him, yes, she did! He was an artist, struggling till she came along. Then she introduced him, you know, to the circle. They moved to Paris. Then they left for Beijing…the Nazis, I suppose."

Their conversation thereafter avoided any more discussions of art (which were painful and joyful at the same time), the Russian avant-garde and who had made the biggest contribution in terms of technical or aesthetic innovation. They both knew they would never have agreed on that. Instead, Valentia told Olga what she knew of the fates of the people she knew. And perhaps Olga knew them, too? Who had been killed and how difficult it was for most people to get away. Few wanted to take the artists or the Old Bolsheviks unless there had been money or prestige involved. Valentia herself had saved quite a few, with Willy's help, she said. Olga was impressed.

"So, how is the play coming along?"

Olga waved her hand. "Oh, yes, very well. You know Chekhov. There is so much to work with."

"What about you and I, Olga? Is it alright that we work together on the play? I on the sets?"

Olga waved her hands and replied, "Oh, of course! I will be honoured!"

Valentia held her thoughts. The time would come when they would need to talk more truthfully.

"Olga! So good to see you! How is the script coming along?"

"Coming," Olga said curtly.

Vera held Olga firmly by the arm.

"Thanks for seeing us, Gwen. We thought it might be good, at this point, to chat about it?"

Gwen led the two women into the committee room, and they sat around the table.

"I'm Vera Watson. Olga has asked me to help with the set design…"

Gwen looked askance but said nothing.

"But…" Vera continued, "well, we're here to talk about the play. It's not going as well as Olga hoped."

"Oh," said Gwen. "Anything we can do to help?"

"Well," said Vera, "we were hoping there might be someone who could help with the writing. Olga has ideas, but she says she's not a playwright."

"Dear, dear. Well, I'm sure there must be someone. Oriel? No, I don't think she would do it. Greg has a great way with the actors, and with *Tribune* articles, but I've never seen anything creative from him."

Gwen stopped. "What about Comrade Vassilenko? Wouldn't she be ideal?"

Olga stood up abruptly. "Come, Vera. We must go."

Olga picked up her handbag and exited quickly. Vera followed her outside, through the theatre and onto the footpath.

"Olga. Olga. Don't walk away from me."

Olga stopped and turned.

"You told me about her, Olga. You told her she would be working on the sets, but you know I can do that. It seems there isn't anyone else to help with the writing of the play. You have to face that."

Olga turned on her solid heels and walked away again. Vera ran after her and tugged at her arm.

"Leave me, Vera. Leave me."

"No. I won't. I won't, Olga."

Olga sighed and moved to sit on a bench nearby. Vera sat next to her.

"I don't know what your objection is to Valentia, your mistrust, Olga. But I know that there are people relying on you to produce a script. Gwen isn't the first one to suggest Valentia. She's been suggested by your own mind, Olga. And that's because she's probably the only person who can help you do what you are being relied on to do."

Olga sniffed the fume-smoked air and wrinkled her nose.

"What is between Valentia and I? Perhaps all of Russian history, that's all."

"You're being melodramatic, Olga."

"I don't really know her, Vera."

"And yet," Vera replied quickly, "here you both are. And she has what you need."

Olga looked at Vera and her shoulders dropped.

"The strange bedfellows."

"I'm surprised you would let that stop you, Olga."

THE WORK OF PLAY

Vera brought the two women together again at the little café in Lygon Street. Vera ordered *küchen und kaffe* as confidently as any European. Her time with the Slodkowicz's was having a good impact, Olga thought.

Vera had telephoned Valentia, and while she didn't tell Olga the details of their conversation, she told Olga that by the end, Valentia had agreed to be the co-author of the play, but that Olga would keep her title as Honorary Meyerhold Playwright. That, Vera knew, Olga would share with no one.

Valentia had suggested to Vera that whilst they would infuse the play with the spirit of Chekhov and *The Three Sisters*, they could use a very different play for their framework, and that was Mayakovsky's *Mystery Bouffe*.

"You know it?" Vera had asked Olga.

"Know it! I was head of theatre when it made its debut!"

"Well, that's good, because from what Valentia told me, you will need to remember a fair bit of it. I understand it wasn't written down."

"Not quite true. But we can talk about that."

Olga had forgotten a lot of the play (but not the controversy), though she knew the basic plot. And, she reflected, better it than *Victory Over the Sun* — oy vey, what a disaster that was in Olga's mind. Though she had to admit the sets were at the very pinnacle of artistic expression.

"So, Olga, you think the *Mystery Bouffe* will work for us?" Valentia asked.

"Da."

Vera was worried that Olga had been quiet during the first few minutes of being seated, ordering and now, in conversation. Valentia had taken up the slack, perhaps a little nervously Vera thought.

"Oh, what a scandal was *Mystery Bouffe*! Someone writes a play and says 'here, anyone else want a turn? Change anything you like, I don't mind.' And then the second time, he had already changed it himself. I saw it then. And you, too, Olga?"

"Yes, I saw both. It is big task. We have our memories, basic outline. But we will have to make it all up again."

Valentia clasped her hands together. "Yes, we will!"

Valentia outlined what she recalled of the play. "You know the strangest thing was, and I do remember this very distinctly, there was a character called 'The Australian.' Yes! In the play, he had escaped the flood from the other side of the world. And here we are."

The two women traded recollections of the play, back and forth, back and forth. They recalled for Vera that it had consisted of characters arranged in two groups: the Clean and the Unclean. The Unclean were the workers, and the Clean the rich and powerful. There was a flood, and the only habitable place left was the Arctic. That was a real Mayakovsky joke.

"Ah, if it wasn't for our friend Lunacharsky, we would have a film of it."

"Oh?" said Olga, "I didn't know. And it was he who all but stopped the first production, you know."

Olga felt like a schoolgirl in a running race, striving to get ahead of her nearest rival. Valentia knew some things about events she, Olga, had been intimately involved in. She was not used to this. She had usually known more than anyone; often things you wished you didn't, such as who was on the list. (She had known that the NKVD would come for her, she just didn't know when. And of course, her suitcase had been ready.)

"But that doesn't matter, actually. Because we have to make it all up again as our Maya would have wanted. And who in Australia would see the Arctic joke? That, after Siberia, it could be a warm worker's paradise!"

Olga said nothing. What would Valentia know of Siberia? "That's what they think they already live in, the paradise. My neighbours do."

"So, we still start with Chekhov's sisters? And what about the Clean and the Unclean? Do you want to keep those categories, Valentia?"

"Yes. I have always liked those sisters. I know that Mayakovsky thought our Anton quite dull, with all his talk of uncles and aunts, but I think he misunderstood."

Olga seemed deep in thought for a few moments. Then she said, "but what is the struggle? *The essential struggle?*"

"Well, yes. That is important. Perhaps we could start with the sets? What would we like to see, visually? Then we could work on the ideas that inform them."

This seemed like a ridiculous proposition to Olga, but nevertheless, she went along with it. There was something that made her do this, but she couldn't quite put her finger on it. It felt like a kind of guilt.

Valentia continued, "well, whether we call our characters Clean or Unclean, there will have to be a struggle, and those on the side of the poor and the workers will win. It's a what do you call it — a pantomime! We will have fun on the way!"

Vera drew several quick drawings in pencil on the serviettes. She had seen a lot of photographs of Soviet art and posters brought back by her comrades. The first drawing was of a factory, with infernal machines that could be broken up at the end of the play. The factory owners versus the workers.

"Could be something like Vsevolod's biomechanics brought to life once again," said Olga approvingly.

"Yes," Valentia agreed. "And you, Vera, you can do the set design? If I am doing the play with Olga?"

Vera replied, enthusiastic. "Oh, yes. I have thought about it. Can I also talk to you about that as we go along, Valentia?"

Vera could feel Olga's eyes on her. "We'll figure something out."

Vera felt her stomach drop. The drawings could easily be done while her adopted family was away during the day. But how would she explain any of this to the Slodkowicz's, once the play was in production? That she had become involved in Communist theatre?

"*Mystery Bouffe* was chaotic after all," Valentia continued. "This needs to be similar. With music and singing. Russian songs? Bring on the circus!

"Yes, and Jazz and folk songs. Above all it is to entertain, so must be comic, farcical, light. Shall we have nudity? *A Slap in the Face of Public Taste*, like Mayakovsky's manifesto?"

"A slap in deadly earnest," Olga reminded Valentia.

While they talked, Vera busied herself with the second drawing. This one was of a set that resembled a garden with all kinds of bizarre constructions overlooking it. Vera quickly sketched in characters and Olga's brow furrowed. Then she nodded her head.

"This one is much better."

VERA BEGINS AGAIN

Beryl was turning out to be a delight. Vera was past wishing that her mother could see her daughter. Past wishing for the support of her sister. It was in this spirit that finally, resolving to take advantage of the new, Vera started to embrace life with the Slodkowicz's. Vera felt she had never known such kindness. She received hand-me-down clothes, toys and gifts from Sarah and family friends, so many wanting to look after Beryl. The family were quite proud that they had rescued Vera from the clutches of the Catholic Church, telling Vera in great detail how the church had tried to collaborate with the Nazis and had failed to denounce them.

Vera had worked a little for Mr Ford, the lawyer. The first time Vera had left her daughter since the birth was a wrench, letting her out of sight, especially with the thought of the child-snatchers in the back of her mind. Beryl was now the thing that held her steady, which was so surprising to Vera. At the same time, she craved time alone. It was a thread leading back to her old life. She still needed it, and she carefully kept one imagined end in her pocket, where she could reach in and wrap her fingers around it.

Her confidence had grown anew in breaching the space between Olga and Valentia Vassilenko. Vera needed to continually reassure Olga that they had made the right decision. Through Olga's reports on the phone of the writing process, Vera had listened and simply agreed with Olga's criticisms, even though she really knew nothing of the play or how it should go. She had agreed to design the sets, and that meant meetings with the carpenters and construction crew, who mainly consisted of building union workers. She had to work out how to incorporate this element into her new life, a part of the old life she was dragging along with her.

She had been drawn more into the life of the Slodkowicz's, which she was prepared for — dive right in! Olga would say that.

Vera had come to know Joseph better. He had started looking after Beryl, as well as having Sarah mind her. Sarah told Vera that there was no one she trusted more. He was incredibly diligent, even chasing the toddlers in his wheelchair when they ran where they shouldn't. Vera had already spent quite a lot of time with Joseph. Not only had they been in the Slodkowicz home together, Vera had also driven

Joseph to his medical appointments at the nearby rehabilitation centre in Caulfield. Joseph's legs were quite withered because of the polio that had struck him down, but he considered himself quite fortunate. "It didn't kill me," he said, "or put me in an iron lung."

Vera was careful not to show all of her political knowledge when talking politics with Joseph. She stuck to current affairs, Australian party politics. Joseph was quite convinced of his own conclusions, so Vera did not see a lot of point in confronting him or arguing too vigorously. Keep your cards close for a while. Olga taught her well.

She had shared enough to demonstrate she was no fan of the Labor Party, and that she held the conservative parties in contempt. Joseph had almost clapped his hands when she told him what she thought of Mr Menzies and his pathetic attempts to ban free speech and stifle dissent, conservative policies like the marriage bar and...well, she probably went on for a long time.

"He did end butter rationing, for which I'm eternally grateful," Joseph joked.

They had spent a lot of time in each other's company. There was a compatibility, an understanding that surprised Vera, since they seemed to her to be from such different backgrounds. Beryl was happy to be lifted into his lap and stay there, Joseph making faces and strange noises to delight her.

When Olga next came to visit, Vera had something she wanted to tell her. She had made some decisions about her life, and she wanted Olga to know.

Vera found that she could not get a word in for quite a while. As usual, Olga had asked to nurse Beryl, and Vera obliged. Beryl was at the age where she had started to be interested in faces other than her mother's. And she was particularly fond of glasses and with ruthless repetition, reached up her little hands to Olga's as Olga gently defended them.

Olga talked volubly about her 'collaboration' with Valentia Vassilenko and the tug of war over the direction of the play.

She stopped. "And Beryl? Is she well?"

Vera smiled. "She is so well. Putting on weight, finally."

Olga snuggled into the baby's face and took a good long sniff of her skin. "She is so delicate. Like little sparrow."

"She doesn't take after me, that's for sure."

"Yes," Olga agreed. "You have put on some weight after the convent?"

"Mrs Slodkowicz's cooking. Dumplings! I love them!"

The two women sat together for a few moments, playing with the baby. Then Vera said, "I have some news for you, too, Olga."

"Not same news as last time you had news!" Olga quickly joked.

"No. What I want to tell you is…Joseph and I are getting married."

Olga responded quickly, "I trouble you for more tea?"

Olga followed Vera into the kitchen where she re-boiled water and added it to the pot. Beryl was safely perched on Olga's hip.

"You have fallen in love with Labor man?"

Vera stirred the tea in the cups for a few seconds longer than needed.

"It's more a practical matter. Joseph has found a little work with the Jewish welfare, and he wants a house of his own near there so he can wheel to work. I can work for Mr Ford two days. He will look after Beryl when I'm working."

"So why marry? You want more children?"

"No. One is enough. And Joseph, well, he isn't capable of having them, Olga."

Olga nodded knowingly. "Ah, the polio."

"Well, I could let you think that. And his parents will think that. But I will tell you the truth. Something his parents don't know."

They took their tea back into the living room.

"Joseph, well, he is a very kind man. He is very good with Beryl. He really loves her. We have different political views, but we will work that out. What we talk about and what we don't…"

"What you don't?" Olga was aghast. "You should not be silenced by this…relationship, Vera."

"No. Of course not. All I'm talking about is a little compromise, Olga. Really, you do act the purist sometimes."

Vera had stopped short of snapping. Olga was secretly pleased at Vera's response.

"Anyway, I will tell you that Joseph…well, he won't be fathering a child, though he tells me he is capable of it...physically…he doesn't want women in that way. So, I'm very safe in that regard."

Olga was silent for a moment. She put Beryl down on her back and put her hand gently on the baby's stomach.

"Coo coo coo," she said. "So, you and Joseph. What will happen if you fall in love really? With other people?"

"Olga, it's a practical arrangement, don't you see? Joseph continues to be admired by his community. He will even stand for pre-selection one day. So, there will be no issue. He will be a happily married man. Beryl will have a father. His parents will be relieved.

"And, for both of us, we will look the other way, I suppose. I don't know how it will go. I might even have an affair with a married man! Then again, so might Joseph…"

Olga giggled. "You are not the same Vera I met in your mother's house, my dear one. You have learned. But I am most unhappy about the need for hypocrisy."

Vera grimaced. "You aren't telling me that there was no hypocrisy in Russia? Didn't your experiences tell you it never goes away?"

Olga could not let this go. "Hrrmmph. Tearing down the organs of hypocrisy was what we fought for, and we succeeded! Church, aristocracy, judges who flouted their own laws. Business owners who *pretended* to care about their workers, the Petersburg socialites who put on stupid balls for the orphans and drank themselves rotten so they could hand over a little cash. We broke it all up!"

"I wish you could see my point of view, Olga. I feel like there are a lot of things I could do now that I never would have done. I have you and the Slodkowicz's to thank. But Joseph is, well, thwarted…in a way I don't agree with, and I've agreed to help him. He will do good, Olga. You'll see. He will help people. But he needs to hide behind me to do it."

Vera could see Olga's cheeks puff and turn red.

"Vera, you astound me. Astound! You should be on side of revolution! Not…crumbs from the table. People cannot live on crumbs!"

Vera snapped now. "And I suppose that's what you're going to do with your production? Make a revolution?"

"Vera, I hardly need to tell you about role of 'Art' in consciousness. Perhaps you have not read my brother's book on the subject? No, we will not make revolution. We will entertain masses with proper workers' theatre. Somewhere they can see the mirror of themselves, of society. That is Meyerhold way. That is my way."

Vera dropped her shoulders. "Let's not argue. My mind is made up. And we've told Joseph's parents. I am sending my mother an invitation, as well."

Olga shifted in her seat.

"Well, perhaps your mother will be pleased. But be careful. Hypocrisy is, how you say, the slippery slide?

"I didn't fight the Tsar of all Russia for nothing! If only I had someone there to send back a little bit of money, if I had contact with my old comrades, I would feel connected to the Revolution still. What people, ordinary people, could do once they were freed from old ways…it was extraordinary. Banish hypocrisy, because everything is laid bare."

Vera breathed deeply before she spoke. She couldn't help herself, and she replied, "but you used their hypocrisy to your own ends when you were fighting the Tsar? Isn't that the beauty of it, that it, too, can be thrown back in their faces? I was able to hide at the convent by pretending to be pious and accepting of my fate. Isn't hypocrisy a weapon, too? You can twist and turn it. *They* must stay silent in case the hypocrisy would be revealed. That's what I learned at the convent. And it was a good lesson."

"Be careful. It will twist you, *your essential nature*, in ways you cannot know. That is why we wanted to change the world."

"Yes," Vera responded. But she could not let it go.

"Joseph has a backbone, but no support for his…essential nature. You must know that. I have analysed the situation. There is no broad support in society, no 'movement'. He would be crushed, as a person…and shunned in his community…"

"Have you learned nothing from me? The road to revolution is paved with the bones of those who came before."

"And the road to reactionism."

"Backbone! Mine was hammered into place by the Tsar. Then that man, Koba, tried to break it in many places, but it stood firm."

"The situation is not the same here, Olga. You can't keep translating your experience to mine! Or Joseph's."

The two women sat in silence again. Vera had seen that Olga's lip had trembled a little during their exchange, but it had not stopped Vera from putting her point of view. In fact, she knew that Olga would reflect on these hard truths and would secretly be pleased at how Vera had come along. *You taught me everything I know!*

"Come, we'll walk you to the train."

Vera placed Beryl, who had fallen asleep, into the pram. At the train station, Olga told Vera she would visit her mother again and Vera thanked her.

"At least I'm now doing what she would have wanted."

Olga nodded. "Yes, in a way."

MY FRIEND, ANTON CHEKHOV

"When did you last see Anton?"

Olga did wonder why Valentia was asking. Tired the night before, Olga had tossed and turned instead of sleeping, her legs had shot out at angles and she had turned onto her stomach with no relief. By morning, she had realised what it was she was wrestling with.

It was Valentia, who was coming to visit. Olga had tidied the flat as best she could but felt that Valentia disapproved of her lowly circumstances the minute she stepped through the door.

Valentia was the interlocutor, the interloper, exhausting Olga, overwhelming her. Olga reflected on her own character (as was her wont), and that after everything she had been through, perhaps she was still the same girl who had attended her first democratic socialist meeting in Kiev where the fire had lit in her, crystallising all her experiences of life under the Tsar and hardening it into a diamond deep within. This diamond had proven difficult to dislodge over the years, even in the camps, but here was Valentia. Here was someone who would have a go at it.

They had come from such different backgrounds. Valentia eschewed her wealthy roots but had used them when it suited her. Olga thought Valentia was fooling herself more than anyone else; and there was proof — had she not married an aristocrat, finally?

When they had inspected the props at the New Theatre, Olga remembered the painters, of whom Valentia had been a minor one on her own admission. How tiresome the debates had become back then, about which type of art to support, which style of painting. But Valentia had regaled her with her tales of Malevich and Chagall and the others, and like Goncharova, Valentia seemed to have joined and left many of the aesthetic movements.

Olga thought of loyalty as a strength, one she decided that Valentia did not have. And why flit from one movement to another anyway? As if there was one way to make art and in joining another exclusive group, you would find that one, true way. Better to join all the groups and never leave! After all, art is not politics, it is only the fellow traveller of politics, Olga concluded.

She was conflicted about whether to challenge what was essentially Valentia's takeover of the play. It was undeniable that she needed her help. Gwen would help with the production, organising the rehearsals, the actors, the printing of the actors' parts, the scheduling; Vera would design the sets, and Gregor would supervise the set building and the actors.

Olga had seen so many plays, she knew their mechanics. But Valentia, she had to admit to herself, had a way with words. She was a poet, a persuader. Olga was composed of more solid material, and she knew her efforts would be too didactic. Valentia, she decided, would act like the leavening in the bread.

Olga had wrestled with her own emotions, her own history, but the future won. So, when Valentia asked her this question about Chekhov, she answered it graciously, to share what she knew, seeing it as an opportunity to practice what she had resolved.

"It was some time before his death. At the Moscow Theatre. He was there with Olga Knipper and there was a lot of clowning around. You know, he did like to laugh. He had that sad twinkle in his eye, like a fading star. That chest of his… we were always worried, but there was no point in saying anything, because he did not listen. Koba…he was like Anton's tuberculosis. Ignore the rattle until it comes for you. Just get on with it."

Valentia laughed. "I like your humour. I never met him, though I met his wife. She was widow then, and I liked her very much. So dedicated to his art, and her own.

"Fusing him and our dear friend Mayakovsky together, that is what we are doing. It is a pity they never knew each other either."

"Yes, I can imagine Anton clapping his hands and stamping his feet and calling out on that first night of *Mystery Bouffe*, amidst all the clamour. I am not certain about what he would think of Meyerhold's biomechanics. But we need to add them, as they were so much a part of what *I* promoted, Valentia."

Valentia slapped her leg. "Yes, it is our genius! Meyerhold, Chekhov and Mayakovsky. A real Holy Trinity! We need to rehearse the biomechanical sequences. Shall we? You must have seen them more often than me, Olga."

Olga nodded brusquely. She stood up. She created an arc with her hands then pretended to stab someone. Moving from side to side, she appeared to be finding her way in a crowd. Then she appeared to fall over in a faint.

"Who will do 'leap from the horse'?"

Olga shook her head. "I'm too old now. But I remember this one."

Olga pretended to juggle while moving backwards and pretended to lose one of the balls.

"Meyerhold wanted to turn us all into circus performers. Such good idea!"

"Circus, Russian folk plays, anything that contained the ba-sic emotions. They knew how to appeal to the hearts, and through that, to the minds."

It struck Olga that if anyone had peered through the curtains, they might not believe what they were seeing: two old ladies in tweed skirts and stout shoes chasing each other around the room, limbs moving in a crazy fashion.

Olga was puffed by the exertion. "We will be able to train all of them in the method. Whoever they are, the workers, anyone. No need to be actor! Meyerhold was against elitism."

Valentia nodded. "But I did wonder whether it wasn't just rivalry with Stanislavski that spurred him to create his system. Creating the opposite."

Olga laughed. "That is point exactly. Dialectics! He invented something because he compelled himself to think about the opposing ideas. True Marxist!"

The women wrote down a sequence of biomechanical actions for the actors that they could hand out at rehearsals.

"Do you remember Hungarian Tokaii, Olga? Here, I brought this all the way from London. Perhaps, just for this purpose."

Valentia took the bottle from her bag. Olga brought out a tray and two small, elaborately etched glasses.

By the time they had finished the bottle of Tokaii, they had sketched out the three acts of the play, the main roles and the story. The three sisters were to be a mix of Clean and Unclean — Mayakovsky's original categories for the actors in the play. The Unclean, Mayakovsky's working class, would encounter a priest, an aristocrat, then an Inuit man who is just passing through their village and threatens to evict them all from his reclaimed land. The three sisters would be there, too and would react according to their differing class consciousness.

"So juicy!" said Valentia after she had drained the dregs of the bottle. "And I love it that Masha can, potentially, transcend her bourgeois origins."

Then she said more quietly, "thank you, Olga."

Both sat, listening to the quiet around them. Then Valentia spoke.

"Do you ever wonder what would have happened if the Mensheviks had won? You, and Lev I recall were against the Revolution at the start…"

Olga swayed a little. Her head had felt cloudy and dizzy with their theatrical foray, but no longer.

"It is true. We had many reservations. Things are not straightforward, Valentia. Those who were on one path, well perhaps history has been on their side — or at least the way it is told. It looks like a straight path when, *in actuality*, there were dead ends, unexpected turns, crookedness, detours. Robbers to pull you into the bushes."

Then Olga said the following to turn the tables: "And you, Valentia? You swayed a little yourself, you say?"

"It is true that I flirted with Futurism for short time. Suprematicism. Then…"

"How long you spend in each one?"

"Oh, I don't remember precisely."

Valentia was quiet for a few moments.

"Perhaps a year? I soon tired of them. It was like wearing a corset again, which I did when I was a young heiress to attract a husband. It became very difficult to meet their expectations. Unless you were Malevich or your friend Maya, nothing was good enough! They kept you on the hook…" Valentia's voice trailed off.

Olga took up the slack. "And let's not forget Soviet Realism! Perhaps you flirted with that, as well, Valentia? Eh? It was pure fantasy! Chekhov would have laughed if he had been around then. Our Anton wanted to strip away the ill-u-sions, and that is why he is the man for us, here. This play, Valentia, we write people's theatre. Nothing needs to be explained. The people reveal their characters in response to the situation in which they find themselves. We expose the *bourgeoisie*. We pour scorn on their pursuit of individual interests above anything else — their own individual character, their guiding purpose. Never, properly, being social an-i-mal. My feeling is same about the painters…"

Olgas realised she had broken the bargain she had made with herself and had showed Valentia her hand.

She continued, trying to be more conciliatory, "of course, there is nothing wrong with individual creativity, Valentia. Nothing on Earth! But they were stupidly competitive with each other instead of helping each other to find new discoveries. Artists really are the least socialistic of people! I did not miss Chagall. Nor Malevich, not really. Natalia, yes. But how they fought, criticised each other as if only one could be right! The people were starving…and they fought over…what?"

Valentia had fallen asleep and had not heard this, but a short silence woke her, and she did not think that Olga had noticed.

In any case, Olga had lost the thread of what she had been saying, and she thought (fuzzily), that perhaps Valentia was not so interested.

Properly awake, Valentia walked to the tram. As she walked, she realised the Futurists had diverted her attention from the real things she had wanted to discuss. Damn Olga! Damn Chekhov!

NAVIGATOR, DIRECTOR, COLLABORATOR

Gwen Shoebridge could see that Valentia Vassilenko had already started to talk to the actors. Gwen sat in a chair where she knew Valentia would see her, and she put her handbag on her lap and listened. Olga, to whom she had given a lift, sat beside her.

Valentia was explaining with grand gestures the physical preparation that the actors would need for the play. Olga sat still. Gwen was concerned on her behalf, that Olga might feel snubbed. She gestured to Olga that she should join Valentia, but Olga smiled and shook her head.

The actors bombarded Valentia with questions. Greg was there, and he listened intently. He was wary of what he was hearing, but they had thrown in their lot with these two, after all, with their unpredictable energy. Valentia answered them patiently and Greg could see Olga listening as well. She looked almost content.

The session went on for some time, and Valentia explained the principles of biomechanics; that character was created through action. Truly a revolutionary gesture! She demonstrated some of the movements and guided the actors to mimic them. "This is necessary," she said, "to master basic movement techniques which would be drawn upon in constructing the character on stage."

The production working group was due to meet after the rehearsal, so Greg and the women moved to the committee room. Gwen had brought scones and set about spreading the jam and cream and handing them around. Lilia Monk had already made the tea. She sat, poured and handed around the cups and saucers.

Lilia raised her cup and crooked her little finger. "Here's to the Revolution!"

There was business to transact.

The working group had already been acquainted with the script outline, so the first item was the proposal for the set — one set only. Olga took charge.

"I, as Honorary Meyerhold Playwright, have recruited very talented set designer, Miss Vera Watson. The design of the set will be simple, yet monumental. Something that will hold the attention and praise the *hum-an* achievement. Interior to depict where the three sisters live, and platforms in two levels, representing the hills and outside world. Inuit man — you call him Eskimo — will come back to claim his land. We will paint igloo on the backdrop."

"Does the Inuit man have a name?" Lilia asked.

Valentia intervened. "Not yet. We must fix that." She made a note in the small leather-bound notebook that she carried everywhere.

"How will the audience know the platforms are the outside world?" asked Gwen.

Olga broke in quickly, "that will come from the action. We will not have sign saying 'this is this!' We look to the actors to show us the way. Gregor, you must take note of this."

Greg nodded.

"So, that is what we will ask Vera Watson to design. Is everyone in agreement?" Gwen asked.

"One more thing," added Valentia. "We intend to leave the back doors open before the show and while it's in progress so that the audience is cold."

Olga nodded enthusiastically. "Yes. This will mean that everyone will know what it is to be cold."

She added, "it will be as cold as the gulag in there."

They all shivered involuntarily.

Lilia spoke. "Doors open? Perhaps not for the whole performance unless we have guards. We may be rushed by Nazi thugs. Or the government. The police. They will be able to come straight in if we leave the doors…"

Olga interrupted, "No guards. Let them all come! We have nothing to hide."

"But we do want people to be safe," Lilia added. "Otherwise we won't have a season."

Olga was silent. Lilia continued, making her hands into fists as she gently placed them on the table.

"Besides that, the government may try to shut us down completely. We need contingency, other venue we can switch last minute if we hear from comrades who stay close to police."

Lilia became more insistent. "We are familiar with clandestine tactics. Comrade Kameneva may not know that Australian Communist Party was banned, we do know how to organise against the state."

Gwen spoke next. "But Lilia, remember the Odets play. They did us a favour by trying to ban that, because we put it on anyway and hundreds came. That notoriety went our way, though it was a hard slog…*Reedy River*, of course that's been a godsend to us, but it built on the popularity of the Odets play. Don't worry, Olga, we're used to raids. We're not scared."

"We should send Mr Menzies the invitation to opening night," Olga said.

No one could tell whether she was joking, but they treated her comment seriously as they were in a formal meeting.

Gwen said, "Well, Olga, we could think about that. You know what they say: 'there'll always be a Menzies while there's a BHP.' So perhaps we should ask Mr Essington Lewis, as well."

"Is that a resolution?" Lilia asked.

Gwen replied. "Yes. Let's send them. The police know everything we do anyway."

"Our *Slap in the Face of Public Taste*!" added Valentia and she drew the gaze of those around the table. "You are familiar with that manifesto? No?"

Gwen felt the discussion was all going a little off topic. "We don't have time to discuss manifestos now, Comrade Vassilenko, — interesting as they may be. And your play? How is the script coming along?"

"Yes, we having to spend much time on it. In doing so, we honour our Russian playwriters: Mr Chekhov, Mr Mayakovsky and of course our dear director, Mr Meyerhold. Praise his glorious legacy."

Lilia spoke next. "I understand you are using the format of the *Mystery Bouffe*? Even I heard about this play through the German Communists. They told me that Lenin didn't like it. It was not to his *liking*," she emphasised.

Valentia spoke. "It is true that it was not to our dear departed comrade's taste. He liked the worker's triumph, I believe, but he did not like the play's *feel*. But you'd be surprised what people do and don't like — some peasants I knew loved it. It reminded them of the folk plays, the Purim and such. The topsy-turvy world. And isn't that what the Bolsheviks did? Turn the world upside down?"

There was pride in Valentia's voice as she spoke, and Olga calmed herself, for she was planning to speak again, and this time, not kindly. But Valentia had said all that was needed.

After the meeting, Gwen took Olga aside. "Why did you sit back and let Valentia do all of the directing of the actors? Don't you know more than she does about biomechanics? You were so close to him, Comrade Meyerhold?"

Olga responded, "We collaborate. I am writer and director of the play. Valentia works under my direct-ion."

Gwen nodded but looked unconvinced. There was a history of emotion, tactics, speculation, action that these women had experienced. But for her, it was as if this was hidden behind a heavy curtain, and all she could hear was a muffled conversation.

After the meeting, one of the young actors came into the committee room. She came up to Olga and asked her quietly, "Is it true that Leon Trotsky was your brother?"

"Da."

The young woman breathed deeply. "What was he like?"

"Well, I knew him as a younger man, not in last years. As a young man, he was humourful and incisive. Once when I was still at home, he visited and told us about his first visit to the theatre. The play was called *The Tenant with a Trombone*. He roared with laughter as he recounted it. Every time he re-told the story, he added more outrageous details, the tenant playing the trombone with his farts…"

The young woman giggled.

"Later, when he joined the Party, he could smell fault like the light-ening striking and became impatient with those who did not see as he did. He knew best. But he could change his views with new information, so that was perhaps his best quality. We had this in common, he and I — just peasants reading the weather patterns and predicting the storms. But he did not speak up against Stalin when he had the chance. We were all guilty of that at one time.

"My brother Leon said that Mayakovsky, our playwright, described love as if it were the migration of nations — so dramatic! But Leon did admire his work. Lenin did not, but Maya was very popular. Not everyone agreed with Lenin! Never have there been so many people at a poet's funeral. Thousands. Many thousands."

Olga thought perhaps that she had talked for too long. The young woman smiled her understanding, then she turned on her heels to join her friends.

Olga had wondered, while the young woman was asking about her brother, why they did not ask about her own history and positions in the Party *apparat*. She had worked so closely with Meyerhold, taking forward as much new thinking as she could — guilty as charged!

More memories flooded back to Olga as she stood in the empty theatre space, so recently dusted that she could still smell it. How much she had laughed at Meyerhold's work, great big laughs from deep in her stomach as she would transport herself back to the Purim of her youth, to the Buster Keaton and Chaplin films they had watched in Moscow and Switzerland. But these memories went as quickly as they came, as Olga stuffed them into the recesses of her brain again, much as one would an old quilt in the back of the cupboard.

She sat quietly on the drive home with Gwen. She knew Gwen had questions that she, Olga, would not be able to answer or would refuse to. Olga was still thinking of Beverly. She still suspected that much had happened in Beverly's life, though she had no real evidence, just the way Beverly held herself in as she spoke and the whites of her bony knuckles.

This, she acknowledged to herself, was Stanislavski's genius with the actors — that all of emotion could be represented in a twitch of the face or a crossing of the arms or legs. All so different from her beloved Vsevolod's grand and generous movements.

No, if she had her way, she would put on both plays, she realised, *The Three Sisters* and *Mystery Bouffe*, facing one another like two boxers shaping up in the ring, dialectically opposed but each watching the other and learning. She was pleased with the thought and felt like telling Gwen, but hesitated.

Gwen was happily talking about one topic after another while Olga gradually brought Gwen's voice back into her consciousness. Gwen was talking, Olga realised, about the farm where she had grown up, in the foothills of the Victorian Alps, where the pastures were lush with snow melt and the forests thick with wallabies and mushrooms and tree ferns and hiding spaces.

"Was there real, actual snow?" Olga asked earnestly.

"Yes," Gwen replied. "Often there was, but it did not stay long on the ground."

"It had somewhere else to go," Olga said firmly. "Probably to Moscow."

A SLAP IN THE FACE OF PUBLIC TASTE

"Nude?"

"Da," said Valentia, and she folded her arms.

Gwen grimaced. "Could they wear nude costumes, perhaps?"

"Ny-et," Valentia replied.

Olga sat back, leaving the discussion to the others. Actually, she and Valentia had not agreed on the nudity aspect of the production, though they had discussed it at some length.

Gwen said, "well surely not all the actors?"

Valentia nodded then said, "perhaps."

"Even Caroline? You know she is four months pregnant? Well, have you asked her?"

Valentia shook her head.

Olga added, "it is just idea at present. For consider-ation."

"Alright." Gwen said. "I'm the producer, so I have to be ready to take the outrage. And face the fact we may be shut down as a result."

Olga replied, "we are involved in entertaining the masses. We give the people spectacle. This is not intellectual pursuit. This is life as we would like it to be, something to aspire to, some fun-i-ness. But we will get back to you on nudity."

The rehearsals had been going well, and the actors seemed to accept Meyerhold's vision and his spirit in the way Olga had intended. Olga had explained the background to his vision, the folk plays and the mystery plays and Comrade Vsevolod Meyerhold's discovery of mime. The actors did not seem to have heard of Commedia dell' Arte or Japanese Kabuki, which Olga considered a gap in their education that she quickly tried to fill.

The cast particularly liked the biomechanical movements of horse and rider, and when Olga explained it would be the women carrying the men on the stage, but that the women would be dressed as men, there was a lot of confusion and questioning and discussion. Why would we be reinforcing old stereotypes, fixed roles for men and women, when the whole point is to overturn them? Olga explained that this was precisely what they were meant to be doing, displaying the topsy-turvy world post-Revolution, but she agreed, perhaps they could have some actual men carrying women, dressed as men, as long as the female riders made it clear they were in charge.

"But isn't the point that no one is 'in charge?'" asked Gwen.

Olga pointed out that Revolution was not anarchy, and, in any case, theatre can only be, "*prox-y for re-al-ity,* not reality itself."

"That is its beauty," Valentia added, and Gwen felt that void between her and them open up again.

The discussion turned to the Inuit man who came to reclaim his land from the three sisters. Elaine, who had asked Olga about Trotsky at the first rehearsal, asked why they would not use this opportunity to highlight the treatment of Australia's own Aborigines? Olga explained that because they had mixed up *The Three Sisters* and *Mystery Bouffe* and both were set in the north, it seemed more plausible to use a person native to that area, one who magically steps across the Bering Sea.

"How plausible do you want it to be, anyway? I guess…" Elaine added, as she cast a knowing smile around at the other actors.

Olga responded. "The people must believe in our vision. And there are no Aboriginal people in your Party, perhaps? And there is no snow in Australia — not really," she added for emphasis.

Gwen smiled. She had prepared a short report on the progress of the production side of the play, which she tabled.

"Vera Watson, your colleague, has given us some early drawings, Olga. She has been to meet with the set builders. I must say, the execution of your and her ideas will be interesting to see. I have heard about the avant-garde, of course, but this will add immensely to our exposure. And the baby! Well, Beryl is a delight to have about the place. She just sits in her pram. Very observant. I have no hesitation in saying it will all be ready on time. And the script is coming along, I believe?"

Valentia weighed in. "Yes, we have a first draft. We are merely refining it now."

Olga nodded quickly, knowing they were barely half finished.

Olga and Valentia Vassilenko were having a disagreement. A real one. One on which life and death depended. They were in Olga's flat, since the journey to Valentia's house would have been a trying one for Olga.

Olga wanted the Inuit man to burn down the house of the three sisters and build an igloo in its place; Valentia wanted the three sisters to invite the man into their house where they would make a great painting together, and after that, the Inuit man would move in.

"And the sisters? I suppose they move to Moscow after the house burns?"

Olga responded, "the sisters never go to Moscow."

"But they must, in our re-writing of it. Don't you see?"

Olga shook her head emphatically.

"No. Definitely not. I have thought about it. Anton was right. They never get there."

"Do we always want the sisters to lose?"

Olga drew a breath.

"Valentia, don't you see? If they did get to Moscow, it would be the end of the world, not the beginning. We need always to be at the beginning of something, not the end."

Valentia sighed. "I feel the loss. So much."

She started to cry, and it was then, right there in Olga's tiny living room, with the sun on her face and the steam of the samovar in her nostrils, that she broke down.

"Olga, there is one thing I must tell you. I *need* to tell you. I thought I could stay silent, but I cannot."

"Tea?" Olga asked.

Valentia choked back some tears. "Why not?"

She sipped the hot liquid and felt the sun on her face again, and it seemed that she could go on, as the heat warmed her outside and in. If it were not for that, she might still be unable to go on...

She began. "Regarding that first writers conference. You attended?"

"Da," said Olga. "1934."

"I did not attend," Valentia added. "But there is a reason that I know you were there."

Olga stood up as if she remembered something important. She picked up the tea glasses and returned them to the kitchen. She walked back into the living room and opened the small cabinet she had bought from the Catholic secondhand shop — one of the few times she had paid them for anything — and she pulled out a bottle of vodka and the two small, etched glasses.

She placed them in front of Valentia. Valentia looked up and into Olga's dark eyes, at her dark, droopy skin, and took the glass handed to her. She downed the vodka in the glass in one gulp.

Olga had sat down, nursing her own glass. Valentia's tears had stopped flowing, her cheeks were wet and cool.

"As you remember, Bielinski was attacked, for many things. So many things! Not attending October Revolution Day celebrations. For leaving a room when *he*, the General Secretary, walked in — Bielinski had to relieve himself and returned, but that was not recorded — then the attacks on his poetry. It was quite merciless. With one speaker after another on how he ignored the principles of Socialist Realism, that he was not sufficiently optimistic. Other things I don't remember now. How Mayakovsky would have laughed. He would have written a poem about it."

Valentia downed another glug of vodka. "You spoke, Olga."

Olga had forgotten. "I did?" Then, "yes...I remember him, I can't say I knew him. Small glasses perched on his nose. You were in love with him?"

"I was. But at the time I was with Eric Holiman, the Negro sculptor. I was with him, but I was in love with Bielinski. But he had a wife..."

Olga raised her glass and said, "da. *Na zdarovye!*"

"Love. Yes," Valentia mused.

Olga spoke, "I said what I believed. I thought his poetry was lazy, I thought he used the Russian themes...motifs, for his own selfish ends. He threw them about like he was scattering stars. Not to illuminate. To make sparkle."

"Yes, you thought he was a fake. And you told everyone in your speech. I did not think him the best poet myself. But the context, Olga! The context! After all the speeches denouncing him?"

Olga smiled. But it was not a smile of pleasure, Valentia thought. There are those who relish the fight.

"I said what I thought. I was honest. I could not help that he was bad poet. He was handsome and charming, but poetry no good. I have *the standards*..."

"Your...standards are what got him killed, Olga."

(A GREAT PAUSE IN THE ACTION)

"How you know I spoke?"

Bielinski told me who spoke against him. Later, I saw the minutes of the Congress in the newspaper. And I went through the names of those who spoke, one by one...and I have not forgotten."

"Not my standard. If he wrote good poetry, I would have said so."

Olga said the last two words slowly, theatrically. Then she continued, "Socialist Realism. I didn't defend it, Valentia! That was not the logical conclus-ion of my comments on Bielinski. I had the devil's time defending Meyerhold and his experiments against the criticism of Lunacharsky."

"But, don't you see, Olga? Attacking my Egon in same forum, after the denunciations…you became a supporter of Socialist Realism…"

"You think too much. He was gone already. And not for the poetry."

They both sat for a moment with that thought. Valentia's brain was frying-pan hot with memory. Olga sat convinced of her righteousness. And she spoke.

"The rot was already there with the writers, with RAPP. And Prolekult for that matter. We should have known, those who had lived under the Tsar. It was one thing my brother and I agreed on: there is no such thing as proletarian literature! We should have smelled the stench when those institu-tions started to give it off, but we still believed in what we had started, Valentia. As if we learnt nothing from the Tsar! Well, Stalin did. He continued what they had started with his censorship; his Socialist Realism. And your painters, Valentia, they were no better. Criticising each other, every artistic decision was life and death. Is good Russian joke. Oy!"

"I tried hard, too, Olga. But I can't forgive you for Bielinski. My Egon. I can't. I wanted to tell you."

Olga nodded. "*Ya znayu.* You tried. Yes. We all tried." Then she shrugged her shoulders and drained the vodka in her glass.

"That is why it is so important that we write the play, Valentia, and bring it to Australia. Not even the Communists are imm-une from the myths about Russia! We show them, eh? That we shook the tree and brought down all the branches and the leaves on our own heads!"

Valentia sat back for a moment and regarded her empty glass. Her tears had dried. She said, "you remember Ehrenburg, of course, on the presidium of the Congress. He spoke for Babel and Pasternak."

"Yes. He was right to do so. But the cause was already lost."

Valentia poured herself another drink. She could not wait for Olga, and perhaps Olga had forgotten they were drinking.

"I had an affair with him, too," she said. "Later. He survived. He was as clever as the wind."

"You surprise me, Valentia. He was not so charming. But many did survive. Stalin had to be careful. He saw how many people turned up to Mayakovsky funeral. He could never manoeuvre against

Akhmatova. Or Sholokhov. How that man berated them about the treatment of the kulaks. But Stalin stayed out of it. Perhaps that was his genius: to know how to pick your targets."

Valentia felt relaxed. She knew it was almost certainly the vodka, but what harm could Olga do now?

"And Zamyatin: his spirit was there. But fancy, him writing to Stalin about censorship. And *asking for* exile."

"And *getting it*," Valentia added, knowing that by now she was quite drunk, and given that Olga had matched her glass for glass, she knew Olga was, too.

Olga (slurring), "And if he took a set against you, if you *offended him*, like Pilnyak, the hurt would simmer for years, and even if you recanted like he did, it would never erase this sin. But actually, to understand Koba is not so difficult. He could not afford to kill everyone — he still needed the cloak of Revolution to hide his acts. And us, some of the Old Bolsheviks and the artists, he gave us some freedoms, so as to mask his actions. That way, there was always hope you would survive, and the Revolution, as well.

"You know, Valentia, one thing that I really appreciated about the camps, and I don't tell many people this…"

Olga took some deep breaths. Then she burped, long and satisfyingly.

"We talked there, we never stopped. Karl Marx, how we talked! Maria Spiridonova, Kristian Radovsky — yes, he was there, too. Many others. We talked about everything and about nothing depending on our moods. We argued, dissented, became angry, didn't speak for days, then we would speak again. Because we couldn't help it. To speak is to think. *At…leasht für mich…*

"Maria, ah, we argued all the time. The camps gave us the freedom to do this. The camps! We created something together, there in that camp. We kept it alive for as long as we could…out of our own minds came a unique *persp-ective,* something that didn't exist before. The *dialec-tic!*"

As Olga emphasised the last word, the glass flew from her hand and landed with a thud on the carpet.

Valentia laughed. "Can you imagine how it was, Olga, visiting with the English upper classes, my husband's friends, and not talking about what matters? You have never heard such silly conversations! They rivalled the Politburo! Ha, the Polite-buro! But of course, all the important conversations happened behind closed doors. Never with the *women*."

"Perhaps we should put…it…in the play." Olga's voice trailed off.

"Perhaps I should go, and we should talk again tomorrow."

Valentia Vassilenko hauled herself up from the sofa, fatigued and a little unsteady. Olga had slumped, and she seemed to be falling asleep, but she replied to Valentia after a few moments in a clear voice. "Yes. I would like that."

Quietly, Valentia gathered her coat and bags and left.

"We're here for the fire inspection."

Gwen and Olga were looking at the drawings Vera had made of the sets for the play, which Valentia and Olga had titled *Anton Chekhov's Mystery Bouffe*. Vera had brought some revised drawings to the theatre on the train, balancing them on the back of Beryl's pram.

Gwen turned from the drawings to see two men standing in the hall. They both wore ill-fitting dark suits and pork-pie hats.

Gwen replied, "we haven't a fire that needs inspection, thank you."

The man who had spoken smirked fleetingly.

"The facility, madam, must be inspected to make sure all the necessary fire precautions are in order."

"You're from the council, then?" Gwen answered in a tone that told Olga this visit was no surprise. "Show me your paperwork."

The man handed over a letter and attachment. Gwen scanned the contents.

"I'm sure you have a good idea of where to find everything."

Tipping their hats, the men walked towards the side cupboards that stored the fire equipment, opened and closed them a few times, then walked towards the stage.

Gwen said, "I'll go with them. They can't be trusted."

Olga and Vera retreated to the committee room. Beryl had started to squirm, so Olga took her from the pram. She dandled the baby on her lap, who tried to reach up towards Olga's ear, having spotted the glint of an earring. Olga took the baby's fingers and pretended to eat them.

"Let us look at those drawings."

Vera unrolled the large, paper squares. Olga looked at them intently. She could see that Vera has taken notice of what she had told her, her memories of the sets from the avant-garde. But Vera had made them her own.

Olga had trawled through her own memories to give Vera a sense, memories at least thirty years old, but the colours and the lines were so true in her mind, they had never faded. The drawings for *The Magnanimous Cuckold*! The mill, conveyer belts creaking and the cranking wheels — ripe for the application of biomechanics — completely in harmony in meaning and action. With Popova, of course, Olga thought, it was the women who were at the forefront with the men. How vivid were her and Ekster's works for the ballet, opera, plays — they reminded Olga so much of the paper doll costumes she had cut out or made as a child: crisp colours, angles and shapes. And those strange beings created for the production of the *Queen of Mars*. Olga did wonder where the ideas had come from and clapped her hands at how Eisenstein and Popova had created something new by working together on the one idea.

Olga had described *Victory Over the Sun* in detail for Vera. It had blazed across all of their horizons with its cosmic, alien language and the costumes — yellow, red — the primal colours, the cut-out look, from the scissors of children and futuristic both at once. In fact, they had defined the future. They used motifs from engineering and industry: Science meeting Art in a new construction.

Vera's conception was very simple, which was fine with Olga. The simpler the better, to highlight the action.

"At least I will have snow, *fig-uritively* speaking," said Olga. "I will ask Gwen to pass these on to the set constructors. They are wonderful, Vera."

"I managed to get some time when Joseph was at work and his parents at the community centre. I haven't told them. Yet."

"But you will need to. Once the production happens."

Vera rubbed her daughter's back as Olga held the child.

"I've sent you an invitation to the wedding, Olga."

"Thank you, Vera. I will be there. But promise me you won't stop working."

"Luckily, I don't work for the government, Olga, otherwise I would have to resign once I am married. No, I'm the main breadwinner in the household. I'm taking on more hours at Mr Ford's. And I'm thinking of going back to university on my days off. Possibly I'll study law."

Olga moved the baby up close to her body and patted her back. "*Krasivaya devochka*," she murmured soothingly.

She didn't talk again in case her voice betrayed her deep emotions. The feel of the baby's back against her hand, the quick rise and fall of her tiny nostrils, a reminder of the preciously short time her sons' childhoods had comprised, and of the few weeks she had spent with her mother with her youngest baby. The snow had come early and hard, and Olga had been forced to stay longer with her mother than planned when she had needed to return to Moscow for a women's committee meeting. Her mother had cooked winter stews and soups over the fire and helped her settle the baby, who refused to breastfeed. She had sat in the evenings at her mother's feet reading from the few books there were around the house, and both of them sang songs from Olga's childhood to soothe the fractious child.

"Your mother, Vera. Did she reply?"

"Not yet. Barbara and her family were also invited, and I haven't heard back. The Slodkowicz's know and understand."

"Do you want me to visit her? You should invite the other women. I'm sure they...I'm sure they will know. Gossip will come out. It is small place, this Melbourne. Even in Moscow, you couldn't hide."

"Hmmm. Part of me thinks I should invite them, just to be, well, you know...honest. Another part thinks I should not bother them. I mean, do I care if I see them again?"

"Yes. You do. You grew up with their children. They will be forever wondering what happened to you, but too polite or too anxious about the answer to ask your mother. You owe them the truth."

Oh, so you're the truth warrior? Vera thought to herself, but said, "I suppose I might run into them in the street."

"You need to ask them to come."

"It will be a surprise. What should I say? That I 'went away'? That I was ashamed, but kept the baby? And then I met a nice man? Fairytale ending?"

"Just invite them. They will work it out."

Olga rolled up Vera's sketches. Gwen walked into the room.

"Well, I think there will be a list of things we have to fix. As usual, the authorities have threatened to stop us putting on the plays this season. But we are made of sterner stuff, eh, Olga? Yes, we are."

Gwen and Olga had more business to do. Vera took the baby and settled her back in her pram.

"Will you visit my mother, as well, Olga? Let me know if she is coming?"

While they worked, Olga and Valentia Vassilenko drank regularly. Back in Olga's childhood, it had not been unusual to have fruit wine along with breakfast before tackling the fields and other agricultural labour. Valentia had found many different types of spirits in the European delicatessens she visited all over the city. These were invariably very pleasant, and her selection reminded Olga of home. She admitted that Valentia had been very kind to bring them.

There were so many decisions to make about the play — the scenes and characters, who was to say what. Actually, Olga had rarely drunk alcohol in over twenty years. But now it seemed to help. Not only did it remind her of home and the times she had spent with family and friends, but it helped with writing, too. It seemed to make it easier for her and Valentia to reach agreement.

On one of these occasions, they had become crazy, dizzily celebrating the playwrights and the painters and the actors who burst — fairly burst! — through heavy stage curtains, as if Tsarism were on one side and their new world on the other. In fact, that was exactly what had happened that night in 1906 when Vera Komissarzhevskaya's theatre let a fledgling Meyerhold fly the nest and bring the house down: after the actors burst through and invaded the audience, the curtains were shredded by actors with bayonets reciting poems by Blok, their uneven rhythms accented by invisible drummers.

Let's put a bullet into Holy Russia...fat-arsed Russia...

Valentia and Olga traded words. Back and forth. Now, it didn't seem to matter who said what; it was one stream of consciousness:

— It was Meyerhold who broke through.

— But Kommissarzhevskaya dismissed him, because he could find no place for her 'individual talent' to shine in his more collective productions.

— And painting? Those silly men fell out over whether a darting arrow or a mysterious black square represented truth. What was real was that they fell out over power and reputation.

— We exiles, excluded from some clubs and admitted to others. The exiles' club? Who wants to be a member of that?

— Never mind! Meyerhold went on to greatness. And early death. You can't have everything.

And so on about Meyerhold.

"He was INDEED WUNDERBAR!" Valentia said finally, and she sang the words and poured a little more of that delicious apple brandy.

"Olga, did you ever see Kharms? His funny hats? And his strange performances, much like our Meyer! I was there, at the one where he came onto the stage dressed as a wardrobe! Imagine! And then he read his poems for two hours, oyyiii…one after another. Lucky I had a flask of vodka with me!"

"I liked him very much," Olga remembered, though as she did, she could barely remember his face.

"Remember The Smithy? Oyyii… the arguments. So much headache for so little enlightenment. All of those manifestos! Everyone had one, all competing. I wish I still had copies." Valentia's voice trailed away. "That oaf Gladkov and his *Cement* book. He's probably under the real cement by now!"

"Valentia, be careful."

"Do we not speak ill of the dead now? That is *bourgeois* concept."

"You call *me* a *bourgeois*? Me? Valentia!"

"I apol-o-gise," Valentia said. "I know you think *me* as bourgeois because of my origins, Olga. No matter how hard I tried, I was never accepted as real comrade. I never joined, but that didn't stop others from being close to the inner circle. I could do nothing about my origins, but I was never allowed to forget them. But I — now, *I* can tear down all of the walls, *I* can speak ill of the dead, *I* can spit on writers feted by any regime. It is duty of the writer to spit on the current order! Mr Menzies and his ilk say what they will. Writers, painters, they should only do what is unexpected!"

"You are very critical of me," Olga replied after a few moments, letting Valentia's words sink in.

"No. Actually not. I am critical of everyone, including myself. But when I remember that time, we were all just feeling our way, but how critical we were! How critical of each other!

"And yes, I flitted around…and I flirted. It was the time for that, as well. So much experimenting. What do you think our neighbours would say if they knew how many men we slept with?"

Valentia looked across at Olga and added, "or the women…"

Olga laughed, a deep sounding from the bottom of her lungs. It welled up. It echoed.

Valentia was contemplating her empty glass, swirling the lees of the drink around.

"Did I tell you already about my affair with Ehrenberg? Yes, perhaps I did. Well, it was a secret. We didn't even want his mistress to know about it. And certainly not his wife, or other writers. He was as slippery as water, he survived. I mention him again to say that people think there is a science to survival. No. If they took a set against you, if that happened, you were doomed. Like poor old Pilnyak. But if they were only half-hearted about you, then you might survive. They were quite half-hearted about me, I assure you."

The two women dozed into a light sleep for perhaps half an hour, then gradually woke each other with thoughts spoken out loud.

It was time for work. They had reached the fulcrum of the play previously, the point at which the topsy-turvy world asserts itself. The women had been in disagreement about what form this should take. Valentia was still in favour of nudity. Olga had voiced her opposition many times. This time she had another reason: she told Valentia she thought it would distract from the circus atmosphere and the audience would focus only on the nakedness and not on the whole production and on Mayakovsky's and Meyerhold's brilliance.

They had been over this issue several times and had always fallen into discussion of other issues or reminiscences.

"It is not the nudity which worries me Valentia, but the distraction."

"Meyerhold would love the distraction, Olga. To get away from the everyday."

"But you need to enjoy whole spectacle, see the whole, not just one part."

They kept going just like that. Eventually, Valentia said, "we must stop the discussion, because we have all become completely confused!" They veered away — Olga unwillingly — then came back to discussing other problems with the play.

"Can the Clean become Unclean?" Valentia asked. "That will give surprise element. Some drama."

Olga thought for a moment. "I am tired again, Valentia. It seems that you use me to think." Olga was smiling.

"Perhaps for once, we are not talking at each other. Unless you disagree, you can't create something new. You told me that — your discussions with Maria. I must talk to think. If I can't talk, I can't think, and I can't collaborate."

Olga's thoughts seemed to crystallise at that moment. They worked their way back to the issue of nudity and found a new compromise.

"At the end of the play only?" Olga said, surprising Valentia.

"Yes, Olga, alright. That may be best way to end."

Sitting back contentedly, Olga took her well-thumbed copy of *The Three Sisters*. "There is a passage I want actors to read. One of the sisters. Towards the end, Valentia. Olga opened the book at a quote. I know Anton gave the speech to Vershinin in the script, but in our play the women should talk."

Olga read in her low rasping voice:

'It goes without saying that you cannot conquer the mass of darkness around you...Life will get the better of you, but still you'll not disappear without a trace. After you there may appear perhaps six like you, then twelve and so on until those such as you form a majority. In two or three hundred years, life on Earth will be unimaginably beautiful, marvellous. We, the people, need such a life and, though we haven't got it yet, we must have a presentiment of it, expect it, dream of it, prepare for it.'

"That is my gift to Anton, our friend, to honour his memory. How he would laugh to hear his words spoken with reverence. Words are as a shroud for real meaning. I heard him say that once to Olga K."

"Hmmm. That Vershinin," said Valentia, finally. "So full of himself."

OLGA AND BEVERLY READ CHEKHOV

INTERIOR: Mrs Beverly Watson's home in Box Hill. Olga Kameneva has arrived, and the two women are seated in the sitting room at the front of the house. Olga sits in her chair, rigidly holding her body. The usual tea and cake are absent.

> BEVERLY

I haven't seen you for quite a while, Olga.

> OLGA

Vera asked me to come.

> BEVERLY

What does she want?

> OLGA

She wanted me to ask if you are coming to her wedding.

Beverly's face betrays a faint grimace as if a deep pain were subsiding.

> BEVERLY

Oh, I've been thinking about it.

> OLGA

And your husband? Will he come?

> BEVERLY

Oh, he doesn't know. I haven't shown him the invitation.

> OLGA

The wedding is in two weeks. She wants both you and your husband to come. She would like to invite the other ladies, as well.

Beverly's brows arch.

> BEVERLY

I haven't decided whether to tell Les. I gather Joseph isn't the baby's father?

OLGA

No. He is good man.

BEVERLY

Oh. And his parents?

OLGA

Very good. Father a schoolteacher. Mother is nurse.

BEVERLY

She works for a living?

OLGA

Yes. She does. Vera is living with the family now.

BEVERLY

Who are they? Migrant friends of yours? How does Vera know them?

OLGA

The family name is Slodkowicz. They live in St Kilda.

The grimace returns to Beverly's face.

BEVERLY

I saw the name on the invitation. I had thought perhaps they were Russian friends of yours. But the address, I should have realised...no, no, no — Jewish. I can see it on your face. My hopes raised. So quickly disappointed. They never last!

Quickly Beverly stands, straight as a human spring. She walks around the room, gesticulating.

BEVERLY

Little B-I-T-C-H! Barmaid! She's worth bottling! The cow. She's marrying a Jew! I thought...if Russian...they might be people who escaped the Communists. Aristocrats, perhaps.

Beverly turns her back towards Olga and starts to waggle her finger.

It's all your fault, Olga. Did you introduce them? Did you play Jewish matchmaker? It was bad enough I had to send her to the Catholics. But the Jews! I know we're supposed to feel sorry for them. Let me tell you, they are not the only ones who've suffered in this world. Not by a long shot. And she's had the nerve to call her...progeny...after my mother. My dear departed mother!

Olga is silent for a moment, absorbing the blows.

OLGA
Vera thought that would be an honour, but perhaps mistake. The Slodkowicz's are good family. Nice family. Not religious, just nice Jewish family. They are my friends. They are Vera's friends.

BEVERLY
She's marrying a bloody Jew, Olga. And you want my friends to witness it?

Olga stands up. Beverly lets out a miserable sob. Olga moves to put her arms around Beverly but pulls back. Beverly holds her body rigid and still.

BEVERLY
Everything Les and I have worked for. Her sister. She will be mortified. Her husband's family. I will not tell them about Vera. I will not.

Olga sits down.

OLGA
Sit, Beverly. Sit down. Something there is stopping you from letting Vera re-join your family. It is making you ill. I fear your rigid-ity is making you sick. What is the end? What is this future that you seek without your daughter or grandchild...?

Beverly sits down, no less rigid, as if her limbs are made of stiff cardboard.

BEVERLY

Olga. I have worked all my life for what I have. I will not give it up now. There is a pride in achievement I see that you don't seem to understand...

OLGA

Very well. I do see. You are following something through, something only you can really know to be true. I will tell Vera.

Olga stands and gathers her coat and bag.

OLGA

The ladies will receive the invites, too.

BEVERLY

I can't help that. I can't help it that Vera is flaunting herself in public. All will know of my betrayal. But I will hold my head high, because I will continue as I am. I will retain the moral high ground. Unchanged by this scandal.

Olga reaches for Beverly's hand and squeezes it briefly, then leaves the house. She walks to the tram stop and waits. A tram slides ponderously towards her and as she looks up, the door opens and Clarissa steps down in front of her.

CLARISSA

Olga, love! Haven't seen you for a while!

Clarissa kisses Olga on both cheeks in the European style.

Have you been to see Beverly? How is she?

Olga gestures to Clarissa to step back onto the footpath and they sit down at the tram shelter.

OLGA

She is...well. Yes, well. She tells me that Barbara and the children are well. They have just been on a holiday to Bairnsdale, and Beverly and Leslie looked after Chappy.

CLARISSA

Oh, they love that little dog. I'm surprised they gave him back!

Olga smiles, but in a way that anyone seeing it would know that it was a prelude to something more serious.

OLGA

Do you know that Vera is living in Melbourne?

Clarissa looks puzzled.

CLARISSA

Oh, we thought she had moved to Sydney for her studies...

OLGA

Well, you and I know Clarissa that when a young woman is said to have moved to another city suddenly, there is often another explanation.

CLARISSA

You mean...Vera...

OLGA

Yes. And she has kept baby. And she is getting married to man not father.

Clarissa looks straight ahead.

CLARISSA

I can't imagine Beverly is very happy about that. And she hasn't told... I'm not surprised about that. Married you say? Well, that's probably for the best. Beverly is probably a bit too old to raise the child.

OLGA

Vera will invite you to the wedding.

Clarissa looks directly at Olga's face.

CLARISSA

I gather Beverly isn't going? No. Well. I would have to tell my husband. And the children, if I do go. My husband... well, his sister was the same, but she was young enough that the child was brought up as their sibling. The boy thought his grandmother was his mother. So, it all worked out.

OLGA

But everyone around you knew?

CLARISSA

Oh yes. No one said anything. You had to get on with things. And during the war. Well, you know there are a few children running around who look like they've got a bit of the tar brush.

Clarissa looks knowingly at Olga. Olga bids Clarissa goodbye and hails the oncoming tram.

OLGA KAMENEVA'S SKAZ

Skinny man with bad smell. *Zlovonnyy*, stinking! Narrow my nostrils, breathe more shallow-ly-ly-ly-ly.

Tea and Sympathy-thy-thy-thy, there — two smiling women in a poster as the tram pulled up.

Cheer-me-up! Cup!

Screee-cchhh! From Beverly-ly-ly? Nothing. *Nichego*.

Clarissa, kind, airs and graces! Clarissa will tell, and the DREAD-FUL SECRET will be out. Old life never coming back. Beverly never read Chekhov?

Skinny man's bones stick-spike my arthritic leg. Owwww!

Skin and bone — Beverly when she raved. Beverly without skin. You see the bones, sinews and muscles. Her heart, beating. B-bm. B-bm. B-bm.

Beverly without skin. In the camps, nowhere to hide emotions. Knowing the number of each and every day. Count down to a wedding, to a death.

Moscow — Ah! The memories that make pain disappear! A warm salon, late afternoon sun, weak. Lace curtains glowing and branches tap, tap, tap on the window, darkly, gently with the wind. Her two infants dead, the woman spent her days with religious mystics and soothsayers... taking after those parasites, the Romanovs...to contact THE OTHER SIDE. (Other side! Other side! Where are you???)

My visit: the tiny biscuits served, that I try to find in this new country (Olga, Olga, always searching for the past, pawing over old rubbish). The woman fawning over my Yuri, calling him Andre. Andre! Andre! My son! My son!

The grief: it drives you mad! What will become of us? Of us all-lull-lull-lull.

Husband left for the mistress. Divorce. "When Ilya comes home, I will tell him you asked after him," she say to me. "I expect that Ilya will be late tonight and I have asked the servants to hold back his food until he arrives.'

He is never coming back. Never, never, never. Never coming back. Meyerhold, Mayakovsky, Leon. Maria. Never. Ever, ever, ever.

After the Revolution, the cocooned salon opened up: ah, the artists! Passing quickly through with somewhere else to go, chasing words. Never stopping — reaching out to a new world, oh world oh world. If you don't change, you go mad. Beverly. Ly-ly-ly.

Torture yourself through your own mind: better than a gun! Wait! An unseen force moves Beverly: where are your seances now, Mrs Watson? The GREAT CHEKHOVIAN HEROINES fight the cage of the mind, but not TRAGIC BEVERLY, the one who does not fight for her own freedom!

Valentia Vassilenko is here....why now? Valentia shapeshifter, more agile. Shapeshifting is admirable. Not trustworthy. Thy-thy-thy.

Beverly and Valentia: one rigid, the other malleable like lead. Have strong spine, but wave your arms and legs like puppet. Zzzzzzzzzzzzz...schree....ch...

Olga could feel the tram sway on its tracks, and it shuddered to her stop and her arms and legs went flying as her consciousness returned from its drowse.

Fly-fly-fly!

Exit left.

BREAK THE GLASS!

She was walking.

Olga thought (perhaps inevitably) of the gulags, where she had walked perhaps thousands of miles, but she was thinking more of the endless, ruthless time with Maria and the others: even Shakespeare had been recited to pass the time. But Chekhov had been popular with everyone. Some had speeches from his plays ready, and favourite passages would be requested over and over. Maria (of course!) had no time for Chekhov. But Olga saw that sometimes Maria's eyes would glaze with pleasure as she listened.

Taking Chekhov to the people — Olga felt the weight of responsibility. Let alone Mayakovsky!

She was on her way to Vera's wedding, and all of these things were jumbling in her mind like a pile of old clothes you could choose from in the gulag.

Suddenly, she realised she felt free. It was an odd feeling, as if a heavy chain had been lifted from her body. Perhaps it was the play, finally being able to put ideas on paper. It felt that she had shouted the whole play from the top of her lungs; the experience of writing (of working, she had to admit, with Valentia) had been compelling, exhausting, exhilarating.

Olga felt she had dressed well for the wedding: a narrow-brimmed, camel-coloured hat with a strong, orange and brown feather stuck in one side, jaunty, as well as an old brown coat she had bought from the Jewish charity shop in Balaclava, fox trimmed, and though the pockets were thin at the edges from wear, that was not particularly visible. Perhaps only to Olga. And isn't that often the way? The things that you are most concerned that others will see, pass them by as if they were clouds, for they are focused on their own realities.

Olga corrected her thoughts immediately. There was Chekhov again, but today he was banished. Today she would enjoy herself without reflection or the judgement of dead playwrights.

Olga had thought at length about the gift she would give to Vera and Joseph. She had decided on linen. Very practical.

She had found the linen — just what she wanted! — at a small Ukrainian delicatessen in North Melbourne that sold kielbasa and salo, but also folk outfits and embroidery from the homeland. It was a cream, linen tablecloth — she avoided those with religious symbols. This one had a muted blue thread worked into geometric patterns and lozenge shapes to herald fertility. Well, the last pattern was hard to avoid in traditional designs, but neither Joseph nor Vera would know what it signified. She had carefully wrapped the tablecloth in embossed gold and white wedding paper.

As she walked along Balaclava Road, Olga began to limp. Her hip ached. In the camp, she had fallen down an embankment when they were out gathering wood. She slid on the snow all the way to the bottom and hit a tree. She had laughed out loud as she fell, at the air rushing against her face, her uncontrolled body and limbs flailing.

At the time, the pain had been bearable. But a few more winters saw arthritis set in, and now, in these hobbling shoes, she felt it sharp and tender. She stopped and tried balancing herself on a narrow fence. She felt a little faint and took herself a few steps more inside the gate so that she could sit on the brick gate support that stretched back along the driveway.

She intended to rest but a minute. A man flew out of the house, the front door flyscreen banging behind him as he walked briskly towards her.

"You're trespassing, lady," he said.

Olga tried to smile. "Sorry," she replied. "I get pain…"

"Yeah, I'll give you pain if you don't git."

He was close to her now and his hands were on his hips.

"Dago, eh?"

Olga had heard this word. She was breathing heavily. "From Russia," she said matter-of-factly.

"Then git going a bit quicker. I lost my son fighting you lot…"

Olga stood up. She had taken off her shoes and held them in her hand. Her fur collar was starting to irritate her neck and her face was still flushed.

"I am sorry to correct you," Olga said, "but we were allies in the war, side by side. We Russians lost millions. Millions. My family…"

"Bloody commo, get out! My son died…"

By this time, Olga had hobbled to the footpath. She did not look back.

Once she reached the Jewish Hall, she sat in the first chair she could find. She looked around quickly but saw no one she knew. A chuppah had been set up at the front of the chairs, white cloth with blue trim strung across the ceremonial area and decorated with red flowers. A rabbi stood talking to Joseph's parents. Olga scanned the crowd again. No Beverly. Vera was standing with some young women and with Joseph's sister, Sarah, who was holding baby Beryl.

Olga spotted Barbara, sitting stiffly at the end of one row, wearing a smart, dark green cloche hat and matching coat. She was alone. Olga walked over and sat next to her.

"My dear Barbara," she started. "So nice to see you."

"Olga," said Barbara, her face pinched. "My mother blames you for all of this."

Olga smiled. "I have been blamed for many things. If I am blamed for keeping a beautiful child with its mother and union of two decent people, perhaps not so bad. You mother not coming? I think this is sad."

"She could never come here." Barbara seemed to relax a little. "Actually, my father wanted to come. He wanted to walk Vera down the aisle. He called her and told her so."

"I am pleased to hear he did. The other ladies?"

"I know Clarissa isn't coming. I think out of some kind of loyalty. I think Betty is coming, and Margaret is coming, too."

Margaret was Betty's daughter who had grown up with Beverly's children and was the same age as Barbara. Margaret had married a man and moved to Ballarat before Olga moved to Box Hill, so Olga did not know her well. Olga had heard from Betty that just quietly things were not going well with the marriage — some talk of loose morals.

"Barbara, do you greet your sister?"

"I said hello and kissed the baby. We haven't talked. She wrote to me to tell me what had happened. I didn't suspect a thing. I thought she had gone to Sydney like Mother said. And then this. Well, I suppose it's a better ending than it could have been. She told me that this man, Joseph, is going to look after Beryl while she works. Imagine what people will say."

"I think his parents and whole circle are very happy with the idea. They are progressive people."

Barbara looked askance. "I don't even know what that means, Olga. But I don't like the look of him, Olga. He has a look about him."

"He is Jewish, Barbara. I'm not sure if you…"

"I hear they don't eat pork."

"This is true for many. Some are not religious, but some Jewish people, they do eat it. I eat it myself."

"My mother told me you are Jewish. But I didn't think…anyway, with everything that's happened in my family…"

"You don't know any Jewish people, Barbara? You probably do. You will find they are very normal people. Family people. Especially the Slodkowicz's."

"I don't expect we will be seeing much of Vera once she's become a Jewess."

"Joseph's family is not religious, Barbara. Con-version not needed," Olga replied, holding back the frustration from her voice.

"Why is there a rabbi, then?"

"Well, people like traditions. I have some partiality myself, but I am atheist. Everyone is ridiculous in their own way."

"Speak for yourself," Barbara shot back quickly.

Before Olga could respond, which she fully intended to do, Betty, Helen and Margaret arrived and sat behind them. Their brief conversation was halted by the swell of an accordion, with violins following, playing a solemn tune. Everyone turned their heads to see Vera walking slowly from the back of the hall and Joseph wheeling himself next to her, followed by his parents. Vera wore a long, ankle-length dress of a dark burgundy velvet and a velvet ribbon tied at the side of her hair. She carried a sheath of white lilies. Olga thought she looked proud of herself. Joseph wore a grey suit that hung limply around his legs, but he was smiling. Joseph's mother was beaming.

They walked past the chairs to the chuppah where the rabbi was waiting. The music stopped and the ceremony started.

Olga could hear Beryl whining a little at the back of the hall. A sole singer stood under the chuppah and sang a slow, ethereal tune as the rabbi placed blue-trimmed linen scarves around the necks of the bride and groom.

Olga recognised the tune from her childhood. Her throat started to vibrate and tears well, whether bitter or sweet, whether from regret or from a feeling of homecoming, she did not know. She let them come. She did not reflect! Her lungs pulsed with tiny convulsions as she re-imagined her own wedding, standing next to Lev, her brother and sister and their parents with them. Never again would they stand together. And yet, that day had been one of the happiest of her life. Everything in front, nothing behind.

Olga looked around her and recognised the features of people long persecuted in Russia and other countries, some of them would be survivors of Hitler's camps and the Soviet gulags. Such a variety: blonde, young women; tall and short men and women, some with red hair. Many would 'pass' for Christian and used it as a survival strategy (alas for Olga, she had always looked *too Jewish)*. These same Christians who always seemed to know who the Jews were — singling them out in the pogroms. So many of the Old Bolsheviks were Jewish. The persecutions quietened after the Revolution as they had longed for; Jewish people were even given citizenship, but the Kremlin Highlander re-discovered its power to divide people again, to set neighbour upon neighbour. She stifled one last sob.

The breaking of glass brought Olga back to the present. She raised her head to see Vera lean down to kiss Joseph on the cheek.

The music took over, and after the shouting and clapping, Vera and Joseph mingled with guests, and a small group of men removed the chairs to the sides of the hall to create a space for dancing. Women started to bring our food from the kitchen. The band played klezmer tunes, joined by another wedding singer, an energetic young woman who exhorted them to start dancing.

Olga, Betty, Helen and Barbara moved to the chairs, and Margaret offered to get drinks. There was a sweet wine on offer, beer, vodka and raspberry tea. Chocolate milk for the children, who were eagerly queuing.

Margaret ferried drinks to them. Betty and Helen looked around with smiles plastered onto their faces. After a few minutes, Olga asked, "Are you enjoying typical Jewish hospitality?"

Betty replied, "yes, thank you, Olga."

Helen said, "We'd never even met any Jewish people. Except you Olga… but you don't observe, so… I got the invite. I thought to myself, 'Vera's getting married, it looks like her mother won't be there. A Jewish wedding. Probably food I've never tried before. Drinking…dancing…'"

"Helen!" Betty interjected.

"So, I said to Ronald, 'you try and stop me!'"

Helen clinked her glass with another imaginary one. "Well, to be a bit more serious, I surprised myself. When I read that Vera had a baby, I said to Ronald, well, a child should be welcomed. You know, Olga, we tried so hard to have a child. And I thought perhaps I should be jealous, but no, I don't have it in me. It's sad Beverly won't see the baby. I know Iris thinks different. She stayed away. And Clarissa, too — she said her husband objected in the end and she had to keep the peace. But things should be different now, shouldn't they? Wasn't the war meant to change things? Don't look at me like that, Betty!"

Betty replied quietly, "well I'm here, aren't I?"

Helen whispered, "after I twisted your arm. Margaret and Vera were good friends as kids. They went to school together. You had her in your kitchen every day after school. She's not a different person now she's had a baby and married a Jew. I'm sorry, Betty. But she's not. She's still the same girl we all thought would do something with her life. And I reckon she will. Can I have another drink, Margaret? Maybe a vodka this time?"

Barbara was sitting with her legs firmly crossed. She was wondering how long she should stay. How long would be polite? Perhaps when someone else left, she would take her cue. She hadn't congratulated Vera yet. She knew she should. But she was finding it difficult.

"You were married, Olga?" she said by way of making conversation.

Ah Lev! thought Olga. Always interrupting my train of thought.

"My husband and I, Lev, we were…more or less divorced. I cannot say it was unhappy marriage. But he went off with a painter. First a writer, then a painter."

"Oh, I see," said Barbara. "I'm sorry to hear…well, that your marriage failed."

Olga let out a loud guffaw and drew the attention momentarily of Betty and Helen who were deep in conversation.

"I'm not so sure what might be considered failure. We were drawn together by politics, Barbara. We made common cause. There is no better way! But come the Revolution, everything was upside down, and you could change partners as quickly as you changed coats. And we did! Oh, it was glorious. But we were ahead of our time. We had not built the necessary means for women to look after themselves and their children, so it became impossible. Nothing was, how you say, in synchronicity? What you ask about? My husband? He was executed, Barbara."

Barbara's face had blanched considerably. "I don't know what to say. It must have been hard."

"Yes. My sons, also. When they shoot me along with a line of other people, it was not fatal and I hid underneath other dead bodies until night when guards left and I could escape."

Barbara sat and was quiet.

When Olga heard that her children had been killed, her brain refused to function. She found it impossible to get out of bed, and had to be pulled out, cajoled, by the other women in the camp (though bedbugs also helped). Maria had looked on with suspicion. Olga felt that Maria was contemptuous of her sorrow, that a comrade like Olga would have such ties that would weaken her strength. Maria had no children. She was as unbending as the steel rod the guards used to beat the prisoners on a whim, or for stealing food or shirking the work.

Barbara recovered. "Communists, were they?"

Olga sighed. "Yes," she said. "As was I."

"Well, I suppose I had better go over and see Vera," said Barbara quickly and as she rose, her sister caught her eye and walked over. Vera kissed Barbara on the cheek.

"Thank you for coming. It means a lot to me, Bub."

"Well. You came to mine," was all Barbara could think of to say. She had been at a loss for words all day. She was her own person, and even though she was bubbly on the outside, (everyone would say so), she didn't give her thoughts away easily, (she had heard her mother say that). Now she had her own children, people didn't seem to want to know what she thought anyway.

"The baby is beautiful, Vera. A real pet. Can I hold her?"

Vera nodded and walked over to Sarah to fetch Beryl. The dancing was in full swing, and as Vera wended her way through the dancers, they stopped to pat Beryl on the back of the head, or gently pull at her little cheeks to coax a smile.

"There you go."

They were interrupted by Betty singing loudly to her sister-in-law, "sparkle-arkle-arkling, tingle-ingl-ingling, make mine Marchants please!"

Barbara and Vera looked on as Helen had to steady Betty on her chair.

"Oh, she has your eyes. And Dad's chin. Are you breastfeeding?"

"I did. But not now. I'm working three days a week, so it's not practical."

"Oh, that's a shame, Vera. It's such a wonderful time to spend with them…"

Vera looked bemused. "I'm lucky to be spending any time with her at all, Bub. Don't you remember? Mother tried to have her adopted?"

Barbara's face coloured.

"I wasn't talking about that…"

"No. It hasn't been the easiest of times for me. I am really sad about not getting any support from Mother. It's been just the opposite!"

"Well, you distanced yourself from us, Vera. At university. That life."

"Yes, I made my own bed. That's what Mother said."

Vera started to shake her head and took Beryl back.

"Don't shake your noddle at me, Vera! I won't have it."

"I'd rather have your help, Bub. Not your judgement."

Barbara wondered why she had stayed. She imagined herself on the tram, heading for home.

"It's hard, between you and Mother…"

The two women fell into a long conversation about whether they could see each other, whether their children could meet; if their mother would ever come around. Vera told Barbara about the play and the sets she had designed.

The look on Barbara's face was one of disguised terror as Vera explained the play and finally, the topsy-turvy world and the nudity.

"Vera, I wouldn't be able to hold my head up. I wouldn't be able to talk to you again."

"Well, you don't talk to me now."

"Well, I won't talk to you even more after that."

They laughed a little, and Vera decided to go in harder.

"What kind of society is it that tears mothers away from their babies and justifies it by saying it's best for the children? That's what I call a topsy-turvy world!"

Barbara wasn't biting. In her mind, she was already alighting the tram and walking in the moonlight towards her home.

THE STAGE IS SET

My soul is like a wonderful piano that is locked and the key has been lost.
> — Anton Chekhov, *The Three Sisters.*

Olga woke with the magpies' call.

She ignored her arthritis. She ignored the facial tic, which had developed again, this time because of the stress of the production. The tic had not been part of her physical life since the camps. She ignored the churning of her stomach as she alternately weighed the possibility that the stage props would seize because the young man with the oil can had forgotten certain spots, or that they might not hold the weight of the actors, or that someone might fall off the stage with an over-exuberant leap. She and Valentia Vassilenko had drilled the actors ruthlessly to make sure they understood the dimensions of the stage and didn't get carried away.

Getting *carried away* was largely what the play was about — but Olga worried even so. How do you control chaos once the mechanism is set? She, of all people, knew you could not.

Olga was eating toast for lunch, and she followed it with some sweet, warm tea to ease it down her dry throat. Gwen was coming to fetch her at four o'clock. What to do till then, to occupy her mind so that it did not descend into a kind of madness?

One of the actors had helpfully typewritten the script and used a machine to copy it for everyone. Olga had taken a copy and added her own notes and directions. She poured herself some more tea and, sitting in her fur-collared coat, she read through it. She liked this coat, the one she had bought for Vera's wedding. She had taken to wearing it around the house, suiting herself, letting go a little. Perhaps she was under Valentia Vassilenko's influence. If she wanted to lie in bed all day reading a book, she did. She would answer the door in her nightdress and fur-collared coat, startling the postman when he delivered a small package. On that occasion, she had forgotten the buttons, and her breasts were hanging forward in a most unruly manner, but what did she care if a postman saw the breasts of an old lady, that had been poked out for two children or caressed by lovers?

She made more notes as she made her way through the script. Actually, Olga was quite disappointed with the product. She and Valentia had set out to do something new. They had tussled, like tumbling acrobats. But finally, they had produced a more conventional play, Olga thought. Which force had more sway, Chekhov or Mayakovsky?

As Olga went through the script, she realised they had made a fundamental error. She had given in to Valentia, who had argued that the form needed at least to be accessible to the audience, if the content was not. But Valentia had forgotten the exuberance of the crowds that had cheered to the antics of Kharms and his declarations and funny songs and...

Meyerhold's 'unleashed humanity': that's what he called the people with no knowledge of plays except religious ones (knowledge that Meyerhold used to advantage); those who instead ended their days drunk with the exhaustion of toil in homes, factories or fields. Those who had never been inside one of the big Moscow or Petersburg theatres for lack of suitable clothing or the price of a ticket. Those were exactly the people Meyerhold wanted to come to his plays.

If Olga had not been convinced of the need to upend the world before she saw those productions, they, with their spontaneous glee and liquid wailing when the hero died or was disgraced, those people were the reason for the chaos, the cause of upheaval. She was never more convinced of her purpose than when she saw them in all their dirt and starvation and squalor, laughing and cheering.

Valentia had proposed that they stick to the conventional format, several acts leading to a conclusion. Olga favoured something more akin to a two-ring circus, with the Clean and Unclean vying for superiority through slapstick acts like a Buster Keaton or Charlie Chaplin. Valentia was not in favour of slapstick as much, because it made fun of *both* the Clean and the Unclean. But surely that was the point! Olga felt that Valentia had unleashed something inside her, something she had hidden behind her administrator's mask for many years: her own creativity.

But she had given in on the structure, and she felt Meyerhold shaking his head behind her as she read the script. He would have wanted her to go further than even he did, even further than Mayakovsky! She did not know if she dreamt his presence or had truly perceived it, because she fell asleep and was only woken by the sound of Gwen knocking at her door.

As they drove into the city, Gwen recounted all of her preparations for door staff and volunteers to hand out the play's program and manage the seating. She was excited.

"Oh, Olga, I can't believe we are seeing some of the best from the Soviet. And you, Olga! You are like a gift!"

Olga puffed her chest a little.

"Oh, I can't wait to sit down with you and talk about the Revolution. And Comrade Lenin — you knew him. Actually knew him. And his wife. She sounds like the most amazing woman."

"Yes. I can talk to you one day. But what happens here, Gwen, that is of most immediate interest. The unions. The Catholic infiltrators. Mr Pig Iron, the Prime Minister."

"Oh, Olga, you're a wag. That's what he's called by everyone who can see through him."

Olga was not looking forward to the day when she might be asked to sit down and tell these comrades about her life. They will ask the same question: was Stalin the sole architect of the deaths of so many? If not, who takes the blame? You and the other Old Bolsheviks, Olga? Why didn't your brother challenge Stalin when he had the chance? Why did your husband recant? Who was to blame?

Always the same questions. If she lived for a hundred years, she would be asked perhaps a thousand more times. She had rehearsed her answers and used them like handkerchiefs. Her usual way was to tell a well-worn anecdote about an interaction with Lenin or Stalin, disposable stories usually forgotten by the hearer as soon as they walked away. And that's what passes for history!

She could be more forthright, but mostly people didn't want to know what she really had to say. That *they* want to erase the real revolutionaries, our achievements, from history. We lost. But the vanquished never stop calling out for justice. *They* keep interrupting us, constantly, inconveniently. That is the beauty of the past! It is never silent.

She had made a confession to herself of sorts, many years ago. She was not an intellectual. Not in the same way as Lenin, her brother or Kollontai or Krupskaya. Neither was Lev, her husband, an intellectual. Lev had chosen sides badly, several times, and the recanting was worse than useless.

All of them were very smart. But none of them were able to solve the riddle: how do you build a worker's state, defend and dismantle it all at once? All Olga had was action, bustling, incessant action. She was never still, not when there was something to be done. What is to be done? Lenin had asked, and she would have replied, *I'll show you.*

The sun is in the sky, the priest is in his counting house and the Tsar is far away. Time to make mischief!

"Are you nervous, Olga? You shouldn't be," Gwen said to break the silence when they were in the car. She had worried that Olga was too frail for the task she had set her. But, after seeing the rehearsals, she had to admit that the production was what they had hoped for: a real slice of Art. Revolutionary Moscow. Something to inspire the people and to tempt the press: we are still here!

Gwen had won the battle to move away from Socialist Realism. She had reminded the executive of the rich history of revolutionary art, enough ideas to flood a gorge. Some of the artists had visited Melbourne in the late twenties, just when she was becoming involved with the Party. They had talked of artists' colonies taking over sprawling aristocratic mansions and hotels and of the support provided to develop their ideas. Stories of the Smithy, the Serapions, the Futurists, the Symbolists, graffiti writers, actors. Another world, just glimpsed like a far, twinkling light.

Olga's reply was considered. "Not as nervous as I was when Lev was arrested. I knew I was next; I just didn't know when. At least this has the executioner's certainty."

Gwen laughed. "Oh, Olga, you are so dark."

Olga smiled, too. But she had meant what she said. She liked that about Gwen: her ability to keep her eye on the best when you were in the middle of the worst. Gwen would certainly be at home in Russia.

Gwen parked the car in an unused lot close to the city and they caught a tram the short distance to the theatre. She had leaflets for the play in her bag, which she methodically handed out to every passenger — young people out for a night on the town, older couples going to show and supper clubs, a young woman in need of some help who turned away when Gwen approached her — she had a look of fear on her face.

Gwen returned to sit next to Olga. "We expect less than a full house, I might as well tell you. Good sales, but be good to get a few more."

As they neared the theatre, Olga could see a modest queue of people outside the theatre. A few men were smoking on the footpath, their smoke trails disappearing above them into the cooling night air. They could see that Vera was waiting for them just outside the door.

"Tonight we make history, Olga," Gwen exclaimed, clapping her gloved hands in front of her.

Olga sighed. "Tonight we make something that can't be erased," she said, wanting to sound optimistic.

They stood next to Vera now, and she kissed Gwen and Olga on both of their cheeks, saying, "well, there is nothing more we can do, darlings. It is now up to the actors!"

Olga watched the seats fill, the ushers making sure that the first rows were occupied in accordance with Gwen's instructions. She saw that there were a few workers amongst the crowd. From their rough hands and weathered faces, she thought they were probably the building union workers. There were quite a few old people, perhaps older even than Olga. The stalwarts. An ancient man in a very worn suit, stooped and unshaven, his short collar grubby and fraying. He sat down and took out a filled pipe and lit up. He looked like he knew a lot of discarded stories, Olga thought.

Olga spotted Betty, Helen and Iris in the front rows, but there were too many people between them, milling, finding seats, for Olga to greet them. They waved and she waved back and pretended to kiss both cheeks in the European way.

Joseph had arrived, as Vera warned he would. Olga was surprised to see Pawel and some of his Bundist friends with him. Vera told Olga she had persuaded them to come. Vera took a shocked Olga aside and told her she would explain everything, that it had not been an easy time for her. Olga noticed that some of her comrades — Gregor, Ron and others — also looked askance at the Bundists, whom they clearly recognised.

Nevertheless, Olga greeted Pawel warmly. She had seen him at Vera's wedding. She was introduced to the other two men and noticed all were smartly dressed.

"This is Mr Terry Seville and Mr Jacob Adamson."

Olga thought the first man's name was an obvious pseudonym. He was tall and thin, with a long pale face, sandy hair and green eyes. The two men looked uncomfortable.

"Olga here wrote the play," Pawel said. "There's a lot we don't know about you…"

Olga turned sharply and spoke to Joseph. "You should be very proud of your wife, Joseph. Her creativity should be allowed to flourish."

Olga sometimes wondered to herself why she held out so much hope for Vera, why she seemed to invest so much in Vera's success, her transcendence. Continue, continue, continue. When she thought of Vera, this was the word that sprang to mind.

Joseph replied, "I will do what I can, Olga. Tell me, do you speak Yiddish?"

"No, my family…we were not taught…in that way. You understand?"

"Would you like to learn? I am teaching it to small groups. Keeping *our* culture alive."

"Thank you, Joseph. I will think about it. Now, I will go. I hope you enjoy the play."

"I hear you are quite the provocateurs, you and Mrs Vassilenko."

Olga smiled and took her leave. Valentia had not yet arrived. Olga had some final words to impart to the company and something to give them. This time she would take advantage of Valentia Vassilenko's absence.

ANTON CHEKHOV'S MYSTERY BOUFFE

The time is at hand, an avalanche is moving down upon us, a mighty clearing storm which is coming, is already near and will soon blow the laziness, the indifference, the distaste for work, the rotten boredom out...I'll work, and in another twenty-five or thirty years everyone will have to work. Everyone!
— Anton Chekhov, The Three Sisters.

"Just sit there quietly", they say to you
"either straight or sidewise,
and look at a slice of other folks' lives."
You look — and what do you see?
Uncle Vanya
and Aunty Manya
parked on a sofa as they chatter.
But we don't care
about uncles and aunts:
you can find them at home — or anywhere!
We, too, will show you life that's real — very!
But life transformed by the theatre into a spectacle most extraordinary!
— Vladimir Mayakovsky, *Mystery Bouffe.*

THE CURTAINS PART. CYMBALS CLASH.

The STAGE is set for:

Anton Chekhov's Mystery Bouffe: a play written by Olga Kameneva and Valentia Vassilenko

The audience is hushed. The stage is set. The stage backdrop is painted with a scene of a looming storm, grey clouds and black lightning bolts and high winds are sketched across. Double-storey trestles are lined up in front, painted bright red. A vaulting horse and a small barrel topped by a wooden pivot stand in front. A huge, cardboard tree sits in a 24-gallon drum painted with symbols. A large vase of enormous multi-coloured cardboard flowers is at the other end of the stage. A cardboard igloo is situated on the left front of the stage.

ACT 1

A MAN ENTERS the stage from the left. It is the Revolutionary Playwright himself, holding a proclamation. There is a sign around his neck that reads MAYAKOVSKY.

MAYAKOVSKY
In the future, all persons performing, presenting, reading or publishing this play should change the content making it contemporary, immediate, up to the minute.
Everything anew!
One thing's for certain: you'll never be bored!

MAYAKOVSKY exits stage right.

ENTER the actors, half in drab, uniform garb — men and women dressed in long peasant smocks over wide trousers. These are THE UNCLEAN. The other actors are THE CLEAN — a man in a long Edwardian dress, his beard long enough to cover the high lace collar; a woman dressed as a priest; another woman, big busted, wearing a papier mâché mask in the likeness of the Prime Minister, Mr Pig Iron Bob; an industrialist; a woman in a crinoline wearing a huge wig in the style of Marie Antoinette; a man and a woman, both wearing glasses and male Edwardian dress.

The actors all stand to attention as THE THREE SISTERS walk onto the stage, dressed in dark velvet crinolines with their hair in tight buns on top of their heads.

ALL ACTORS
TUM TUM DIDLEE DEE!

THE THREE SISTERS *(in unison)*
Unhappy sisters are we
Toiling at embroidery

gossip and childminding are our trades
and supervising the maids...
Lazy, deceitful maids!
Can we ever be free?
Ah, the mystery!

A man in the audience sprang up from his seat and yelled and waved,
"go for it, Bridie!"

*The actors line up on either side of the stage. The THREE
SISTERS are in the middle. THE CLEAN hold teacups and
talk to each other, backs to the UNCLEAN. The UNCLEAN
are performing circus tricks: cartwheels, juggling, falling
about. The UNCLEAN turn their attention to the CLEAN.*

*The CLEAN throw some large pieces of paper with pound
symbols painted on them at the UNCLEAN. The UNCLEAN
pretend to eat the paper, chewing and spitting it onto the
stage. They cavort across the stage, spluttering as they
go.*

*The THREE SISTERS look from one side to the other, back
and forth, back and forth, back and forth.*

The audience laughed and pointed at the stage.

PIG IRON BOB
Gentlemen, since we are all so immaculate
Is it fitting that we should work and sweat?
Let's make the Unclean work for us.

PRIEST
I'm all for that!
But what can I do?
I'm delicate — and each one of them has the strength of
two!

PIG IRON BOB
Oh, there'll be no fighting, God forbid!

We'll have no mayhem.
But while they're gobbling up their meal
We'll cook up a deal — to betray them.

The CLEAN cup their ears to the UNCLEAN and murmur amongst themselves. One of the UNCLEAN starts to cut off long braids with scissors. He/she throws them at the CLEAN on the other side of the stage. One of the UNCLEAN takes off his/her trousers and long smock revealing a fitted dress underneath. He/she rips off a fake beard. THE UNCLEAN start to murmur.

THE UNCLEAN

Open up the cellars
Today the rabble will have fun!

Some of the UNCLEAN take off their trousers and smocks and long-haired wigs, revealing short hair underneath. They are wearing tight-fitting leggings and short tunics.

As the Unclean cavorted on stage — pivoting on the barrel, jumping the vaulting horse, carrying each other in pretend horse races — the audience murmured, laughed, shouted, shook their fists at the stage.

The CLEAN and the UNCLEAN tussle, they occupy the highest point of the trestles, chasing each other, almost falling, stopping short of the precipice.

A woman in the audience jumped up from her seat and let out a loud cry amidst the cacophony, then said, "O-OHHHHH! Do be careful, Neville!"

THE THREE SISTERS run about the stage making imploring gestures.

THE THREE SISTERS (in unison)

Stop! Stop! You are fouling our carpets! You are marking our floors with your grubby feet!

Another of the UNCLEAN with a long beard and bushy, black eyebrows throws off the brown smock, revealing women's underclothes. She is holding a sign, which says BEHOLD THE FLOOD.

The audience gasped and hooted as water was flung from buckets at the actors. A man ran for the back of the theatre.

UNCLEAN ACTOR
The flood has arrived. The Unclean will sweep away the Clean. Afterwards, who will be able to tell them apart?

Solemnly, the actor walks across the front of the stage, and flips the sign. On the other side, there is a picture of a house on fire.

THE THREE SISTERS (in unison)
FIRE! FIRE! FIRE!
Our house is on fire!
Where are our diamonds?
Where our attire?
Gone is our wealth
And all we earned by our stealth!

An actor dressed in fur skins and a fur hat enters the stage.

KALLIK (INUIT PERSON)
I am Kallik!
Sisters, I will tell you your fate
As you told me my own
Chained at the foot of the Tsar's throne.
The flood subsides, and everything has changed
The topsy-turvy world has arrived
There are those who want retribution
To make a contribution
Overturn institutions
To feed themselves from the hoarded food of the rich
And cover the churches with pitch.

The CLEAN retreat to a corner of the stage.

KALLIK
Who is here to part the seas?

THE UNCLEAN
We are! We are!

The UNCLEAN play-attack the CLEAN and the CLEAN retreat again, then push forward.

CLEAN ACTOR
I'm going to register complaints about all of you! I'm going to set the spies on you. You émigrés — I'm going to deny your citizenship. Then I'm going to deport you.

The people in the audience shouted, "Boo! Boo!"

After more tussling, the CLEAN are hounded from the stage, fighting each other as they go. The priest is the last to leave, brandishing his cross as if to exorcise the UNCLEAN. THE THREE SISTERS look on in horror.

Another actor stomps onto stage. He wears an oversized hat, corks dangling, and shorts tied up with a rope.

A roar went up from the people in the audience.

THE AUSTRALIAN
A fine lot, I say.
No better than a bunch of thugs!
There are no empires left today,
Yet still they punch each other's mugs!

The curtain closed. The audience began to chatter. Olga was seated in the front row with Valentia, who arrived late. Behind them, she heard a man say, "This is bloody unbelievable! Unbelievable I tell you!"

ACT 2

The curtain opens again. The UNCLEAN gather at the tree, and the vase of flowers has now been placed next to it. This is a GARDEN. KALLIK stands in front of the tree with hands folded in front.

One of the UNCLEAN holds up a painting of a black square. She/he steps forward.

UNCLEAN ACTOR

The shape and the colour of the box have changed. We cannot be forced back into it.

THE THREE SISTERS *(in unison)*

Where are our maids?
How will we live?
Our hopes for fulfilment foiled
We have such accomplishments to give!
We who toiled with you...
We lift our fingers, too!

UNCLEAN

The sisters are twisting!
Their fog is lifting!
Blow it away with your voices!
Join us! Join us!

Shouting, singing, whistling, clapping and stomping erupted from the audience.

THE THREE SISTERS look on in horror. KALLIK approaches them and tries to take their hands, but they recoil. The UNCLEAN re-enter stage left and move to centre stage. The CLEAN re-enter stage right. They stand together, pretending to murmur.

THE UNCLEAN AND KALLIK

We remember the dead. We remember the native peoples slaughtered like seals, their land usurped. The rich man stands on a bloody stage. Empires fall, and when they do, they make sure you pay the price.

THE THREE SISTERS rush over to the UNCLEAN and KALLIK.

THE UNCLEAN
Do we know you?

Two of the sisters stay with the UNCLEAN. One of the sisters walks to the other side of the stage and stands with the CLEAN.

THE TWO SISTERS
Our illusions are stripped away
Now we shall join the fray!

A flurry of confetti drifts down onto the actors from above, and KALLIK takes a bucket from the igloo. It is filled with confetti, which he throws at the actors.

THE ACTORS
Now the snow! The snow has come at last!

One of the UNCLEAN picks up a broom and beings sweeping the confetti off the stage, pretending to sweep away the other actors who run about on the stage.

THE UNCLEAN
We sought no aid from Him on high
Nor did the Devil lend a hand
The workers went into the fray,
And seized the power in the land.
We've made the world one great Commune!
It's ringed round by the working class
Just try to snatch it back again
From our determined grasp!

UNCLEAN ACTOR WITH BROOM
History is a broom.
Sweeping together

— wars, events, words, books, speeches, people, men, women, babies, children, paintings, plays, poems, theatres, bookshops, train stations, factories, houses, igloos, roads, bridges, workers' councils, parliaments — It piles everything into the corner
— for sorting later.

SUDDENLY, all the actors tore off their clothes. They stood naked before the audience. The actors were given buckets of water and they began to fling water towards the audience, bucket after bucket. Some ran into the audience throwing water.

The back doors of the hall were flung wide open, and cold wind started to whistle through. The audience stood up, some scrambled for the entrance, others stood on the sidelines. More clapped. Some stomped. Laughter erupted from those dripping with water.

Olga heard cries from the audience: do it again! Do it again!", and "that'll show the wowsers!"

The actors re-assembled on the stage, hair dripping and hastily dressed. Volunteers handed out song sheets to the audience.

Gwen Shoebridge appeared on stage and shouted, "three cheers for the New Theatre, three cheers for the actors! Three cheers for our playwrights, our set builders and our volunteers! Three cheers for the working class!"

The audience deafened with their shouts and yells and ya-hoos, Gwen put her fingers to her lips to signal quiet. Then everyone sang from the song sheets:

TA-RA-RA-BOOM-DE-YAY
I had a job once threshin' wheat, worked sixteen hours with hands and feet.
And when the moon was shining bright, they kept me working all the night.
One moonlight night I hate to tell, I 'accidentally' slipped and fell.
Ta-ra-ra-boom-de-ay!

That stingy rube said, 'Well!
A thousand gone to hell.'

But I did sleep that night,
I needed it all right.
Next day that stingy rube did say, 'I'll bring my eggs to town;
You grease my wagon up, and don't forget to screw the nut.'
I greased his wagon all right, but I plumb forgot to screw that nut,
And when he started on that trip, the wheel slipped off and broke his hip.

Ta-ra-ra-boom-de-ay!
It made a noise that way,
That rube was sure a sight,
And mad enough to fight.
Ta-ra-ra-boom-de-ay!

But still that rube was pretty wise. These things did open up his eyes.
He said, 'There must be something wrong; I think I work my men too long.'
He cut the hours and raised the pay, gave them ham and eggs every day,
Now he gets his men from union hall and has no "accidents" at all.
Ta-ra-ra-boom-de-ay!
Ta-ra-ra-boom-de-ay!

More volunteers rushed through the aisles scattering confetti made of cut-up poetry. Olga waited at the door and many people congratulated her as they left the hall. One of the building workers shook her hand and said "Comrade, I'm spent! And I don't even think I'll mind getting up at sparrows tomorrow — that's if I can sleep at all!"

AFTER THE FLOOD

ASIO file: The Melbourne New Theatre, 1949-

Report dated 19 September 1954.
Report by Agent ████████████

THE TOPIC:
A fundraising supper after the production of Anton Chekhov's Mystery Boufe (see separate note on the play and press coverage thereof).

THE INFORMATION:
About a hundred people gathered for the play. Price given as two shillings for families and one for single people, fivepence for the unemployed or free for the destitute. About forty of these people attended the supper.

In attendance at the fundraising supper:
Writers:
Judah WATEN
Brian FITZPATRICK
John MORRISON
Oriel GRAY
Kevin TEMPLEMAN (formerly known as Kelvin TELEMANN, German émigré active in metalworker's union)

CPA executive members:
Gregor KRACHSTEIN (also a member of the Realist Film Association, a known Communist front organisation and of the New Theatre Committee)
Gwen SHOEBRIDGE (also a member of the Communist front organisation, the Union of Australian Women and of the New Theatre Committee)

Bruce MILES (also a member of the Broadmeadows Ford Factory Fishing Club, a known Communist front organisation)

Chandler MYER

Solomon HANDLER

"Chiller" WILLIAMS, a well-known waterside agitator.

James SHOEBRIDGE, CPA member

Hetty SHOEBRIDGE, sister of James and CPA member

New Theatre Committee members:
Lilia MONK, German Jewish émigré and CPA member

Bob MUNRO, CPA member

Italian Communists who were involved in the Bonegilla riots in 1952:
Giuseppe SCOLINO (source)

Augusto CARMINI (source)

Other Emigrés
Olga KAMENEVA

Valentia VASSILENKO (source)

Members of the building unions (one a man called Noel); a German man (strong accent, bearded) named Fritz.

Three lovely women from Box Hill, Betty, Iris and Helen who told me they were there on a friend's invitation. (We had a shandy together and there was no suggestion these ladies are Communists, although I did see them kiss Olga KAMENEVA and throw their arms around her).

Various other attendees unknown to this agent, actors from the play, not identified by my sources (NOTE: check separate record from Agent ████████ of car number plates parked outside the venue).

There was a lot of talk about the nudity. Most of the people present seemed to approve. After a while, Gwen SHOEBRIDGE gave a short speech thanking the authors Olga KAMENEVA and Valentia VASSILENKO and said the play and the attendance was proof that The New~~s~~ Theatre was still a bold experiment. It showed just how far we have come ~~to~~ as a society. KAMENEVA said she was pleased to have contributed to class conscienceness. She said the nudity was a necessary part of the production, to show solidarity between all peoples, and thanks them for their fourbearance.

I overheard Judah WATEN talking to Brian FITZPATRICK, complaining about his writing grant and he said the Prime Minister had stopped it. The writers in general discussed the difficulty they have publishing their work, which they called 'a form of censorship the proletariatins know nothing of'. Kevin TEMPLEMAN said he was outraged.

SHOEBRIDGE asked Giuseppe CARMINI what was he doing these days and he said he had recently qualified but was finding it difficult to gain work because he had been blacklisted by the yellow union because of his Communist credentials. SHOEBRIDGE commented that it was a pity and she would try to find him something herself and CARMINI commented she was a good stick.

Bruce MILES asked Oriel GRAY why she left the CPA and she replied that she had become disillusioned with the Soviet pact with Hitler, and that had led her to question the unwavering allegiance the CPA had to every line that came from the Russians. Then she said the Communists had led the miners badly. WATEN overheard GRAY and responded that we are all friends of the Soviet Union here and added that there is still hope for its future, now the iron heel of

Stalin's purges is off the throat of the Russian people, and especially the Jewish people.

Mrs KAMENEVA butted in and said she had warned comrades about the pact herself, and that it would lead to no good end. She talked about her brother, Leon, and how he had tried to warn everyone about Stalin.

WATEN was talking to the other writers about The Jewish Bund (make note on Melbourne Bund file that several of their members attended the play). WATEN said he himself was happy to talk to them and tell them where they went wrong with their support of the Labor Party. Brian FITZPATRICK said I was taken in myself by Socialism Without Doctrine (NOTE: my source told me this is the name of a book about Australia and New Zealand Labor parties) for a time, but the Labor Party failed with that disaster with the banks, don't they understand?

WATEN thanked FITZPATRICK for his advocate the cause of Jewish refugees. He became angry at the Bund who he said told Jewish people that the Labor Party was the best hope they had for an improvment in their standing in Australia. Then WATEN laughed and said that the Bund needed to take a clearer stand against capital bloodsuckers and warmongers and piggy bob, but how difficult that must be when your community leaders are capitalists themselves?

Gregor KRACHSTEIN said he had talked to Pawel Jankowski himself before the play. He said Jankowski became defensive and said that all of the Bund's members supported progress, not only for Jewish people but for all working people. KRACHSTEIN said this sounded like something Pig Iron Bob would say, and that he asked, by working people, do you mean the working class? Jankowski had laughed and called KRACHSTEIN a trickster, a real Herschele. (Source told me how to spll this).

I next stood near the building workers who had drunk their fair share of beer. They were laughing and the tallest one (ginger hair, blue eyes) was remarking that it was a rum thing, and it had taken him a while to work out that the men were dressed as woman and the women dressed as men and what possible reason would there be except to make as all laugh at how silly everyone looked?

The building worker identified by the others as NOEL said he didn't think it would be too many years before the differences between men and women disappeared altogether — isn't that the logical outcome of revolution? You mean we'll lose our tackle? asked another. No, he said, just look at what women have achieved in the Soviet: free kitchens and creches and have you seen those films about the women fighters and the tractor drivers? Blood oath, I bet they have strong hips, if you get my drift. One of the others asked if they thought the play should tour through the building sites, and they agreed it should, though what about the nudity? They couldn't agree on that. But the song at the end definitely should be sung.

I turned my attention to the two Iti Communists, SCOLINO and CARMINI. They were talking to KAMENEVA. They proceeded to tell her that they were mistreated when they arrived in the camps from Italy after the war. They said after some roughhouse treatment by the guards and four men hanging themselves in despair, they protested and were surrounded by armoured cars and troops ready to shoot.

KAMENEVA asked where that was, and SCOLINO replied it was at Bonegilla, at which point KAMENEVA gasped loudly and said that's the place I stayed when I came to Australia. SCOLINO laughed and said half the people in this room were from there!

CARMINI said we were promised work and it never came, we were in a prison not a hostel, as we told. The promised land, hallelujah! Don't be alarmed, Olga, there will be spies here amongst us tonight! They have followed Giuseppe and me for years, since the camps. They have stopped us working, blacklisted us, told us our passports are being taken away. Some of us deported. And if there is another bloody war, who knows, perhaps they will shoot us!

Don't worry, said KAMENEVA, I've handled my fair share of spies. They won't come after me again (cross-reference to KAMENEVA file).

SCOLINO laughed and said, they are always with us, like blowflies they keep on multiplying around the fresh meat. Our kids, the Eureka League ones, they were handing out leaflets about the cane cutters and the terrible conditions, and my cousin was one of them and they arrested him for offensive behavior and threatened to take his citizenship away. And when we protested that they let off the Nazis and the mussos (Source: followers of Mussolini) — they ignored us, even our lawyers' letters, even though the Nazis deface our houses and buildings.

Valentia VASSILENKO had joined the group and added, yes, they were present at my lecture on Russian folk music. I know their kind. I went up to one after the lecture and kissed him three times on the cheek. She laughed.

VASSILENKO turned her attention to KAMENEVA and kissed her on both cheeks and said, Oh those young men! How delicious they looked with their naked chests. If I were any younger...so. Olga, you surprised me with your song!

Not my song said KAMENEVA, it is revolutionary worker's song from America.

And not my song either, said VASSILENKO — the one I wrote for the production?

KAMENEVA nodded her head brusquely. No, not your song Valentia. This one was right one for the occasion, she said. And to make the worker's feel more close to us.

(Agent's note: there may be some tension between these two women we can exploit later).

KAMENEVA and VASSILENKO moved to one side and I did not hear the rest of their conversation.

I excused myself from remaining conversers and when no one was observing me, I exited the building at approximately 10.18 pm.

DA-DA!

Olga rose early.

She had been unable to get a reasonable sleep. Tossing about, her limbs had moved in restless synchronicity with her overstimulated mind. That song, *"Ta ra ra boom de yay"*, stuck in her head, over and over…the supper, the talk with the writers…ta-ra-ra boom… Then she had an idea. She slowed the melody to a calm, snail pace, like a Russian dirge. Perhaps that was when she fell asleep.

The day was well awake, milk at the front door, post delivered. She filled the stray cats' saucer. The light bore down like a thousand suns on her sleep-deprived eyes. Too much brandy! She made tea in her dressing gown.

Gwen had said there would possibly be a review of the play. She thought she recognised a critic in the audience. Olga anticipated the congratulations — that was audacious, wonderful, I could have watched it over and over it's the best thing the New Theatre HAS EVER PRODUCED! She could have been back in Moscow in the salons, late-night meetings of the artists with pamphlets drawn as if they were weapons, the deadly furious discussions.

Of course, there would be a write-up in *The Tribune*. Gregor had taken on this task. Then there was the second performance to get through, which was to be the following Saturday night. By then the reviews would be out. And they would be the talk of the building sites.

"We will get noticed," Gwen had said, "come hell or high water."

Today, Olga busied herself with chores she had neglected, remembering the conversations of the night before. The writers had known who she was — Gregor must have told them. The admiration for Lunacharsky, well, that was expected. She tolerated it. She wanted to settle in with Judah Waten and John Morrison. The playwright, Oriel, whom she had wanted to befriend, had gone home early. But Waten and Morrison proved good company. The talk soon turned to Socialist Realism. What did Olga think?

"Did you see my play?"

They laughed and Olga deflected their question. "If you are artist, you start somewhere and you finish somewhere else you don't expect."

Morrison had told his own stories, which Olga was eager to hear. "The only short story worth writing, I never got to write because the bloke said he didn't want it written. Too ashamed. He was a wharfie, but he cried when he told me about the Depression, on the road with the drovers having to kill and boil up the newborn lambs and feed them to the dogs. He knew the lambs didn't have a chance, but he was thinking of his own children who he'd had to leave in an orphanage, which he'd told me about earlier. He yearned for a different world, but he cried because he was stuck in this one."

Morrison had tapped his nose and sniffed. "Cheer me up with a story about Comrade Mayakovsky."

Olga had pulled out one of her handkerchiefs. "Our Maya went to the USA, America. He found it very drab. It troubled him. 'America is waging war against its own people, the workers,' he said, 'not land of free at all'.

"I went to Maya's flat to hear his American poems, so packed with people. Some perched on the windowsills, in the hallway. Coats, hats piled in the doorway high to the roof. Lunacharsky was there. He was opportunist, but he let the futurists decorate Moscow's streets, painting the market stalls with the gigantic flowers. I digress.

"Maya read his three poems and I cannot say there was silence throughout. Many people interjected, shouting condemnations of America, singing Soviet songs. Quiet! Quiet! Then another song. It took three hours. Maya beamed from ear to ear, like that man Lewis Carroll's cat. He had infinite patience — except with Love! Ah, it was his downfall in the end…

"I remember some lines —

> Regarding America, here's what I would do:
> I would shut America and slightly clean it
> Then I would open it anew."

Judah Waten had laughed out loud. "Gwen tells me you live in Box Hill, Comrade Kameneva. I can give you a lift. And perhaps we can have coffee together sometime?"

Judah Waten drove her home. They talked. Olga was not tired, and she loved to hear the once-familiar inflections in his accent as they rolled through the night. They talked about food, the food of their childhood — the Rumanian food his mother cooked and he rejected, preferring the fare of his young Perth friends. His parents would catch him out trying to be Australian, but he was quite defiant. "From an early age," he said. "And you, Olga?"

"Da."

Judah talked of his life as a wanderer, to New Zealand and in an English prison, from job to job, house to house. As his father had observed of Judah's mother, living on one leg like a bird.

Olga felt that agitation, too. But she had some peace, sitting in his car. Something accomplished. A little freedom punching a large hole in a wall. Olga flexed her arthritic fingers and then tried to form fists with them. She could still manage it. Just.

"My father would have loved the play," Judah said. "The comedy, how he loved the old Purim spiel and masquerades. He was a dancer, he would dance around the kitchen and try to involve my mother, with no success.

"And you, Olga? Tell me what you know. Trotsky?"

"Ah. My brother? Yes? About him? Lenin often gave my husband Lev tasks, jobs to do, but my brother was the independent thinker. If Lenin agreed with him, all the good. If he didn't, then Leon would go his own way, and Lenin would give tasks to others. Rather than seeing this as a slight, my brother saw it as recognition from Lenin that they were equals. That was Leon.

"I remember that my brother and my husband met to discuss Lenin's support for Stalin. This was just before Lenin died. Lev, my husband, came home to us, pale and agitated. He paced around our tiny apartment, as much as the space would allow. Krupskaya had told Lev that her husband Lenin was about to break off all relations with Stalin.

"But…we know the rest. Anyway, perhaps such things are…let us leave it all for another time. We have the play. It is all in there."

Judah rasped a laugh as rough as a metal file. "We should still never forget that you and the others sacrificed their lives to protect the Revolution. Their lives!" He talked at the top of his voice and sounded to Olga like a demented rabbi at the Bimah in *shul*. Olga laughed, as well, suppressing some tears.

"I used to have an hourglass, Comrade Waten, as a child. The sand, it ran down a few grains at a time, and when it was finished, I would instantly turn it upside down and watch the sand again. As a child, you can do that for a long time. But as you grow, you forget about the sand. It fascinates a child but as an adult, your focus is somewhere else —

food queues, whether you will be interrogated yet again. And what you also saw as you grew up plays its part: the woman stripped to the waist in the village square, called a whore and paraded through the streets till she could no longer stand, the peasants flogged for letting the horses stray into the wheat field. This is what comes back to you. The simple things are buried under all that weight. That is the life, here in Australia, yes, as anywhere else. I have seen slums here, and people starved during the capitalist Depression just the same. And now there is the show trial of Royal Espionage Commission to distract from real issues."

Pulling up to the traffic lights, Judah Waten had shaken his fist out of the window and shouted, "Dissent! Dissent! Dissent!"

They heard the putter of a motorbike as a policeman pulled up beside them. If the rider had looked inside, he would have seen two people singing *The Internationale* in Yiddish — *shtyat oyf ir ale ver vi shklafn- in hinger leybn miz, in noit* — at the top of their voices, but he was at the end of his shift and rushed away just as the lights changed.

Olga had always wanted to write a manifesto. So she did.

The Manifesto of Olga Kameneva

Do Not Make Art! Everyone express themselves continuously! Disturb the peace! Make trouble; paint the doors, walls, roads. Workers! Make slogans and plays in your factories and fields, dance your way through your work; sing whenever you feel like it.

Welcome each new expression of human creativity like a newborn baby.

Speak loudly and clearly whenever you have something to say.

Do it in a public place.

Never write letters to the newspapers. If you do and are published, you will know you have joined the wrong club.

Join the local Theatrical Society. When someone asks you what you are doing there, reply "just biding my time."

Don't write anything down, or if you do, leave it somewhere it can be found.
Make sure there is sausage in your pocket whenever you leave the house, and also chalk.

There, she thought. It is done.

What is done cannot be undone.

She signed it: Olga Kameneva, revolutionary socialist, peasant, worker, comrade, playwright, woman, mother, sister, wife, friend, Ukrainian, Jew, mourner, camp survivor, displaced person, Australian, library member, failed gardener, tea drinker, liberator and (officially) dead person.

CODA! CODA!

Vera stood outside the front door of Valentia Vassilenko's sprawling house, a little fear catching in her throat. This would be the first time she had seen Olga since the play, the newspaper headlines, the police raid and the closure of the New Theatre.

She had visited Valentia many times now. They had collaborated on another project. Three young women were living in Valentia Vassilenko's house, together with their babies. Vera had waited patiently for hours at a time, clutching leaflets for young women being walked into the convent by their families and she would shove one determinedly into their hands. The young women knew from her look that she meant business and usually took the leaflet. So far, five had made the trek, heavily pregnant, to Valentia's house.

Vera had not told Olga what she was doing. She knew that Olga would be proud of her. An exchange of words was not necessary. Her aim was to create a network of refuges for the girls whose only other choice was to give up their children. The refuges she was planning were in the homes of Bund members, friends of Joseph's and his parents who were willing to take the women in for a period of time.

She knew Olga would be proud of her; at the same time, she knew Olga would be disappointed that she had not gone far enough. Why had she not organised the young women to protest in the city square? Why had she not organised to slap the face of so-called decency?

Vera had no answer — guilty as charged. Lenin had said one man alone won't make the weather, Olga told her.

Something else Olga had said: what if it doesn't work out with Joseph? What if you find someone else later on? It's not so easy to divorce. You say, eyes open, but reality is different, Olga had said. Her decision had already been tested. Twice, she had found Joseph with a stout young man she did not know. There was something other than friendship between them, she knew that, though she said nothing to Joseph.

You will find fault with each other, she had told herself. Singularly-minded people will often rub each other the wrong way. And the political differences they had papered over? Well, they had reared their head like a mighty, ruthless animal tearing at a carcass.

Vera admitted to herself — as she would need to do to Olga in no doubt what would be a long, protracted discussion — that she would take responsibility for bringing the Bundists into the picture, for the closure of the New Theatre.

She pressed the doorbell and waited.

Olga was seated in the dining room. Valentia was busy in the kitchen showing two of the young women how to preserve fruit. The smell of stewed peaches wafted.

Olga was breathing deeply after the long trip to Valentia's house. She approved of this new project. She and Vera had not seen each other since the newspaper articles with all of their repercussions. It was some months since the play had debuted and the yellow press reviews had damned them.

Valentia had said, "it's time you saw Vera. Besides, you have not seen Beryl and she is so big now."

Olga had worked through the events following the opening night many times in her mind. Vera had been naïve to bring the Bundists. She did not know what Vera had told Joseph about her involvement with the New Theatre, or what she was thinking, but she admitted to herself that if she'd had alarm bells ringing herself, she had done nothing about it. But there had been so much going on, and isn't that always the way?

Vera lifted Beryl out of the large perambulator and handed her to Olga. Olga asked if Beryl had any teeth and Vera replied she had five and was chewing meat very enthusiastically.

They talked for a few minutes about Vera's work with Mr Ford. Vera added that she had been drawing consistently since her work with the New Theatre. She was thinking of taking some commercial art classes and changing over to advertising.

"They seem to pay higher wages," Vera said.

"Good for you," said Olga, tickling Beryl under the chin.

Valentia emerged from the kitchen with the young women. She was carrying lemon biscuits dusted with icing sugar, piled onto a plate.

"Have you talked about the newspaper articles yet?"

Both were silent. Olga did not think she should be the one to start.

Vera said, "I know I owe you an apology. I hope you know I had no idea what they had planned to do. I thought they would see what 'Great Art' could be, the quality of the Revolutionary arts…how it could inspire people, and I thought about leaving Joseph afterwards. I really did."

"But you didn't," said Valentia.

"No. I resolved to do my best with the situation I find myself in. I hope I gain your trust again, Olga."

Valentia interrupted. "Well, I never thought that you could have known beforehand what Pawel was going to do. Did they apologise to you?"

"Not really. It's just politics. That's what Pawel said. Joseph said I would realise in time that the exposé had been necessary to distance real, working people from the avant-garde, who would never be accepted in Australia. I made completely the wrong call."

Olga and Valentia exchanged a glance.

"Rubbish. Their motive was altogether different. It was to give them a firm position in the public mind as the champions of *bourgeois* values, to cement their credentials with the Labor Party," Valentia added, her arms crossed in front of her. "And the newspapers duly obliged them," she added.

Vera continued, "I know, Olga, that you want more of an explanation from me. I tried to tell Joseph it was just art that I was interested in, but he saw through that. We ended up having the whole discussion: about Beryl's father, my political views. That's when I invited him, and then he invited Pawel and..."

"And what about the people who were injured? Arrested?"

"That's when I nearly left him. I have found it hard to live with myself..." Vera had tears in her eyes as she spoke.

It had been the second night of the play. Olga and Valentia had both attended. Vera had stayed home, but not because she knew anything about what was planned. Against Olga's wishes, the back doors of the theatre were closed. The theatre was packed with patrons — word had leaked out ahead of the reviews, of the play's provocative acts.

The play had begun, the hooting and howling of the audience followed, even more enthusiastically than the first night. Once the actors were naked, the banging started at the doors, just as they were about to fling them open. At first, Olga thought the crew had added sound effects to the play, and she hooted and clapped along with the audience. Within seconds, the thuds had escalated, the doors were forced open, and the police rushed in. Olga counted at least forty of them.

The audience stood and tumbled, chaotically, in different directions, falling over themselves to get out of the way of the truncheons, boots and fists. Olga was not struck, but Valentia was, right on the cheek. The actors scattered and ran behind the stage. Gwen, Greg and Bob were arrested for an offence against public decency, as the newspapers put it.

Several people were badly injured, sustaining broken limbs and jaws. Olga saw that a man was helping Lilia Monk get up from the floor. The ambulances arrived very quickly. Olga was holding Valentia up, lest she collapse, and she was one of the first to be loaded into an ambulance. Lilia was next, and Olga squeezed her arm as she passed her on the stretcher.

"I am so sorry, Lilia," Olga said, but Lilia had not met her gaze.

The newspapers were on cue; they were right there and must have been tipped off. They photographed the fleeing crowd and there they were the next day, on the front pages of the dailies.

REDS FLEE!

MORE REPORTS INSIDE!

The editorials bayed for the production to be closed. 'Indecent, the inane ramblings of a deranged mind.' 'Nothing funny to see in the glorification of violence and insurrection.'

The *Tribune* review had been effusive. There was a quote from Gwen and Greg about their arrest, and how they would use their trial as a platform to champion free speech.

The front pages of the tabloids had been accompanied by some quotes. One was from Mr Terry Seville who had been at the opening night and claimed to have been 'blindsided' by its graphic content. Another quoted Pawel, who had a similar refrain and tightened the screw further by linking the play to the Failed Soviet Experiment.

Olga and Vera traded words, back and forwards.

Finally, Vera said, "you can't blame the Bund for the publicity, Olga. Pawel and that Mr Seville were only saying what the tabloids would have printed themselves. But they took advantage of the situation, I grant you that."

Valentia added, "Imperialist stooges! But let's all face facts. After the first night, we were bound to be in the police's sights. I think we knew that, deep down."

Vera continued, "anyway, I had it out with Joseph, Olga. There are some things about me he has to learn to accept, just as I do with him."

"After the play?"

"We argued badly. But I put on my brave face. I told him I was proud to be part of the play, and that you, Olga, would have liked nothing better than being denounced by the yellow press."

"Good for you," said Valentia.

"I sent a letter to the paper. They didn't print it.

"The Petrovs and the Royal Commission mean Labor and its followers will distance themselves even more from the Left. I know that from talking to Joseph about it," added Vera.

"Joseph said Pawel told him it was best to use the play as another example of decadent Communist influence on young people. We should be natural allies against imperialism, but it never turns out that way. The ruling class get fat and we get sent to the slaughterhouse."

Valentia laughed. Vera sounded like a Russian. "I notice they didn't talk about our ages. Imagine that! Seventy-year-old decadents! Taking the nud-ity to the people!"

Olga added with some resignation, "see what happens when you let Communist émigrés into country to make new life. Look how they reward us. Corrupting the young people…"

"Anyway, the trial and the coverage mean they'll get plenty of publicity for the fight to re-open the theatre. They've had that lawyer offer to represent them: the cove that represented Frank Hardy. Campbell's his name," said Vera.

"Well, I know what I will say to Pawel if I ever see him again."

"Olga, you will be invited to any occasion I am invited to," Vera reassured her.

"I do not want friends of the fair weather. I will tell him what I think. Their gains are short term — illusions only. They will rest on their haunches and keep taking the king's gold. They are betraying the working class, and all Jewish people."

"Well, there will be an opportunity to tell them soon. Sarah's son is having his *bar mitzvah*."

Olga raised her eyebrows, then nodded and folded her arms tightly.

"That will depend on the date and time. Valentia and I have joined the Box Hill Repera-tory Society. They are rehearsing Strindberg. Strindberg, I ask you! But never mind. Valentia and I have a plan for them."

Vera laughed inwardly. "I'm sure it will work out, with you two behind it."

"Well, you know I am already a Box Hill lady, Vera. So, there should be no problem at all," Olga replied.

The young women brought in lunch from the kitchen: roast vegetables surrounding a piece of lamb on a platter. There was mint sauce, made with mint from Valentia's garden. Boiled silver beet was heaped on another plate.

Everyone sat around the table.

"Go on, Carol, out with it," said one of the young women to the other.

"We want to know…well," said a hesitant Carol, "Mrs Vassilenko told us you were famous, Mrs Kameneva. You know, back in the old country. You went to opening nights at the theatre and films. Did you wear nice clothes? Did you meet any film stars?"

Olga was quick. "You could say I had some fame, but that is just my bad luck. Fame was invented to justify war. War and fame: both are unnatural."

"Oh," Carol said, disappointed. She blushed. "I suppose you could say Betty Grable was made famous by a war. She was pretty, though."

"Actors in Russia are workers like anyone else," Olga added definitively and there were no more questions.

Valentia had placed white wine on the table, together with cut, crystal glasses from the cabinet. The young women declined, but Valentia poured herself, Olga and Vera a glass each. Olga hacked off a small piece of the lamb for Beryl. The child sucked on the meat as if there were no more to be had. Olga smoothed her hair and kissed her head.

Continuing their previous conversation, Vera said, "I did object when the so-called reporter, who did not even see our play, called it Stalin's depraved propaganda. As if Stalin *would* allow anyone to make anything like that! Besides, he's dead, isn't he?"

Olga laughed. "They say that is so. He must be, or they would never have courage to kill Beria. How did the sainted Molotov keep his head? If Koba had lived, Molotov would not be alive now and Beria would not be dead. So it seems, yes, Koba must be dead. And since we are all atheists, he cannot come back from the dead and haunt us again."

Olga began to feel light-headed.

Valentia continued talking, but to Olga, her voice seemed blurry, and she found it difficult to concentrate on what was being said.

Then Vera said, "I told Joseph that we should never be on the side of censorship. They'll always use it against *us*, and eventually, anyone they can scrape into the category of 'The Left". You know Hardy was put on trial, and something you probably don't know, so was William Dobell, one of our painters, for a portrait that wasn't 'sufficiently lifelike' Don't think he was a leftist! I told Joseph, 'Socialist Realism seems alive and well here!'"

"You tell him in private, yes?"

Vera blushed borsch-red. "Yes, in private. And he said to me, so much for socialism. Where did it get the Russians? After what we Jews have been through, a two-bed flat with a private bathroom is socialism."

"Yes, this seems to be a common refrain," said Olga.

Vera pecked at the meat on her plate, feeding a little more to Beryl. "We are having an ongoing discussion, Joseph and I. I said I've always been curious as to why, when we talk about Hitler, we talk about the history of Austria and other European countries as anti-Semitic, and people nod, yes, he inherited something he could use to manipulate the German people. But when we talk about Stalin, no one talks about what people faced before the Revolution, what continued from those times, and what didn't. That's where we are. Joseph is thinking about it."

Olga smiled but looked pained and said, "I need to lie down, Valentia."

Vera was still thinking about Joseph as she watched Olga hobble to the bedroom, aided by Valentia. The idea had struck her then: it was not only Joseph who could carry on affairs. She had observed the comings and goings and ins and outs of the New Theatre comrades, frequently changing partners, including the married ones. There were jealousies, flare-ups, but Vera liked that it was all out in the open, not swept under the carpet with the dust and the mites.

ONE PIANO, 64 KEYS

Vera could hear the two women talking as Valentia settled Olga into bed, the conversation muffled by the space between them, and then, Vera realised, by time, as well.

Vera worried that Olga lived on her own. She wondered why the two women had not moved in together. But what did she really know? Olga had told her only glimpses of her life. And whenever she did, it seemed to be fused to another story that Vera could only call a lesson.

The story of the piano had run just like that. After Vera had been rescued from the convent and they had been wondering why anyone would keep piano keys in a bag in the corner of a room, Olga had told her another story about a piano.

During the Revolution, peasants came upon a deserted country manor and while exploring the rooms, found a grand piano in a large ballroom. They had been busy dividing the contents of the house between themselves, but when it came to the piano, they were stumped. After a discussion, they decided to extract all of the keys from the piano and share out the ivory keys equally. The piano itself became firewood.

What is the meaning of the story? Olga had asked Vera, but Olga went on to answer the question herself.

Perhaps it shows how stupid the peasants are, how ignorant, that they need educating, civilising?

Or, how acquisitive they are: see I told you peasants are greedy!

Maybe how people dream but fail to act when it comes true. Imagine the peasant folding the keys over in his rough hands, dreaming of the music he could create if only he knew how.

How short-sighted peasants are: all they did was destroy something beautiful and turn it into a heap of rubbish.

Perhaps the peasants really were socialists and understood the piano keys had to be divided equally.

Or perhaps they simply wanted to feed their families and took the keys to sell later.

And who is to say each of them had the same idea, even though they all agreed on the act? Olga had said she had told the story many times to countless people. In the gulag, it became a point of conversation, something which at the same time took them to an abstract realm but also grounded them in their own reality there in the camp, dealing with the legacy of those who built the piano, those who bought it, those who hauled it to the manor in the countryside, those who played it, and those who smashed it up.

Vera's experience was of the nuns separating the piano from its keys and keeping both. No one else could play the piano, and neither could they themselves. Denial for everyone, equally. Chekhov's 'locked soul'.

Vera had asked herself repeatedly if she had betrayed Olga. It had driven her mad, this incessant questioning of her situation. She and Joseph had argued about Olga many times. Joseph said that she represented a 'discredited philosophy'. We should examine the lived experience and draw our conclusions from that.

Vera had felt the thunder build in her lungs. "What of my lived experience?" she had shouted at him.

Joseph had laughed at her, how she effortlessly brought all of world suffering back to her own experience. She didn't bother responding.

"You are always defending her. It's an admirable quality," he had said finally, and she had kissed him on the top of the head.

She had worked it out: to the Bund, she had to defend Olga, and to Olga she had to defend the Bund. Up to a point. This was not a contradiction, and she had found her peace with it.

Olga lay on Valentia's bed under its thickly quilted satin covering — dusky pink, a colour much in vogue with her Box Hill friends. In this land of milk and honey, husbands 'allowed' their wives to decorate the bedrooms, choose the colours and furniture and wallpaper as if that were a kind of freedom. She would always think this a strange country.

She could hear Vera telling Valentia and the other women about something that had happened in Carlton near one of the Jewish halls, something about Nazi slogans and swastikas painted on the walls and the Bund mobilising people to defend themselves. There was a fight...

The wine had gone to her head, or perhaps it was the stress of travel and walking up the long hill to the house. Thoughts were running through her mind like falling water.

Olga was remembering a séance she attended on a dare from Chekhov's wife, Olga Knipper. Ahh! Oohhh! The knocks and moans were human, but no one else seemed to care. The noise so obviously came from behind a curtain. Olga had laughed out loud, but even she had wondered for a fraction of a moment if her mother could be on the other side. Betty had mentioned that Beverly was fond of séances. Olga wondered now who it was Beverly had wanted to contact. Perhaps her own mother?

Mother! Mother! The coach trip she had taken across the wide plains leading from her home towards Kiev. She was a young girl. A dark red woollen cloak warmed her shoulders and a cloth hat, her head. The hat was too small, and she had pulled at it incessantly to stop it from riding up. And what did she do, all those hours on the way to Kiev? She looked out the window of the coach at the boundless plains and the stretches of rye and infinite bunches of stipa and the whirling birds and darting marmots, and she thought of her mother, how her hair hung in a long, dark waterfall when she let it down to go to bed.

Olga adjusted the pillows beneath her head so her neck rested more easily. Perhaps what she was remembering was not her own journey, but that of the boy in *The Steppe*, a Chekhov story she had read over and over in a book Esther had given her, *The World's Best Travel Stories*. Had she really seen the rye and the wild hemp and felt the yellow rays of the sun, or was that from the story?

She could feel that sun warming her bones even now. Such a timid child transformed: a fighter, an advocate, a bureaucrat, a wild animal. Perhaps even her memories were not hers, or not only hers, they had fused with the memories of others recounted — ah! the long nights of stories in the camps — and the thought pleased her, that even her own memories were not those of one person, but from a cauldron, a soup.

She could hear Vera's voice again. The words floated to her, about the work Joseph was doing to gain the migration of loved ones, old parents who were not really welcome, barriers put in their way, even though their children had made money in this country and could provide for them. Too many Jews already, we are told.

We are mismatched with our times! Machines are invented to plough, and afterwards, the peasant uses a talisman to ward off its evil spirits. And yet there is an itch for something else beyond the fields. That makes the peasant keep singing her songs.

That song…

She heard it float from the piano as Valentia played it. It was the song Valentia had written for the play. Olga and Gwen had substituted the Joe Hill song from *The Little Red Songbook* for Valentia's song at the last moment without telling her. But finally, Olga did discuss it with her, when the fire died down.

OLGA

You were late. I would have told you about the song if you had been on time.

Valentia laughs.

VALENTIA

I don't care.

OLGA

You do.

VALENTIA

No, I don't.

OLGA

Gwen asked me to substitute a worker's song, one everyone in the audience would know. She said it would reassure them. How could I say no?

VALENTIA

We are the same now.

OLGA

Are we?

VALENTIA

Yes. But I will have my revenge on you, and Gwen. I will write more songs!

Now, the song that Valentia wrote for the play floated around Olga.

We who made the flood
The flesh
The blood
We break ourselves
We don't need others to do it for us!

Whistle to me
Take my hand, take me far
Build me that ladder to the stars
To the stars!

Valentia seemed to be playing the song over and over. Or was Olga's mind playing tricks?

My comrades...Maria...my brother...Lev...my Alexei. Yuri...I can almost touch them. Maya, Kristian, Meyerhold, Lenin.

The trees: Olga suddenly wanted to see the trees of her homeland. The branches laden with snow. Snow is magical for a few days. Had she forgotten? Soon it turns to slush.

Sleep, memory! And dreams. One and many. Olga felt her head-fog lift. Perhaps she had snoozed for ten minutes. Was she awake, even now? She felt light, as if the light of the Steppes shone through her. There were days when Olga felt as if she might be dead, and she could imagine this new country as a kind of heavenly, abundant forest that the folk tales foretold, and she could go along as if she had not lived the life she had.

It felt as if there was something stuck between her teeth.

"Valentia. I need a toothpick!" she shouted suddenly. "And fetch me an axe!"

POSTSCRIPT

After her death, Olga Kameneva's memoirs were discovered in her flat, including fragments of the earlier manuscript Olga claimed to have consigned to the backyard incinerator. She wrote little about herself in these documents, which was more about the movements she had been part of and the role of debate and the dissection of particular turns in these movements. She had written in detail about the episode involving Vera and Beryl and the practices they had exposed. These memoirs were lodged by Vera with historians of Jewish people in Australia and were used many years later as evidence that the illegal practices against unmarried mothers were always known and were abetted by churches, the police, social workers and others in authority.

Vera Slodkowicz forged a career in advertising and eventually managed several large accounts. She also designed the posters for Communists who stood in local government elections, anti-nuclear protests and women's peace protests. She signed the posters as Olga K. She never reconciled with her parents. Her mother left strict instructions with her sister Barbara that Vera was not to be allowed to attend her funeral, should she attempt it (which she did not).

Valentia Vassilenko survived for five years longer than Olga. Valentia cohabited for the rest of her life with the émigré Hungarian painter Viktor Gregas, with whom she been having an affair for many years back in Europe and who eventually followed her to Australia. She continued to run an open house for unmarried mothers until she died.

THE HISTORY

Short biographies follow of the main historical persons, organisations and some cultural references mentioned in this novel, generally in order of appearance. Some better-known historical persons mentioned do not appear in this list, for example, the painter Chagall or the writer Pasternak, to keep this section to a modest length.

The BOLSHEVIKS: The leaders of the Russian Revolution, many of its members formed the first and subsequent Soviet governments. Many of the Old Bolsheviks, the members of the Party since its earliest formations, were systematically killed or exiled by Stalin.

Olga KAMENEVA (born Olga BRONSTEIN): Olga was politically active all her adult life, engaged in revolutionary politics as a member of the Bolsheviks. She held many posts in the Soviet government, appointed the chief of the Foreign Section (All Russian Society for Cultural Relations) and head of the Theatre Division of the People's Commissariat for Education, as well as being a member of the Famine Relief Committee and the Soviet Communist Party Women's Section. Olga married Lev KAMENEV, who was a member of Stalin's first governing troika. She was also the sister of Leon TROTSKY. She was executed in 1941 after Lev was convicted of treason at the first Moscow show trials.

Lev KAMENEV: Olga married Lev when she was around twenty, and they led a life of revolutionary politics together until he left the marriage and took up with the painter, Tatiana Glebova in the late 1920s. Often on the opposite side to LENIN and STALIN in the political foment of pre- and post-Revolutionary Russia, Lev fell out with Stalin in 1925 and briefly collaborated with TROTSKY before capitulating to Stalin again. After the murder of Sergei Kirov in 1934, which Stalin used as an excuse for a wave of repression and reprisals, Lev and others were tried for conspiring in Kirov's murder. He was convicted on these trumped-up charges and executed in 1936.

Josef STALIN, (also called the Kremlin Highlander and Koba in this book): A Bolshevik who organised bank robberies to fuel political activities, he was a key organiser, strategist and eventual leader of the Soviet Union after LENIN's death, gradually accreting sole power and ultimately, the power of life and death over millions. Died in 1953.

Lev BRONSTEIN aka Leon TROTSKY: Olga's brother, one of the fiercest of all the Old Bolsheviks, head of the Red Army after the Russian Revolution and sometimes collaborator but ultimately opponent of Stalin (and therefore of Olga and Lev KAMENEV). Assassinated in exile by Stalin's agent in 1940. Trotsky was a Menshevik until 1904, then an independent Marxist who joined the Bolsheviks in 1917 in the foment of revolution.

DISPLACED PERSON (DP): A person resettled from Europe by the International Refugee Organisation. They included war refugees, political exiles and others unable to return home post World War Two. Those coming to Australia came via resettlement camps such as Bonegilla and were contracted to work for two years. Little regard was had to previous qualifications and women mainly worked in 'domestic labour'.

WHITE RUSSIANS: A loosely-based confederation of nationalist, anti-Bolshevik and anti-Communist forces that fought the Red Army, they opposed the Russian Revolution at every turn, leading to the Civil War of 1917 to 1921. The Whites allied with foreign forces, such as the United Kingdom, France, Germany and the United States who all invaded Russia. The Whites included ex-aristocrats and their supporters, many of whom fled to other countries during and after the Civil War.

Yuri KAMENEV: The youngest son of Olga and Lev, he was executed at age 17 in 1938.

Aleksander KAMENEV: Olga and Lev's oldest son, he was executed at age 33 in 1939.

Maria SPIRIDONOVA: A member of an opposition party to the Bolsheviks, the Socialist Revolutionaries (SR). Maria assassinated a local landlord in 1906 and spent 11 years in prisons until freed by the Russian Revolutions of 1917. She led the Left SR and sided with Lenin in the October Revolution but fell out with the Bolsheviks over the forced requisition of grain from the rural peasantry. Her party's assassination of the German ambassador led to further repression and arrest. She was arrested and exiled many times until her execution along with Olga KAMENEVA in the Medvedevsky Forest in 1941.

THE GULAG: A system of Soviet forced labour camps used for political prisoners and other dissidents as well as criminals. An instrument of political repression, such camps had been used since Tsarist times against political opponents. Terms of imprisonment varied, and it wasn't uncommon for people to be forbidden from returning to their homes once their term was served.

OKHRANA, CHEKA, GPU, OGPU, NKVD, MGB, KGB: All were variations of Russian security agencies, commencing with the Tsarist Okhrana. The Soviet apparatuses demonstrated continuity from the Okhrana in terms of their methods (interrogation, spying, torture etc).

ITI (or EYETIE): A shortened version of 'Italian', used by Australians in the post-war period when referring to Italian immigrants. Other terms included 'Dago'.

Anton CHEKHOV: One of Russia's foremost playwrights and short story writers, writing before the Revolution. Chekhov was a doctor by profession who refused to have his own tuberculosis treated.

Konstantin STANISLAVSKI: A leading Russian theatre director and actor. He is most famous as the developer of an acting 'system.' He was a collaborator and sometimes aesthetic rival to MEYERHOLD. He died of natural causes in 1928.

Vsevolod MEYERHOLD: A leading Russian theatre actor and director, younger than STANISLAVSKI. He is most famous as the developer of biomechanics, an acting method championed in the radical theatre after the Revolution. He was a key collaborator of Olga KAMENEVA's during her leadership of the Soviet theatre. He was an opponent of Soviet Realism and was arrested in 1939 and executed in 1940.

Natalia GONCHAROVA: One of the most prominent of Russian artists across painting, costume design, writing and set design, she was a member of the Blue Rose artists and was exhibited in the later Knave of Diamonds exhibitions, splitting from that group to form the Donkey's Tail. She was associated with Rayonism, Cubism, Futurism and Primitivism as art movements, as well as Everythingvism. In 1921 she moved to Paris and designed costumes for the Ballets Russes.

El LISSITSKY, RODCHENKO, MALEVICH: Russian avant-garde artists, working variously in the Constructivist, Futurist and Suprematist art movements in the pre- and post-Revolutionary period.

El Lissitsky was responsible for the famous Soviet 'Red Wedge' poster and Malevich's most famous work is his 'Black Square'.

Vladimir MAYAKOVSKY: A Russian poet and playwright, he was famous for such poems as "Talking to the Taxman about Poetry" and "A Cloud in Trousers" and his plays, *The Bedbug* and *Mystery Bouffe*; this latter play was produced only twice in Russia, both times with different lines. Mayakovsky encouraged anyone who produced it to re-write it. He helped craft the *Futurist Manifesto, A Slap in the Face of Public Taste*. He created posters in support of the Revolution, but increasingly fell foul of Soviet authorities and resisted censorship. Although some think he died in suspicious circumstances in 1930, it seems likely he killed himself as the result of failed love affairs.

The BUND: The General Jewish Labour Bund (with followers known as Bundistn). Founded in the late nineteenth century, this secular group organised Jewish workers across Europe to resist exploitation, pogroms and discrimination. Supporters of the October Revolution, they were inclined to side with the Mensheviks and were dissolved by the Bolsheviks in 1921 on the grounds that a separate organisation based on ethnic origins was not necessary. The Bund survived and even thrived in Poland, but the rising persecution of Jews saw their organisations crushed and the Bund's adherents dispersed to the four corners of the globe. With their philosophy of 'hereness' (the Jews' right to live in freedom and dignity wherever they settled), the Bund has contributed culturally in many countries, with one of the most vibrant communities established in Melbourne, Australia. There, the Bund established a youth organisation, SKIF, and has stayed active, running cultural and educational events.

IMPERIALISM: the expansion of control, usually said to have started in the mid-1800s, both formal and informal, where Western countries extended their economic and often political control over other countries, especially in Africa, Asia and South America. This happened through the co-option of local elites, the establishment of ruthless business practices, religion, slavery and military force, extracting wealth and leaving centuries-long trauma and poverty as their lasting legacy.

Vladimir LENIN: The leader of the BOLSHEVIKS and main architect of the October Revolution. Died of illness in 1921 after warning his comrades about the ambitions of STALIN.

The MENSHEVIKS: A revolutionary party in opposition to the Bolsheviks, the two parties split in 1903 over tactical differences, with the Mensheviks more prepared to work with social liberals and favouring a more gradual approach to change. TROTSKY was a member until 1904 when he became an independent Marxist.

Anton LUNACHARSKY: Prominent Bolshevik, though not always aligned with them. Appointed Commissar of Enlightenment in 1917, he was effectively Olga's boss. He was also in charge of censorship, but at various times supported open discussion about art and artistic movements. He removed Olga KAMENEVA from her official position as head of the theatre in 1919.

Alexandra KOLLANTAI: One of the most prominent of Russian revolutionaries, she was a member of the Mensheviks before becoming a Bolshevik in 1915. She was the foremost Soviet theoretician in support of women's rights. In her personal life, she had many relationships and two marriages with co-revolutionaries. Sidelined from politics from 1922, she served in diplomatic posts until 1945. She was one of the only members of the original October Revolution Central Committee to die of old age (other than STALIN and one of his supporters).

Inessa ARMAND: Born in France, she migrated to Russia with her husband and left him for his younger brother. She became politically active and, after a period of exile and meeting Lenin in Paris, she undertook dangerous missions for the socialist movement. Then, after the October Revolution, she was head of the Moscow Soviet, then director of a key women's organisation, Zhenotdel. There was some suggestion she and LENIN were lovers. She died of cholera in 1920.

The SERAPIONS, the SMITHY: Groups of Russian artists. Founded in 1920, the Smithy touted itself as the first association of proletarian writers and published their manifesto as the Declaration of the Smithy Proletarian Writers and did not agree with political interference with art. The Serapion Brothers was a literary group, which included ZAMYATIN (see below), founded in 1921 with no specific program. Both groups lived in small artists' communities.

PROLEKULT: An organisation formed from a number of cultural and literary organisations after the Revolution. LUNACHARSKY was an early sponsor. Funded by the government, Prolekult sought autonomy, which brought it into conflict with the Communist Party hierarchy and state bureaucracy, and this was the subject of much wrangling over the three years of its life. Extensive reading about this organisation will reveal to the reader the turmoil and vicissitudes of artistic movements in the early Soviet era.

Vyacheslav MOLOTOV: One of STALIN's key collaborators over many years and a senior member of the Soviet government. He signed the Ribbentrop- Molotov Pact, the non-aggression agreement with Hitler, on Stalin's behalf. An Old Bolshevik, he was one of the few of them who survived Stalin.

CADRE: Term for a group of activists in revolutionary or communist politics. The term was used by activists to delineate those relationships which were the closest between revolutionary comrades.

Nadezhda KRUPSKAYA: Married to LENIN, she was an early Bolshevik and shared his years in exile and in the Revolution and was an organiser and prominent advocate for women's rights. A prominent Old Bolshevik, she was a member of the Central Committee of the Communist Party in 1924. She fell out with STALIN, but retained a position of Deputy Commissar of Education until her death in 1939.

Lavrentiy BERIA: Chief of the Secret Police under STALIN. A thoroughly nasty and cruel individual. He was tried on hundreds of rape charges and treason after Stalin's death in 1953 and was executed before the year was finished.

Vasily BLOKHIN: STALIN's chief executioner, he oversaw many political executions. He personally executed 7,000 Polish officers in the Katyn Massacre of 1940. He died in 1955, with his death officially reported as suicide.

Olga KNIPPER: A Russian stage actress, she married Anton CHEKHOV in 1901 and was one of the original members of the Moscow Art Theatre. She was Chekhov's model for Masha in *The Three Sisters*.

OBLOMOV: 1859 novel by Ivan Goncharov, about a man who rarely left his room or bed. It was considered a satire of Russian intellectuals.

Oriel GRAY: An Australian playwright, from 1937 to 1949, she wrote and acted for the Sydney New Theatre. 1942, Gray was appointed as the first paid Australian playwright-in-residence. Her play, *The*

Torrents, was awarded the 1955 Playwrights' Advisory Board award for best play, jointly with Ray Lawler's *Summer of the Seventeenth Doll*.

Dr Hilda BULL: Married to playwright Louis Esson, Bull worked as a medical practitioner, but acted in Australian plays and later produced them for the New Theatre in Melbourne. She is reputed to have had wide knowledge of the theatre, set a high production standard and introduced the theatre to the techniques of STANISLAVSKI.

THE ODETS PLAY: *Till The Day I Die* by Clifford Odets, a left-wing American playwright, was produced in 1937 by the New Theatre. The play had been banned from production in Sydney, but Melbourne members went ahead, only to find they were locked out of the hall. They finally put the play on after many sabotage attempts. On the night of the lockout, Catherine Duncan from the New Theatre told the waiting crowd "…the government and the censors need not think for one moment we are going to accept their dictum. We will fight for freedom of expression in Australia even if it takes till the day we die."

REEDY RIVER: A 1953 Australian musical, produced by the New Theatre. Written by Dick Diamond with songs chosen by John Gray, who was Oriel GRAY's husband. It played around Australia and in England for over three years and is considered the New Theatre's most successful production.

Trofim LYSENKO: Responsible for the major scientific scandal in the Soviet Union (involving misguided genetic and plant propagation theories). Promoted by STALIN, he discredited accurate scientific research and is often assigned responsibility for some famines, due to his theories of agricultural production which he imposed on farmers.

FUTURISTS, CONSTRUCTIVISTS: Early twentieth century Russian artistic movements which spawned some of the best and brightest of Russian artists of the times, across most of the arts – painting, writing etc.

RED LOVE: A novel written by Alexandra KOLLANTAI in 1923 and translated into English in 1927. It centres on Vassilissa, a Bolshevik, worker and community activist, her travails and love affairs, and shows the new possibilities for women developing in Soviet society, as well as the difficulties faced in developing an entirely new kind of society.

PEOPLE'S ART SCHOOL: Established by Marc Chagall in 1918 when he has been appointed a Fine Arts Commissioner by LUNACHARSKY, the school was intended to further the avant-garde in revolutionary arts. MALEVICH joined the school in 1919 and the two clashed in a major way over artistic perspectives, with Chagall leaving in 1920. The school only lasted for another two years. NB: The other artists mentioned in the conversation about the school are fictional.

THE GOVERNMENT INSPECTOR: A 1836 play by Nikolai Gogol. the play is a comedy of errors, satirising greed, stupidity, and the extensive political corruption of Imperial Russia.

VICTORY OVER THE SUN: Russian avant-garde (Futurist) opera, premiered in 1913, poster by EL LISSITZKY and set design by MALEVICH. The plot was about a group of people who want to get rid of time and destroy reason by capturing the sun. It provoked violent reactions when performed. The libretto written by Alexei Kruchenykh, used his own made-up language, called zaum, which he intended as the first language to be based on reason.

A SLAP IN THE FACE OF PUBLIC TASTE: A manifesto issued by a Futurist group, Hylea. MAYAKOVSKY was a co-signatory. It called for poetic rights, eschewing past writers such as Tolstoi and their previous use of language, and aimed to provoke outrage.

Essington LEWIS: A mining engineer who rose to become Chairman of BHP in 1950, he supported conservative politics, calling the Depression a 'fiery furnace', which clarified what he saw as false values. Menzies made him his chief of munitions at the beginning of World War Two, and he had easy access to the War Cabinet. The Labor Government of 1941 increased his power. He required his wife to keep a methodically clean house and he disapproved of women smoking, drinking beer or whisky, using nail polish and wearing shorts or slacks.

RAPP: The Russian Association of Proletarian Writers was established in 1925 and was folded into the Soviet Union of Writers in 1932. It attacked writers who didn't measure up to its definition of a Soviet writer. Among its first targets were ZAMYATIN and PILNYAK.

Ilya EHRENBURG: His most famous novel, *The Thaw*, gave its name to the post-Stalin era in the Soviet Union and is felt to have tested the limits of Soviet censorship. He was an early BOLSHEVIK but opposed them in 1917. He worked as a journalist and writer in various capacities, spending much of his life abroad. He stirred up emotions against the Germans during the war with his incendiary journalism. He was active in the Jewish Anti-Fascist Committee, which was banned by STALIN, and championed the cause of Jews in the Soviet. He survived to old age.

Yevgeny ZAMYATIN: Most famous as the author of a work of dystopian fiction, *We*, set in a police-state, he was an Old Bolshevik who became increasingly disillusioned after the revolution. His works became increasingly satirical, and he was eventually blacklisted from publishing in the Soviet Union. He wrote to Stalin to ask permission to emigrate, and after an intercession by Gorky, this was granted.

Boris PILNYAK: Not a Bolshevik sympathizer, Pilnyak was a popular author from an early age and often sailed close to the wind with themes critical of the government. He recanted on several occasions and was eventually given privileges. His recanting was not enough to save him, and he was executed in 1938.

Lyubov POPOVA: A Russian avant-garde painter and costume designer who experimented with Cubo-futurism and Suprematism, she also exhibited as part of the Knave of Diamonds Group. Her Constructivist projects included theatrical sets and costumes for productions such as MEYERHOLD's *Magnanimous Cuckold*.

Aleksandra EKSTER: Involved in similar movements to Popova, Ekster was a very experimental avant-garde artist, becoming director of the Color course at the Higher Artistic-Technical Workshop in Moscow in 1921. She also designed theatrical sets and costumes and had a long career after emigrating to Paris in 1924.

Vera KOMISSARZHEVSKAYA: Famous late-Russian Empire actress, early patron and collaborator of MEYERHOLD's, helping him establish his experimental theatre techniques.

Daniil KHARMS: Expelled from school, Kharms soon joined a group of poets and experimented with different forms and absurdist themes. He was a talented and eccentric writer who indulged in public acts of decadence and illogicality. He was arrested in 1931 as an anti-Soviet children's author. The world of his adult work, mostly unpublished in his lifetime, incorporated irrationality, dreams, fantasy and comedy. He did not survive the Siege of Leningrad, having been committed by the authorities to a psychiatric ward where he is said to have starved to death.

Fyodor GLADKOV: A dyed-in-the-wool Socialist Realist writer. His novel *Cement* was considered one of the best examples of the genre and grappled with issues of reconstruction in the post-Civil War and post-revolutionary Soviet Union.

John MORRISON: A realist Australian writer of short stories based on working class experiences, including his own as a wharfie. He worked as a gardener after he left the waterfront. He was a member of the Realist Writer's Group.

Judah WATEN: A Jewish immigrant, Waten wrote novels and short stories and was politically active in several countries, including England and New Zealand. He was gaoled for his activities in England. He had an on-again, off-again relationship with the Australian Communist Party. As a result of Waten's nomination for a Commonwealth Literary Fund award, Prime Minister Menzies ensured that all future nominees were investigated by security agencies.

Brian FITZPATRICK: An Australian historian, Fitzpatrick was also one of the founders and key advocates for the Council for Civil Liberties and active in support of post war refugees. A left-wing sympathiser, he held few academic posts during his life and mainly sustained himself through publication, print and media journalism. His daughter, Sheila Fitzpatrick, is a noted and prolific historian of the Soviet Union.

Alexander BLOK: A prominent Russian and Soviet playwright, poet and multi-talented artist, Blok was a fellow traveller of revolutionary politics, but had grown disillusioned by the time of his death in 1921. One of his most famous poems, "The Twelve", follows the march of Bolshevik soldiers through revolutionary Petrograd.

AFTERWORD

Imagining that Olga Kameneva survived her execution was the inciting idea for this novel. I fashioned the narrative from limited facts about Olga: namely, that she was Trotsky's sister, married to Lev Kamenev; was the head of the Russian theatre for a time, collaborated on radical theatre projects and participated in the women's movement. She was one of the tens of thousands of Russians whose contribution to one of the greatest events of the twentieth century, the Russian Revolution, remains largely unknown — consigned, as her brother said of the Mensheviks, to the 'dustbin of history'.

When I came across her stance against contraception, I knew I had to be true to Olga's views, and it led me to construct the story of Vera's rescue. Olga's experience in the theatre led to her imagined involvement with the Melbourne New Theatre. The other key fact I used was her execution along with Maria Spiridonova, who I knew was a political opponent. Therefore, the plot evolved from the bare bones of Olga's life and her historical context. Her character is a composite, crystallising what I learned about the Old Bolsheviks, in particular better-known and documented women such as Krupskaya, Kollantai and Armand.

In my mind, the History section, with its cast of characters and events, is essential, telling much more about the factual basis for the material than could be covered in the fiction. For completeness, I have also listed the books, articles and online resources I found of most interest during the writing of the book, as well as a few explicit textual references. I hope that you are inspired to read more about the years before and immediately after the Russian Revolution when so much political, radical, artistic and intellectual effort flowered, and especially about the Russian avant-garde and writers of the 1920s and 30s. Mayakovsky was a revelation, and I hope you are motivated to read his poems and plays, which I think put him at the forefront of any of the twentieth century's writers. This all had an impact on Australia too, that also should not be consigned to the 'dustbin of history'.

I wish to thank my family and friends who assisted me by reading drafts of the book and providing me with rich feedback. These people are my brother, Michael Roberts; my life partner, Robert Hodder and my niece, Conor Roberts. Peter and Aemelia Wilkins also proved valuable feedback. My thanks and acknowledgement also to Brice Fallon-Freeman, who provided editorial advice.

Gratitude is owed again to Conor Roberts for designing the cover; to my brothers and sisters, Michael, Rob, Lisa, Paul and Kim; to my wonderful mother, Gail, and my Dad Pete, for all their encouragement and support throughout my writing life. Thanks to them, friends and colleagues who have put up with me prattling on about my various writing endeavours over many years.

I would like to acknowledge all those people I have met in various left and progressive campaigns over many years. They are the reminder we need that there are still thousands of people, even in a relatively privileged country like Australia, and millions worldwide, who fight oppression wherever they find it. I especially acknowledge those who support refugees, the true dispossessed of this world. No one should rest easily until the world stops creating more of them.

NOTES ON CERTAIN REFERENCES IN THE TEXT

These notes are listed by chapter title.

Olga Kameneva in church: "…drivers carrying wheat," Trotsky, *My Life*, p43.

What is to be done? "She fondly remembered the times…" adapted from Leon Trotsky, *My Life*, p80.

A Slap in the face of public taste: Bielenski and Holiman are made-up characters. American jazz musicians, including African Americans, did visit the Soviet Union at that time.

 "Olga had trawled through her own memories…" is adapted from *The Guardian* article, *"Russia's stage revolution: when theatre was a hotbed for impossibly space-age design,"* October 2014.

"Let's put a bullet into Holy Russia…fat-arsed Russia…" Alexander Blok, *The Twelve*.

"It goes without saying…" Chekhov, *The Three Sisters*, Act 1. Speech by Vershinin.

Mrs Kameneva's Skaz: Skaz is a Russian oral form of narrative using dialect or local idiom with the feeling of improvisation.

Anton Chekhov's Mystery Bouffe: "The time is at hand…" Chekhov, *The Three Sisters*, Act 1. Speech by Tuzenbakh.

Mayakovsky, *Mystery Bouffe*. All quotes from the play are from the translation in Mayakovsky, *The Complete Plays of Vladimir Mayakovsky*. The following lines from the translation form part of *Anton Chekhov's Mystery Bouffe*:

"In the future, all persons performing, presenting, reading or publishing this play should change the content making it contemporary, immediate, up to the minute."

The passages from "Gentlemen…" to "…betray them."

The passage from "A fine lot I must say!..." to "…punch each other's mugs!"

The passage "we sought no aid…" to "…powerful grasp!"

Alexander Blok, *The Twelve*:

"Open up the cellars

Today the rabble will have fun!"

The song at the end of the play is abridged from the song, "Ta Ra Ra Boom De Yay," by Joe Hill, first published in *The Joe Hill Memorial Edition of the Industrial Worker Little Red Songbook*.

P 166 Mayakovsky quote is from his American poems, quoted in the introduction to Mayakovsky, *Poems*.

Da-da! "Living on one leg…" Waten, *Mother*, p3.

"Ah, my brother?..." the story is adapted from Trotsky, *My Life*, p383.

One piano, 64 keys: The story of the piano is adapted from Orlando Figes, *A People's Tragedy*, p182, where he reports that on encountering a mansion, some peasants broke up a grand piano and shared out the ivory keys amongst themselves. The musings about their motivations are entirely Olga's.

BIBLIOGRAPHY
Primary sources

Alexander Blok, "*The Twelve*", retrieved online at:
https://kuscholarworks.ku.edu/handle/1808/6598.
Anton Chekhov, *The Three Sisters*, Retrieved online at:
https://www.ibiblio.org/eldritch/ac/sisters.htm. Based on the copy-text *Plays by Anton Tchekov,* translated from the Russian by Constance Garnett, New York, Macmillan, 1916. Scanned by A. S. Man. Translation revised and notes added 1998 by James Rusk and A. S. Man.
Anton Chekhov, *The Steppe*. Retrieved online at:
https://www.ataun.eus/BIBLIOTECAGRATUITA/Classics%20in%20English/Anton%20Chekhov/The%20Steppe.pdf.
Anton Chekhov, *The Duel and Other Stories*, Penguin Books, 1984.
Ilya Ehrenburg, *Memoirs, 1921-1941*, Universal Library, New York, 1966.
Oriel Gray, *Exit Left*, Penguin Books, Ringwood, 1985.
Alexandra Kollantai, *Selected Writings,* Allison and Busby, London, 1977.
Alexandra Kollantai, *Red Love*, retrieved at:
https://www.marxists.org/archive/kollonta/red-love/index.htm
Leon Trotsky, *My Life*, first published by Charles Scribner's Sons, New York, 1931. Transcription and HTML Markup: 1998 by David Walters. This edition: 2000 by Chris Russell for Marxists Internet Archive.
Vladimir Mayakovsky, *Poems*, translated by Dorian Rottenberg, printed in the Union of Soviet Socialist Republics, 1972. Retrieved online at:
https://ubu.com/historical/mayakovsky/Mayakovsky-Vladimir-Vladimir-Mayakovsky-Poems.pdf.
Vladimir Mayakovsky. *The Complete Plays of Vladimir Mayakovsky*, translated by Guy Daniels, Simon and Schuster, New York, 1971.
Victor Serge, *Memoir of a Revolutionary*, Translated by P. Sedgwick, New York Review of Books, 2012.
Clare Sheridan, *Russian Portraits*, 1921 (extract on Sparticist International website).

The Joe Hill Memorial Edition of the Industrial Worker Little Red Songbook, 1916.

Song published online at: http://www.folkarchive.de/tarara.html.

Judah Waten, *"Mother"*, published in *Coast to Coast*, Australian Short Stories, 1949-50, Angus and Robertson, Sydney, 1950. Retrieved from:
http://www.egyankosh.ac.in/bitstream/123456789/26871/1/Unit-13.pdf.

Secondary sources

Jean Aitken-Swann, *Widows in Australia,* 1962 (Council of Social Services of NSW).

Australian Dictionary of Biography online, for Essington Lewis biographical information.

Walter Benjamin, On the Concept of History, 1940.

Joy Damousi, *Women Come Rally*, Oxford University Press, 1994.

Zelda D'Aprano, *Zelda*, Spinifex Press, Melbourne, 1995.

Orlando Figes, *A People's Tragedy,* Random House, United Kingdom 1998.

Orlando Figes, *Just Send Me Word*, Metropolitan Books, New York, 2012.

Sheila Fitzpatrick, *Everyday Stalinism*, Oxford University Press, USA, 1999.

Sheila Fitzpatrick, *White Russians, Red Peril*, LaTrobe University Press and Black Ink Books, Carlton, 2021.

Kristen R. Ghodsee, *Why Women Have Better Sex Under Socialism*, Bodley Head, London, 2018.

Angela Hillel and Dot Thompson, *Against the Stream: 50 Years of New Theatre*, New Theatre Melbourne, 1986, (accessed through *Reason and Revolt* website).

Oleg V. Khlevniuk, *Master of the House: Stalin and his Inner Circle*, Yale University Press, USA, 2009.

Vladimir Kataev, *If Only We Could Know!*, Ivan R. Dee, Chicago, 2002.

Tamas Krausz, *Reconstructing Lenin*, Monthly Review Press, New York, 2015.

Kristina Kukolja, Lindsey Arkley, with John Zubricki and Nathan Kopp, Special Broadcasting Service (SBS) Australia, *The Unwanted Australians,* retrieved from SBS website.

Greil Marcus, *The Dustbin of History,* Picador, London, 1995.

Owen Matthews, *Stalin's Children*, Walker and Company, New York, 2008.

Zhores and Roy Medvedev, *A Question of Madness*, Penguin Books, Ringwood, 1974.

Mara Moustafine, *Secrets and Spies: The Harbin Files,* Random House, 2002.

The staging of Mystery Bouffe, (online article) at tutorhunt.com.

Sparticist International (website), entry on Olga Kameneva.

Francis Spufford, *Red Plenty*, Faber and Faber, 2010.

SovLit.com, website containing English translations of many Soviet literary works, including contemporary critical works.

Ronald Grigor Suny, *Stalin: Passage to Revolution,* Princeton University Press, 2020.

Lynne Viola, ed, *Contending with Stalinism,* Cornell University Press, 2002.

Oliver Wainwright, *Russia's stage revolution: when theatre was a hotbed for impossibly space-age design, The Guardian,* 15 October 2014. Retrieved from:
https://www.theguardian.com/artanddesign/2014/oct/15/russian-theatre-design-revolution-avant-garde-v-and-a.

Wikipedia entries on Olga Kameneva, and many others listed in the history section.

Elizabeth Wood, *The Baba and the Comrade*, Indiana University Press, Bloomington, 1997.